This wasn't the way it was supposed to be. I'd never imagined, when I got the foundation grant that paid half my tuition to law school, that six years later the reward for my labors would be to be yoked in judicial servitude with some condescending, self-infatuated whiz-kid lawyer half my age. Worse, I had to admit in my most candid moments that I was just a little bit jealous of her. I mean, she was always *right*. I wondered, if I'd gotten my act together decades earlier, if I could have been a woman without obstacles or uncertainties too. Unfortunately, the critical decades had passed, and now I wasn't too thrilled about Lauren's well-meaning exhortation to put my life on hold and my nose to the grindstone, a position that was unlikely to be anatomically advantageous or a great deal of fun. I thought I'd spent enough time on hold already.

What is that saying—"Life is what happens when you're making other plans"?

EXIT STRATEGIES

"Quick and likable."
Kirkus Reviews

"Slick, sassy . . . Becky's balancing act is fun to read and told with wit and compassion."
Oklahoma City Sunday Oklahoman

"This terrific book illustrates the humor, irony, disasters, and unexpected joys life can throw at women."
Romantic Times

Other books by
Catherine Todd

STAYING COOL
MAKING WAVES

CATHERINE TODD

EXIT STRATEGIES

HarperTorch
An Imprint of HarperCollins*Publishers*

This is a work of fiction. Names, characters, places, and incidents are products of the author's imagination or are used fictitiously and are not to be construed as real. Any resemblance to actual events, locales, organizations, or persons, living or dead, is entirely coincidental.

HARPERTORCH
An Imprint of HarperCollins*Publishers*
10 East 53rd Street
New York, New York 10022-5299

ISBN: 0-06-000878-4

First HarperTorch paperback printing: November 2002
First William Morrow hardcover printing: January 2002

Printed in the United States of America

Visit HarperTorch on the World Wide Web at www.harpercollins.com

10 9 8 7 6 5 4 3 2 1

For Denise Marcil,
with thanks

ACKNOWLEDGMENTS

SPECIAL THANKS TO SEVERAL PEOPLE WHO HELPED ME with excellent suggestions for improving this book as well as with a generous gift of time and expertise: Maureen Baron, Allison McCabe, and Krista Stroever. I'd also like to add my voice to the chorus of grateful authors in praise of Larry Ashmead, my editor at HarperCollins, and thank him for believing in my work.

Thanks too to all the people at HarperCollins for their part in the production and publication of *Exit Strategies:* Lorie Young; Brenda Woodward; Lisa Gallagher; my publicists, DeeDee DeBartlo and Chelsea Meeks; and the sales and marketing departments and the representatives on the road.

As always, I would like to thank my agent, Denise Marcil, not only for her enthusiastic representation but also for her encouragement and editorial advice. This book is dedicated to her.

Jay Bartz very kindly provided background information on trusts, offshore accounts, and the ever elusive Rule Against Perpetuities. Needless to say, errors of fact, interpretation, and law are strictly my own.

EXIT STRATEGIES

CHAPTER ONE

THE MEETING HAD STARTED WITHOUT ME. I SNEAKED A peek at my watch—I was still one minute early. I flashed Taylor Anderson—partner in charge, Armani Adonis, and the object of countless fantasies, including mine—a rueful smile, which he appeared not to notice. I took a seat. The client, Jason Krill, head of a tiny Internet start-up company, looked at me expectantly. Members of the legal team, no matter how junior, are usually introduced.

Taylor went right on talking. Krill's company was trying to raise venture capital, the kind of shoestring deal that could explode profitably overnight given the right combination of luck and more luck. The venture capitalists wanted seats on the board of directors and a reasonable amount of stock. The CEO wanted to give up as little as possible. Taylor was explaining the Facts of Life.

"This isn't Silicon Valley," he said apologetically. "I'm afraid you have to give something to get something back."

The client had the geeky look of someone who had spent a lot of time in front of his terminal and not much outdoors. He probably wasn't a day older than twenty-five, with a hint of stubble on his chin that spoke of neglect rather than style, but in a year he might be driving a new Bentley Continental SC and squandering vast sums on a vintage pinball machine collection. Or not. That was the fun of start-up companies.

Melissa Peters, my senior in experience but not in years, crossed her admittedly awesome legs beneath a skirt that was definitely born the runt of the litter. "You might want to rework your business plan," she suggested.

The leg-crossing appeared to have short-circuited the client's brain. He stared at her, his mouth opened slightly. She obviously did something for his hard drive.

Melissa (called "Missy" by her friends, but not by me) and her ilk are the reason a lot of men in positions of authority treat their female colleagues with a wary formality inspired by fear of lawsuits. She gave off so many conflicting signals you were derailed before you knew what hit you. Her awesome self-confidence in her own ability was no less irritating for being justified, at least most of the time. On the other hand, instead of the you-touch-me-you'll-be-sorry professional demeanor of a female associate on the make, she had a kind of post-feminist exhibitionism about her body. She could stop a firm meeting dead (and had) by hitching up her skirt and massaging her calves. She was also taking classes in Tae Kwan Do and early Norse literature. For fun.

Taylor frowned momentarily. I knew what was the matter—the rule for associates at Roth, Tolbert & Anderson was that in meetings with a client, silence was not only golden but mandatory. Only one person at a time speaks for the firm, and it better not be you. My job, as the lowest in seniority, was to sit in the corner like Jane Eyre and take notes. Melissa's was to nod sagely at everything Taylor said. She wasn't supposed to make suggestions on her own.

"The firm feels that a review of your plan might be helpful," Taylor said, resuming command. He glanced in my direction. "Becky, could you get Mr. Krill's business plan for us?" He turned to the client. "Jason, can we get you anything? Coffee? Tea? Soda? Wine?"

Jason closed his mouth and swallowed. "Do you have Sprite?" he asked hopefully.

I stood up. Taylor caught my eye and then he stiffened. I knew, and he knew I knew, that he'd forgotten I was the lawyer and not the gofer.

Again.

If I'd come into the firm in the normal way, fresh out of law school at twenty-four and incandescent with ambition, I wouldn't have had these problems. Instead I'd spent the last six years becoming the oldest new associate in the law firm where I had, not incidentally, spent the same six years working as a receptionist while putting myself through law school at night. If I hadn't received a foundation grant for older graduate students returning to the workforce, it would have been more like eight and a half, or never. Not such a lofty pinnacle, I admit. But if this wasn't success, I didn't have a clue which way to turn.

The trouble was, for all those years I'd been a fixture at the front desk—a pleasant fixture, probably, but only slightly above the Italian-style furniture in rank. Receptionists come in two categories—twenty-year-olds who didn't go to college and can't get another job and forty-something divorcées who went to college years ago and can't get another job. Moreover, firms like the forty-somethings better because they don't chew gum into the phone, don't come to work wearing halter tops, and don't (usually) throw themselves at the partners. Anyway, when you're used to seeing—or, more accurately, not seeing—someone in a certain way, it's difficult to alter your perception.

It was bad enough that the attorneys sometimes forgot to take me seriously, but worse by far was the attitude of most of the staff. Putting yourself through law school at night—however grueling, grinding, or boring the process—is seen as a kind of rebuke, a suggestion that being a secretary or a receptionist isn't Enough. It isn't, financially, but that's beside the point. I mean, how much did the stepsisters like taking orders from Cinderella after the ball? I hadn't married the prince, but it was like pulling teeth to get anybody to do my work.

I might have done better seeking employment somewhere other than Roth, Tolbert & Anderson, which was an aspiring law firm but definitely second tier. Unfortunately, night law school is not the career path of choice for the upwardly mobile, and topflight legal jobs do not grow on trees (or even shrubs) for the chronologically challenged. Law firms, particularly top law firms, like to mold you into their own image, and grads with a few years under their belts are presumably less malleable and far less willing to devote their associate years to Nothing But Work. RTA, however, suffered from a geographical disadvantage—everybody would like to vacation in San Diego, but no one looking for big bucks wants to work there.

Not that I wasn't grateful. The firm paid for me to take the bar exam and gave me time off to study. I didn't have to uproot my children from their schools or my mother from her security. I could stay in La Jolla, home of the improbably fortunate, even if only on a shoestring. Jamison Roth, the only partner over sixty, took me to lunch. In a burst of optimism, I even allowed my college roommate, the alumni class secretary, to publish news of my promotion in the Class Notes. So what if all the other first-year associates called me "ma'am"?

All of which goes to explain why I gave Taylor Anderson another smile—this time a reassuring one—in the face of his little faux pas. "I'll get it," I said, noticing when I stood up that my slip had worked its way up around my hips like a life preserver. Great.

Melissa gave me a you'll-never-make-partner-at-this-rate smirk. I didn't care; it was exactly what I hoped for her, though probably only one of us would get her wish. "I'll be right back," I added. And I would have been too, except that the career god chose that moment to deal me another low blow.

Wendy Richards, legal secretary and office administrator, stuck her well-coiffed head around the door. "Excuse me," she said, looking directly at Taylor, "but there's a phone call for Ms. Weston." Taylor made an impatient little gesture, and Wendy turned to me. "Your mother," she mouthed.

"Could you tell her I'm in a meeting and I'll call her back?" I asked desperately. I knew what was coming next.

"She says it's urgent," Wendy said sympathetically. My mother always said it was urgent. Since she was eighty years old, there was always the chance that this time, after a lifetime total of 956 false alarms, there might actually be a real emergency.

I was already standing, so there was no way to make an inconspicuous exit. "I'd better take it," I said to all and sundry, carefully avoiding looking at Melissa. *Her* mother was probably my age, fit and tanned and playing a round of tennis every day before she went off to be chairman of General Motors or whatever.

Taylor's quick grimace passed for permission to leave. Or maybe I just imagined his exasperation, because a second later he said pleasantly, "Sure; go ahead. Wendy, would you get us the rest of the papers from Mr. Krill's file? It's on my desk. And if you wouldn't mind, Mr. Krill would like a Sprite."

"Ice?" Wendy was asking as I left the room.

"WE'RE OUT OF ice cream," my mother told me when I picked up the phone.

I closed my eyes and made a conscious effort not to hold the phone with my neck. I could feel the tension spreading through my shoulders. "Is that what you called to tell me?" I asked her. I thought I sounded wonderfully patient, but my mother apparently thought otherwise.

"You *said* to remind you," she said in an aggrieved tone.

"Yes, but, Mother, you said it was urgent. I was in a meeting with a client."

"They always say you're in a meeting," she protested, unruffled. "That's how they put you off. If I didn't say it was important, they wouldn't have called you to the phone, would they?" she asked reasonably.

I had to swallow hard to stifle an audible sigh. "Mother, I'll pick up the ice cream on the way home, but *please* don't say it's urgent when you call if it's not." I paused. "We've had this conversation before."

"Don't use that tone with me, Rebecca. I'm not a child."

But sometimes she was, of course, in the ways that counted. Not a child who was growing outward and more independent but one who was dwindling and becoming needier. The relationship was constantly being renegotiated.

Before I could say anything more, she added, “I can’t find my blood-pressure medicine.”

“What time did you last take it?”

There was an edge of panic beginning in her voice. “I’m not sure. I don’t remember.” Pause. “Maybe this morning.”

I went through the litany of all the places her pills might be.

“I checked there. I checked *everywhere.*”

“Okay, try to relax. I’ll help you find them when I get home. You know it doesn’t matter that much if you miss one dose.”

Her voice fluttered a little. “I think I need them now.”

Whether she did or not, it was pointless to argue. She wanted me to come home and find them for her, and I couldn’t. We reached this impasse a couple of times a month. I looked at my watch. “Did you ask Allie to help you?”

“Alicia is not home,” she said triumphantly.

I wondered if that was the hidden agenda behind the conversation. My mother adored her granddaughter, but she couldn’t resist pointing out the flaws in the elaborate domestic construct I had made to try to keep everyone happy.

I felt a flicker of annoyance. I paid Alicia to come straight home from high school every day she didn’t have a scheduled activity so she could check on her grandmother. Not that my mother needed constant surveillance, but it was supposed to head off problems before they got serious. Not incidentally, it made sure that my fifteen-year-old daughter was not wandering around unsupervised while I was working.

I thought it was a brilliant solution. When it worked.

"I'm sure she'll be home soon," I told her. "What flavor ice cream do you want?"

"Whatever you like," said my mother, infuriatingly. "Becky?"

"What?" I asked, more curtly than I intended.

"If you got one of those phones . . . you know . . ."

I knew. "Cell phones?"

"That's right. A cell phone. If you had one, I wouldn't have to call the office."

I felt a measure of panic at the thought of being available in the car, the market, even the ladies' room. "I don't think so," I said sharply.

"Oh," she said forlornly.

Then I felt a wave of guilt, the kind you feel when you think you've been really, truly selfish.

The Older Parent Game is a game you can't win. It's not their fault, but it isn't yours either. Ambivalence, guilt, responsibility, tenderness—they're all part of a complicated package. My mother had moved in with Allie, David (my son), and me after my divorce, and her presence made it possible for me to go back to work and to school. Her Social Security tided us over when the support payments were late and in the awful period after my ex-husband died.

On the other hand, her needs were becoming a large, powerful drain that threatened to draw everything close into the maelstrom, and I was the only one around to meet them. As she reminded me rather frequently, she'd given up her friends, her life, and her house to help me out, and she wasn't about to start over. I loved my mother, but love wasn't enough anymore. A sense of jeopardy hung over my life like mist—letting up occasionally but never entirely evaporating.

"Well, I'll look into it," I told her. "They're very expensive, but . . . I'll look into it."

"Becky?"

"Yes, Mother?"

"Chocolate," she said. "Bring home chocolate."

WENDY STEPPED INTO my office as I was replacing the receiver. "Everything okay?" she asked.

Wendy was about fifty-five, a decade my senior, and had been my ally ever since I discovered her sneaking into the office one morning very early to call *her* mother at firm expense. "She lives in a nursing home in Toronto," she'd said then. "I don't do this very often, but it's so expensive. . . ." She seemed to expect me to turn her in to the partners. I didn't.

"We were out of ice cream," I told her.

She laughed sympathetically. "Sorry. I guess I shouldn't have called you out of the meeting, but your mother insisted."

"I know," I told her. "She wants me to get a cell phone so I can be more available."

"Don't do it," she warned. She rolled her eyes. "I can't say who, of course, but someone in this firm has a mother who calls with daily soap opera updates. Four calls an afternoon. Well, three, now that they've canceled *Another World*."

I shuddered. "I'll keep it in mind. Is Jason Krill still here?"

She shook her head. "He's catching the Nerd Bird to San Jose tomorrow and wanted to go home and pack." The Nerd Bird was the early flight to Silicon Valley, awash in laptops and pocket protectors. "Sheesh. I hope he remembers to put in his deodorant."

"He'll probably be a billionaire by Christmas," I told her.

"Then he ought to be able to afford soap," she said with asperity. "Not that that stopped our Miss Peters from throwing herself at him."

I didn't say anything, although I was dying to.

Wendy gave me her best attempt at a leer. Since she resembled no one so much as Pat Nixon in her heyday, the effect was almost macabre. "And he's not the only one she's dangling her . . . wares in front of," she said. Her eyes shone a little, as if she was excited by the idea of RTA as a hotbed of illicit lust.

"I don't think . . ." I started.

"Yes you do," she said. "But you're too nice to say so."

I couldn't think what to say to that.

"Don't mind me," she said. "I'm just your generic sex-starved middle-aged divorcée."

That makes two of us, I thought. But of course I didn't say that either.

CHAPTER TWO

TAYLOR ANDERSON WAS SITTING AT HIS DESK STARING out the window. Despite his polished demeanor, his office looked as if he hadn't put anything away since approximately 1982. Even the chairs were stacked with papers. I thought it took a certain confidence to entertain clients in those surroundings, because it looked impossibly chaotic. What if your will was at the bottom of one of those piles? By the time its whereabouts were discovered, your hated nephew could have absconded to Brazil with your estate.

I tapped on the door and went in. Law firms are more informal than big corporations, where nobody dares disturb the person above him in the chain of command.

Taylor looked startled, as if I'd caught him in a fantasy of his own. Maybe I had. "What's up?" he asked distractedly.

"Not much," I told him. "I just wanted to apologize."

He raised his eyebrows. His sleeves were rolled up at the cuffs. It made him look adorably boyish. "What for?" he asked.

"For having to leave the client meeting," I told him.

He looked blank.

"Jason Krill. The phone call," I prompted him.

"Oh, right."

This was worse than I thought. He hadn't even remembered I was supposed to be there. He watched me patiently, the way people do when you interrupt them at a cocktail party and they're just waiting to get back to their conversations. I couldn't think what to say next. The seconds ticked by.

"Was there something else?" Taylor asked finally. His fingers toyed longingly with the edges of the papers in front of him. He softened the dismissal with a smile.

"My mother," I blurted out. The words were hanging there before I knew what I was saying. Damn, damn. Why did I say something like that? "I'm sorry," I said hopelessly.

Taylor truly focused on me at last. "Becky, is there something wrong? Is your mother ill?" He actually sounded a little concerned. That only made it worse.

I shook my head. "No, she just . . . calls. A lot. Sometimes it's hard." I shrugged. "She's old." I couldn't believe I was making such a fool of myself, babbling about my personal problems when I'd hoped to impress him with my professional dynamism. I started to back away.

He looked at me. "I'm afraid I don't understand. Do you need some time off?"

I shook my head.

"Would you like to leave early? You don't have to ask."

"No, not that," I said.

"What, then?"

I took a deep breath. *Be assertive. Cool. In charge.* "I need to get up to speed on the Krill matter," I told him.

He picked up his pen and glanced down at the papers on his desk. "Oh, okay," he said, sounding relieved. "Melissa can fill you in. She's on top of it. Why don't you talk to her?"

"Thank you," I told him with a cheeriness I was far from feeling. "I'll do that right away." I made for the door, not before noticing that my panty hose had a gigantic run right down the front of my right leg.

"Good," he said. He didn't look up.

I SHOULD PROBABLY explain about Taylor Anderson. But then again, maybe I don't need to. If someone's been a fantasy object for six years without anything much happening, there probably isn't a lot more that needs explaining. Besides, it is *so* trite to have an unrequited crush on your boss. So giggly. So unprofessional. So desperate.

Not that I was alone. Before I took up jurisprudence as a money-making activity, I had leisure to notice that plenty of the staff were similarly afflicted in Taylor's presence. The female attorneys were a little more subtle about it than the secretaries, but let's face it, the man was almost too good to be true. I've already mentioned the part about being an Adonis (a Scandinavian Adonis, but no less mythical for that) and the Armani suits. Shallow qualities, maybe, but when you consider the Harvard Law degree, the private pilot's license, the conversational knowledge of French and Spanish (I'd heard him talking with clients on the phone), the bequests to the art museum and the zoo, the entry in *Who's Who in the West, plus* the aforesaid physical attributes (they encourage you to use words like *aforesaid* in law school, along with other electrifying expressions such as *herein* and *the party of the first part*), the total package was pretty attractive.

For some of the time I'd worked at the firm there had been a Mrs. Taylor Anderson, a pretty, petite salon-blonde who'd been an engineering undergraduate at Stanford, where they met. I saw her at several Christmas parties for the staff, where she gushed with insincere bonhomie and kept a watchful eye on Taylor at the same time. Well, who could blame her? Her husband was the walking embodiment of the brass ring, and that counted more than a wedding band, at least in some quarters.

Not in mine, though. I'd been around enough to know that affairs, not marriage, are what men like Taylor have with their underlings, and affairs were tacky and time-consuming, not to mention rude. Besides, I didn't even have time to date—an affair was out of the question. I didn't have the wardrobe for it either, much less the body. I mean, the younger generation could engage in serious debates on the virtues of a return to Modesty, but mine didn't have a choice. Before the maniacally aerobicized eighties it might have been easier, but now it was impossible.

Like all fantasies, Taylor's personality was mostly a projection. He might have slurped his spaghetti and eaten peas with a knife at home, but to me he was like some exceptionally attractive painting on a wall—unchanging and essentially unreal. Since I had never, in the six years I'd spent at the firm, had a real conversation with him that didn't involve work, this was a surprisingly easy illusion to maintain. I was free to imagine him in any situation I wanted without ever encountering any messy disappointments. I entertained a sneaking suspicion that he didn't have much of a sense of humor—all right, I knew it for a fact—but what do you need jokes for on Mount Olympus? He was great to look at, fine to listen to (on legal topics at least), satisfying to think about, and, in light of my divorce and its aftermath, reasonably safe as a love object.

If only his wife hadn't left him.

I don't know the particulars, though there was certainly enough speculation about it around the firm. I can't imagine who you would leave Taylor for. Brad Pitt? Steve Jobs? It boggled the mind. Anyway, Taylor was suffering. Not the teeth-gnashing, hair-pulling, weeping and wailing kind of suffering, but a toned-down WASP version of an alluring melancholia. He lost weight. His eyes developed little lines of strain at the corners. He lost his train of thought in midsentence. He looked vulnerable. But underneath it all there was a tiny signal being transmitted like pheromones. He probably didn't even realize he was doing it.

He was looking.

If he ever really saw me, he would want me too. He would get up from his desk and walk into my office, closing the door behind him. He would come toward me, arms extended. His kiss would be soft, at first. Everything in the right place. Expert . . .

Bad. Very bad. Don't even think about it. A sure road to professional disaster.

My superego was working overtime.

My id wasn't so sure.

The one thing (in addition to common sense, not to mention lack of invitation) that had so far kept me from testing the waters was the certainty that Wendy would be sure to notice, and I would be forever classed with Melissa as some hysterically hormonal office hussy.

Anyway, between my mother's phone call and the meeting with Jason Krill, I had a pretty alarming view of my status, both professional and otherwise. I have to say that while it was bad enough to be ignored as a woman, what really galled me was that I'd worked my tail off for six years to land on the attorney's side of the desk and it looked like a hollow victory. Unless I did something soon, I could be back to answering the phones in no time.

"I'M DOOMED," I SAID, picking at the run in my hose with my fingernail. They'd been brand-new that morning. "Sabotage by wardrobe."

"Don't be melodramatic." Lauren Gould, senior associate, mentor, and all-around good person, sat across from me and sipped her tea. "You should just keep another pair of panty hose in your desk drawer, or wear pants, like me."

I glanced involuntarily at her legs as she sat in her wheelchair. She always wore pants, she'd told me, because her leg muscles were so emaciated from disuse she thought she looked terrible in anything else.

"That's not the only problem," I told her.

She laughed. "I know, but you have to admit I have a point. Weren't you ever a Girl Scout? 'Be prepared.' Don't you remember?"

"I hated Girl Scouts," I told her, with only slight exaggeration. "I was too shy to sell cookies. It was torture. I ended up buying boxes of them with my allowance so my mother wouldn't drag me door-to-door through the neighborhood. Then I ate them." I looked at her. "Remember *badges*?"

She nodded. "Badges weren't so bad. But camp . . ." She was getting into the spirit, I could tell. "Jollywood, they called it. There were concrete paths to the cabins, and if you stepped onto the dirt someone yelled, 'Stay on the path,' through a bullhorn. And there were *tarantulas.*"

"In the cabin?"

"No, on the trails. But anywhere was bad enough."

I tried to imagine her as a girl, hiking, before the accident. At least I assumed it was an accident that put her in the wheelchair; she didn't talk about it, and I didn't want to pry. She'd only been at RTA about a year, a lateral hire from a firm that had broken up over some legal shenanigans of one of the partners. We didn't know each other well enough to share personal calamities. Besides, there were enough things in my biography that I didn't feel like broadcasting to the world either.

She saw me looking, so I said quickly, "I didn't like all those planned activities: canoeing, tennis, archery, softball. Somebody was always going around with a clipboard telling you what to do next." I laughed. "My ex-husband could never understand why I wouldn't go to Club Med."

"I liked all those things," she said, and I suddenly wondered if I'd been tactless.

"That's probably because you weren't the last one to be chosen for every sport," I told her. "I was pretty uncoordinated."

She looked at me.

"It's true. It's still true. My ideal in the exercise department is Fran Lebowitz."

I expected her to laugh, but she looked serious. "Becky, don't," she said.

"Don't what?" Even though she was ten years younger than I was and the closest thing I had to a friend in the firm, she was still a senior associate (soon to be partner, if the grapevine was correct), and when she said something in that tone, I listened.

"Don't be self-deprecating, even as a joke. I mean it. Especially not here. It won't get you very far in the law."

"Not even if it's true?" I joked.

"Especially not then," she said earnestly. "Clients don't want their lawyers to have flaws. It's like doctors. Do you want to know that your surgeon drinks too much and paws the nurses? I don't think so."

I repressed a shudder. I knew about doctors and their public image. "I see your point," I told her.

"Look," she said, leaning toward me conspiratorially. "I know you're worried about being taken seriously as a lawyer around here."

I looked around quickly, hoping I wouldn't catch Melissa lurking in the doorway listening.

Lauren smiled and lowered her voice. She was very perceptive. "What you have to do first is prove you're one of the guys. And I mean that figuratively. It includes the women partners too."

"How do I do that?" I asked her. "I don't have any business."

She shook her head. "Nobody expects you to have your own clients as a first-year associate. That will come later. Right now you have to work harder and longer than you probably want to in order to show everybody you've got the right stuff."

I stared at her.

"I'm not kidding. I know it sounds like macho nonsense or hazing or something like that, but every self-respecting attorney thinks he works harder than everybody else. Especially in a firm like this that has something to prove. It was the same at Eastman, Bartels, where I worked before. In the beginning, you've got to show that you buy into it, or nobody will trust you. Keep your billable hours up. Way up. Later on, you can get your life back."

"How much later?"

"Much later." She gave me a pitying look. She knew I had a son in college, a rebellious teenage daughter, and a mother constantly hovering near disaster. I thought about Diane Keaton in *Baby Boom* and wondered if there was some nifty business I could run out of my house that would net me a couple of million dollars.

"I'll try. I just hope I can pull it off," I said.

"Are you sure you want to? You've got a lot on your plate already."

By the time my name came up for partnership, she might be one of the people deciding my fate. So I didn't say, "I really don't think I have any choice," which was the truth. Instead I told her, "I can handle it."

CHAPTER THREE

I HUSTLED MY DETERMINEDLY ASSERTIVE, JUST-ONE-OF-the-guys self down the hall to Melissa's office for an update on what I'd missed with Jason Krill. She was talking to Ryan James, a volcanically ambitious associate who virtually seethed with intrigue. The conversation stopped abruptly when I entered the room.

"Can I help you?" Melissa said coolly, as if I'd shown up on her doorstep hawking Tupperware.

"Sorry to interrupt," I said, "but Taylor thought you might be able to fill me in on Jason Krill's business plan."

Ryan stood up. "I'll catch you later," he said to Melissa in an undertone. "How's it going, Becky?" he asked me, in a normal voice.

"Fine," I said. I thought he still looked furtive, but that was his usual expression. When you're a first-year associate, doors are always closing on you, literally and figuratively. It comes with the territory. Other people go into rooms and talk about things you know nothing about. The message is, It's none of your business, at least not till you're one of us.

It was firmwide too. The secretaries did it to the Xerox operator, the paralegals did it to the secretaries, the associates did it to the paralegals and to each other. The partners did it to everybody.

"Sit down," Melissa said when Ryan had left. "As a matter of fact," she said conspiratorially, "I'm glad you interrupted us. Sometimes he's a little too intense, if you understand what I mean."

Directly across from me on her desk was the latest edition of *Metro* magazine, its hot-pink cover proclaiming articles on "131 Ways to Be a Prodigy with His You-Know-What" and "Aardvark to Zebra: How to Be an Animal and Drive Him Wild Wild Wild." Underneath it were copies of *PC Week* and *Fortune*. Conflicting signals indeed. No wonder poor Ryan felt "intense."

"I imagine I do," I told her.

Melissa looked at me suspiciously. She had an excellent brain, and she could detect sarcasm when she heard it. I shouldn't have given in to the impulse, but I mean *really*. What did she expect me to say—"That swine!"? Besides, I was already suspect for not sharing her enthusiasm for running in marathons, a topic on which I had virtually nothing to contribute.

"Well," she said eventually, "did you bring the meeting notes?"

I handed them to her. "They're not very useful," I said. "I was called out early."

She tossed them back at me. "Oh, yes. Your mother, wasn't it?"

"Yes, as a matter of fact it was," I said steadily.

"Well," she said again, "do you know what to look for in a business plan?"

"Not entirely," I told her. One of the things you learn very fast when you start working at a law firm is never to pretend to know something you don't. Never.

She sighed. "Don't they teach people *anything* in law school anymore? Lawyers need to know this stuff."

I waited. I knew she hadn't learned it in law school either. Law school operated on the theory that if you understood the general principles, you could find out the practical details on your own.

She sighed again. "All right," she said finally. "Think about what you need to say to convince someone to give you money. You have to tell who you are, what you're proposing, what the market is, who the competitors are, and why you can beat them, as well as how much money you need and when you'll need it. You have to construct a spreadsheet of monetary milestones timelined out—showing things like when you'll need to pay rent, buy equipment, hire employees, et cetera. With me so far?"

She looked dubious so I nodded.

"Can you guess what one of the most important elements of the plan is?"

I did know that one. "An exit strategy for the investors." Venture capitalists wanted out of deals in about five years, depending on the circumstances. They didn't want their money tied up forever.

She looked surprised. "That's right, Becky." She made it sound as if I'd just won the Middle School Spelling Bee. "How did you know that?"

"I read *Business Week,*" I said.

She seemed nonplussed and unsure whether to believe me or not. Finally she said, "Here. Why don't you take this and see what you can do with it? If you don't mind, I need it on my desk by Monday morning."

Strictly speaking, only partners had the power to order you to do work for them, but I'd more or less asked for it, and this was how you learned things. And much as I hated to admit it, I could learn a lot from Melissa.

"I'll be happy to help you out, Melissa," I told her. "As a matter of fact, I do have one or two ideas for improving it."

She looked at me. "Do you? That should be . . . interesting."

THIS WASN'T THE way it was supposed to be. I'd never imagined, when I got the foundation grant that paid half my tuition to law school, that six years later the reward for my labors would be to be yoked in juridical servitude with some condescending, self-infatuated whiz-kid lawyer half my age. Worse, I had to admit in my most candid moments that I was just a little bit jealous of her. I mean, she was always *right*. I wondered, if I'd gotten my act together decades earlier, if I could have been a woman without obstacles or uncertainties too. Unfortunately, the critical decades had passed, and now I wasn't too thrilled about Lauren's well-meaning exhortation to put my life on hold and my nose to the grindstone, a position that was unlikely to be anatomically advantageous or a great deal of fun. I thought I'd spent enough time on hold already. What is that saying—"Life is what happens when you're making other plans"?

What I *had* thought when the Medallion Foundation offered me the way out was *I'm saved!* Saved from my own stupidity, in part. Once upon a time—in the days of the Volvo in the garage, the shopping trips to Saks, the lunches that didn't require the removal of Saran Wrap first—I'd rarely given a thought to what I would do if the money were to vanish. I mean, money may not solve your problems, but at least it keeps the wild things away from the fire. It's not as if I missed all those warnings from Betty Friedan (*get a job, protect yourself*) either. I heard them; I just didn't want to listen. I was a doctor's wife with a teaching credential and two kids, and doctors' wives didn't have to work. My husband, my parents, my in-laws, and even my friends (at least the ones I had then) all bought into it. Besides, the thrill of working is definitely overrated. I hadn't changed my mind about that, but nevertheless, if I could go back and start over I wouldn't be so naive.

The only thing the foundation asked in return for its money was a letter on the first of every month (or more often, if there was anything to say) reporting on my professional progress. Since the board members chose to remain anonymous, I didn't know whom I was writing to, and of course I never got anything back. All I had was a post office box and my imagination to go on. In my gratitude and intoxication with my change in prospects, I imagined a kindly old gentleman who got my jokes (someone like a slightly younger Alistair Cooke) reading my letters, and turned them into a combination journal and letter home.

Dear Members of the Board, I'd write, imagining him, Pendleton Silverbridge (I'd read too much Trollope at an impressionable age), in a navy-blue cashmere sweater and Bally loafers, with an aristocratic nose and beautiful white hair.

Law school is the most amazing combination of the lofty and the down-and-dirty. [Okay, scratch down-and-dirty and substitute nitty-gritty. I had to make some concessions to age.] For example, to-

day, in my Torts class, we learned the concept of "res ipsa loquitur." That means "the thing speaks for itself," and it's used in reference to a situation that by its existence confirms a tort (a legal wrong) without any other evidence. (It goes to the concept of negligence and exclusive control of whatever might have caused an injury, but never mind.)

Do you know the example that's used to illustrate this concept? A rat in a soda bottle! In other words, if you find a rat in your soft drink—or even in your Chardonnay—something bad (actionable) has obviously happened. Very obviously.

After I heard about it, I couldn't get that poor rat out of my mind. I mean, how would it get in there? The bottle neck is too narrow, unless we're talking about a very small rat or a very big bottle. Or—eeuuw—what if it crawled into an empty bottle as a baby rat and grew too big to get out until one day it met its end in a Niagara of carbonated brown liquid? The possibilities are endless, and all of them are unappetizing. Not only that, but do you know what happens to flesh when it is immersed in a cola drink? We did an experiment with raw steak in sixth grade.

I think I'll swear off soft drinks.

Luckily, the real Pendleton Silverbridge did have a sense of humor, or, more likely, all my correspondence went directly into the round file unread. In any event, the checks kept coming, so I saw no need to crimp my style. Besides, I had all the dignity and aloofness I could stand at Roth, Tolbert & Anderson by day and at law school by night. And anyway, getting things down on paper was good therapy. I'd learned that from the psychiatrist I saw when I was going through my divorce.

The letters had stopped when I graduated, of course, but sometimes even now I composed progress reports in my mind.

> *Despite your unstinting generosity, six years of hard work, two horrible months of studying for the bar exam, and one thousand two hundred and fifty-six frozen entrée dinners, I'm not sure I can go through with it all the way to partnership.*

I tried to imagine old Pendleton, born to a life of privilege and entitlement, reading a letter like that. It would disappoint him severely, I'm sure. It reeked of ingratitude and self-pity. Besides, I couldn't afford a midlife crisis; there were too many people depending on me. I didn't have an Exit Strategy. I'd have to stick it out till the next stage of life, the one where you're happy just to be alive without tubes down your throat or balloons up your arteries.

Lauren rolled by and stopped at the door. Melissa looked up and smiled; Lauren was the firm's most senior associate and the next on the partnership list.

"I'm going to treat myself to a glass of wine at the Grant," Lauren said. "Tom's picking me up in a few minutes. Would either of you like to come?"

"I'd *really* love to," said Melissa, "but I've got a date."

I remembered dates. Dimly. Sex was an even dimmer memory. *Don't go there,* I told myself.

"With Jason Krill," Melissa added, for my benefit.

I wondered if she would drive him wild wild wild. I

thought there was at least a possibility. "How nice for you," I told her.

"Becky?" Lauren asked, looking amused.

"Sorry, I can't," I told her. "I've got to work."

And don't forget the ice cream, said my mother's voice, in my ear.

CHAPTER FOUR

MY HOUSE WAS IN A PART OF LA JOLLA THAT DEFIED even the most assiduous efforts of real estate agents at verbal adornment. The best they could come up with was *single-level convenience* (no troublesome second story) and *peek of ocean view* (from the garage). Real estate is a big deal in La Jolla, where the sale of even one or two multimillion-dollar houses a year is enough to guarantee a comfortable income. In consequence, the competition is cutthroat, and the village newspaper is filled with brokers' ads sandwiched in among the articles on rotting whale carcasses on the beach and advertisements for personal chef services. All the real estate agents have their pictures in it too—most in double-decker pairs of many possible combinations (husband and wife, mother and daughter, mother and son) and all sporting identical have-I-got-a-cream-puff-for-you smiles.

Our house was not a cream puff. It wasn't even plain French bread. What it was was affordable on the proceeds of the sale of my Mediterranean-style (*Warm and inviting, 4 bedrooms, 3 baths, luxurious master suite with spa, contemporary gourmet kitchen, hardwood floors . . .*) house in the Muirlands—which I had to split with my ex-husband after the divorce—and located in the same school district so my kids wouldn't have to be uprooted. Before my son, David, went away to college in Los Angeles, Alicia and I had shared one bedroom with a closet the size of a hot-water heater, and he and my mother had each had their own equally diminutive quarters. There was one bathroom, with ancient green tile, mold-gray grout, and a big sink that still had separate spigots for the hot and cold water. The bathroom window had been painted so many times it would no longer open, so whenever you took a shower (a short one, with so many people waiting), condensation streamed down the walls and rendered the mirror useless.

Not that I was complaining. It was a struggle to make the payments every month, but one day, after my mother was gone and Allie was out of the house, I could sell it for an absurdly princely sum. The zip code alone guaranteed it. After I paid off the first and second mortgages, I'd have a couple of hundred thousand, or maybe more, left over. It was just about all the retirement I would have, if you don't count Social Security (and nobody my age should count Social Security).

I shifted the carton of chocolate ice cream into the crook of my left arm and fumbled for my house key on the dark porch. I could hear the television going as I pushed the door open. My mother had command of the set in the living room, while Alicia watched in her own bedroom. Neither was an admirer of PBS, but that was all they had in common. The second set had solved no end of problems and turf wars, although in principle I objected to making it too easy for your child to watch TV, as opposed to uplifting activities like reading or homework. In principle I objected to a lot of things, but sometimes expediency was the only thing between me and the Prozac.

My mother looked up from the couch when I walked in. Burdick the cat was stretched out next to her. He wasn't supposed to be up on the couch, but I'd given up trying to enforce the prohibition, since the minute I left the house my mother encouraged him. The cushions had little rips in them where he'd flexed his claws. Now he no longer even bothered to open his eyes when I showed up.

"How was your day?" my mother asked me. Her eyes strayed back to the set. Television was a big part of her life now, her companion. I didn't blame her. She'd reached the age where most of her friends were in rest homes or reposing someplace more final. My father had been dead ten years. At least on TV your favorites never really left you; you could almost always catch them in reruns, if you stayed up late enough.

"Fine," I told her. "How are you feeling? Did you find your medicine?"

She looked startled. "You know, I don't remember." She smiled. "I guess I made quite a fuss over nothing. Would you mind looking for it for me? I'll take it right now."

"Sure, Mom." I patted her shoulder with my right hand. My left was still holding the ice cream. "Just let me put this down."

My mother had nine bottles of pills arrayed on top of her dresser, for daily use. The blood-pressure medicine was first in line. I picked it up, wondering whether she had found it and put it back in its place or just overlooked it. Had she taken her pill? Would I need to start counting them out for her, checking against the contents of the bottle? I would have to talk to her doctor soon. Meanwhile it was safer not to risk giving her another one.

My daughter was lying on her bed wearing jeans and a Delia sweater that barely came to her waist. Her uniform. I wish I could say that she looked like me, with her blond hair and green eyes, but no such luck. My eyes and hair were straight brown all the way, and I'd probably never looked that good in jeans even in my prime.

The door was open, but I tapped on it anyway. "Hi," I said.

She swung her legs over the edge of the bed and sat up. "Hi," she said. "I didn't hear you come in. Want some help with dinner?" Her offer was overenthusiastic, so I knew she knew something was up.

"In a minute, thanks. Could we talk a little bit first?"

Her expression changed to one of wariness. "What did I do now?" she asked me.

I don't know why all those medieval artists bothered to conjure up such elaborate visions of Eternal Torment. If any one of them had had a teenage child, he would have known that perdition starts long before the afterlife. How about "The only time you ever talk to me is when I've done something wrong" for laying on a major guilt trip?

I took a deep breath and wished that the secret to serenity really did lie in respiration. I waited; no such luck. The self-improvement books always lied to you. "Grandma called me at work this afternoon," I said. "She couldn't find her blood-pressure medication."

"I didn't do anything with it."

"Allie, she needed help finding it, and you weren't here."

She let out her breath in a little puff of exasperation.

"Mom, you worry about her too much. She's fine. She doesn't need someone watching her all the time."

"I haven't said she does, but she does need someone to check on her now and then." I looked at her.

She squirmed. "I was just a couple of hours late. Vanessa and I were watching the softball game after school."

"We agreed that checking on Grandma would be your responsibility," I said. Reasonably. Calmly. "Like a job. When you have a job, you have to do it, even if you'd rather be doing something else." I hated the way this conversation was going. I knew that lecturing her was the least likely way to produce results. But I was powerless to stop it. It was as if I were listening to a tape of somebody else's sermon, somebody who wasn't going to win a lot of converts.

She lifted her chin. "Then fire me."

"Oh, Alicia."

"I mean it, Mom. We didn't agree to anything. You *told* me I have to do it. What choice did I have?"

"Nobody has a lot of choice here, Allie. Not you, not me, not Grandma. We have to do the best we can."

She squirmed on the bed, her eyes shifting away from me. "It's different for you," she said in a distant voice. "You've had *your* life."

I gasped, but she didn't notice. She wasn't even trying to wound me, which made it worse.

"I love Grandma, really I do, Mom," she continued, "but it's *boring* spending all this time with her. She used to be sort of fun when I was younger, but now all she does is watch television and talk about her health. I can tell you every single thing that's been wrong with her since 1968, and I wasn't even *alive* then."

"I know," I said not unsympathetically.

"I want to be with my friends. I want to be able to stay after school for activities whenever something good is going on, not just when I've arranged it with you in advance. I want . . ." She shrugged.

"You want to do whatever you want, no strings attached," I told her. "But you can't; nobody can."

"You do. You can go to work or bring home dates or whatever you want, while I have to take care of Grandma." She was getting teary and unreasonable; if we kept on, one or both of us would end up yelling. I took a breath.

"Allie, you know why I have to work, so let's not go over it again. And you also know I haven't brought home a real date in a year and a half." And when I had, she'd refused to speak to him when he came to pick me up on the grounds that just because somebody speaks to *you*, why should you be obligated to answer back? Between that and referring to the poor guy as "that dork" in a not-so-sotto voce, she generally made things so unpleasant I decided it wasn't worth the effort. Her father was not long dead, and I hadn't wanted to do anything more to upset her life. "To understand all is to forgive all," the French say. Well, maybe.

"That's no reason to take it out on *me*. It's not fair."

I shifted tactics. "Maybe not," I told her. "But what do you think I should do?"

She looked exasperated. "You're the mother. Why are you asking me?"

"Because you're the one who's complaining."

She ran her fingers through her fine blond hair. "I don't know. But do *something*. I'm already a sophomore. I don't want to miss my entire high school career."

She made it sound as if she'd been forced to turn down a seat on the Supreme Court. "I wish . . ." she added.

I knew what she was going to say before she said it. *I wish Daddy were here. Daddy would understand.*

CHAPTER FIVE

DADDY, AS IT TURNS OUT, PROBABLY WOULD HAVE UNderstood. My husband, Richard Pratt—*Doctor* Richard Pratt, as his mother always emphasized when mentioning his name to anyone who, however unwittingly, gave her the least conversational opening to do so—had had his own problems with my mother, especially in the early days of our marriage.

"Does she have to come so often?" wasn't even the half of it.

"I don't think Richard likes me," my mother said, as if she was stunned by the possibility. "He never says anything."

"Nonsense," I told her more than once. "He's just tired."

"He seems to be tired a lot," she observed.

It isn't easy to explain about my mother, still less about my ex-husband.

My mother, Mary Alice Weston, was the youngest and best-looking of five children, an adored family pet—at least to hear her tell it—who grew up with a somewhat exaggerated sense of entitlement and the high-handed manner that sometimes falls to those lucky enough to be treated with an excess of deference. Since my father was, to all intents and purposes, willing to devote himself entirely to her comfort and happiness, their marriage was perfectly agreeable, at least for her. He even called her "Baby." Would Freud have liked that one or what?

My husband, on the other hand, was smart and handsome, brilliant at his studies, athletic, and the only boy. Maybe just a little supercilious, but wasn't he entitled? His sister might have resented him, but his parents could read his destiny from the cradle. His first name was Doctor before he ever left kindergarten, although it would take him twenty more years before the M.D. was officially added.

In short, he thought he was a prince. Unfortunately, my mother knew she was a queen. A queen looking for courtiers. The combination was bound to be disastrous.

Not that the skirmishing was overt. Richard was polite to my mother whenever he dragged himself home to our apartment, exhausted and barely sentient, after hours in the lab or classroom or, later, the hospital, and found my parents visiting. He just didn't talk to her, not really. He never said a word when she occupied the only comfortable chair, insisted on sitting in the passenger seat of the car, or stretched out on our bed—the only one in the apartment—for "an hour's beauty sleep." He smiled numbly when she criticized the furniture or replaced the lamp shades uninvited. I was a little numb myself—I was working on my credential and practice teaching, and I didn't have the energy to protest. Besides, I was out of the habit; it was so much easier to go along with what she wanted. What did a few alterations in our bare-bones student apartment matter? We weren't home that much anyway.

"Mary Alice is like some giant ocean liner," Richard grumbled on one of the rare occasions when he could summon up the stamina for both sex and conversation. We were lying, spent, on sheets that needed changing. "She leaves little eddies in her wake wherever she goes."

"She doesn't mean to interfere," I told him insincerely.

He gave me a disbelieving look and turned out the light. Well, how could I guess from that that he was seething inside?

I didn't know how much anger he'd accumulated until my mother scheduled some minor surgery for the day of his med school graduation. As soon as I reminded her, she changed the date, but Richard refused to believe she hadn't done it as some sort of bizarre gesture of one-upmanship. He would not be cajoled out of his feeling of affront. By that time I was pregnant with David, hot and uncomfortable most of the time. I'd developed a love-hate relationship with the toilet bowl. I didn't feel like arguing. "It's not that big a deal," I told him.

He looked at me as if I'd confessed to an adulterous liaison with Pee-wee Herman.

"I don't mean your graduation," I said hurriedly. "I mean Mother. She just made a mistake. She didn't mean anything by it. You know how she is."

"I know how she is, Becky. That's precisely what I'm talking about. I am sick to fucking death . . ." He never finished the sentence, but he punctuated it by throwing an ashtray (people still smoked then, even, or especially, doctors) against the wall. It broke into ocher ceramic smithereens. It had been a wedding present.

I was so surprised I fell back in my chair. It wasn't the

comfortable one either. I probably should have laughed, but instead I started to smooth things over. "Richard . . ."

Richard bent and picked up the scattered shards. "Don't say anything," he said. "Just . . . don't say anything."

And sometime after that, he stopped talking to me too.

Okay, we were married for another decade and we managed to conceive Alicia, so of course I don't mean that he really never talked to me again. Or that a fit of pique over my mother's overbearing ways was sufficiently venomous to poison our relationship. But for whatever reason, some cork had been pulled in our marriage, letting out the air. The sense of cooperation, of being in the business of life together, had altered.

Years later, when I finally realized that the marriage was really over, mutual outrage brought Richard and my mother together at last.

Richard was livid. "You want *me* to leave? Have you lost your mind? How are you going to support yourself? Christ, if you think I'm going to let you take me to the cleaners, you're mistaken, I promise you."

My mother was in perfect accord, albeit at a different end of the equation. "Are you crazy, Becky? Do you know what you're giving up?" Her voice shook a little on the phone. "What about the children? How *can* you be so selfish?"

Good question. In my own defense, in defense of everyone at the outset of the divorce rather than in its aftermath, I knew it would be hard for them, but I really thought they'd be better off in the long run. It came to me that, while I had led a perfectly satisfactory traditionally *female* existence—clothes, children, a beautiful house, Buccellati silver, lunches at La Valencia Hotel—I hadn't really sampled a masculine life. What this consisted of was fairly obvious, I thought. A career, certainly; not just a job. Strong opinions, expressed without equivocation. Map-reading. Football. Sexual adventures.

With the exception of map-reading (hopeless) and sexual adventures (ha), I thought it might be good for me and for the children if I crossed over into the other camp. I had to admit that thus far in my life I'd been something of an underachiever, less than a stellar example to my daughter in particular. Besides, I reasoned, a marriage where one of the partners is holding back isn't a healthy environment for children. Did I want them to watch it wilt on the vine and just hang there?

Now, after years of battling rebellion, resistance to any intact strange male over the age of eight who might conceivably develop an interest in me, and out-and-out war with their stepmother, my certainty had vanished along with my optimism. If I had it to do over, I wasn't sure I'd have the courage or the stamina to go through with the divorce. I wasn't sure it *wasn't* selfish either, because it was hard to demonstrate that any of us were all that much better off.

Not only that, but Richard found the perfect way to get back at me.

He died.

NOT, OF COURSE, before he had married his office assistant (trite), fathered a baby boy (cute but spoiled), and changed the beneficiaries on his life insurance policy (expectable but devastating). And not before devising the most vengeful postmortem property arrangement imaginable either. But death is, not to put too fine a point upon it, the end of the discussion, and Richard had had the last word. There weren't going to be any more chances to renegotiate the past, to arrive at some kind of peaceful acceptance. Plus, when Richard keeled over from a heart attack right in the middle of an operation to remove an ovarian cyst ("the size of a grapefruit," the OR nurse told me in hushed tones at the funeral), everybody said it was my fault. Richard's mother, whose affection for me had never been profound even at the best of times, broadcast to all who would listen that my unreasonable demands (child support, visitation, the usual) had placed an unbearable strain on her son, that he couldn't bear to see his children abandoned by their own mother—I was working at RTA and going to school—but was powerless to stop me because of the ruling of the unfeeling courts. Richard's widow, Carole Cushman Pratt, by then retired from the working world I had entered, seconded every motion with unrestrained enthusiasm.

Never mind that he still smoked, that he'd married a woman half his age with a 38D chest and an array of excitements I couldn't even begin to guess at, and that he had a new baby who sabotaged his sleep. Or that he was, and always had been, a workaholic, a heart-attack-in-waiting. It was all my fault. You might have been pardoned for thinking I'd taken a gun and shot him right in the middle of Prospect, in front of half of La Jolla, God, and La Valencia Hotel.

My children, who had been mad as hell ever since the divorce, got even angrier because, as Allie told me, if I hadn't made Dad move out, he never would have married *that woman* and died. Richard was instantly reborn as a fairy-tale father who had fallen into the clutches of an evil witch, like Snow White or Hansel and Gretel, and I had sent him there. I'd tried to encourage David and Alicia to treat Carole civilly despite her all-too-apparent reluctance to be saddled with inconvenient stepchildren, but they were jealous of the marriage and of the new baby, Andrew. It didn't help matters that Richard put the money for their support and their education in trust and made Carole the trustee after his death, which gave her very broadly defined powers to wreak havoc in all our lives. Since she and Andrew were beneficiaries of the trust as well, the potential for conflict was almost unlimited. I will never believe that Richard set it up that way for any other reason than knowing how incredibly tense and awkward such an arrangement would be, and on my worst, most mean-spirited days, I indulged the sneaking fantasy that he'd died on purpose, just to get even.

Plus his dying hurt so much. I wasn't prepared for that.

MY MOTHER SAID, "I never liked him, but it's a shame. Wear black to the funeral, and do something about your hair. You look like an unmade bed."

CHAPTER SIX

ON THE SUNDAY AFTER THE JASON KRILL MEETING, TAYlor Anderson called me at home. This was a first, an event portending, I feared, nothing good. It was always possible that he had come to the belated recognition that I was the woman of his dreams after all, but barring that, I couldn't think of anything positive Taylor would want to talk to me about that couldn't wait till Monday morning.

Unfortunately, or fortunately perhaps, I wasn't home to get the message.

"Mom, that guy called," Allie said as I dumped the fresh produce I'd picked up at the Farmer's Market in Hillcrest on the kitchen counter. She picked up a head of cauliflower as if it were roadkill, wrinkling her nose. Like most of her generation, she had little enthusiasm for vegetables.

"What guy?" I asked. Usually if I didn't press her too hard, the relevant information would eventually emerge.

"That guy from your firm." Usually but not always. My heart started thudding.

"Which one?" I prompted her.

"Ummm . . ." She shoved her hand into her jeans pocket. "Oh, yeah. I wrote it down." She handed me a crumpled sheet from a notepad.

I read: *Taylor Anderson. Pls. come to work early tomorrow.*

"Thanks," I told her, despite my immediate misgivings. "Did he leave a number? Was he at the office?"

"I don't *know,* Mom," she said in an exasperated tone, something like the one I sometimes found myself using with my mother, despite my best efforts. "He didn't say. He just said, 'Come in early tomorrow.' That's all I know."

"How early?" I could see the shrug beginning, so I added quickly, "If there's anything else, Allie, please try to remember. It might be important."

She looked chagrined. "He might have said 'eight.' Yeah, I'm sure he said 'Come in at eight.'" She looked at me, picking up on my anxiety. "That's really it, Mom, honest."

I would definitely have to look into voice mail.

"Thanks," I said again.

"WHAT ARE YOU worried about?" My best friend, Isabel Kingsley, was staring down at the business end of a taco, holding it aloft gingerly to keep the sauce from sliding down her fingers. We were sitting under an umbrella in the outdoor restaurant of the Bazaar del Mundo, enjoying the sunshine. Our monthly lunch date was the one tradition I had been faithful to despite work, law school, or minor emergencies.

"I really need not to have screwed this up," I told her. "So far, I haven't had a chance to make a great impression. Things keep coming up. I might as well be wearing a sign saying 'Middle-Aged Woman with Baggage.' "

She stuffed some more guacamole into the top of her taco with a spoon. I watched her with envy. I myself had been at war with food ever since I'd started rolling excess flesh upward whenever I pulled on my pants. The food always won, though; if I didn't eat it, I wanted it, and if I did, I was sorry. I took a spoonful of my tortilla soup suspiciously; the menu touted it as low-cal and "heart-safe," but it was far too rich-tasting to be healthful.

"Everybody has baggage," she said with authority. She should know; in addition to her day job as a math teacher, she ran a very profitable business out of her house as a private investigator for potential partners, checking to see if Mr. Right is really Mr. Wrong.

"Not Missy," I said grumpily.

"With a name like that, she has baggage, I promise you." She laughed. "Anyway, you're being totally paranoid. Do you think some partner in your firm is going to call you at home to come in early so he can fire you? I don't think so!" She chewed her taco thoughtfully. "Besides, is it your professional image you're thinking about, or is it Taylor Anderson?"

Isabel was the only one to whom I'd confided my Taylor fantasies, and sometimes I regretted it. She was singularly unsympathetic, despite knowing more about bad dates and doomed relationships than almost anyone I'd ever met. Isabel was one of those rare people with the confidence and substance not to care whether she found anyone or not, which of course acted on the opposite sex like catnip. It didn't hurt that she was also quite beautiful, with black hair pulled back from her face, and carried herself like a dancer or an equestrienne. She'd been married, once, to a man whose business success, she belatedly discovered, was the result of numerous surreptitious trips to Colombia, a bombshell that ultimately inspired her sleuthing service. "I don't want anyone else to have to go through the mess I did," she'd told me. But she'd laughed when she said it. Isabel had no dark edges.

"Probably both," I admitted reluctantly. I began to wish I'd ordered a margarita.

She looked at me. "Is it time for the pep talk again?"

"No," I said. "And you have some guacamole on your lip."

"I do not. You're trying to distract me." Nevertheless, she blotted her mouth with her napkin and then checked the napkin for spots. Nothing smears like avocado. "So tell me again, what is it you get out of this thing you have for Taylor Anderson? And stop glaring at me."

"I'm glaring at you because you already know the answer," I told her. "Is this friendly badinage or a serious discussion?"

"Both," she said calmly. "You're only relaxed when we talk about my life. The minute we talk about yours you tense up. Besides, I'm worried about you."

"Don't be. I'm fine, as least as long as I don't get fired." I looked at the chip basket longingly. Maybe if I limited myself to just one . . .

"Then answer the question. What do you get out of this—I won't say *relationship*."

"I don't get anything out of it," I admitted. Well, I did get a face to put with the vibrator, but I wasn't about to confess *that*.

"And this whole time you've known him, you haven't talked about books or music or a play or Strom Thurmond's sex life or anything like that?"

"Strom Thurmond doesn't have a sex life, so what could we talk about? And we did discuss movies once. He went to see *The First Wives Club* with his wife. He didn't get why women liked it so much."

"How insightful." She wrinkled her nose. "Becky, hasn't it occurred to you that this guy is incredibly dull?"

"You haven't seen him," I pointed out.

"I don't for one minute believe that's enough for you."

"He's very wrapped up in his work," I offered. "They're—we're, I mean—trying to build up the practice."

She looked at me. "Like Richard."

I smiled. "Thank you, Dr. Freud."

"I'm serious," she said.

"So am I. Look, Isabel, I went through this when I was seeing Dr. Lawrence. Not only that, but I took psych in college. I can see for myself that I'm using Taylor to excuse not having a real relationship with someone else. But so what? It makes me happy. . . ."

She raised an eyebrow. "Does it?"

I reached for the basket of chips and scooped out a few into my hand. "Well, to be perfectly honest, not entirely. But I don't have room in my life for a relationship right now, even if I could find one that was more appropriate than having the hots for my boss, which even I know is a really dumb idea. I have all I can do just keeping my little ship afloat." I sighed. "I want the sixties back."

She sat back and looked at me, amused. "What for? You want to get stoned and forget about the whole thing?"

I laughed. "That's not the part I want back. I want the

Peace Corps. I want the civil rights movement. I want . . ."

"Becky, you weren't old enough for those things in the sixties."

"I want that sense that what you did could make a difference," I persisted. "I want to have everything ahead of me again. I want *possibilities.*"

"Oh, I get it," she said. "You want to be young again."

"That too," I admitted.

"Why don't you just settle for having some fun?" she asked.

"Pass the chips," I told her.

"I'm serious."

"So am I."

She passed me the basket.

"Anyway, I do have fun," I told her. "I go to galleries. I go to the opera when I can afford it. I read when I have the time. I like doing all those things."

"You're on a permanent quest for self-improvement, ever since you divorced Richard," she observed.

"Don't go there," I warned her.

She made a face. "Okay. But I mean *fun.*"

"You mean men."

"Of course I mean men." She leaned forward confidentially. "Don't you get the urge?" she said.

"Sure, but I've forgotten what it's for."

She sat back in her chair. "You're hopeless."

"Nope. I just remember that there's nothing lonelier than a bad marriage. Anyway, I have other priorities now."

"I know. Your work."

It was my turn to be serious. "Well, of course. My children and my mother have paid a big price these last few years while I was never home. If I don't make a go of it now, it will all be for nothing. I *want* to be a success. I want everyone to see I'm a better lawyer than Missy." I scooped up a few more chips. Maybe just a *little* guacamole. "Besides, it's not as if I haven't had any dates," I told her. "Remember the guy who kept referring to his ex-wife as 'the late, great Mrs. Mifflin,' only she wasn't dead? Or the one who kept dissecting the flowers on the restaurant table while he talked about 'respecting the carbon' of the knife? And what about the guy who changed the spelling of his name to Gym because he thought it sounded distinguished? What about—"

She waved her hand helplessly. "Okay. I get your point."

"My point is that there isn't any point. It's just setting yourself up with fresh opportunities for disappointment, and I don't have the time for that."

"You have a bad attitude," she said. "That's why you attract all these losers. You shouldn't take such a hang-dog view of your own appeal. Be more open to what comes along."

"How can you say that? Your whole job is exposing how people are trying to dupe each other into believing they're something better than they are."

"My job is finding out if they've got prison records, or a wife in another state, or larcenous tendencies. I don't do spell checks."

"Maybe you should."

She stuck out her tongue, a gesture she managed to make look insouciant and charming rather than dumb. "Didn't you say you wanted possibilities? Think about it—there's nothing more possible than a new relationship, before all the neuroses and guilt set in."

I laughed. "The baggage?"

"Exactly. Becky, let me set you up with somebody. I'll check him out very carefully, I promise. If he so much as dots an *i* funny I'll eliminate him immediately."

"I can't right now. I'm supposed to be piling on the billable hours even as we speak."

"Becky—"

"I have responsibilities," I said, picking up the check.

She tried to grab it away from me, but I held on tight.

"You have excuses," she said. "Think it over."

CHAPTER SEVEN

TAYLOR WAS WAITING FOR ME IN HIS OFFICE. I'D dressed carefully for the occasion; when you walk into a situation not knowing what to expect, what you wear is part of the conversation. Tailored skirt, silk shirt, good shoes, gold earrings. A uniform, but a nice one. I'd even gone in for what used to be called a foundation garment when we swore off them (forever, we thought, in our optimism) in the sixties and seventies. Now they're called body shapers, but the task is the same.

Taylor smiled at me so warmly I almost turned around to see who was standing behind me in the doorway. "Becky," he said, as if my presence were the most delicious sort of surprise. "Come in. Have a seat."

I looked around at that. There was something different—the office was clean. In fact, it was very clean, and there wasn't a file in sight. I was puzzled, but I began to relax. Unless he was a world-class sadist, his tone hadn't sounded like bad news. I sat.

"The others will be here in a few minutes," he said, still beaming. "I wanted to fill you in before they got here."

I didn't know if I was supposed to know who the others were, but I didn't have any idea what he was talking about. I had a sudden brief urge to throttle my daughter and her sloppy message-taking. Voice mail definitely, before the day was out.

"You've been holding out on us," Taylor said, as if that were an adorable thing to do. I'd been waiting for this conversation for six years, and now I didn't know what it was even about. "How long have you known Bobbie Crystol?"

I tried not to gape. I *knew* it had to be some mistake—the appreciative tone, all this collegial warmth. "Bobbie Crystol?" I asked, like some obtuse parrot.

"Yes," he said encouragingly. "*Doctor* Bobbie Crystol. The anti-aging guru, if that's the right word."

I felt dismayed. Of course I knew who Bobbie Crystol was, now that he reminded me. Her book, *You Don't Have to Die,* had made every bestseller list from the *Times* to the *La Jolla Light*. You'd have to have been comatose to ignore the kind of media hype she'd received. But while I knew *of* her, I didn't *know* her, not in the way he obviously meant. I hadn't even read the book. That combination of zealotry and showmanship didn't appeal to me. "More séance than science," as one reviewer put it.

Although I wasn't eager to disillusion Taylor and forfeit all this unwarranted approval, I knew I had to say something, fast. "I'm afraid I—"

The phone buzzed on his desk, and he lifted a finger to signal me to wait. "Taylor Anderson," he said crisply into the receiver. He listened for a few seconds and then frowned. "Give me two minutes, and then show her in. Offer her some cappuccino, or whatever she'd like."

He put down the phone and looked at me. "She's here

early, so we won't have a chance to go over the game plan. Now, you're nominally in charge, but I know you won't object if I back you up. You don't have the experience yet to handle a major client entirely on your own. And if you don't mind, I think it might be a good idea to get Melissa Peters involved too. But of course that's up to you."

My mind could only absorb one phrase from what he'd said. "I'm in charge," I repeated.

He smiled as proudly as if I'd won the Nobel Prize, or maybe just the lottery. I would have given a lot to have earned that smile. "Dr. Crystol asked for you specifically. I've explained to her that she'll need a team to handle all of her legal matters, but after today, you're the billing attorney."

"She asked for me?" I knew I was sounding less than quick-witted on this topic, but I couldn't help myself.

"Yes, and I'm sure I don't need to tell you that if we handle this right, it could be worth a lot of money to the firm. Not only is there a great deal of ongoing legal work, but the publicity is priceless." He gave me a little wink, the closest he had come to being playful. "I guess I don't have to add that there are substantial rewards in line for an associate who brings in a client like this," he said. "Nice going, Becky."

It didn't seem the optimal moment to tell him that I couldn't imagine any possible reason why Dr. Bobbie Crystol would ask for me to work for her in any capacity, including janitor, and that in all probability this entire construct would come tumbling down as soon as she realized that she had, in all probability, made a colossal mistake in identity. I was trying to frame some graceful explanation that would extricate all of us from this embarrassing situation when Wendy opened the door. "Right through here, Dr. Crystol."

I put on my best meet-the-client smile. I'd seen Bobbie Crystol fleetingly on television, so I knew she would be tall and vanilla-blond, with an operatic sense of style and a manner to match. I extended my hand and stepped toward the door.

And was enveloped immediately in a cloud of hand-painted silk. "Becky," Bobbie Crystol said, embracing me as if I were the last Godiva chocolate in the world. "How marvelous to see you again."

Because my face was buried in silk, I couldn't see her very clearly, but there was something just a little familiar about her voice. *Please, God,* I implored, squeezing in a prayer before she released me. *If I know this person, please let me recognize her. It will be so embarrassing if I don't.*

But I didn't. She had an oval face, flawless skin, and eyes too blue to be natural. She looked about a decade younger than I did, and gravity had not yet begun its evil work on her form, which was encased in a flowing tunic top and matching pants that had probably set her back a month's worth of my salary. She wore big shiny earrings reminiscent of Christmas ornaments on steroids.

She smiled, showing a very large number of very white teeth. "You don't recognize me, do you?" she said.

I flirted briefly with the idea of trying to fake it but rejected it as too risky, as well as unlikely to impress. "Well," I began apologetically, "I'm afraid not. . . ." I could almost feel Taylor wincing, although Dr. Crystol still absorbed the lion's share of my view.

She released me and stood back, giving me a better

panorama. "Thank God," she said. "I would have been so mortified if you had!"

Hope, which had momentarily flared up when Dr. Crystol seemed to recognize me, flickered out again. She might be fortune's favorite, but she was evidently a few cards short of a full deck. I answered her with the sort of friendly wariness I'd perfected as the firm's receptionist. "Oh, yes?"

"Yes," she said firmly. "Think Holcombe Hall, Becky. Does that help you remember?"

Holcombe Hall was the dorm I'd lived in as a freshman in college. Could she have been someone's younger sister? I mentally traveled down its dingy corridors, following the scuffed tiles and acoustic ceilings, opening the doors of memory. I stopped, horrified. *Not—*

Dr. Crystol was watching me closely. So was Taylor, but I was lost in the past more than twenty-five years before.

It couldn't be.

I lifted my eyes to Bobbie Crystol and she nodded, smiling. Delighted, in fact. "That's right. Barbara Collins."

No wonder she'd been thrilled that I hadn't recognized her right away. The Barbara Collins I'd known had been an overweight, peevish premed student, bright enough to succeed ably in class but not original enough to be labeled brilliant. There was very little resemblance to the svelte, dynamic creature who'd turned herself into a mega-celebrity mind-body-spirit guru whose shtick was eternal youth. If we'd lived in seventeenth-century Salem, they'd be piling the kindling around the base of the stake for sure.

I didn't know what to say. "I can't believe it" didn't

sound quite right. "Why me?" didn't sound like a good idea either, but it's what I was thinking. The Barbara Collins I remembered hadn't liked me in the least, certainly not enough to do me any major favors.

Maybe it was bad chemistry, maybe it was the antiquated and cruel phone system, which (in the days before anyone had a phone in her own room) alerted whole corridors to who was (and wasn't) getting outside calls through an elaborate code of blaring tones. I remembered, in the distant way you do when something is no longer relevant, like finger painting or sex, that my phone used to ring a lot, and Barbara's didn't.

Or maybe it was something I did or said or wore. I remember noting the animosity and snide remarks with amusement, which in retrospect I hoped I hadn't let show. It was college, and there were other fish to fry. There was always somebody who didn't like you. No big deal.

Still, even your friends didn't usually look you up out of the blue after a quarter of a century to drop riches and rewards into your lap. More likely it was some classier version of *Revenge of the Nerds*. Anyway, what difference did it make? This was a gift horse far too big to look in the mouth.

The "horse" was clearly expecting a gracious response, which I, gathering my wits, attempted to muster. "I'm overwhelmed," I said, which was true. "You look fantastic." I turned to Taylor. "Dr. Crystol and I went to school together."

He smiled disbelievingly, as if I'd claimed Leo DiCaprio as an intimate.

"It's true," Barbara—Dr. Crystol—told him, clearly delighted by his incredulity. "We were in the same class."

"In that case," Taylor said, holding a chair for our client with as much panache as the Scarlet Pimpernel, "you are certainly an excellent advertisement for your own program."

Not to mention liposuction, a platoon of well-compensated plastic surgeons, and, I was virtually positive now that I thought back, tinted contact lenses. Meow. Still, I thought I was entitled to a little cattiness since Taylor had implied she looked practically young enough to be my daughter. It didn't help in the least that it was perfectly true.

"What I don't understand," Taylor continued, looking at me curiously, "is why you didn't know your classmate had become so famous."

What could I say? Because she used to be everybody's idea of somebody with no activities under her name in the yearbook? There was no nice way to explain it. Come to think of it, it was surprising that news of the transformation hadn't trickled down. That's what alumni magazines are for, after all. "Well, I, uh . . ."

Dr. Crystol rescued me. "I left after two years," she said firmly. "I transferred to UCLA." I hadn't known—or noticed—that, a fact I was not about to admit. "I've changed my name, and, as Becky will tell you, I don't look the way I used to either. My mother still gets my old alumni magazines at her address, and that's how I found *you*, Becky." She smiled at me, and Taylor and I both smiled back. "My publicity materials are purposely vague about my past, although if anyone cares to look it up, of course I don't mind. I reinvented myself, and that's the way I like to present myself to the world. I'm *Bobbie* Crystol now," she said, stressing the name for my benefit in case I should be so gauche as to slip and call her commonplace Barbara. The earrings flashed and clinked a little, as if to second the motion.

I thought of Mark Lawrence, the psychiatrist I'd seen when I went through my divorce, and of how much I'd enjoy telling him about this situation. Unfortunately, I'd reached the point of impecuniousness some time ago when it was a wild extravagance to pay someone to listen to your stories, but nevertheless I thought he'd like it. Though I'd always felt a little shy of him, he wasn't one of those impassive therapists who never reacted to anything you said.

"Perhaps you two should get together for lunch and catch up on the old days," Taylor said, throwing us at each other like a matchmaker. "You must have a lot to talk about." He was hardly to be blamed if he thought we must have been bosom buddies in the sweet mists of our youth. How else to explain the choice of a first-year associate to hand your legal business to?

"That would be lovely," said Bar-Bobbie, now and ever after to be Bobbie, if that's what she wanted. She consulted her watch. I refused to check whether it was a Rolex or a Patek Philippe. "I'm not free today. Tomorrow? One o'clock? I *think* I'm free, but if I'm not I'll have my assistant get back to you."

I didn't have an assistant, but at any event I was certainly going to adapt my schedule accordingly. I said I thought that would be lovely too.

"Then shall we get down to business?" Taylor asked. We all beamed at each other as if this were a splendidly original idea. "We *are* a full-service law firm, so perhaps you could tell us what your needs are at this time, Dr. Crystol."

"Bobbie, please." She crossed her legs, showing pink toenails on her sandaled foot. I could see that Taylor was having an effect on her not dissimilar to that of walking past a bakery and catching the fragrance of fresh-baked cinnamon rolls. Her body inclined ever so slightly in his direction, following its instincts. I wondered if there were a Mr. Dr. Crystol, and if so, what he was like.

"Well," said Bobbie, "naturally my business affairs are such that I already have representation. Largo and Longueur, in New York."

I could almost hear the air go out of our inflated hopes. "Naturally," murmured Taylor. "A very fine firm."

"Naturally," I said, Taylor's echo.

"But . . ." She hesitated.

"But?" Taylor prompted.

"This is confidential, of course?"

"Of course," Taylor and I, the lawyer chorus, said together.

"Good. Some of my patients are famous, *very* famous, and require the utmost discretion. I've acquired a clinic in Mexico, which I hope to transform into the premier longevity spa in the world. In time I would hope to add others as well. So there will be real estate and tax issues, and of course, since we are a nonprofit corporation, there are compliance issues as well. I'm looking for someone in Southern California to represent my interests in these areas. Later, perhaps, there will be even more. I like it here, and I might be moving my base of operations to La Jolla." She tore her gaze away from Taylor with apparent difficulty and looked at me. "Does that interest you?"

I knew what I was supposed to say without the benefit of Taylor's piercing, encouraging look. "Certainly," I told her.

"We work with excellent firms in Mexico," Taylor added.

"Good, because that's one of the reasons I'm here," she said. "When I bought the clinic, the red tape got out of hand, and the bribes have been endless."

"I'm sorry to say that bribes—*la mordida*—are inevitable when you do business in Mexico," Taylor said, with a First World sophisticated chuckle. "The trick is knowing whom to pay and how much, so you get what you want in the end."

"This is what they teach you at Harvard Law School," I joked.

Taylor smiled faintly.

"You went to Harvard?" Bobbie asked, all but batting her eyelashes at him.

He inclined his head modestly.

"What kind of clinic?" I asked.

The ornaments swung in my direction. "Shark cartilage," she said, without blinking. "For cancer."

I'd heard this called "the great white hype" in medical exposés. It ranked up there with coffee-grounds enemas (another South of the Border favorite) as a target for ridicule. "And, ahem, will you be continuing that sort of treatment?" I asked her.

Taylor was frowning at me, but I wanted to know how bad things were.

"Of course not," said Bobbie. "There's no medical basis for those treatments whatsoever."

I let out a small sigh of relief. I mean yoga and aromatherapy are one thing, but deceiving the desperate is something else.

"We have something much more effective than that to offer our patients," she said, her voice rising a little in pitch. "We harness the immense power of the mind and spirit to the latest in scientific innovations to not only heal the body but extend the life cycle well beyond the norm."

"Very impressive," Taylor said neutrally. He was not the mind-body-spirit type; even I could see that.

"You're skeptical," Bobbie observed. She didn't sound annoyed. "I'm used to that. I'll send you some literature explaining what we do, and maybe the two of you would like to come to one of my presentations. I'm giving a seminar at the Convention Center next week."

"I'll try to be there," I assured her.

She looked at Taylor expectantly. "Taylor?"

His face momentarily took on a harassed look, which he wiped off just as quickly. "Why not?" he said.

"Excellent," Bobbie said, smiling complacently. "Now why don't I give you these documents to review?"

I wondered if attendance at the seminar was some kind of test. Since we'd apparently passed so far, I felt I should clarify something before we went any further. "Bobbie," I told her, "I really appreciate your contacting the firm in some way because of me, but you aren't restricted to using me for your work. You know that there are more experienced attorneys here too, all of whom will be very happy to work with you." I felt I owed her that much. I would already get credit for bringing in the client, even if I didn't do any of her work.

"Becky, that is so—"

"Am I late?" Melissa Peters appeared at the door, all teeth and eagerness, in a skirt so short it was less suggestive than demanding. "I'm Melissa Peters," she said, striding into the room energetically, bristling with expertise. I felt instantly slothful and inert. "I'll be helping with your legal work, Dr. Crystol."

I waited for her to say, "Please call me Bobbie," but she didn't. She turned her body slightly. "How lovely to meet you, dear." She turned back to me. "I understand that there are more experienced lawyers. I expect you'll get any help you need. But I'd like to make it clear that I'm here because of you, and I hope you'll take the leading role in handling my work."

I took back every mean thought I'd ever had about her and had to restrain myself from planting kisses on her sandals. "Thank you," I told her.

"Dr. Crystol—" Melissa began.

"I'm sorry," she said grandly, "what was your name again?"

"Melissa. Peters."

"Oh, yes." She flashed Melissa a brilliant I'm-pleased-with-everything-I-see smile. "Do you think you could get me another cup of that delicious cappuccino?"

Yessss!

CHAPTER EIGHT

I WAS SO ELATED AT THE QUANTUM LEAP IN MY PROSPECTS that I stopped at Jonathan's on the way home and bought a pork tenderloin. I could have bought it at Albertson's or Von's or some less exalted (and cheaper) purveyor of foodstuffs, but it was so unusual to have meat that actually had to be cooked from scratch that I decided the occasion justified it. If price were no object, the makings for a fairly awesome celebration were right in front of me. I passed on the caviar, but I picked up asparagus and baby lettuces, for once not caring if my mother and Allie ate them or not. Then I headed for the wine aisle, wondering what would go best with pork. I looked around for one of the ubiquitous and knowledgeable Jonathan's clerks, who could probably help me select something decent and affordable.

I almost backed into Dr. Lawrence, who was studying the Merlots.

I felt a momentary sense of confusion, the way you do in high school when you happen to meet one of your teachers somewhere outside school. Should you say something or head in the opposite direction? I'd run into my former psychiatrist two or three times since I finished therapy, and every time I felt the same way: unsettled.

To demonstrate that I was now a professional woman with clients of her own, rather than the mixed-up divorcée he had known several years before, I made myself go up to him. "Hi, Dr. Lawrence," I said.

He turned. For just a second his face was a psychiatrist's mask, showing nothing. Then he smiled. "Hi, Becky. And it's Mark, remember?"

I remembered. It was just hard to say it. He looked older; his hair was grayer and was beginning to get thinner around the crown. But his brown eyes were warm, the way I remembered them. I wondered if he still told very good very bad jokes. "Mark," I said.

"How are you?" he said, like a normal person.

I was the one having trouble. The patient-to-doctor manner I'd bestowed on him for years didn't fit anymore, and I hadn't come up with a suitable substitute.

"Fine," I told him heartily. "Really fine."

He looked amused. "That's good."

"So, um," I said awkwardly, forgetting to ask how *he* was, "what are you doing here?" The minute the words were out of my mouth I felt like an idiot. What was the matter with me? I shouldn't have conjured up high school.

His eyes flicked to the bottle he was holding.

"Sorry," I said, before he could say anything. "It's obvious. I guess I'm just a little surprised running into you like this."

"I drink," he said, deadpan. "Occasionally I eat too."

I laughed. "I'm glad to hear it." I studied him. "You're looking well," I said, like a grown-up.

He was. His olive skin made him looked tanned and healthy, even in winter.

"Thanks," he said pleasantly. "So are you. How are things going at the law firm?"

"You picked a good day to ask," I said, flattered that he'd remembered. "I—"

A sultry beauty with dark hair and heavy-lidded eyes stuck her head around the end of the aisle. "Marky, do you have the wine? We're going to be late!" She looked at me. "Sorry," she said, and disappeared again.

Marky?

He looked at his watch. "She's right," he said. "Sorry, I'd better run. It was really nice seeing you."

"Same here," I said to his back as he headed for the checkout counter.

His back looked friendly and substantial. I felt a little pang of regret at the missed opportunity and a flicker of annoyance at that "Marky."

Transference, I said to myself. *Get over it.*

Still, I thought it wouldn't hurt to treat myself to a bottle of the same wine Dr. Lawrence had selected. I lifted the bottle and turned it around.

The tag read $37.50.

I put it back on the shelf.

BURDICK WAS ASLEEP on the couch again, orange belly exposed and a paw flung over his eyes. He looked like some aging, impossibly world-weary Hollywood producer taking a brief respite from the attentions of importunate starlets. I made cooing noises at him, and he opened one amber eye with moderate enthusiasm, probably due to the groceries I was carrying in my ecologically sound recyclable bag. He closed his eye again. Cats all know *The Rules* instinctively: Make 'em come to you.

My daughter greeted me with a little wave as she passed through the living room. The phone was pressed up against her head as if it had been grafted on. She moved on into the kitchen and momentarily reemerged with a bowl of cereal, still talking into the receiver. Her dexterity never ceased to astonish me. "Don't spoil your dinner," I said, waving my grocery bag in her general direction. "I've got something special."

She gave me a look of polite incomprehension and floated into her room, closing the door behind her.

"She's been like that all afternoon," said my mother, coming out of her room. "On the phone, I mean." Her tone was a combination of amusement and disapproval. *Her* daughter (yours truly) had been limited to half an hour of phone time per day. It was useless to try to explain the futility of imposing phone limits when you weren't going to be home to enforce them. "Whispering and giggling," she added.

"Ohmygod!" Allie's voice rose to an excited squeal that penetrated into the hallway.

"What's up, do you know?" I asked my mother.

My mother looked blank. She shrugged. Once, not long before, she would have made it her business to know, the way she had made my clothes and hair and taste and friends her business when I was Allie's age. I'd resisted her badgering, but at least by her own lights she was participating in my life. Now she was slipping into self-absorption, her interest rarely straying beyond her body and its war against decline. I'd spent half my life trying to hold her at arm's length, and now I missed her giving me a hard time almost as much as I regretted her long, slow retreat.

"We'll find out eventually," I told her. "If we're patient. Are you hungry?"

"My stomach's a little rocky this afternoon," she told me. "But you go ahead. I'll just have a little ice cream later."

"Mother, you know you need to eat a more balanced diet. You can't just live on ice cream; it isn't good for you. Besides, I have some nice pork tenderloin. We're celebrating."

"I guess that would be okay," said my mother. She didn't add, "Celebrating what?"

"I HAVE NEWS," I said, cutting a bite of (if I do say so myself) perfectly cooked pork tenderloin and swirling it in the bitter orange sauce. (Just add some cognac to marmalade and throw in a little orange juice. Heat and serve, as Betty Crocker might have said.) Although I was fiercely devoted in principle (if not in practice) to someday getting my weight down to 121 pounds again, in front of Allie I was the role model of somatic satisfaction, of feeling comfortable with who you are and your own appetites, and all the other things that are the opposite of bulimia and anorexia. I didn't see a way around this hypocrisy other than a very long run of very expensive therapy in an attempt to root out years of being told by every magazine from *Seventeen* to *Cosmo* that More is Less in the size department. Hence the lovely steamed potatoes, the fresh asparagus, and the mixed baby lettuce salad sharing the plate with the pork slices. I made an ostentatious show of sampling everything, which quickly became something more than an act, while Allie pushed her food into piles on her plate. It was clear that her mind was not on dinner.

"I'm going to need your cooperation," I added. Both of them looked up at that. I knew it had an ominous ring. Allie set down her fork and gave me a worried look.

"It's nothing bad," I said. "Quite the contrary, in fact."

"That's nice, dear," said my mother absently.

Well, what did I expect? Work and family are parallel universes, intersected only by guilt. I couldn't demand enthusiasm, however much I might have enjoyed it. The most I could hope for was to slog along reasonably well in two worlds at the same time without wreaking havoc in either one. Like it or not, this was probably what my life was going to be from now on. Not an altogether cheerful prospect, on the whole.

"I got a new client today," I went on relentlessly. "Maybe you've heard of her: Dr. Bobbie Crystol."

"Is she on *Oprah*?" asked my mother.

"Not that I know of," I admitted. "But she is sort of famous. She's a medical doctor working in the anti-aging area and—"

My mother snorted.

"What does that mean, *anti-aging*?" asked Allie.

"In my day it meant dying your hair and lying about your age," said my mother surprisingly. "Now it means stuffing yourself full of hormones and freezing your head after you're dead."

"Oh, cool!" cried Allie. "Is that where they, like, store you in a Thermos so they can bring you back later on? Grandma and I saw that on TV. It costs a *lot* of money."

I could see that I had seriously underestimated the informational value of afternoon programming.

"Giving new meaning to *The Big Chill,*" I murmured.

They both looked at me without comprehension, locked out of the generational reference by their positions at opposite ends of the age spectrum. I *hated* it when that happened; it was like having Old Fogy tattooed on your forehead, except that tattoos were a generational marker too. Like saying "You sound like a broken record" and realizing your teenage child has no idea what that would sound like. How did this happen so fast? When did the Grateful Dead get edged out by Dr. Kevorkian?

"Anyway," I said, "I don't know exactly what's involved. I haven't read her book yet."

"Oh, a *book,*" Allie mumbled in a tone that struck daggers into my heart.

"Called *You Don't Have to Die,*" I offered.

My mother choked on her asparagus.

Allie looked startled. "Really?"

"That's really the title. I don't think she can actually be claiming that she's found the secret to eternal life or anything like that. I mean, the public is gullible but not *that* gullible."

Allie looked disappointed.

"Hubris," said my mother.

"What does that mean?" my daughter asked.

"Getting too big for your britches."

Allie made a little face. This was one of my mother's favorite criticisms, used to stamp out Ambition before it took root and caused permanent damage. We'd both been on the receiving end more than once.

"I'd like to live forever," Allie said.

My mother shook her head. "No, you wouldn't."

Allie and I looked at her.

"You can only stand things for so long," she muttered darkly. "Trust me."

"Anyway," I said hurriedly, before she could expand on this topic, "it might be mumbo jumbo, but it's going to be *my* mumbo jumbo. I'm going to be in charge of Dr. Crystol's legal work."

"That's nice, Mom," said Allie. Her tone told me she'd lost interest.

"It's a very big client. It means a lot of work and undoubtedly some nights and weekends at the office."

"Oh, Mom." My daughter sighed. She knew what I was going to say.

"I really need to be able to count on you to keep things running smoothly while I'm not here," I said, encompassing both of them. Allie knew what I meant and started squirming. "It won't be forever, but ultimately it could mean a lot more money for us."

"What good will that do?" she mumbled, rolling her eyes.

College, a car that starts reliably, a vacation somewhere without canvas walls, I thought. I didn't say anything.

Her eyes flooded suddenly. "May I please be excused?" she asked, dabbing at her tears with her napkin. "I have to call somebody."

"You didn't finish your dinner," my mother pointed out.

Allie looked at me desperately.

"It's fine," I said. "Go ahead."

"Humph," said my mother disapprovingly.

"I wonder what that was about," I said after Allie had departed for the sanctuary of her room, phone in hand. By now I was used to adolescent mood swings, but this was more sudden than most.

"Spring formal," said my mother, surprising me again.

"This early?"

My mother shrugged.

"I thought you didn't know what was up."

"I forgot," she said.

I CORNERED ALLIE later in the kitchen, after her grandmother had gone to bed. The one constant with healthy teenagers is their requirement for frequent infusions of sustenance.

Her look said, *Don't crowd me.*

All innocence, I got a glass of water from the tap (no fat, no calories, good for you, and tastes *terrible*, plus the city of San Diego keeps trying to get voters to approve recycling sewage water treated to make it potable) and sipped it, watching her spread a piece of bread with honey from the nearby Laguna Mountains. She always insisted that honey you could buy in the grocery store tasted "plastic," so we made the hour and a half round-trip to Julian once every two or three months. As soon as she got her license, she declared, she would make the trip by herself over the narrow and winding roads. Ha.

"So," I said, sidling up to the topic with astounding subtlety, "are you thinking of asking somebody to the dance?"

She looked away, embarrassed. "I don't know." She

put down the half-eaten slice of bread. "Maybe. It's not for a couple of months yet."

"Have someone in mind?"

She looked at me. "Mom, *please* don't ask me who. You don't know him, okay? I'm not ready to talk about it yet."

"Fine," I told her. "I understand. I only want to encourage you to go, if that's what you want. Remember what you were saying about making the most of high school?"

She nodded mutely.

"I just want to say that no matter what happens at work or with Grandma, I won't let anything interfere with this, barring unspeakable acts of nature or fate. We'll go get a dress, and we'll make time for whatever else is necessary. Shoes, the whole bit."

She laughed. "Promise?"

"Promise," I said. "But first you have to ask somebody."

"I know," she said, looking at her feet like a shy kindergartner, in one of those abrupt changes of attitude that twist your heart when you're a parent. "But what if . . ."

"What if?" I prompted her gently.

"What if he says no?"

"It'll hurt," I admitted. I couldn't even begin to tell her how much. "But you'll live through it. And if you're as brave and smart as I think you are, you'll just shrug your shoulders and ask someone else."

"You make it sound so easy," she said.

"Oh, Allie," I said, "there's nothing easy about it. It's just . . . the way life is."

She looked away. "Did Dad . . . ?"

"What?" I asked her.

She half smiled. "He told me once you turned him down the first time he asked you out."

"That's true," I said. "Imagine your remembering that."

"I remember *everything* about Dad," she declared. "So how come you said no?"

A million answers sprang to mind, none of which I wanted to share with my daughter. "I was seeing somebody else when he asked me, someone I thought I liked better."

"But Dad won out in the end," she said.

I smiled. "He was very persistent," I told her. "You should remember that."

"Are you sorry?"

I looked at her. She was serious. "Of course not," I said. Which, in most of the ways that really count, was true.

She gave me a quick hug. "Thanks, Mom."

I flicked her cheek with my finger. "Don't mention it," I said. "Advice is my specialty."

"I know," she said, rolling her eyes. But at least she laughed.

Afterward, I thought how much I missed having someone to share this with. Somebody to ask, "Do you think she'll get a date?" who would understand the worry that she might not. Somebody to relive the excitement and the fear of being rejected that comes with asking someone out. Somebody to say, "How could anybody not want to go with her?"

Somebody like her father, in fact.

Most of the mental dialogues I still had with Richard

were arguments, part of the unfinished business between us. At moments like this I was reminded that there had been good times too, and I knew he would have understood, even if he'd been impatient or busy. If Richard had still been alive, I wouldn't have wanted him back as a husband, but I wanted him back as a father, Allie's father, and David's too.

SIGHING, AND FEELING sorry for myself for reasons that were unclear even to me, I went to check the voice mail I'd acquired earlier in the afternoon. There was already a message in my "mailbox."

"Hi, Mom," said my son's voice, in his usual breezy tone. "Glad you finally got a message service. Grandma always forgets when I tell her I called." He hesitated. "Listen, Mom, I'm really sorry to ask you this because I know how much you hate to deal with it, but Carole's late with Dad's portion of the tuition payment again. Could you, like, call and remind her? The administration office has been on my case, because it happens, like, every quarter. Sorry, Mom. Thanks. Bye."

CHAPTER NINE

BOBBIE CRYSTOL SWOOPED INTO THE RESTAURANT LIKE an actress auditioning for a starring role she knows she's already won.

"Sorry I'm late," she said, disengaging her hand from the maître d', who looked as if he'd like nothing more than to kiss it. She had on tight jeans, a black T-shirt, and the most dramatically beautiful Navajo squash blossom necklace I had ever seen. Heads turned.

I gave her a smile worthy of a publicist or an escort. "No problem," I said, although my seat was already numb from sitting.

"Use the firm credit card," Taylor had told me. "Go somewhere expensive."

I picked George's at the Cove, although it fell more into the "reasonable" category, because of its zillion-dollar view over the La Jolla coastline and because of the black bean soup, which is outstanding and famous. I had to confess to a certain curiosity about what or whether my old acquaintance would eat. On the basis of her metamorphosis, I wasn't so sure I shouldn't follow suit, even if she expressed a preference for steamed kale and seaweed.

"You look terrific," I told her. "I still can't get over it." I didn't know if this would be a nostalgia lunch or a business lunch, but either way I was sure the remark would please her. Besides, it was true.

"Thank you," she said, shaking out her napkin, which seemed far too ample to cover her tiny lap. "You look nice too." She studied me. "It's been a long time, but I'd still recognize you."

I wouldn't have minded if it hadn't taken her quite so long to arrive at that conclusion. "Thanks," I said.

"Look, Becky, would you mind if we didn't talk business today?" she asked. "I've got to eat and run, and I'd really like to catch up with you personally first."

"If that's what you'd like," I told her. "We can go over the time-sensitive issues at the office."

"Something to drink, ladies?" inquired the waiter.

"Iced tea," I told him.

"Vodka tonic, no ice, with a twist of lemon," said Bobbie.

"You drink?" I asked her, surprised.

She laughed. "I'm over twenty-one," she said. The waiter looked as if this were a wonderful joke and he'd like to card her on the spot.

"I just meant that I didn't know it was part of your program."

"I'm off duty," she said. Catching my look, she gave me a big toothy smile. "Just kidding, Becky. It's all very carefully worked out. You really should read my book."

I said I was planning to. I hoped I sounded more enthusiastic at the prospect than I felt. "I'd heard of you and your book, of course, but I didn't have any idea it was anyone I knew personally," I told her. "How did you get interested in anti-aging?"

She raised an eyebrow. "Are you serious? Every ten seconds a Baby Boomer turns fifty, and people are desperate for help. Nobody wants to age the way their parents have. People are *ready* for my message."

"Which isn't really that you don't have to die, surely?"

She shrugged. "Well, in the sense that you don't have to die when you thought you did, yes, that is the message. That you don't have to be sick and old in the sense we think of it now. That you can take responsibility for what happens to your body by changing what you do and how you think. As for the long run"—she smiled—"we're still working on that."

The long run? What was that, eternal life? "Working on it how?" I asked her.

She tapped a long, perfectly manicured fingernail on the table. "Cryonics, maybe. Nuclear cell transfer. There are so many things going on you wouldn't believe it."

"Cryonics? As in freezing the corpse?" I couldn't wait to tell my mother she'd been right. "You're kidding," I added tactlessly.

Dr. Crystol—momentarily forgetting she was my friend Bobbie—gave me a frigid smile. "Freezing the *body*," she corrected me. "I personally expect to take advantage of such technology myself. I hope that by the time it becomes an issue for me, the research will have found a way to circumvent the cell damage that now accompanies the Freezing Event. At all events, I hope so. I have made a reservation for the neurosuspension of my entire body."

"Ready to order?" asked the waiter.

* * *

BOBBIE ORDERED A GRILLED chicken salad, like a normal person rather than someone who had plunked down a fortune to pump her veins full of antifreeze in the afterlife. I had the same. I passed on the black bean/tomato/broccoli soup on the grounds that, although it gets points for the broccoli (*fights cancer, attacks free radicals!*), major points must be deducted for heavy cream, which is, of course, what makes it so delicious in the first place. There is something so unfair about the inverse correlation between taste and benefit. Still, I didn't want to risk another Freezing Event.

"So what about you?" she asked me, sipping her drink.

"I don't even own a cemetery plot," I told her.

She laughed. "I mean, what about your life? Are you married? Children?"

I gave her a very edited sketch of my life since college, without any lamentations or regrets.

"I see," she said. She looked at me. "Were you happy in school?"

"College, you mean?"

She nodded.

"It was probably the happiest time of my life." I was always surprised that anyone could doubt it. I mean, how bad could things be when you were given four whole years to focus on nothing but your own development and pleasures? Four years, if you worked it right, without even having to pick up after yourself, much less worry about the mortgage or the car payments. Other kinds of happiness—marriage, children—were more intense, but they were rarely as uncomplicated. And then there was always the fact that in college you were—not to put too fine a point upon it—young.

She frowned. "I hated it, you know. I had to work really hard while the rest of you had a good time. I guess it paid off, though, didn't it?"

I felt it would be impolitic of me to mention my Phi Beta Kappa key. Besides, premed really was awful, and if she wanted to paint me as Cindy Cheerleader by comparison, I wasn't going to argue with a Client. "It certainly did," I agreed.

"So you're not thinking of getting married again?"

I shook my head.

"Sleeping with anyone?" she asked, looking at me over the top of her drink.

I wondered what the ultrapolite version of "None of your business" would be. Dear Abby always said you should say something like "Why would you want to know that?" but by this point in the conversation I was beginning to suspect that I knew the answer to that already. Unless I missed my guess, I was about to be treated to a recitation of Dr. Crystol's triumphs at the altar or in the sack. My role, clearly, was to be the appreciative audience.

"Bread?" I temporized, offering her the basket.

She smiled. "No, thanks." She leaned forward earnestly, resting a blossom (or is it a squash?) against the tablecloth. "You know, Becky, you're really very attractive. Of course, we prefer to start before the client is forty, but I still think I could do a lot for you. Why don't you think about entering one of my programs? We could do a *complete* body, mind, and spirit makeover. If finances are a problem, I could give you a special rate."

I nearly choked on my breadstick. "Well, that's very generous, but . . ."

She gave me a shrewd look. "Ever had anyone fantasize about you? I mean lately?"

I laughed. "I sincerely doubt it," I told her.

"Well, *I* have. Men write me letters all the time. Some women do too." She glanced around the dining room as if to see whether any of them might be looking at her now. She turned back to me. "It's not just my physical appearance. They sense something in me they want. It's, well, I'd call it the possibility for self-regeneration. People are hungry for it." She looked down at her salad and then lifted her eyes. "It's a turn-on too, I can tell you that much."

"I'm sure it must be," I murmured.

"You think I'm a total narcissist, don't you?"

Of course I did. I smiled. "How can I possibly answer a question like that?"

"Never mind," she said, waving her fork dismissively. "I don't care what people think of me. At least not anymore. My ex-husband cured me of that."

"You were married?"

She shrugged. "Twice. Once to a very conventional M.D., like you were. I met him in med school. We came to a parting of the ways when we realized all we had in common was a preference for 69 and a mountain of debts. We bifurcated the debts. The sex lasted a little longer." She sighed. "I haven't seen him in years. He's probably a GP in Stockton or something like that. I wish him well. He was a nice guy. He just . . . thought *small,* if you know what I mean. My second was an Indian. That only lasted a few months."

My glance moved involuntarily to her necklace.

She saw me and laughed, a little too loudly. "No, no.

I got this when I was speaking at a conference in Santa Fe. Sameer was from *India*. He was an Ayurvedic practitioner. I met him in the Amazon, where he was studying with the local shamans."

"Wow," I said.

"I learned a lot from him," Bobbie said with uncharacteristic reticence. "But I came home with amoebic dysentery." She sighed. "Of course, it was entirely my own fault."

"For drinking the water?"

"For abandoning the path of righteous living," she said seriously. "Also for eating raw shellfish."

"What happened?" I couldn't help asking.

"Eventually he went back to India," she said. "I followed him, but I found that, once there, his views . . . reverted to something I couldn't live with. Particularly with regard to his mother."

I wondered what Sameer's mother, expecting a dutiful and perhaps reverent daughter-in-law, had made of Bobbie Crystol, M.D. "I suppose she had someone more traditional in mind for her son," I suggested.

She snorted. "That's putting it mildly. I always suspected suttee might eventually be part of the package, but I didn't want to risk waiting around to find out. Anyway, it certainly wasn't a waste. Many of the therapeutic herbs I use in my program I discovered in India. That's one of the pillars of my success." She looked at me. "Here's an example. Have you heard of guggul?"

I shook my head.

"It's excellent for the control of obesity."

I didn't want to inquire whether this general observation was made for a more specific purpose, so I said nothing. An appreciative audience *and* a target for the occasional well-placed jab, apparently. I *knew* I'd been right about that lingering hostility. What I wasn't clear about was why I'd been anointed counsel at all.

"And for other things as well," Bobbie said. "Most of Western medicine is completely ignorant of such treatments, and there are dozens of them."

"Are they safe?"

She gave a smug little smile. "They've been used for thousands of years in the East. We in this country are far too suspicious of anything we didn't invent."

Nevertheless, you had to wonder if the life span of those Third World denizens privy only to such enlightened treatment was really the equal of their First World cousins treated by harassed GPs and unfeeling HMOs.

"Hmmm. Sounds interesting," I said noncommittally. I mean, I wanted to keep an open mind about a client, particularly a big client, but I didn't trust Bobbie's oversized ego and undersized evidence. Still, as long as it didn't hurt anybody, what difference did it make?

"Well, it is, actually," she said. "You know, I probably shouldn't insist on this, but you *really* should let me help you. You need to let go of so many things. I can feel the tension in you from here. My program will not only extend your life, but it will restore harmony and balance to your existence. I've told you, it's much more than just a physical regimen."

"You want to make me a test case?" I asked, laughing. It seemed prudent not to take her too seriously.

She fixed me with a piercing stare, the look of a zealot. "I'm not kidding, Becky. I've worked with much more difficult cases."

I felt like some powerless furry animal hypnotized by a cobra on a PBS nature program. If I wasn't careful I wouldn't get out of this with my psyche intact. It seemed less amusing to let her rattle on than it had a moment before—clearly it was time for a bit of what Jameson Roth called "client management." "I think we should decide right now that if we're going to work together, this sort of thing is off-limits," I told her. "I appreciate your concern, but we both need to maintain our objectivity."

She shrugged. "Have it your way," she said. "But if I might make one *tiny* suggestion, you could start with trying to get rid of the people who cause you anxiety and pain," she said.

Easy for you to say, I thought. She was incorrigible. Nothing short of a firehose would stop her. Why not start right now?

"I'll get the check," I told her.

"CAROLE," I SAID, finally placing the call I'd been putting off all afternoon since getting back from lunch, "it's me, Becky."

My late ex-husband's second wife greeted me in a tone appropriate to time-share salesmen or mechanical messages. "Yes?" she said frostily.

"How are you?" I asked, trying for a conciliatory note. I could hear Andrew—adorable Andrew, my husband's second son—talking about something in the background.

"Fine," she said shortly. "A little busy at the moment."

"Well, I won't keep you." I paused. "I've spoken to David recently. . . ." I always expected her to leap in with "The tuition money! I forgot! I'll send it right off!" but she never did. We had had this conversation numerous times already.

"Yes?" she said again, more impatiently. "Just a minute, Andy. Mommy will be off the phone in just a second."

"The college hasn't received this quarter's payment. I was wondering if you'd sent it yet."

She sighed gustily. "I don't remember off the top of my head," she said.

"Well, would you mind checking? The administration office has sent him two notices already."

"I don't have time for this right now," she said. "We're on our way out."

All the things I would like to have said went screaming through my brain, exploding like little meteors. I knew that getting angry wouldn't help, and, unless I was prepared to finance a major court battle to try to remove her as trustee (virtually impossible without cause), I had to preserve a veneer of civility in our relationship. But it galled me nonetheless. I mean, it was my *children* she was manipulating to get even with me. If I provoked her she could make things worse for them, but that didn't stop me from indulging in a few sadistic fantasies.

"Could you check tomorrow, then?" I asked as pleasantly as I could through clenched teeth. "If you haven't already sent it, that is."

I knew she hadn't. I knew she did this on purpose. I knew what would come next too.

"Fine," she said. "Since you're so concerned about it, you can come over here and pick up the check anytime after ten."

She occasionally made me come to her house, her big beautiful villa on a hill, to pick up what she should have just dropped in the mail. I suspected it was a way of reminding me of—all right, make that rubbing my nose in—the difference in our economic circumstances, my downward mobility. I had to keep paying for being Richard's first wife, at least till the kids collected on the principal of the trust when the last child—Andrew—turned twenty-five. That was so long in the future I felt as if I would be chained to her forever. I'm sure she felt the same way about me. I think she hated me so much that it was worth suffering the irritation of proximity in order to have the opportunity for punishment. In her place, I hope I would have turned the trust over to some nice bank officer who would collect a fat fee and act as referee.

Still, if she insisted on handing the check over personally rather than sending it on, it suited me more to go there than to have her come to my office or my house. I had a superstitious fear that if she saw my *things*—my desk, my taste in furniture, the art on my walls, the contents of my bookshelves—she might get some insight into my personal life or my persona that she could use against me later. It was probably a paranoid reaction, but my feeling was, when in doubt, go with your gut instinct.

Besides, Dr. Lawrence, my last access to the fount of psychological wisdom, had said the same thing, albeit in more elegant and professionally appropriate terms.

I wondered if maybe I shouldn't consider taking Bobbie Crystol up on her offer to change my life after all.

CHAPTER TEN

"SO BASICALLY," ISABEL SAID, WHEN I TOLD HER THE story of My Lunch with Bobbie, "she spent the entire lunch trying to bully you."

"Did I say that?"

"What else would you call it?"

"Trying to impress me." I laughed. "With just a *teensy* bit of bullying."

"Humph!" Isabel made a skeptical noise into the phone. "She sounds like a queen dispensing patronage to me. Very noblesse oblige."

"I suppose," I said. "But the patronage is being dispensed my way, so if she wants to preen and beat her chest a little, I'm willing to hold up the mirror. Besides, to tell you the truth, it was more amusing than annoying."

"This reminds me of *Peggy Sue Got Married*," Isabel said. I love talking to people my own age, who have all the same cultural reference points, instead of to whippersnappers who think the special effects in the original *Star Wars* are primitive. Someday we'll all be laughing uproariously at jokes about "dignity pads" and trusses, to the horror of younger, less afflicted generations. Nevertheless, I didn't get it. My favorite scene in the movie was where the heroine renounces algebra as totally irrelevant, but I didn't think she could be referring to that.

"I don't get it," I told her.

"I mean the part about the unpopular nerd who comes back a multimillionaire to the high school reunion," she said. "Remember? This has the same kind of feel to it. It sounds as if Dr. Crystol has chosen you to be the audience to her success."

"You're probably right," I said. "I had the same thought. It's certainly understandable. If you got rich and famous—not to mention great-looking—when everyone remembered you as lumpy and peevish, wouldn't you want those people to see how you'd changed? I would." Isabel herself had won a *Mademoiselle* competition in college and had a brief stint as a model, so she might have had difficulty identifying with such a scenario. When she went back to *her* reunions, everyone would no doubt exclaim over how little she had changed.

"Was she really lumpy and peevish?" she asked.

"Well, sort of. She always seemed irritated about something whenever you talked to her."

"Humph," she said again. "Just be careful she isn't building herself up at your expense, that's all."

"I will," I told her. "I get the showing off, and I can even understand the digs. We weren't exactly friends way back then. What I don't understand is why me?"

"Frankly, I'd watch my back around her," Isabel said. "My theory is that people's characters are formed by age eleven and everything after that is just veneer."

"God, I hope not. I was an awful brat at eleven, to hear my mother tell it. Anyway, I don't really mind being her audience. I see what she's doing, and I can live with it."

"Yes, but that's your motto," she said lightly. "Becky?"

"What?"

"You're not going to let her mess with your head, are you? I mean, you know I think you should allow yourself to have more fun, but you don't need a 'mind-body-spirit makeover,' whatever that is."

"Don't worry; it's probably nothing worse than herbal tea and a good night's sleep," I told her. "And anyway, I told her no." I laughed. "I may go on and on about body parts that flap in the wrong direction occasionally and the extra five pounds I'd like to lose, but I draw the line at major remodeling. I have no desire to be one of Bobbie's 'projects,' believe me."

"Good," she said. "Just checking."

Isabel was the kind of woman I wanted to be; I'd known that from the moment I'd first seen her, picking out paperbacks at the monthly used book sale held by the library. And not just because she'd bagged the best books already—*Animal Dreams* and *The Realms of Gold* and *Persian Nights*—by getting there first. There was something quietly confident about her demeanor, without being overbearing or brash. She had discipline too and the courage to rebuke. Later, when I got to know her, I remarked on these qualities. She told me she'd had a military upbringing, which, if you were the type, was the best possible preparation for life. All that moving and changing, she said, was a tonic. It toughened you or it killed you.

"Isabel?"

"I'm here."

I love you. "Thanks," I told her.

"Don't mention it," she said.

CAROLE'S HOUSE WAS near the top of a steep hill. Statistics published in the newspaper indicated that 131 houses in La Jolla had opened escrow in the million-dollar housing market in the first half of the year. The average price was $1,824,259. That kind of price was the only respect in which Château Pratt would qualify as average. I parked in front and cropped the wheels into the curb. I would like to have leaked oil onto the driveway, but the Lexus was blocking my way.

Carole and I, despite our separate attractions, brought out the worst in each other. The difference between us was that she didn't have to try to hide it for the sake of her children, and I did.

Although she was allegedly expecting me, the wrought iron gate, which would not have been out of place at a monastery in Spain, was locked. I rang the bell. I waited. I rang it again.

Andrew opened the door and walked into the courtyard. He was, I was forced to admit, an extremely handsome child, a miniature of Richard at the same age. He peered at me through the gate. "Hello, stupid," he said.

Carole followed him out the door carrying a tennis racket. Her legs were tanned, even though it was only March. "Andy, that's rude," she said without much conviction. "We don't speak that way to anyone, no matter *who* it is." She looked at me. "Sorry," she said, as if the admission cost her an effort.

"No problem," I told her. And it wasn't, at least not mine. In another ten years I thought she would come face-to-face with the error of her child-rearing ways, but by that time, trust or no trust, I planned to be out of the picture.

We were at an impasse. The check was clearly in the house, which meant that either she would have to invite me in or leave me unsupervised with her son or her property or both.

She chose to keep me where she could see me. "Won't you come in?" she asked formally.

"Thank you," I replied with equal ceremony. We might have been ambassadors of rival nations meeting at court. "I won't keep you. I have to get back to work."

Carole left me in the living room, while the au pair, an exhausted-looking student from Denmark, collected Andrew and whisked him away to the backyard. The house was very well furnished, although to my taste a little too crowded with "collectibles" and a little too lacking in books. Another reason I didn't want her in my house making assessments about *me*.

Moreover, now that I was into noticing, I discovered that the honeymoon picture of Richard and Carole in Bali, once displayed in glorious prominence on the mantel, was missing. I considered Carole's tan, her tennis, and her overall sleek look. I wondered if she was seeing someone. She certainly was an attractive prospect (if you didn't mind serving as an acolyte at the shrine of Andrew); she had looks, and thanks to Richard's life insurance and the trust, she had money. In addition, she was still young enough for a second family. At all events, I certainly hoped she might be. If she remarried, the trusteeship reverted to a bank.

As there was no possibility of asking her outright or even of skirting delicately around the subject, I contented myself with sitting on the edge of a chair, hands folded in my lap. Presently she came back into the room, holding the edge of the check as if it were a dangerous species of reptile. She thrust it at me.

"Thank you," I said, giving it a quick peek to make sure it was for the correct amount. It wasn't, but it was only off by a few dollars. Not worth making an issue over. With Carole, issues had a way of coming back to haunt you.

"It's ridiculously high, the tuition," she said, averting her face from me.

I felt a twinge of discomfort. When people won't look you in the eye, they usually have something unpleasant in mind to say. "Yes, and David gets a scholarship," I said mildly. "Think what the costs will be by the time Andrew is ready for school."

She sniffed. "Still, doesn't it seem a bit... *excessive*... to pay that much when he could just as easily go to a state school?"

Little alarm bells went off in my mind. "A state school?"

She shrugged. "What's wrong with San Diego State? He could save even more by living at home."

I said, very carefully, "Richard and I agreed that it would be best for him to go away to college, years before David even graduated from high school. We wanted both our children to have the residential college experience that we had." Carole had gone to State herself, like half of the rest of San Diego, so it would have been tactless to impugn its academic reputation. "Besides," I said, "Richard went to private school."

"Richard," she said, invoking the name like a talisman to ward off evil, "was going to be a *doctor*. Your son is studying—what?—physical education?"

"Communications," I said, struggling to keep my temper. "He wants to be a journalist."

"A journalist." She closed her eyes. "How . . . useful."

"It's what he's good at." I strove for a tone of levity, despite my pounding heart. "Come on, Carole, it's not as if he's expressed a lifelong interest in opening a Chippendale's franchise. It's still a perfectly respectable ambition. Didn't you see *All the President's Men*?"

"Yes," she said. "We rented it once. It bored me to tears."

Oh.

"After what those dreadful animals did to poor Princess Diana, I wonder how anyone could even consider such a field," she said. "Anyway, I think it's only fair to warn you that we might need to reconsider the tuition payments. I'm not sure that giving him that much is justified, under the circumstances."

I felt an edge of panic. "You're not saying there isn't enough in the trust fund to cover it?"

She looked away again, at a spot over the top of my head. "As a matter of fact, some of our investments haven't worked out as well as I'd hoped. So, yes, the return on the principal has been reduced."

I gasped. "You haven't been putting the money into something superspeculative or anything like that?"

She glared at me. "I have an excellent investment adviser. Unfortunately, no one is right a hundred percent of the time."

"Carole," I said, scarcely breathing, "this is our children's education we're talking about. You have to be responsible. You can't take risks."

"I have other sources of income," she said, "as do you."

"But—"

"I don't want to argue about it with you. If Richard had had faith in *your* judgment, why didn't he name *you* trustee?"

Because he was probably hoping it would work out just like this. Wherever Richard was, he was no doubt looking up (or even down, but I doubted it) and savoring this moment. His little plan to get back at me was working perfectly. I wondered if there was any way to put a stop to it.

"Carole," I said, clasping my hands together so hard my fingers turned white and bloodless, "I know we aren't exactly friends—"

"That's putting it mildly."

"And I know you resent me for reasons that we probably don't need to go into now, but—"

"No, let's do go into them," she said. "I do resent you. I resent the fact that you wrecked your own marriage and then you made so many unreasonable demands you wrecked mine too. You helped kill my husband. You knew he was under a lot of stress from working so hard, but you wouldn't let up. You took my son's father away. Resent? That's hardly a strong enough word for it! And now I have to keep *seeing* you. It's too *much*." Despite her anger, she kept her voice low enough so that Andrew and the au pair couldn't hear. I was grateful for that.

Breathe deeply. Count to ten. I could hear Dr. Lawrence's maxims in my mind. "This is pointless," I said finally. "Can't you see how futile it is to blame everything on me? Richard was a fine man, but he certainly wasn't blameless for what went wrong in our marriage, and—"

"But *you* had the affair," she pointed out triumphantly.

I flushed. "Richard shouldn't have told you that," I said quietly. "It was between us. And anyway, it wasn't an *affair*. But that's all I'm going to say about it."

I'd told Dr. Lawrence, though. I'd slept with someone I wasn't in love with, didn't even like much, in fact. Richard and I weren't separated yet, although the subject had come up. Not that that's any excuse. I'd done it partly out of curiosity, partly out of loneliness, and partly out of motives that probably don't have to be explained. None of them made me very proud, even before Richard found out, which he was bound to since the affairee was another doctor in his hospital whom we saw socially. He was divorced too. I didn't like to think about it, but I'd done the best I could to work through it honestly with the therapist. Nevertheless, I wasn't too keen on discussing it with Carole.

I had to wonder how Carole had dealt with the fact that medicine was the only truly absorbing interest of Richard's life. Maybe it had been different between them, but I doubted it. When we were married, Richard's work was the only thing that really moved him. His conversation wasn't an exchange—it was a series of stories about somatic dramas.

It had taken me a long time to catch on. He had a powerful and conspicuous life, but I wasn't an important part of it.

So what? you might ask. It's not as if there weren't any perks. It's undeniably nice to have a vehicle that comes from Symbolic Motor Cars instead of Leo's New and Used, not to mention a view of the Pacific Ocean, granite countertops, Manolo Blahniks in the closet, and a lot of other tangible benchmarks of affluence. But the trouble with parallel lives is that they don't, well, intersect.

Richard had not been sympathetic to my dissatisfaction, which, in retrospect, was probably tedious. "What are you complaining about?" he asked me. "You have time, you have help with the children. You can do anything you want. You can *be* anything you want."

The truth is, I didn't know then what I wanted to do or what I wanted to be. I thought all I wanted was Richard, the way he was—or the way I thought he was—at the beginning of our marriage. When my heart leaped up at the sight of him, when I didn't have to tease "I love you" out of him as if it were the prize in the Cracker Jack box. By the time I finally asked him to leave, my heart hadn't leaped up at anything in a very long time. Maybe that's why I found the courage to go through with the divorce.

Carole was studying me with dislike. Part of the reason for her animosity toward me was that she obviously thought I should envy her, and I didn't.

"The point is," I told her, "that whatever you think your grievances are with me, you must exercise prudence with the trust. Richard's whole purpose in setting it up was to protect his assets so that money would be there for all of you when you need it. My children are counting on that money for their educations. They're innocent victims here."

"*Victims?*"

I couldn't shriek at her the way I felt like doing or she would take it out on David and Allie, if she could. I decided to try another tack. I drew a breath. "Richard loved Alicia and David just the way he loved Andrew. As you say, he trusted you to do the right thing by them. I'm sure when you remember that you'll try to put our differences aside."

I sounded a bit like a self-help manual, and one glance at her told me she wasn't buying it.

"Actually, I doubt that very much," she said, walking toward the front door.

I rose. "Then why not just give up the trusteeship? Let someone disinterested decide how the money should be invested and spent. You don't want to keep seeing me, and I feel the same about you. This is the perfect way to take yourself out of the picture altogether. It lets you off the hook."

"I don't think so, Becky. That would be letting Richard down."

And you'd lose the administrative fees paid to the trustee, not to mention access to the principal, I thought, but I didn't say it. As both a beneficiary and a trustee, Carole enjoyed a great deal of latitude about how the money got spent. Or wasted.

"Besides, as you know, the trustee is not legally responsible for unhappy investment results, as long as she picks her adviser with care." She smiled enigmatically. I wondered who was advising her.

"If you violate the spirit of the trust, I'll take you to court," I told her.

She regarded me speculatively. "I don't think so," she said. She opened the door and gestured with her head. "And if you harass me any further on this, I'll make you very sorry. Now if you'll excuse me, I have a tennis match."

CHAPTER ELEVEN

"WHAT TIME SHALL I PICK YOU UP?" TAYLOR ASKED ME.

My mouth dropped open, an expression unlikely to be flattering much after infancy. I couldn't help it. Taylor Anderson, in shirtsleeves and tie—not to mention a crinkly smile and mesmerizing blue-green eyes—was filling the door frame of the conference room, offering to pick me up.

It's just a ride. Get a life.

I must have sat there gawking rather longer than the question necessitated, because eventually Lauren poked me under the table.

"Anytime," I said. It came out as a sort of squeak. "If it's not too much trouble," I added.

"No trouble. I don't live all that far from you, so we might as well go together."

He knew where I lived. "Eight-thirty?" I asked him.

"Fine," he said. "See you then."

Okay, so it wasn't a date. We were just going to Bobbie Crystol's command performance at the Convention Center. But until two minutes before, I'd assumed we were going in separate cars. I wouldn't have been surprised if we hadn't even sat together. A cool, professional, independent woman like me certainly didn't need an escort to what was essentially a business occasion. I wondered what I should wear. Suede? Linen? Casual cotton? And loafers, maybe? Or . . .

"Becky?" Lauren was looking at me rather too perceptively, so I hastened to return to Earth.

"Sorry," I said. "Where were we?"

She smiled somewhat enigmatically. "I'm not sure."

I jerked my mind back to the papers on the desk. Leases. FDA guidelines. EPA regulations. Tax codes. There were so many issues involved in advising somebody setting up a company—and in Bobbie's case a laboratory as well—and I didn't have the experience even to identify them all, much less handle them. I had to have help.

"I really appreciate this," I told Lauren. I did too. I might have had to work with Melissa instead. "I couldn't handle all this alone."

She smiled. "Knowing that is half the battle. Generally I don't think it's a good idea for first-year associates even to worry about getting their own clients, as I think I told you." She grinned at me. "No matter how brilliant and talented you are, you need several years of experience before you solo on a client. More, for one like this." She made a wry face, which told me a lot about her opinion of Bobbie. "Taylor's being generous in letting you take a crack at the work yourself," she added. "In some firms, a partner would take over automatically."

The trouble with law school is that you don't know anything useful, in the practical sense, when you come out. You've learned to "think like a lawyer" and, worse, write like one, and you've got a lot of judicial principles down pat. If you've worked especially hard (or are exceptionally lucky), you can explain the Rule Against Perpetuities (the Holy Grail of murkiness) in a reasonably knowledgeable way. But that doesn't mean you know how to write somebody's will. The truth is, nobody should turn over his work to a new associate, whatever the certificate on the wall may say about passing the bar. Every day of my first year I was constantly being reminded of my inadequacies.

"My turn to get the coffee," I said. I went into the coffee room and poured two cups. The staff took turns making fresh pots all day long. Once it had been my job too.

I set Lauren's cup in front of her on the table. I slid a napkin under it, so it wouldn't make a ring on the surface. Wendy had once told me that we would know RTA was in the big leagues when they swapped the oak conference table for rosewood.

"What did you mean about a client 'like this'?" I asked Lauren. "Is there something about Dr. Crystol's work that's more complicated than usual?"

"How honest do you want me to be?" she asked levelly.

"Very," I said.

She shrugged. "Well, initially the work is fairly predictable." She gestured at the piles of paper on the table. "We get her a lease on a suite of offices and some laboratory space. We do the paperwork to deal with the water purification issues, health code compliance, et cetera. We look over her Mexican real estate transactions and go over them with our colleagues in Mexicali. We get the tax guys to review everything to make sure we haven't missed anything. It's complicated, but it's straightforward, if you understand what I mean."

It seemed like keeping a dozen balls in the air at once to me. "If you say so," I told her. "Go on."

She spread her hands wide. "After that, it really depends on what Dr. Crystol does next. Is she going to limit herself to speaking, or is she going to dispense medications and nutritional supplements? If the latter, she has to make sure she meets FDA regulations, and sometimes that means walking a fine line legally." She sighed. "And that doesn't get into issues like what if someone feels cheated because he didn't get eternal life, or boundless energy, or whatever it is she's hawking, and decides to sue for malpractice. The possibilities are virtually endless."

"You sound less than thrilled with Dr. Crystol's life-extension theories," I said. She rarely made a negative comment about anyone, so I was curious.

"I have no idea what her theories are," she said. "It's Dr. Crystol I'm less than thrilled with."

"Oh, dear."

"She's a client, Becky, so we cut her a lot of slack. We aren't a big enough firm to turn that kind of business away. Don't worry. I just didn't take it kindly when she waltzed into my office and said that if I worked on my attitude I might be able to walk again."

Oh, God. "Oh, Lauren. She *didn't.*"

She laughed ruefully. "When you're in a wheelchair, you're a magnet for this kind of thing. It's like being pregnant—you attract a lot of loonies along with the well-wishers, but nobody feels any reticence about jumping right in."

"Is Dr. Crystol a loony?"

"She is if she thinks 'healing waves' or whatever are going to fuse together a spinal cord severed by a bullet," she said.

A bullet? I was speechless.

"Thank you for not asking," she said. She paused a moment and went on. "Anyway, even if Dr. Crystol has the noblest and best intentions in the world, things can get screwed up. There can be unintended consequences. That's where you, the drafter of documents, the adviser and expert, come in. You have to do the long-term thinking about heading off undesirable outcomes. And that isn't always easy. Particularly not with a loose cannon like Bobbie Crystol."

" 'Unintended consequences.' I like that. It's the story of my life."

"It's the story of everybody's life," she said soberly. "But as a lawyer, it's your job to try to make sure all the consequences are intended."

"How can I do that?" I asked her. "How can I control Bobbie Crystol?"

"You can't."

"So what do I do?"

She laughed. "You worry."

"Seriously?"

"Seriously. Also, you protect your ass, and the firm's ass too. You make sure Dr. Crystol is aware of the consequences, and you get your advice in writing. Then you have to do what she wants."

"Or quit," I said.

She made a face. "Get real," she said. "Your job is to help the client do what she wants, as long as it's legal. Period. After that, you get to obsess all the time about not screwing up. You have to internalize it till it becomes like a mantra. *I will not screw up. I will not screw up.* You aren't really a lawyer—certainly not a good one—till you wake up at two in the morning going over every step of your last deal or whatever to make sure you did it all right."

"Oh, Christ. Doesn't that get any better after you've been practicing a while?"

She shook her head. "No, it gets worse. Now you have a history—a whole backlog of things that might come back to bite you. Sorry, Becky. It comes with the territory."

I laughed. "So basically, if I do this right, what I have to look forward to is no affordable scruples, no sleep, and a lifetime of obsessing over details, right?"

"Don't forget outrageous malpractice premiums."

"Isn't there any juridical joie de vivre?" I asked her.

She narrowed her eyes and gave me a dry little smile. "Not at the office," she said. "Not if you're smart."

THERE WERE NO secrets at the law firm.

"I heard a certain partner is taking you to a meeting tonight," Wendy said in a conspiratorial whisper as I was washing out the coffee cups in the sink. "And a certain associate has her nose out of joint."

I dried them carefully and put them down on the strainer, the Sisyphean task of the coffee room. Tomorrow they would reappear magically with dark encrusted rings. "I don't suppose it would do any good to pretend I don't know what in the world you're talking about," I said.

She grinned.

"It's just a business event," I told her.

"*I* know that," she said. "But our Miss Peters isn't so sure. You should have seen the look on her face when Ryan told her."

"Ryan should mind his own business," I said.

She shrugged. "The way she dishes it out, he can't resist the opportunity to stick it to her when the opportunity presents itself. For that matter, neither can I."

"She's not *that* bad," I said. "Maybe just a trifle too confident for comfort." I laughed. "And anyway, I doubt she's worried about me in any sense whatsoever."

Wendy rolled her eyes.

"You know, I don't think this is what all those women in the sixties and seventies envisioned when they fought for their right to compete in the workplace," I told her.

She shrugged. "It beats sitting home and wondering what your husband is getting up to with his secretary," she said. "Which is what law firms were like in 1968, when I first started working." She sighed. "And anyway, Becky, I know you have better sense than to get involved with someone like Taylor Anderson."

I wondered what she meant by *that*. "Or anybody else where you work," I said, fishing. "It's just a bad idea in general."

She looked at me shrewdly. "Granted." She lowered her voice. "Just remember, secretaries in a business know lots more about you than you realize. If you're booking two tickets to Miami twice a month, if you're late with your alimony payments, if you're a heavy user of a certain florist, well, we know."

I wasn't sure what she was trying to tell me. "I'll bear it in mind," I told her.

"You do that," she said.

CHAPTER TWELVE

MY MOTHER MET ME AT THE DOOR WITH UNCHARACTER-istic energy. Even the cat seemed to have caught her mood; he bolted outside as soon as I opened the front door, running right between my legs and out onto the porch. "Just a sec," I said, fending off whatever it was she obviously wanted to tell me. I threw down my brief-case and went after Burdick, who was edging out onto the lawn, pursuing his interests in botany and herpetol-ogy. I moved slowly. I didn't want him to run away. Nighttime is when bad things happen to good cats.

"Gotcha," I said, grabbing him around the stomach. He squirmed in protest. Fourteen pounds of truculent cat is no small handful, but mindful of who opened the cans, he sheathed his claws.

"Got him," I said to my mother, unnecessarily. Bur-dick, affronted, trotted off toward the solace of the food bowl. "What's up?" I asked her.

My mother put a finger to her lips. "She asked some-body," she said.

"Already?"

She nodded. "I'm not sure, but I think he said no."

Oh, God. "Oh, dear. Is she upset?"

My mother rolled her eyes. "She's in her room. I knocked on the door, but she won't come out."

"Well, leave her alone for the time being. If you try to force the issue, she'll clam up. You know that."

My mother gave me one of her you-indulge-that girl-no-end looks and shrugged. Maybe I did, but when I was Allie's age Mother had demanded that I share my every thought and secret with her, at least when she cared to ask. I didn't, of course, but I still remembered what it felt like to have the contents of your mind requisitioned for inspection. I probably went overboard stamping out any traces of the same tendency in my own parenting. The trouble with the gene pool is that there isn't any life-guard to save you from yourself.

Still, it didn't take a mind reader to see that my mother was probably right. Allie didn't come out of her room for the hour it took me to shower and get ready to go to Dr. Crystol's lecture, and when I went to call her to dinner, I could hear her whispering feverishly into the phone. Peer consultations were burning up the lines. I hoped she didn't tell too many people; it would just make tomorrow that much harder to face.

"I don't want any dinner," she said when I tapped on the door.

I knocked again, waited, and then opened it. "Sorry, kiddo," I said. "I need to talk to you for a minute any-way."

She looked unhappy, but in a normal, adolescent kind of way, not anything that signaled a deeper distur-bance—depression, drugs, you name it. If you believed the newspapers, you had to be on the lookout all the time. So much guessing goes on in the parent-child relationship in the teen years. It made me yearn for the days when her needs and emotions were more readable, not to mention less complex, the days when she cried and I picked her up, and that was enough.

"I have to go listen to Dr. Crystol lecture on life extension down at the Convention Center," I told her. "I was wondering if you'd like to come with me."

She looked blank. "Dr. Crystol?"

"You remember. Human Popsicles? Fountain of Youth?"

She smiled. "Oh, right. No, I think I'll pass. Thanks anyway."

"Okay. In that case, here's Mr. Anderson's cell phone number in case you need me. We're going together." I paused. "Ready to join me in tonight's boxed offering?"

The moody look returned. "No, thanks. I'm not very hungry."

"Want to talk about it?" I strove for a gossamer touch. Too heavy-handed, and I'd squash it before it ever started.

She shrugged. "It's no big deal."

Right. I waited.

"I just asked this guy to the dance, that's all."

"And?" I prompted gently.

She sighed, needing an audience. "I'm like, 'Are you going to the dance?' and he's like, 'I don't know.' And then I say, 'Would you like to go with me?' " She looked away.

I hadn't even heard the rest of the story and already I would have liked to kill this person.

"He said he'd have to think about it," she said.

With a hot poker up his nether regions.

She gave me an anguished look. "He's a senior, Mom. He says if he goes, he wants to take a motel room with some of his friends and their dates so they can stay out all night."

With barbs on it.

"Alicia—"

"I *knew* you wouldn't let me," she said, clutching the pillow to her chest in the same fierce way she used to hold on to her Raggedy Ann.

I resisted the temptation to say, "You got that right!" I took a breath, waiting for the inspiration that never comes to rescue you at such moments. "Honey, you haven't even dated this person before. You don't want to put yourself in a situation like that. Too many things can go wrong." *Sex! Alcohol! Pregnancy! Drugs!* I tried to stay calm.

"Nothing would *happen,* Mom. All the kids do it." She didn't sound utterly convinced herself, which gave me a little hope. I wasn't ready for the staying-out-all-night battle yet.

"Allie, why did you ask this boy? How well do you know him?"

She shrugged. "He's cool. All my friends would just *die* to go out with him."

Uh-oh.

She twisted unhappily on the bed, bunching up the pillow under her hands. "I *have* to go, Mom. *Everybody's* going to the dance," she said.

I patted her gently on the back, like a baby. "The last time you said *everybody* like that was when you were trying to persuade me to let you pierce your tongue. I'll say the same thing now that I did then. The *somebody* you're becoming now is the one you have to live with for the rest of your life. Make sure you're making decisions for the right reasons."

"Oh, Mom, I know. It's just . . ." She raised her arms in a gesture of despair.

"Allie . . ."

"What?"

"Ask somebody else to the dance. There's plenty of time."

She looked startled. "How could I do that? What if he decides to go with me anyway?"

I closed my eyes. The words *A lousy jerk who keeps you dangling while he waits for a better invitation?* hovered temptingly close to utterance, but restraint won out. "Tell him that since he wasn't able to make a commitment, you made other plans," I said gently.

"You're kidding, right?"

"Trust me," I told her.

BOBBIE CRYSTOL WAS resplendent in a diaphanous, flowing pink gown that would have been right at home at the Oscars. Her blond hair (chemically assisted or I'd eat my program) was pulled back in a knot to show off her perfect youthful complexion. She swept across the stage clutching her microphone as if it were the gift of the Magi.

The room was packed, so Taylor and I sat in the back.

"She doesn't look much like a doctor," Taylor observed.

"Who'd want to come if she did?" I whispered back. It was true. Medical professionals aren't a very glamorous-looking bunch, on the whole. Too much time squinting into microscopes and staying up late to study. By the time you reach the age where you can afford restorative measures like health spas and ski trips, the years of toil have already taken their toll.

A room-sized screen at the front of the auditorium filled suddenly with a slide of what looked to be a gathering of transparent worms, but maybe it was just something on the projector.

"Nematodes!" cried Dr. Crystol in a celebratory tone more suitable to announcing the Half Yearly Sale at Nordstrom's.

The audience, now fearing they had signed up for a science lecture by mistake, murmured audibly.

"Why do we care about nematodes?" she continued. She paused dramatically, but not long enough for someone to fill it with a rude comment. "They're creepy, right? You can't even see them unless you've got very good eyes. They don't do much either. This group just hangs around a Petri dish, resting on top of a bed of nutrients. *Borrring!* Get a life, nematodes!"

The audience laughed uncertainly, not sure where she was going, but clearly relieved by the jocular tone.

"The thing is," said Bobbie, in a tone of intense excitement, "it's not what they do with their lives, it's how long they have to do it. Outside of laboratory conditions, nematodes might survive nine days if they're lucky. These nematodes, who happen to live in a laboratory in Canada"—she made a sweeping gesture with her arm, embracing the screen—"have been known to live *fifty* days." She dropped her voice in pitch and volume. "If a human being were able to duplicate that kind of life extension, he would live for four hundred and twenty years. *Four hundred and twenty,*" she emphasized.

I had to admit she was good. She had the audience in the palm of her hand, enthralled with the life span of invisible worms.

The picture on the screen changed. I recognized the

subject matter from biology, not to mention rotten bananas.

"Fruit flies!" exclaimed Dr. Crystol. This time there was nothing but expectant silence.

"Fruit flies have a *riveting* life compared to nematodes," she said. I could see the bumper stickers now: FRUIT FLIES HAVE MORE FUN. "They eat, they mate, they fly around. This is a fruit fly community here in California, in another laboratory. In the wild, if some bird or another predator doesn't snap them up, fruit flies might get to live seventy days. These fruit flies can survive up to a hundred and forty. It's not as dramatic an increase as the nematodes, but a human with this kind of longevity could live a hundred and fifty *years* and beyond."

She turned away from the slide to face the audience. "So why am I bugging you with this?"

Heh heh.

"Because in laboratories all over the world, similar studies are going on. Because the world of aging is being remade. The rules are changing. Scientists like me are here to tell you that *what works for nematodes and fruit flies can work for human beings too.*"

Wow, a life span of 420 years. I wondered what that would do to Social Security.

"In nineteen hundred, a child born in the United States could expect to live forty-seven years," she said. "If he's born today, his life expectancy is seventy-six. There's absolutely no reason to believe that we can't keep on extending and extending a person's life, perhaps indefinitely."

In short, *you don't have to die*.

I glanced over at Taylor to see what his reaction was so far. He looked transfixed, like the rest of the audience.

But hey, he was a Boomer too, and immortality sounded just as good to him as it did to everybody else.

"Unfortunately," said Bobbie with a wistful smile, prepared to let us down gently, "science alone, while pursuing many promising areas of investigation, isn't yet able to give us the kind of results we've seen with nematodes and fruit flies."

She walked to the edge of the stage and spread her arms wide. "I believe in science. I am a medical doctor. I believe that in the not-too-distant future, genetic manipulation or nanotechnology or some line of inquiry will produce impressive results for mankind of the kind we've seen here. *But* . . ." She paused dramatically. You could have heard a pin drop in the audience.

"But," she said, "as much as I respect allopathic medicine, I think all the emphasis on pure scientific research is lopsided. It neglects the *mind*. It neglects the *spirit*. If we really want to extend our lives, we can't afford to overlook these essential elements of our being. We *know* that the mind has a profound effect on the body. Did you know that a Japanese acupuncturist has created anesthesia in his patients just by setting the needles next to them on the bed? We *know* that the mind can create disease and dysfunction in the body. Have you heard of hysterical blindness? Does your child get a stomachache before a test? Ever wonder where the term *tension headache* comes from? I could go on and on. I'm sure we all recognize that our thoughts and emotions can create illness."

She paced across the stage, caressing her microphone like a country-and-western singer. "What we *haven't* focused on is this: If our feelings and thoughts can make us sick, they can certainly *cure* us as well. They can actually create the chemical reactions in our bodies that support life." She smiled serenely. "There is a long scientific explanation for how what's going on in your mind and spirit affects the molecular structures of your body to produce biological signals and affect your well-being," she said. "But I won't bore you with it now. Let's get down-and-dirty. Let's talk about *your body*."

She pointed out into the audience, probably right at me. "Are you slipping slowly out of your prime? Do you *hate* to drop something because it's so hard to bend over and pick it up? Have you been laid up with backaches, headaches, stomachaches, and worse? Have you seen the common cold turn into a two-week event? Do you look in the mirror and see the face of a person much older than you think you are?"

Uh-oh.

"All of these things are signs of aging," she said. "And *all* of them are avoidable."

A gigantic blowup of the cover of *You Don't Have to Die* flashed onto the screen.

"The Crystol Program, which is outlined in my book, which you see here on the screen"—she pointed at it with a laser, just in case we might have overlooked the billboard-sized mock-up as a result of our slide into senescence—"is three-pronged.

"*First*, we start with the body. We pamper it, soothe it, rest it, tone it. We give it what it wants. We eliminate toxins from the diet by following a carefully prescribed plan. In some cases we give it natural tonics, based on substances that have been known to heal and enhance physical well-being for thousands of years."

I liked the part about giving the body what it wanted, but I bet mocha cappuccino cheesecake, my own Platonic ideal of a carnal craving, would not be on the list.

Bobbie's body probably lusted for tofu. Thank God there hadn't been any advocacy of caloric restriction, at least so far, unlike those dedicated types who hoped to squeeze out a year or two more of life by subsisting entirely on steamed broccoli sprouts and cherry tomatoes.

"*Next*, we turn to the mind. We focus on various ways to use our brains to change our bodies. We recognize that our emotional and psychological past and present—our 'baggage,' if you will—can make us ill and that we will never get well until we can jettison these things from our lives. Learning to let go, to discharge our negatives, is a big part of healing our bodies, and as we heal our bodies, we get rid of the things that make us *age*.

"*Last*, we address the spirit. Obviously this is a personal and very complicated thing, but harnessing the spirit, finding your individual path to righteous living, is the key to longevity. We hope you will come out of our program spiritually enlightened as well as physically and mentally refreshed."

A picture of Casa Alegría, the soon-to-be-opened Crystol spa across the border, flashed up on the screen. Bobbie obviously wasn't one for subtlety.

She took a sip of water from the glass on the lectern. "I'd like to take a short break, during which time I'll be answering questions and signing books in the area adjoining this room. When we come back, I'll talk more specifically about our program. Thank you."

When the lights came on, Taylor stood up. "Let's get some coffee," he said. All about us, well-heeled types reasonably well acquainted with the period known as midlife were milling and mulling. The demographics were fantastic, even I could see that.

Taylor took my arm and steered me up the escalator

to the refreshment pavilion. In honor of my body (as well as my desire to sleep) I chose decaf. I wondered if I should ask for green tea, but I've always thought it tastes like someplace legions of incontinent water creatures have called home.

Taylor started to take out his wallet, while I agonized momentarily about whether I should let him pay. (It's not a man-woman thing, it's a partner-associate thing.) "I'll get it," I said finally, preempting him. "It's my client."

He smiled.

We took our coffees out on the terrace overlooking the water. The Convention Center occupies one of the most beautiful spots in the city, right on the water's edge, but it was designed to face inward, and you have to fight the architecture to get any view. It's worth the effort.

"So what did you think?" I asked him as we stood side by side facing out to sea. It was a little chilly, but I wasn't about to suggest going in. "She was great, wasn't she?"

He grinned hugely. "I think," he said, all but rubbing his hands together with uncharacteristic glee, "that we ought to seriously consider taking a large percentage of our fees in stock."

I laughed. "That good?"

"I'm serious. I'm going to raise it with the partners next week at the meeting. We're looking at tremendous potential here. She could be as big as Chopra. Did you see the way she held the crowd?"

I was beginning to think that being unlovely and unloved in school was probably the best thing that ever happened to Barbara Collins. She might never have become Bobbie Crystol if she'd been a Little Sister of Minerva or some other social atrocity that seemed ridiculously important at the time.

I nodded. "She was very impressive." I cleared my throat. "I'm thinking books, clinics, tapes, seminars, maybe even TV specials." I hoped I was on the right track.

"Absolutely," he said. "All of those things." He ticked them off on the fingers of his hands. "I'm sure she can pull it off."

"What did you think of her life-extension theories?" I asked him. I was curious to know how he'd reacted.

He looked startled, as if the question was totally unexpected. "I don't know. To tell you the truth, I wasn't really listening to that part."

I wondered what part he'd been listening to.

"What did *you* think?" he asked me.

"Well," I said, considering. "It seemed pretty harmless."

He raised an eyebrow. "Did you think it wouldn't be?"

"Maybe *harmless* isn't the right word. I mean, it's pretty straightforward. You take care of your body. You take care of your emotions because they affect your body. I mean, who doesn't know that? And you take care of your spirit because, well, it's good for you." I shrugged. "It reminds me of hearing about one of these incredibly complex and scientific-sounding weight loss programs and then finding out that what it boils down to is diet and exercise." I looked at him; his eyes were glazing over. Weight control and emotions were obviously not high-priority topics on his list of enthusiasms. "Anyway," I said, returning to subject matter more likely to excite him, "I'm glad to hear you agree that this will be good business for the firm."

He smiled. "It's good business for everybody." He looked at me. "You know, when you wanted to come on as an associate at RTA, I wondered if it would work out."

"So did I," I told him truthfully. "There are certain difficulties involved in changing roles so completely."

"Not that you aren't smart and competent and—though of course I shouldn't say it—attractive," he said.

The night, which had previously seemed a little chilly, began to warm up.

"But the law isn't for everyone," he continued. "If you're going to succeed, you have to have a certain toughness. Quite frankly, I didn't see that toughness in you when you worked at the firm before."

How tough did you have to be to say "Roth, Tolbert and Anderson" into the telephone and "Where would you like me to put this file?" to the firm's attorneys? On the other hand, sitting through Torts and Contracts and Civil Procedure, et al, every week for six years after you've worked all day was tough. Writing briefs on the weekends and staying up till three in the morning reading case law was tough. Trying to find enough time for your job, your classes, and your children was tough. Taylor didn't have a clue.

"I'm not surprised," I told him. "I was the *receptionist,* Taylor."

He looked disconcerted, as if he'd momentarily forgotten. He waved a hand dismissively. "Anyway, that's all forgotten now." He made it sound like a sordid incident. "I think it's safe to say we've never had an associate bring in a piece of business like this so early in his or her career. It's quite a coup."

"Too bad I didn't go to school with Bill Gates," I suggested.

"Umm, isn't he a little bit younger than you are?" he asked.

Okay, so Taylor didn't have the greatest sense of humor, despite all his other favored-by-fortune attributes. But the night was beautiful and so was all the attention I was getting for being the Friend of Bobbie. It was impossible not to enjoy it.

"A tad," I conceded good-naturedly. "Plus he dropped out." Plus he went to Harvard, which I'd never come remotely close to attending. The nearest I'd gotten to the Ivy League was that my alma mater liked to style itself "The Princeton of the West."

"What *was* Bobbie like in school?" Taylor asked me.

This was a question I was not eager to answer with tactless truth. "Well," I temporized, "you remember that I didn't recognize her at first. I didn't know her very well, but, um, she was a bit less glamorous than she is now."

"A bit?"

"The styles were different. You know how it is."

He folded his arms and smiled. "I think I get the picture."

I doubted it, but I didn't want to enlighten him. "Let's just say that her program has definitely succeeded if she's any example. In fact, she wants the firm to come for a 'refurbishment weekend' or whatever when the spa opens."

He nodded. "Do it, if you want. It will be great publicity. The firm will pay."

"She wants you to come too," I stressed. At least there was safety in numbers.

"We'll see. We could send all the associates at least. I'll talk to Jamison Roth about it tomorrow. In fact, you should also come to the meeting with the partners to plan how to make the most of Crystol Enterprises. We might even get to take her public." Even on the darkened terrace I could see happy thoughts of IPOs dancing through his head.

"Great," I said. "Thank you."

"So," he said, looking out over the water, "was she always ambitious?"

"Apparently. I didn't know it at the time, though."

He nodded. "Good. I admire people who are driven to succeed." He turned to look at me. "Like you and Bobbie."

I entertained a moment of indecision about whether or not to accept this compliment gracefully. As a matter of fact, I wasn't too keen on being lumped with Bobbie's knock-'em-out-of-your-path ruthlessness, but what was I going to say? *I'm* not driven to succeed? Dr. Lawrence would doubtless have had something acerbically appropriate to say about this dilemma. I drew in a breath. "I—"

The phone rang.

At first I didn't know where it was coming from, since I myself was still on the low-tech end of the telecommunications technology spectrum.

Taylor made a face. "Sorry," he said, and pulled the phone out of his pocket, flipping it open. "Taylor Anderson," he said crisply. He listened. He closed his eyes in weary resignation.

"It's for you," he said.

CHAPTER THIRTEEN

THE INTENSIVE CARE UNIT NURSES' STATION WAS A POOL of light and noise in the middle of a circle of darker, quieter patient rooms humming with the comforting sounds of watchful machines. The nurses themselves, not far into the night shift, were frenetically occupied—leafing through papers, conferring with doctors and aides, writing reports, giving directions. A few plants and stuffed animals sat on the edges of the barriers, their softening effect largely lost in the absence of sunlight. As in a bank, the interior architecture was designed to keep you away from the important stuff. I shifted from one foot to the other, waiting for someone to look up, although I was standing only a few inches away from the nearest seated person, a tired-looking gray-haired woman with her reading glasses perched on her nose.

"Excuse me," I said for the second time.

"Yes?" she said, looking up at last, probably annoyed at the interruption. She studied me and said, more gently, "Can I help you?"

"My mother." My throat was dry, and I swallowed. "Mary Alice Weston. W-e-s-t-o-n. They said downstairs that she was on this floor, but she's not in the room number they gave me."

She consulted the computer. "She was here," she confirmed. "But she's been moved. Room two-oh-six. Take the elevator and turn right." Her eyes slid to her paperwork again. *Dismissed.*

"Wait, I—"

"Yes?" She indulged me momentarily.

"Can you tell me what's the matter with her? Why she was brought here? No one told me anything on the phone except that she fell."

"That's something you'll have to discuss with your mother's doctor," she said. "Room two-oh-six," she repeated firmly.

"Could you at least tell me . . ."

Her eyes were steely, her lips pressed together.

"Is it a good sign that she's been moved to another floor? I mean, it isn't bad news, is it?"

Surprisingly, she laughed. "Honey," she said, "this is Intensive Care. There's no place to go but up."

MY MOTHER WAS sleeping. There were no alarming tubes or other paraphernalia attached to her body parts, so I was reassured. Still, as she lay there I felt I was really seeing her for the first time in a long time. She looked thin and old and very tired. It was like seeing a house you've lived in all your life suddenly stripped of its furniture and familiar objects. It made me feel forlorn and lost.

There wasn't a doctor in sight. I wondered how I could get someone to tell me what had happened. My neighbor, Louise Kennedy, had responded to Allie's frantic phone call and found my mother passed out on the kitchen floor. She'd called 911 and stayed till the paramedics arrived, but she didn't know much more than that. Bless her, she was waiting at my house with Allie till I got home. The ICU allowed only one family visitor at a time.

"Please," I said to the woman seated at the nurses' station, "I need to find out what happened to my mother."

The nurse looked at me with dark eyes filled with compassion.

Thank God, I thought.

"You're Mrs. Weston's daughter? She said you would come."

Yes. "Yes."

"Try not to worry. Your mother fell, and they've had to run some tests. Right now there's no indication that it's anything really serious. They'll want to keep her here at least overnight for observation. You just missed Dr. Bryan, but she'll be checking in again in a couple of hours."

"Is she unconscious?" I asked.

"Oh, no. Just sleeping, I think. She's probably exhausted. It's natural."

"Oh. I should just let her rest, then."

She nodded encouragingly. "It's probably best. While you're waiting, you might stop by Admissions downstairs and fill in the paperwork. And tomorrow, after they see the test results, the discharge planner and a patient advocate will want to ask you some questions."

"Some questions?" Even to me the words sounded slow and dull-witted. My brain seemed to be numbed.

"About your mother's situation at home and what kind of care she'll receive. It's routine. Nothing to worry about."

Nothing to worry about. Routine. Of course they would want to know how I would take care of my mother, now that she was . . . what? Unable to take care of herself? I still didn't know if she'd had a stroke or a heart attack or something less on the medical atrocity scale. How was I going to take care of her?

"Becky?"

I turned. "Mark?" I almost said, "Dr. Lawrence," but I remembered in time.

"How's your mother?" he asked. "Have you talked to Julie Bryan?"

I shook my head. "I haven't talked to anyone. How did you know?"

"I happened to be in the ER when they brought her in," he said. "I didn't know she was your mother until I saw the chart. I stopped by to see if I could catch you here."

I felt such an immense rush of gratitude I almost cried, except that I'd already done that a lot in therapy and didn't want to remind him, or myself, of any of those scenes. "Thank you," I said. "Can you tell me anything?"

He hesitated.

I had a thought. "What kind of doctor is Julie Bryan?"

"Neurologist," he said.

"Uh-oh," I said.

He touched my arm. "Why don't we go down to the cafeteria and get some coffee?"

"Okay," I said. "Thanks."

The coffee was surprisingly good. We sat in a couple of vinyl chairs of the turquoise color favored by institutions determined to manipulate the mood of the inmates. The cafeteria was largely deserted; the food section was closed except for the portion devoted to caffeinated beverages. "It's a myth, about the bad food in hospitals," Mark told me. "And the coffee has to be good because if it weren't, no one would drink it, and if no one drank it, the staff would be going facedown onto the patients. And that's not good for business."

I laughed. "Sounds like a good basis for a Monty Python skit," I said. I wanted to relax, but I still felt very shy with him, the way I had in the grocery store. He was never in a million years going to bring them up, I was sure, but he knew things about me that no one else did. He knew that I'd faked orgasm for two years before Richard left. He knew about my affair. He knew how vulnerable I was and how insecure I'd felt about my ability to make a life for myself without a husband. In short, he was aware of all the things I hoped no one would ever find out.

Besides, how can you not feel wary when someone knows your darkest and most intimate secrets and you know next to nothing about him? The only really personal things I knew about Mark were that his wife had died of breast cancer at age thirty-four, which was very sad, of course, but could hardly be counted as his fault. And that some sultry Dark Lady knew him well enough to call him Marky. In a relationship of therapist and patient, even when it's in the past, the balance of power is permanently skewed, unless you can get him to confess to a previous episode of erotomania or an excessive enthusiasm for feet.

If Mark had a lascivious interest in my shoes, which were perfectly serviceable Cole Haans, he certainly hid it well. He also looked too tired to be caught in the toils of obsessive love for anything other than his coffee. Still, you never know. Everybody is somebody with a past.

"TIA," Mark said, interrupting my speculations.

"Pardon?"

"TIA. Transient ischemic attack. That's what they think your mother might have had. It's like a mini-stroke of a brief duration. She might have felt dizzy and fallen, or her leg might have been temporarily weak."

"What do the tests show?"

"Inconclusive," he said. "But she has high blood pressure and a partially blocked carotid artery, so it's certainly a possibility. She might need an endarterectomy to unblock the artery. Julie will talk to you about it. How has she been acting at home?"

"Sort of listless, to tell you the truth. I've tried to interest her in going out, in joining groups or clubs or something that would give her a chance to socialize with someone other than the three of us, but she fights me every time I suggest anything. She watches a lot of TV." I sighed. "I don't suppose that's a medical condition."

"Depends on what she watches," he said. "Seriously, she might be clinically depressed or something like that. I'd mention it to Dr. Bryan."

"I think," I said, trying to explain it to him, "that most of it is that she hates being old." Also, she hated not being the center of someone's universe, as she had been for my father. But it seemed a betrayal to tell him that.

He nodded. "The Golden Years are definitely overrated," he said. "The prospect of prune juice cocktails and a fixation on roughage is enough to depress anyone. Not to mention dentures, hip replacements, and Depends."

"You surprise me," I told him.

He looked pleased. "Why is that?"

"You're a psychiatrist. Aren't you supposed to make people feel better about things?"

He smiled. "I try to help people cope. I don't try to change the facts. People do that on their own. If people took an unflinching look at the way things really are instead of spinning little stories for themselves to help sugarcoat reality, a whole lot of the world would have trouble getting out of bed every morning."

I stared at him, trying to decide what he was really saying. "How do you get out of bed in the morning, feeling that way?"

He grinned. "One leg at time. That's what I'm talking about. You adjust, according to the circumstances. Some things can't be helped, you know that."

I knew that. "But—"

"What? Did you think that because of what I do I don't mind when I can't remember where I put my keys or that the print on the *Thomas Guide* has suddenly shrunk? I'm not immune."

"You sound like a candidate for Dr. Crystol," I told him. I had just realized, hearing even Mark Lawrence—M.D., Ph.D., and extremely centered human being—complain about the depredations of age, why Taylor was so excited about the economic possibilities of Bobbie's appeal.

Mark was frowning.

"Oh, sorry," I said. "I just came from hearing her speak tonight, so she was on my mind. She's—"

"I know who she is," he said shortly.

"You don't approve," I observed.

"I wouldn't put it like that." After the comradely chat we'd been having, his manner suddenly seemed stiff and reserved.

"She's a client," I explained. "My client."

He nodded. "That's great," he said neutrally.

"It is, actually," I told him. "It could mean big things for the firm."

"Great," he said again.

I felt annoyed. I wanted his approval, and he wasn't giving it. I knew I wasn't supposed to need his approval, but I still wanted it. So much for eight thousand dollars' worth of therapy. "Mark?"

He smiled pleasantly. "Yes?"

"Level with me."

"I thought I had."

"Is there something I should know about Bobbie Crystol?" I persisted.

He sighed. "Oh, Becky." He rubbed the bridge of his nose with his fingertips. "I don't mean to rain on your parade. It's just that I have reservations about this whole anti-aging thing."

"Reservations." The word had an ominous ring.

He looked unhappy. "I know. I've just been complaining about it myself, but the gist of this movement seems to be that aging is some ghastly but treatable disease—like typhoid or the Black Plague. Find the magic bullet—the penicillin or the Salk vaccine—and *pow!* you're cured. A whole industry has grown up around a lot of unorthodox remedies, a number of which are medically questionable, to say the least." He shook his head. "It's just that I find it disconcerting to see all these people who won't buy a blender without checking *Consumer Reports* stampeding toward health regimens that are unproved and possibly dangerous." He shrugged.

"That's fair enough," I told him.

"Also," he said, warming to his subject, "as a psychiatrist I feel more than a little uncomfortable with some of the mind-body nonsense I've heard spouted. I mean, of course the mind has an effect on the body; I'd be out of business in a week if that weren't the case. But some of these guys seem to be suggesting that the patient is responsible for his own illnesses because of spiritual or metaphysical failures. That's dangerous and cruel." He spun the saucer around and around under the cup. "Christ, there are people who claim they can heal you over the phone just by intuiting your emotional state. It's smart marketing, actually. You change your emotional biography, and you get better. If you don't, it's your own fault. The practitioner can't lose."

"Look," I said to him seriously, "I've been around Bobbie Crystol long enough to see that she's an egomaniac who's probably skating on thin ice scientifically. But I thought that if people want a little feel-good therapy to delude themselves into thinking they're going to live longer or sexier or whatever, where's the harm? We're helping her set up what she calls a longevity spa in Mexico. It's really big business, in the legal sense. What I guess I'm asking is, do you know anything derogatory about her personally?"

"Derogatory in what sense?"

"In the sense that I'd want to reconsider representing her. *Seriously* derogatory."

He looked pained. He hesitated and then shook his head. I wondered if he was going to say something else but decided against it. "Cautionary maybe, but not derogatory. Not if that's the test. If that's what you want."

That "if that's what you want" stung me. "I've

worked so hard to make a success of myself, Mark; you know that. This business could make my entire career."

He gave me one of his noncommittal Freudian nods. "Just watch yourself, that's all," he said finally. "Please."

CHAPTER FOURTEEN

THE PHONE JARRED ME INTO CONSCIOUSNESS AFTER less than four hours of sleep. My heart was still pounding from an excess of caffeine and stress, and my mouth tasted like rust. My mind trailed along behind my body into wakefulness.

"Hello?" I said, not optimistically.

"This is Dr. Bryan," said the crisp voice on the other end of the line.

I attempted to sit up rapidly and bumped my shin on the bedside table. I tried not to yell into the phone. "Is my mother all right?" I asked, after a moment.

"She's fine. She's resting. I'm sorry I missed you last night. Dr. Lawrence said he talked to you."

"He did. He's an old friend," I added by way of explanation, knowing how much doctors hate to poach on their colleagues' territory, in this case, information.

"That's what he said. I gather he told you we might want to operate?"

"On the carotid artery? Yes, he did."

"Well, Dr. Van Gelder, the neurosurgeon, and I have conferred, and we feel it's probably not necessary at this time. Her blockage is about fifty percent, which we feel is not life-threatening. We'd like to monitor the situation with Doppler tests and revisit this again in about three months."

"Why not just do it now if she'll need it eventually?"

There was a moment of silence. "There are certain risks involved. The operation itself could trigger a stroke. And at her age . . ."

"I see."

"Will you be visiting her today?" Dr. Bryan asked me.

"She's not coming home?"

"She's complaining of dizziness. We'd like to keep her another day, just to be sure. After that . . . You will be coming in?"

"Yes," I said.

"Then I've arranged an appointment for you with our patient advocate, Nancy March. She'll talk to you about arranging for your mother's release. Is ten all right?"

She made it sound as if Mother's parole officer would be checking her out of the Big House. "Fine," I said.

"HOW'S GRANDMA?" ALLIE asked me when I came into the kitchen. She still had her pajamas on and was carrying around a piece of dry toast. The words *Is that all you're having for breakfast?* leaped immediately to mind, but I didn't utter them. There ought to be parental merit badges for omissions.

"She's fine," I said. "They decided not to operate."

I expected the worried look to vanish, but it didn't. "Mom, can I go with you today to the hospital?"

"Sure," I said. "I'll pick you up right after school."

She frowned. "I don't feel like going to school."

"Honey, you can't do any more for her right now.

She's in good hands. I expect she'll be coming home in a day or two."

She looked at me, and her eyes filled with tears. "Mom?"

"Yes?"

She hesitated. "I'm not sure I *want* her to come home."

Oh, Christ, what was I going to do with a confession like that? There were some things I didn't want to know.

She sighed noisily. "I'm afraid, Mom."

"Afraid?" I asked, as gently as I could.

"I'm afraid something will happen again. *I didn't know what to do,* Mom. I didn't know how to help her. What if something happens again and I don't know what to do and she dies and *it's all my fault*?"

I let out my breath in relief. It was fear, not resentment. I could deal with fear. "Allie, you did absolutely the right thing. You called Louise, didn't you?" I put my arm around her shoulders but she pulled away.

"Yes, but I didn't know what to *do,*" she said again. "I mean, should I do CPR? I learned it in school, but it's not the same when it's somebody you know. I didn't know if I should move her. I just let her lie there, Mom. I couldn't think. After a while I thought of calling Mrs. Kennedy, but I don't even know how long it was, I was so scared."

This time she did accept my embrace. She said into my collarbone, "I'm so sorry, Mom."

My heart twisted. I stroked her hair. "It's okay. There's nothing to apologize for. When these things happen, you just do the best you can, that's all. You did fine."

I wondered if I'd been beguiled by my daughter's confident demeanor into giving her too much responsibility for her age. Maybe it hadn't been fair to load so much onto her shoulders. Maybe I'd been unrealistic too. My mother had been such a formidable presence in my life for so long that I'd never really expected her to become fragile and dependent, despite the obvious evidence before my eyes.

"Grandma's eighty," I told Allie. "She's been lucky so far. But at that age, things can happen. It's not anyone's fault."

She looked at me without comprehension. The decay and indignities of age were too many decades in the future for true understanding. When you're young, everything is fixable.

"We could take a first-aid class," she said. "Like the ones they have at school. Only this would be for old people's problems."

"Great idea," I told her. "For the record, Allie, I think you've been really terrific about this whole thing."

"Oh, Mom," she said, squirming. But I knew she was pleased.

MY MOTHER WAS sufficiently recovered to be directing the placement of floral tributes with obvious relish. "Not there," she told the nurse, raising the head of her bed the better to scrutinize the operation. "I want to be able to see the irises when I'm lying down. And move that big one"—she pointed at a huge spray of orchids and freesias that would not have been out of place at the funeral of a much-lamented head of state—"into the corner. The boy tripped on it when he brought in my breakfast."

I walked in and kissed my mother's cheek. "Feeling better?" I asked her.

A wary look settled over her face. "Maybe a little," she said reluctantly.

"You look good," I told her, although in truth she didn't. I was so used to seeing her with makeup that her pallor without it was a little alarming.

"My back hurts," she said. "And so does my head."

"I'm sorry," I said. I looked around the room. "Wow. Who are all these flowers from?'

"I don't know," she said, brightening. "They've just brought them in. Maybe you could hand me the cards."

"Sure," I said. I reached over and plucked the envelope from a perfect basket of spring flowers in blue and purple and yellow. The principles of flower arranging had always eluded me, but I knew art when I saw it. I handed my mother the card.

"Could you read it?" she asked. "The light's a little dim in here, and I have a headache."

"Oh," I said, smiling with pleasure, "it's from the partners at the firm." *Wendy picked these out,* I thought.

"The firm?"

"My law firm," I told her. "Roth, Tolbert and Anderson. You remember."

"Of course I remember," she snapped. "That's very nice. What about that one?" She pointed at the huge floral spray in the corner. "Who sent me that? It must have cost a fortune."

I opened the envelope and took out the card. It said:

Be strong. I care.
BOBBIE CRYSTOL

I read it aloud to my mother.

"Who the hell is Bobbie Crystol?" she asked.

* * *

NANCY MARCH, THE patient advocate, was not impressed with my elder-care arrangements.

She fixed me with a piercing gaze made more formidable by her electric blue contacts. She was at least fifteen years younger than I was, a freshly minted MSW without a heart. I still felt as if I'd been summoned to the vice principal's office and found wanting.

"You can't expect a teenage girl to be responsible for an elderly person," she said. "It might be convenient, but it isn't suitable."

I tried to keep a rein on my irritation. "It's worked for us for a long time. It's only now, when my mother has had these health problems, that it's become an issue."

She tapped the desk with the edge of her pen. "I don't mean to sound unsympathetic. I know what a burden caring for elderly parents can be, particularly when you're working. But your mother is having dizzy spells, and frankly, she's a bit confused. I don't think you should have been trusting her to take care of your house."

"Actually, *I* take care of my house," I told her. She made it sound as if my mother had been some sort of indentured servant.

"That's not what she says," she suggested.

I sighed. "She might be prone to exaggeration." How could I explain my mother and a complicated forty-year relationship in some way that this judgmental creature, decades from any such situation herself, could understand? I felt defensive, and I didn't want to give her any information in case she used it against me or against my mother. I needed to know what her agenda was first.

I suddenly realized I was thinking like a lawyer, a goal I had always professed to seek. I didn't feel comforted. *Be careful what you wish for.*

"Why don't you tell me a little more about your mother?" she said. "What sort of activities does she engage in? Does she get any exercise? How much does she go out? Does she have friends? That sort of thing," she said encouragingly.

I was not deceived. She disapproved of me, I could feel it. She would disapprove even more when she unearthed the truth—that my mother's principal activity was watching television. I suppose it was only fair; I disapproved myself.

"Umm," I said. "Actually, she favors passive entertainment."

She leaned forward eagerly, a hound on the scent. "Passive entertainment?"

I leaned away from her automatically. "Yes," I agreed.

"And that would be . . . ?"

"The opposite of active," I said sincerely.

She smiled broadly, by which I knew she found me as irritating as I did her. "So . . . no exercise?"

"Not much," I admitted.

"Friends?"

"Not many," I conceded.

"Hobbies?

This was definitely not going well. "None I can think of," I said.

She sighed and sat back in her chair.

"Rebecca—may I call you Rebecca?" she said, consulting the papers on her desk. "Don't you think it would be better for your mother to spend some time with people her own age?"

I sighed. "She says she doesn't like old people." I knew how that would sound, but it was perfectly true.

"Sometimes people say that as a defense because

they're lonely and they don't want to hurt anyone's feelings," she suggested.

I refrained from remarking that that had scarcely been my mother's modus operandi. It was pointless. What I did say was, "I agree with you that it would be good for her to be more socially involved. In fact, I've tried to interest her in women's groups, the church, the senior center, anything. She always resists me."

"And you haven't forced the issue?"

"I can't *make* my mother do anything she doesn't want to do," I said with transparent annoyance.

"Ah."

I didn't like the sound of that "Ah." I waited.

She shuffled the papers on her desk. "Well, under the circumstances, I think it's best that we make alternative arrangements for your mother."

"Define *alternative arrangements,*" I said.

"Well, ahem, for a few days I think she should be admitted to a nursing home, probably at the subacute level. Just so you know, Medicare will take care of that. After that . . ."

"After that?" I was doing the parrot trick again. I couldn't seem to help myself.

"After that, I'm going to recommend that she go into some kind of residential facility where she can live independently but still have her needs provided for." She handed me a manila envelope stuffed with papers, obviously pre-prepared. "Here are some brochures and a list of assisted living facilities in this area. You might also wish to speak with one of our financial consultants, who can help you come up with a strategy for meeting the payments." She shook her head sadly. "I'm afraid Medicare doesn't cover this kind of care."

"Assisted living?" I asked. My mouth felt very dry.

She frowned, as if I were a little slow. "Yes, I'm sure you're familiar with that kind of facility. The residents have their own rooms or apartments, or they might even share. There is a common dining room and all meals are provided. Also, laundry service and cleaning. And there are *lots* of activities. Bingo, exercise groups, Spanish classes, macramé, all sorts of things. I think it will be just the thing for your mother," she added brightly.

Bingo? "I doubt if I'll ever get her to agree to it," I said. Even if I could afford it. "I'm afraid she'll insist on coming home."

She leaned forward again and patted my hand. "Rebecca, she may not have that option."

I jerked it away. "What do you mean, she may not have that option?"

She said, very softly, "I thought you understood. I can't recommend that she return to your home under the existing circumstances, at least for the foreseeable future. If she gets stronger, we can reevaluate her then, but I have to tell you, I don't think that will happen. You need to make alternative arrangements, as I told you. You could arrange for someone to stay with her while you're working, but I must warn you, that can be very expensive. And it would keep her isolated and bored. I'm sure you can see the advantages of assisted living." She gave me a toothy smile. "This will all work out for the best, I'm sure you can see that."

"You can do that? You can impose *conditions* on somebody because you think you know what's best for them?"

She looked at me sympathetically. "Not personally,

no," she said. "But Protective Services can, if they feel your mother is in danger. That's a long and unpleasant process. I'm sure we don't want it to come to that, do we?"

CHAPTER FIFTEEN

TAYLOR WAS GRACIOUS ABOUT MY NEED TO TAKE A FEW days off. "It must be difficult for you," he murmured sympathetically. "I'll get Miss—er, Melissa—to cover for you here. Don't worry about a thing."

Ha, but I appreciated the sentiment. Sort of.

Isabel left a message on my voice mail. "Call me," she said. "Let me help."

My mother said, turning her face away from me so I could scarcely hear her, "I just want you to know one thing. No matter what happens, I'm not ever going to be happy again."

THE NURSING HOME in which my mother found herself recuperating was a surefire antidote to life-extension wannabes more interested in longevity than quality of life. It smelled; of what, specifically, I'm sure it isn't necessary to say. A buzzer rang in the nurses' station every time a patient pressed the call button, and continued to sound until it was answered. It rang incessantly, buzz, buzz, buzz, buzz, at intervals approximately thirty seconds apart. After ten minutes, I was ready to strangle anyone I could get my hands on. Fortunately, or unfortunately, there was no one there.

"Please," said the woman in the bed next to my mother's, who was incontinent following a stroke. "Please. I need changing. Please."

"I'll try to find someone," I told her when no one answered the bell after she'd pushed it for the third or fourth time.

I stepped out into the hall. A woman in a wheelchair with unkempt hair and vacant eyes grabbed my hand. "Please help me to get up," she said.

"I can't," I said. "I don't know if it's allowed."

"I want to go home," she said.

I let go of her hand and patted her shoulder. "I'm so sorry," I said. "So sorry." I clutched at a passing person who might have been a nurse. "Please," I said, "there's a person who needs changing in room three-oh-three."

He hesitated. "I'm just going on my break. I'm sure someone will be there in a few minutes."

"But I can't find anyone. How do I get someone to come?"

He looked at the big clock on the wall. "Shift change," he said.

"Shift change?"

"Sure. You know: the old shift goes out, the new one comes in. Someone will take care of it as soon as the new shift's signed in. You know how it is."

"How long will that be?" I asked, as desperately as if I needed changing myself.

"A few minutes. Ten or fifteen at the outside. Gotta go, bye."

"Get me out of this hellhole," said my mother when I reentered the room.

* * *

WHEN I GOT HOME, two envelopes were lying on the floor underneath the mail chute. I picked them up gingerly. I was feeling fragile and pessimistic. The house was very quiet. It was the first time I'd come home in a long time, daytime or evening, when the TV wasn't on.

I slit open the first one, which looked like a formal invitation, using the Victorian silver letter opener that had been a wedding present from an old friend. It seemed baroquely luxurious and superannuated in my reinvented life, and it required polishing, but I loved it. I read:

DR. BOBBIE CRYSTOL AND
CRYSTOL ENTERPRISES
request the honor of your presence
Opening Weekend
Casa Alegría, Alegre, B.C.

At the bottom she had written, "Please come for our opening weekend program! I think you'll really enjoy it."

I set it aside for later. I could not deal with it just then.

The other, more ominous envelope lay in my hand. I think I knew what was in it before I even opened it. It gave off bad vibes, as we used to say. It didn't help matters that Carole's return address was on the outside.

They haven't invented a word for the combination of anger and despair I felt when I read the enclosed letter, although if they had, the word would probably have been German. Carole was giving me notice of a reduction in the trust's contribution to David's tuition payments, effective the following school year. Rising costs . . . Diminishing principal in the trust . . . I collapsed into a chair, feeling the adrenaline pumping through my veins, preparing me for fight or flight. I wanted to do both. In my pumped-up state I might have been able to lift the couch with one hand, but what good was that going to do? Civilization had complicated everything. It was pointless to act on my instincts, which at that moment called for a combination of throttling the life out of Carole with my bare hands and packing my bags for some beach resort on Kauai. Both options had their drawbacks, so I was left to stew in my chair, wondering what to do.

Think. I went to the drawer and pulled out the trust documents. Other than the annual accounting statement, I hadn't had occasion to look at them in some time. The name of the accountant—Carole's presumably—was on the envelope. I looked up the number and dialed.

The trust accountant was unexpectedly helpful when I told her what I wanted.

"You don't want that," she said. "A full accounting will spell out every transaction of the trust in detail. Every original holding, every change in investment, every collection of dividends and interest, every distribution to beneficiaries, every payment of expenses and fees."

"That's it. That's what I want," I told her.

"No, you don't," she insisted. "Are you thinking about trying to remove the trustee?"

It had occurred to me. "I'm just looking for clarification," I said.

"Well, look," she said calmly, "we handle many, many trust investment statements, and I can tell you that generally it's the trustee who asks for the accounting when he or she has been challenged. It's quite involved, really, so many issues can come up—are the investments appropriate, are the fees and expenses justified, that sort of thing. Lawyers"—she said the word with mild distaste—"have to have their say on each side of every issue, and then the court decides each and every point in dispute. Even if there are no complaints, the necessary presentation takes a very long time. And that, I can tell you, is very, very expensive."

"So am I stuck, then? I have to accept whatever the trustee tells me?"

"Not at all. We stand by our accounting of our clients' investments. If all you are looking for is an advance on the information that will appear on the beneficiaries' next statement, we can provide that. We will have to charge a fee, of course."

Of course. She promised to call me back as soon as possible with the information. I felt a little calmer. It sounded like a reputable accounting firm, and if Carole was lying about bad investments diminishing the income of the trust, I thought they would tell me the truth.

The phone rang almost as soon as I hung up, so I answered it. I was still hyperventilating, and my hello came out as a sort of gasp.

"Becky?" inquired Isabel. "Is that you? Your voice sounds all funny."

"I'm hyperventilating," I told her.

"Oh. Did I interrupt something interesting?"

Never answer the phone when your glandular system is in the driver's seat. I started to laugh, and the laugh turned into something hysterical, a cackle that was halfway to a sob. The more I tried to stop it, the worse it got. "I thought I was calmer," I said, gulping.

"I'll be right over," said Isabel.

ISABEL ARRIVED WITH a very large bottle of Sauvignon Blanc—what we often drank together, since she didn't like Chardonnay.

"Thanks," I said simply, opening the door for her.

"Storm over?"

"For the moment. I'm too stressed out to make any predictions."

She nodded. "I'll pour you a big glass. We'll take it from there."

She did, and I did, and the whole story, or stories, came tumbling out.

"So that's it," I concluded. "It's been a seriously bad day. I've got to find my mother someplace to live before she goes crazy in that terrible place. I've got to find a way to pay for it after I've found it. I've got to find some way to come up with David's tuition money next year if I can't persuade Carole to change her mind—"

"Ha," she said.

"Ha," I agreed. "Or if the accountant doesn't come up with something fast. Anyway, I'm not even sure where to start. I was seriously contemplating mayhem when you called. I haven't gotten round to anything more productive than the phone call."

"Drink up," she said, holding the bottle poised to refill my glass.

I took a big swallow. "I shouldn't have any more. I don't want to be sloshed when Allie gets home."

"You're not sloshed," Isabel said firmly. "You've had one glass of wine. I don't think Alicia will be shocked."

"That's what I'm afraid of," I muttered, but I extended my glass.

I sighed gustily. No matter what Isabel said, I wasn't used to drinking in the afternoon, and I could feel emotion rising in me like a maudlin tide. "You should have *seen* that nursing home, Isabel," I said. "I've got to get her out of there. You should have *heard* her. She said she wouldn't be happy anywhere, no matter what."

"So you told me," said Isabel with some asperity. "It seems to me that your mother isn't helping matters much."

I looked at her with surprise. "You wouldn't say that if you'd been there."

"I've seen nursing homes," she said. "There are good ones and bad ones. Of course you don't want to be there before you have to be. But we're talking about something a lot better than that after she's discharged. She could try to be more open-minded."

"She's afraid," I said.

"Sure she is. Weren't you afraid when you went off to college? This is just like going off to live in the dorm with a bunch of people you don't know."

"A dorm without the sex and the drinking," I observed.

She laughed. "Not necessarily. Anyway, I've had a passing acquaintance with your mother all the time we've known each other. I hate to say this, Becky, but she keeps you tied up in knots with guilt."

"All mothers keep their kids tied up in knots with guilt," I pointed out. "I do it myself."

She smiled ruefully. "True. Still, couldn't she try to make a life for herself outside of you and the kids?"

"That might be partly my fault," I said. "I needed her to help me. I haven't really focused on what *she* needed."

Isabel shook her head. "Not everything that happens is your fault. Or your responsibility either. Don't be so goddamn *fair* all the time." She waved her glass around, gesturing dramatically. "Anyway," she said, "what were we talking about?"

"Dorms," I said.

She nodded sagely. "Oh, yeah. Well, have you ever considered it might be really *good* for her to live someplace where she'll be forced to have some kind of social life? Where there are classes and activities and things to stimulate her mind other than TV?"

"You sound like the patient advocate," I told her.

"I'm your advocate," she said mistily. "Somebody has to be."

"What if she stays in her room all the time and won't come out?"

"Then they'll force-feed her peanut butter and jelly through a tube. Come on, Becky, they have staff psychologists at these places. There will be all kinds of people paying attention to her. She's not going to starve or go catatonic or anything like that. Anyway, you don't have a choice. She needs to try, and so do you. She'll have to be brave."

"Bravery requires options," I said.

She shook her head. "I know there's an answer to that, but I can't think what it is," she said.

"Isabel, you are a perfect human being," I told her sincerely.

She studied me through narrowed eyes. "Maybe we are just a little bit sloshed," she said. "Before it's too late, we should tackle these problems one at a time. Have you got a pad of paper? Pen?"

I handed them to her. I could see that a military upbringing might have its advantages. Isabel could have reduced D-Day to a "to-do" list.

"What shall we start with?" she asked.

"Carole?"

She shook her head. "Too nasty. Wait till the accountant calls back. Let's pick something easier, like finding an assisted living residence for your mother." She scribbled something at the top of the pad. "Okay, number one: leads?"

I waved the sheaf of papers Nancy March had given me. "Here's a list of all the places in the metropolitan area."

Isabel looked at it and frowned. "God, look at all of them. It shows you the wave of the future." She sighed. "I suppose we could visit them one by one to check them out, but I think it would be a lot easier to network. Do you still have any doctor friends?"

"That's rich," I said with a fruity chuckle.

Isabel raised her eyebrows. "You sound like a P. G. Wodehouse character. Concentrate. Don't you know anyone at the hospital who could recommend someplace?"

I had a thought. "I could ask Mark," I told her.

"Mark?"

"Dr. Lawrence. He was—"

"Your shrink." She smiled. "I remember."

"Why are you smiling?" I demanded.

"Why are you blushing?"

"I'm not," I said, annoyed. Because I had been.

"Becky, it's no big deal. You used to talk about him all the time when you had therapy. It's natural."

"Isabel, stop hinting at some big transference thing, okay?" I tried to scowl at her, but I'd sort of lost control of my face.

"Okay," she said, smiling again. "Anyway, why don't you ask him to recommend a few places? When you have some names, I'll check out their background. Then we can do some visiting." She scribbled some notes on the pad. "What's next?"

"Paying for it," I said soberly.

She tapped her lip with the end of the pen. "Doesn't your mother have any money?"

"Well, she has Social Security. And my father left her about forty thousand dollars in life insurance. It's invested in growth and income funds, so she's made some money on that. But that's it."

She looked at the figures I'd written down. "Depending on the cost, that can probably take you through two or three years. After that, you'll need to supplement the Social Security." She thought. "You could refinance the house—"

"I've done that already."

"Or take out a loan—"

"Ouch."

"Or you could . . ."

"Yes?" I prompted her.

"You could sell the house."

"What?" I screeched. "It's all I've got."

Isabel closed her eyes. "Try to stay calm. Think about it; if you sold the house, you could pay the capital gains, invest the proceeds in the market, and still get a pretty good return. Meanwhile, you could get a nice condo somewhere on your salary."

"Leave La Jolla?" I gasped.

She laughed. "Is that so shocking? There are other nice places. Besides, do you really like this house?" She sounded dubious.

I looked around. "Actually, not all that much," I admitted. "But what about Allie?"

"Allie will be in college by the time it comes up," she said. "But if she isn't, the two of you can live with me while she finishes high school."

"College," I said, stricken. I wondered how I was going to pay for that too if Carole refused to loosen the purse strings on the income from the trust. Or worse, if there wasn't any money left.

"We'll get to that. Stay flexible; that's the key."

"The key to what?"

"I can't remember."

I rubbed my temple. I was starting to get a headache from the wine or the emotion or both. The phone rang. I was going to let it go, but Isabel said, "Answer it. It might be good news, and we could use some."

It wasn't.

"Mrs. Weston?"

It was Carole's accountant. All warmth had left her voice.

"I didn't expect you to call so soon," I told her.

"Yes, well, I do have information, but it may not be what you require."

I put my hand over the receiver. "She's backpedding," I said to Isabel.

Isabel waved me on with a gesture.

"Yes?" I said into the phone.

"As you know," she said formally, "the trust assets have been used to buy annuities outside the United States—"

"I didn't know that," I said.

"It's on your accounting statement," she said in a disapproving tone.

I felt like the Silly Little Woman. "I didn't realize," I told her.

"Many people don't," she said, relenting a little. "In any case, I'm afraid some of these investments seem to have . . ."

"Yes?" I encouraged, although I didn't feel encouraged myself.

"Well, in layman's terms, they seem to have gone belly-up."

"Christ." My head was throbbing. "Were these prudent investments?"

"Apparently."

I wondered if she was hedging. I wished I hadn't had so much to drink. "Apparently?"

Her voice turned frosty. "There's appropriate documentation for the loss. We've also made inquiries of the agent who sold these annuities, but I'm afraid it's impossible to find out any more."

"Impossible?"

"Impossible," she said firmly. "The secrecy laws of the Cayman Islands make further disclosure impossible."

"You're kidding! The Cayman Islands? Why would somebody buy investments there?" Although, even in my semi-inebriated state, I knew the answer to that already.

"I couldn't speculate," she said.

"And there's really no way to find out anything more?" I asked her.

"A full accounting will cost you five thousand dollars," she said crisply. "If lawyers are involved, it will cost a great deal more than that. But very likely you'll be wasting your time and money trying to wring something out of the offshores. They don't give out the kind of information you're looking for." She sighed. "I'll send you the account statement in today's mail. Along with your bill."

"*NOW* CAN WE get to Carole?" I inquired when I had told Isabel about the conversation. "Christ. The Cayman Islands! She's playing some kind of investment games with the trust."

Isabel nodded and topped off my glass. "I've come up with something—why didn't we think of this before?"

"A hit man? I've thought of that already."

Isabel laughed. "Too obvious. There aren't any drive-bys on Mount Soledad. You could follow her around Jonathan's and try to inject her cheese with *Listeria*—"

"Too unreliable. She's too fit. She'd probably kill the bacteria before it killed her."

"Well, then," said Isabel, "I'd say it's time for a little hands-on juris doctoring, wouldn't you?"

"You mean—"

"I mean, what's the good of six years of legal education if you can't use it against a nitwit like Carole?"

I smiled. "Unfortunately, the trust wasn't drafted by the nitwit. The way it's set up, if the trust is attacked, the trustee can simply close the checkbook. And offshore investments are completely out of my league. I don't have the expertise to take on something like that, much as I'd like to."

"Then I guess you'll just have to talk to Mr. Perfect Partner or somebody else at your law firm about finding some way to get rid of her before she squanders all the assets. Sue her skinny ass, dammit!" She hit the coffee table with her fist. The wine bottle, empty, tipped over onto the rug. "Sorry," she said.

"Don't be," I said. "As a matter of fact, I'm sort of warming to the idea of whopping her ass in court. It's just that I'm a little vague on the details of how I'm going to do it."

"So what?" demanded Isabel.

"So what?" I agreed. "That's what the partners are for, isn't it? To provide the details."

"We'll provide the big picture," Isabel said.

"The big picture," I said, "is that Carole is screwing my kids, and I'm not going to let her get away with it!"

"Hurrah!" cried Isabel. "That's that, then. The trust is history, as soon as you figure out what to do about it. Let's open another bottle to celebrate."

"I haven't finished what's in my glass yet," I said.

"Okay, then drink up." She consulted her list. "Next."

"There isn't any next," I told her. "We've made attack plans for everything."

"Not everything," said Isabel.

I knew that tone. "Oh, Isabel, give it up," I said.

She picked up my wineglass and offered it to me. I drained it without protest. "Never," she said. "Look, I know this guy whose brother's in town and needs a date for some party he's going to. Let me give him your phone number, please."

"Isabel . . ."

"What if I promise he won't drool on you or slaver with lust? It's just a dinner. As a matter of fact, I'll probably be there too."

I laughed. "No one's spoken to me with lust since an Amway salesman tried to sell me on some toilet paper," I told her.

"All the more reason," she persisted. "Just the

phone number. Please," she said again. "You could use the diversion."

I started to refuse, but then I figured, what the hell? I mean, what was so perfect about my life that I didn't want to change it? It's not as if an evening away from my simmering domestic crises would be unwelcome. Besides, how bad could it be if Isabel was going to be there too?

"Okay," I told her, trying to sound nonchalant.

"Great," she said. "You won't regret it."

Now why did she have to go and say something like that?

CHAPTER SIXTEEN

ARMED WITH MY "TO-DO" LISTS, I STARTED MY ASSAULT on my particular mound of problems.

At first I was fortunate.

"I'm glad you asked me," said Mark. "I have a really good place to recommend for your mother."

"You do?" I could not believe my good luck. It couldn't be this easy.

"Sure," he said. "I know a number of people there. It's very well run and not too expensive. The residents seem to like it quite a bit." He gave me the name and some other information. "Of course you'll want to check it out for yourself." He hesitated, as if he wondered if he might be coming across as too pushy. "If you like, I could make an appointment for you with the director."

If I liked? "Oh, Mark, I can't tell you how grateful I am," I said.

"Then don't," he said shortly, sounding, I thought, a little irritated.

"I'm sorry," I said. "Did I . . . ?"

"No, no, it's just a bad day. Don't pay any attention.

I'm glad I could help you. Let me know how it works out."

LAUREN LOOKED AT me in disbelief. "That's the most barbaric trust arrangement I've ever heard of."

I liked that word *barbaric*. I felt she'd cut to the essence of things right off the bat.

"But I gather that was the point," she added. "Really, really vindictive. Of course he had to know how difficult this would be for everyone."

I drew in a breath. I knew then that the real reason I'd never consulted anybody at the firm about the trust was the unexpressed question *What awful thing had I done to my husband to make him dislike me that much?* "He's laughing himself silly somewhere right this minute," I said.

She sighed. "I don't have that much experience with trust and estates or tax law, but I can tell you it's not that uncommon for people to try to control things from beyond the grave. Usually it backfires." She looked at the papers I had given her. "Too bad La Rue and Associates—an extremely reputable firm by the way"—she looked up meaningfully to make sure I took the point—"drafted it as a family pot trust instead of distributing out each child's share when he comes of age. The way it is here, your kids won't get their hands on the principal till they're middle-aged."

"If there's any left," I said. "Anyway, I imagine Richard wanted to be sure Carole and Andrew were provided for before any of the principal gets reduced." I tried not to sound bitter. "Look, their ultimate inheritance is not what I'm concerned about here. Right now their educations are at risk. Isn't there anything I can do to stop Carole from making lunatic investments and squandering the assets?"

"I don't want to advise you on this, Becky. It's too important, and I'm not really an expert. Let me run it by the tax guys and see what they say. I can tell you that my experience, limited as it is, is that the accountant is right. The fees—and they can be big for something like this—will be billed to the trust. It's not unheard of for people to run through a substantial amount of what they're fighting over. You lose even if you win. It's usually better to reach some kind of accommodation if you can."

"Fat chance."

She lifted her eyebrows. "Well, I'd have to agree that some genial accord is less likely when the trustee loathes you," she said. "But it's not unheard of."

"I don't think I'll count on it," I said gloomily.

"Count on what?" asked Ryan James, inserting himself into the conversation. He was always lurking in doorways hoping to hear—what? Something he could use to assess his chances of making partner probably. As the magic number approached—six years out, or seven, or eight, depending on the firm—all associates got more furtive and restless, and Ryan was the worst of all at RTA.

We both looked at him.

"What?" he said. "I'm just asking."

"It's nothing to do with you," Lauren told him.

Which naturally convinced him we'd been plotting his ruination. He looked crestfallen.

"I was asking Lauren about offshore investments," I said, taking pity on him, but not so much pity I was eager to tell him about the trust.

He waved a hand dismissively. "Passé," he said. "Put

your money into tech stocks. Never mind the market corrections. That's the future."

"Right," Lauren said dryly. "Let somebody like Jason Krill lead you to the promised land."

"Passé how?" I asked him. "You mean dangerous? Risky? What?" I was clutching at straws asking financial advice of Ryan James, but I figured that if even *he* knew that Carole's investments would have been imprudent at the outset, it might give me some ammunition to use against her.

Behind him Lauren was shaking her head at me, but it was too late to turn off the spigot.

"I wouldn't say that. I mean, foreign mutual funds and securities have been favored investments for a long time. But the Internet—that's the place to be—"

"But no one's making any money," Lauren protested.

He rolled his eyes at our cluelessness. "That's not what it's *about,* ladies. Didn't you read *The New New Thing*? Anyway, if you've got some money to invest . . ."

Ryan continued in this fashion at some length, but my mind—doubtless an old old thing in this context—drifted away. I didn't have any money to invest. I was just worried about how I was going to keep my kids from getting ripped off.

Sometime later the paean came to an abrupt end, startling me out of my daydreams. "Anyway, if you want to know about investments, you might want to ask Taylor."

Lauren said nothing. "Why Taylor?" I asked.

Ryan looked cagey. "Well, he has to be getting money from *somewhere*. The guy drives a very expensive car and lives in a mansion *and* he supports at least two high-maintenance ex-wives. He's not doing it on his salary, I can promise you that. And I know for a fact that he's taken a certain associate in this firm out to a number of very pricey dinners." He snickered like some hormonally supercharged twelve-year-old making obscene phone calls.

"Ryan—" Lauren began.

Ryan shrugged, unrepentant. "I know you're going to tell me to mind my own business, Lauren, but it is my business, sort of. Anyway, I'm not insinuating that he's anything but a smart investor."

"Good," Lauren said.

"Do you think he'd know anything about offshore investments?" I persisted, despite Lauren's disapproval.

"He might. It stands to reason. He's a tax expert, isn't he? Besides, I hear things."

"No shit," Lauren said. She gave him such a reproachful look that he began to edge away.

"I'm out of here," he said finally.

"See you," she said.

"There goes a waste of a very expensive education," she added when he had gone. "Not a lick of common sense to show for it."

I winced at the reminder. What was I going to do if I couldn't prise the trust income out of Carole?

Lauren looked at me, reading my thoughts. "What will you do if you don't get the money?"

"I'm not sure. It's David's future, for God's sake. I want him to have what he's worked so hard for."

"I know what you mean," she said. "It's so tough to finance a private education. My gardener's daughter is at Stanford Law School this year, but she's going to have to take a leave of absence to work full-time. She's taken the biggest loan they'll give her, and even though she'll probably be fifty-five by the time she can pay it back, she still can't get by. Do you know what tuition costs at that place? I've offered to help, but she says she needs to do it on her own. Her parents are from Vietnam and have just about killed themselves to get her where she is. She says she just doesn't want to feel any more indebted than she is already."

"That's silly," I said. "She should accept the help that's offered."

"Do you think so?" she said. "Some people think having to be grateful can be . . . oppressive."

I wasn't sure if she was still talking about her gardener's daughter, but I didn't want to pursue it. There were some things you couldn't ask. Like whether Taylor was *really* taking Melissa out, as Ryan had suggested. "I hope it works out for this girl," I said.

"She's not a girl. She's thirty-two," she said. "She supported her two younger brothers through college before she went to law school."

"Poor kid," I said. I knew what Lauren meant too: *everybody has it tough*.

A COUPLE OF hours later, Lauren called my office. "Taylor wants to see you," she said.

"Taylor?" I asked her. "About the trust?"

"So I would assume," she said. "I was going to run it by one of the senior tax associates, but Taylor heard me asking and said to send you in as soon as you're free."

"Ummm, I hope you kept the lurid details to a minimum," I said. The understatement of the year.

She laughed. "Just the merest bit of luridity. I'm sure he's heard worse. Good luck."

* * *

TAYLOR'S OFFICE LOOKED like someplace you might feel comfortable dropping off your old couch, the one with the springs protruding through the cushions, so I knew it was back to business as usual. He was on the phone when I got there, his chair turned away from the door. "I tell you I can't do it anymore," he was saying into the phone. "You'll have to use someone else." Pause. "Just for the time being." He swung around and saw me standing in the doorway. He started.

"Sorry," I mouthed.

"Listen, I'll have to get back to you later," he said into the receiver. "Someone's here now." He coughed. "Right. So am I. Seven o'clock."

He hung up and smiled at me in his new business-getter to business-getter fashion; I was no longer confused with the secretarial staff. "Hi," he said. "Come on in."

"You wanted to see me?" I asked.

He nodded, still smiling. "Please close the door and take a seat."

I sat, remembering to pull down my skirt and cross my legs at the ankles, as if my mother were watching.

"Lauren told me you're having some difficulties with a trust set up for the benefit of your children," he said. "I'm glad you've felt *comfortable* bringing such a matter to the firm."

Meaning he wished I hadn't. I felt a flush creeping up my chest toward my neck, heading north. "I might need to engage you to remove the trustee," I told him. I wanted to make it clear I wouldn't expect anyone at the firm to work for free, although I certainly wouldn't object to a discount.

Taylor made a sort of strangled sound. "That's putting the cart way before the horse. This is just an informal chat between colleagues. Nothing more, right?"

I didn't understand his insistence. "I guess so," I told him.

"I'm sure Lauren's explained to you how difficult it is to effect any significant change in a matter like this."

I nodded.

"I don't know all the particulars in this case, of course, but you must realize that conflicts of this nature often occur when the beneficiaries of a trust have opposing interests. The current beneficiaries need high-income yields to meet their present needs, while those who expect to inherit the principal eventually have a strong bias toward capital growth. And in this case, where a very young child is involved, so many unexpected situations may arise that could affect the need for income, it's virtually impossible for a trustee to satisfy all those needs without walking on water." He gave me a sad little smile.

"Surely education expenses are a primary need that should be covered by the trust," I said.

"Certainly, but to what extent? Suppose a beneficiary wanted to put himself through law school, then med school, in order to become a medical malpractice lawyer. Should the trust cover all of that? It's discretionary on the part of the trustee."

"But—"

"And I have to say," he said, not meeting my eyes, "that it appears the trustor—your late ex-husband—had a great deal of faith in the trustee. He's given her very broad powers of discretion—including the ability to add beneficiaries, if she wishes—and there are certain—ahem—built-in disincentives for attempting a removal."

"My ex-husband was probably expecting this," I muttered.

Taylor raised his eyebrows. "It's a reasonable safeguard to protect the assets from being squandered in some prolonged legal battle." He smoothed the edges of the papers in front of him. "Look, the trust was drafted by a highly reputable law firm. There is a degree of oversight by a team of accountants. Generally, in such cases, it's very, very difficult to get the courts to overturn the terms of the trust or remove a trustee unless there's some flagrant abuse on the part of the trustee—like taking the proceeds to pay for a new sports car for herself or something like that. Any attack on the trustee would almost certainly result in the trustee's demanding a full accounting, and the cost of the entire process would come out of the assets of the trust. So unless you can prove . . ."

"What about the offshore investments?" I asked.

His hands stilled. "What?"

"The offshore investments. Carole's put the assets of the trust into some harebrained investments in the Cayman Islands—"

"There's nothing 'harebrained' about such investments. There are very good reasons for putting your money offshore," he said.

"Then why did they all go—what did the accountant say?—'belly-up'?"

"Not all of them, surely?" he said, looking pale.

"Probably not," I admitted. "I'm not sure. But enough to reduce the income of the trust and probably a significant amount of the principal. Isn't that reason enough to stop her from losing more?"

He shook his head. "A trustee is not legally responsible for unhappy investment results as long as he or she uses a reputable adviser. There are no guarantees on return of investment, Becky. In any event, what was lost today might be regained down the road."

"How do I *know* the advice is reputable? The accountant says the Cayman Islands have secrecy laws that can't be breached."

He studied his hands carefully. "I'm afraid that's true, actually."

This couldn't be happening. I couldn't be so totally *helpless*. "Well, what would you advise, then?"

"Speaking informally," he said, "what is it that you want?"

"Right now I want the money for my son's tuition," I told him.

He rubbed his temple with his thumb. "Then if I were you, I'd probably go talk to the trustee again. It's worth a try."

"That's it? Go hat in hand to Carole? Let her get away with—"

Taylor raised a hand to stop me. "Getting emotional won't help. It's up to you what you want to do about it. You can fight it and take it to court if you want to, but it will cost you and your children a great deal of money, and in the end I don't think you'll succeed. You asked for my opinion. There it is."

"I appreciate your candor," I told him. I did, in a way. It was better to know at the outset what the likely outcome would be. It's just that I felt as if someone had emptied a very large bucket of ice water on my plans for the future.

He studied me thoughtfully. "I hope you do. Sometimes the hardest part of being a good lawyer is knowing when *not* to fight."

"Lauren said the same, in essence. But if I *do* decide to fight—"

"Let's not even think about that now. Lauren is a brilliant lawyer. You can learn a lot from her." He leaned forward solicitously. "I hope you know I'm very, very sorry about all this." He put his hand on my wrist. I looked down. His watch had a platinum face, a bit on the gaudy side.

"Thank you," I said noncommittally. I was busy with my own thoughts, which were mostly of the monetary kind.

"If money's a problem . . ." he said.

I lifted my eyes to his.

"What I mean to say is, if things continue going so well with Crystol Enterprises, I think you can count on a substantial bonus this year."

"Thank you," I said again, with more enthusiasm.

I stood up to go before Taylor started glancing at his watch.

"Hope it all works out," he said. "Oh, and Becky?"

I turned at the door.

"How's your mother?"

"Fine," I said. "Thank you for asking."

"Good," he said. "That's really great news."

"HOW DID IT go?" Lauren asked me when I had staggered back to my office.

"Not that well," I said. "I'm sort of stunned."

"Is the firm going to represent you?" she asked.

"I'm not even supposed to think about that. I'm not

supposed to do anything but say, 'Pretty please, Carole, won't you give me more money for my children?' " I said bitterly. "I'm just not sure I can leave it at that."

"I did warn you that might be the case, Becky," Lauren said. "I'm sure Taylor gave you the best possible legal advice. He is an expert."

"I'm not even sure it was legal advice," I said, remembering the conversation. "He kept stressing that it was just an informal chat."

"Really?" asked Lauren. "Maybe he just didn't want you to feel financially obligated."

"Maybe," I said.

"So what are you going to do?"

"I'm not sure," I told her.

"Try to do something to take your mind off of it," she said. "Sometimes the best inspiration sneaks up on you." She grinned. "Get out of here. Go shopping."

"I have something else in mind," I told her.

"SHIT," ISABEL SAID, when I told her about my meeting with Taylor. "I can't believe there's nothing you can do."

"It's not so much that there's nothing I can do, but that any victory is going to be Pyrrhic," I told her. "At least if I understand it correctly. He was definitely warning me off taking the issue to court."

"For your own good?" Isabel asked.

"I know. I hate it when people say that too. There's always another agenda." I took another bite of chocolate cheesecake, my surefire take-your-mind-off-it, let-inspiration-sneak-up-on-you remedy for depression.

"Does Taylor have another agenda?"

"I don't know. The advice is reasonable, even if unwelcome—I have to give him that. But he was so . . . I don't know, *elusive*. He kept insisting on the 'informality' of our little talk, like he thought I was going to try to get him to commit to something he found distasteful."

Isabel made a rude noise. "Men!"

I smiled. "Yes, but there's something more to it I can't put my finger on. It bothers me."

"Not, I take it, his devastating sex appeal?" Isabel asked lightly.

"Missing in action, at least for the moment. No. I'll think of it eventually. In the meantime . . ."

"Yes?" Isabel prompted me.

"In the meantime I have to come up with some options. I have to start thinking outside the box."

"Outside the box? That sounds like geek speak."

"My recent association with dot-com billionaire wannabes has not been entirely wasted," I said.

"So what does it mean?" she asked me.

"I'm not sure," I said, licking chocolate off my fingers. "I've read that if you have to worry about thinking outside the box, you're already so far inside the box the whole exercise is futile. But I have to try. If a frontal assault on Carole and the trust is counterproductive, I'll have to think of some other line of attack. I don't know yet. But I do know I'm not giving up!"

"Good for you," Isabel said. "Let me know if I can help. And, um, Portia?"

I laughed. "'My deeds upon my head! I crave the law.'"

"I hate English majors," she said. "Always showing off. As I was about to say, you won't forget my little dinner party, will you?"

I hesitated. I was scarcely in the mood. Plus I might

never be hungry again after my 965-calorie cheesecake orgy.

"You promised," she said in a warning tone. "It's all set up."

"Right, sure," I said, giving in. "I'll be there."

As Taylor said, sometimes the hardest thing was knowing when not to fight.

CHAPTER SEVENTEEN

ISABEL'S LITTLE DINNER PARTY TURNED OUT TO BE A MAjor charity event, a fund-raiser for the hospital, the kind you see written up in the back of *San Diego* magazine or the society pages of the paper. I didn't know until I'd already agreed to go that it was in that category. I'd run the gamut of these parties when I was Mrs. Dr. Pratt—the dedication of the new endoscopy center, the afternoon of food and wine to benefit hunger relief, the opening of the Rat Lab at the medical school.

Okay, I'm kidding about the last one, but really, these events are totally lacking in irony. I mean, does anyone really *want* to stand around munching caviar on toast to celebrate a place that sticks tubes up your hind end or down your throat? Doesn't anybody see the ridiculous incongruity of consuming 5,500 calories in homage to those who don't have enough to eat? What difference does it make whether someone appeared at such-and-such an event in an Anna Molinari jade-green knit dress? Well, it makes a difference to the someone, and that's what inspires attendance at such functions. But I had definitely had enough to last me a lifetime, and now that

I was no longer dispensing my ex-husband's largesse, I couldn't afford them anyway.

Not only that, but my date was a doctor and a Texan, two groups that tend, for various reasons, to make me nervous. I don't have to explain about the doctors. Texans make me nervous because they make me feel undersized and inhibited, plus their social norms are not in sync with those of the rest of the country. They play by their own rules, and if you aren't a Texan too, you don't know what those are. This makes them unpredictable, although interesting.

It was too late to lose seven pounds so that I could fit into the dress I'd worn the last time I went to a formal event. I pulled the dress out of the closet anyway to see if the seams were big enough to be let out. I'd thought that if I starved for a couple of days beforehand and was very lucky it might work. It was just a simple black sheath, the kind you wear if you want to show off really good jewelry. Ha, but at least the style wasn't hideously dated.

"Too tight," the alterations lady at the cleaners told me, her mouth full of pins.

"I know," I told her sadly, looking in the mirror at the zipper, which was losing its struggle to close. "Can you make it bigger?"

She looked dubious. "Very weak material."

"What?" The dress had cost a fortune in the old days.

"Weak. If I let out, there will not be big enough seams. You see?"

I saw. "Try anyway," I told her. "I don't want to have to buy a new one."

She nodded sympathetically. "Okay. But don't bend over, all right?"

* * *

MY DATE, LYMAN Wilson, might have come from a part of the world where it is not unheard of for people to have multiple first names (Johnny Bob, Billy Ray) and wear reptile boots to church, but he bore not the slightest resemblance to J. R., to my great relief. In fact, he turned out to be—not to gush too much—divine—charming and funny and perfectly at ease. He was an oncologist in San Antonio, out visiting his older brother for a couple of weeks while attending a medical meeting at the Hotel del Coronado.

The only *tiny* fly in the ointment was that at the very moment little Lyman was emerging into the world ready to take on the birthright of brains and good looks that was patently his, little Rebecca Weston was riding her bicycle off to fourth grade. Or maybe fifth. Not that going out with someone younger has ever stopped older men, but it made me a little uncomfortable, mostly because I wasn't sure how he would feel.

If Lyman was less than delighted by what he had won in Dating Lotto, he didn't show it. He did ask me if I was a partner at RTA.

"An associate," I told him. "A first-year associate." I smiled. "I got a late start."

He laughed. "Grandma Moses got a late start. Yours is just leisurely. How's it going?"

"I'm not sure," I told him. "It's appalling how much I don't know."

He nodded. "It's like being an intern, or even a resident. You just have to hope you don't kill anybody."

"I guess I should feel relieved that the consequences for lawyers aren't usually that dire," I said. "Although there's always the possibility of getting sued for malpractice."

We both shuddered. It looked like the start of a very promising evening.

HOTEL BALLROOMS ALL have the same look. Glitzy chandeliers, pastel hues, snowy tablecloths over round tables. A big podium in front, from which to be (1) thanked, (2) exhorted to give more money, and (3) bored.

A few acquaintances from palmier days were kind enough to greet me with enthusiasm, although I hadn't seen or heard from them since my divorce.

"Becky," cried Dorothy Beekman, offering me a scented cheek to kiss. As I did, I got a close-up of her Mikimoto pearls, the size of gumballs or sparrows' eggs. They were much more impressive than diamonds. "It's been absolutely *ages*."

"It's lovely to see you, Dorothy," I said obediently. I introduced Lyman, who gave her a long, easy grin and called her "ma'am." For just an instant, I could see the memory of appetite flicker across her face. Despite that and the world-class pearls, however, the intervening years had not been kind to her. Her skin looked dry and stretched, and she had dark shadows under her eyes. Her arms beneath the too-bare sleeves looked flaccid and very thin.

"And I hear you went to . . . what? Med school?" she asked me.

"Law school," I told her.

"So you're a . . ."

"An attorney," I said.

"Oh, a *lawyer,*" she said, in the tone in which people always say it, as if it were a species you'd walk right by at the pound. I was always tempted to remind them that Abe Lincoln and Thomas Jefferson were lawyers too, but recent revelations about the doings at Monticello made it somewhat dangerous to invoke historical icons.

"Isn't that wonderful?" she added kindly.

"Thank you," I said.

"Have you found your table?" she asked.

"We can't just sit anywhere?"

"Oh no," she said, sounding shocked. "It's all pre-arranged."

ISABEL WAS BEAMING and beckoning like a mother whose child has just won first place in the talent show. She wanted to show me how gratified she was that I'd shown up, although I saw her do a quick double take when she got a glimpse of Lyman. So much for her foolproof checkup procedures, I thought, but I was starting to mind less. In fact, I wasn't minding at all that my debut date was attracting attention for his charm and good looks.

"We're at this table," she said cheerily. "They've put us all together."

"Us," so far, consisted of Isabel and Lyman's brother Daniel, Lyman and me, a well-dressed older couple I didn't know, and Mark Lawrence with a tall, thin, glamorous-looking woman who was clinging to him as if he were the last lifeboat on the *Titanic*. She was definitely not the dusky beauty from Jonathan's. He seemed to get around.

There were two empty seats.

Mark smiled at me. "Hi, Becky."

"Hello." Suddenly, all the rules of introduction I'd memorized in Girl Scouts deserted me. Whom should I introduce first? What should I say about each person? Where was Miss Manners when you needed her? "This is, um . . ."

"Lyman Wilson," said Lyman, reaching across the table with a manly handshake.

"This is Maria Oblomova," Mark said. He completed the introductions.

"We're the Seftons," said the woman next to me. She was wearing black, like three-quarters of the rest of the room. "Dr. and Mrs."

"Pathology," Maria said to me.

I wondered if I could have heard her correctly. "I beg your pardon?" I had momentarily recovered my manners.

"Pathology," she reiterated. "My specialty. What's yours?" She looked me up and down in a manner I was starting to dislike.

"Coq au vin," I told her.

She looked blank.

"I'm sorry, I was just joking," I said. "I'm not a doctor."

Mark half smiled and looked away.

"I'm so glad," said Mrs. Sefton, who still had not declared her first name. "I was afraid everyone here would be a professional. Sometimes I don't know what anyone is talking about at dinner."

Fortunately, Maria—who by this time was exchanging passwords with Daniel (nephrology), Lyman (oncology), and Dr. Sefton (urology)—was not privy to this exchange.

"I know just what you mean," I said to Mrs. S. I did too. I had sat through interminable discussions at such functions, during which, although the conversations were in English and English is my native language, I hadn't understood anything but the prepositions.

"What is tonight's speech on, do you know?" she asked me.

I consulted my program. Introduction. Awards. Thanks. Pledges and Fund Drive. Guest Speaker. I smiled. "Alternative Medicine—South of the Border," I said.

There was an audible groan around the table. "Why do they make us sit through this shit?" asked Daniel. Lyman nudged him. Mrs. S. was past the age where *shit* was part of the acceptable social vocabulary. "Stuff," Daniel amended. "It's all anybody talks about these days."

"Because eighty percent of the people in the world use herbs as their primary source of medicine," said Isabel, surprisingly. The things she knew never ceased to amaze me. The Internet, she confided, whenever I asked her.

"God," breathed Maria. "People are such idiots. I hope this isn't going to be one of those talks where they show women with lemon-size holes in their thighs going to Tijuana for 'alternative' plastic surgery. Those slides are so *gross*." This from someone who spent her days peering at tumors under a microscope.

Mrs. S. touched her own temples in horror. "People go to *Mexico* to have things done?" she asked.

"It's cheaper," I explained.

"Also, they offer all sorts of quack cures for things that aren't licensed here," said Lyman. "It's the same in Texas. People cross over to Juarez for alternative therapies."

"That reminds me—" said Mrs. S.

"It's fucking sick," said her husband, interrupting her and signaling the end of linguistic solicitude. "I've heard that some of those clinics claim to cure cancer by pulling teeth. I can't imagine how any sane person could fall for such nonsense."

"Desperation," suggested Isabel.

"Some of them, certainly," said Daniel, "but desperation alone doesn't explain the numbers. Neither does cost."

I hoped no one besides Mark and Isabel knew I was representing a world-class alternative medicine guru who was opening a clinic in Baja California. I didn't want to be put in the impossible position of defending Bobbie to a bunch of doctors on the warpath.

"Part of it's cultural," said Lyman, surprisingly. "Some nurses in our oncology clinic did a study of a number of these places last year. They posed as family members of patients needing care. The truth is, some of these places are incredibly nurturing and supportive, even if the treatments are entirely bogus. Like when you were a kid and your mother fluffed your pillows and smoothed the sheets. That's part of what makes them so seductive—and dangerous."

Maria's mother had probably treated her to a bracing dash of cold water in the face when she was feverish. "Even if what you say is true," she said, in tones suggesting that this possibility was so remote as to be nonexistent, "it doesn't explain how people can believe such preposterous nonsense. Can you imagine telling people that shark cartilage enemas will cure them of cancer? It's vile and cruel to mislead people that way."

"I suppose you could always argue that dead patients are cancer-free," Lyman said dryly.

"I've heard that some of the clinics in Tijuana dump their American patients back on this side of the border when they're near death," I said, getting swept up into the conversation.

"Why would they do that?" asked Mrs. Sefton, sounding shocked.

"Probably so they can say no one's ever died in their care," Daniel suggested.

I smiled. "Yes, and it avoids legal complications as well."

"You're conducting research?" Maria asked me. "Are you a student?"

"No, I just watch the nightly news," I said.

"Becky's an attorney," Mark said, looking amused.

I saw the slight stiffening. Maria looked at me with such disgust that I wondered if I'd forgotten to shave under my armpits. "Not medical malpractice," I added.

Mark laughed. So did Lyman.

She turned to Mark and touched his shirtsleeve with one finger. It was a surprisingly intimate gesture. "I'm sure Mark can shed some light on why people are so credulous," she said. She gave me a smug look.

Mark looked distinctly uncomfortable, but at that moment our salads were served, so he got a reprieve. Maria, however, had an unexpected ally in Mrs. S.

"Yes, do please tell us, Dr. Lawrence," she said after a few moments. "It would be interesting to know."

Mark put down his arugula reluctantly. Being asked to explain human nature was doubtless the party trick expected of psychiatrists, the way people counted on attorneys to be good sports about shark jokes. "Well, of course you can't lump all alternative or complementary medical treatments together. But if you ask me why people want to believe in what Maria called preposterous regimens—treatments that have no demonstrated scientific validity—I guess there are lots of theories." He sighed. "Many people are deeply resistant to the idea that human beings evolved from animals and that our minds derive from our animal natures—our genes and our resulting brains. It makes them more comfortable to make the mind and spirit something other than the body. Once you do that, all the rules of evidence and proof can fly out the window."

Mrs. S. tugged at my sleeve. "I'm getting lost," she whispered.

"He's saying people don't like to dwell on the fact that they're animals," I whispered back. "So—"

She put her hand to her throat. "Well, of course not," she said.

"I think it's the media's fault," said Daniel wickedly.

He was roundly booed.

He laughed. "No, seriously. I mean, look how they're always sensationalizing modern science. String theory, neutrinos, black holes, all that . . . stuff. It leads you to believe that you can't rely on common sense to understand the world. Ergo, anything is possible."

Generally I dislike people who use the word *ergo* in conversation, but in this case I thought he had a point. Besides, he was Isabel's date and Lyman's brother.

Maria looked at him. "You're seriously trying to blame the Discovery Channel for some poor schmuck sticking coffee grounds up his ass?" At least she smiled when she said it.

Mrs. S. shuddered.

"I think he's on to something," Isabel said.

"So do I," I agreed.

Maria gave me a look that said, "You would."

I didn't know what had come over me. Maybe I'd been dateless too long. I'd forgotten all the rules. All I wanted to do was talk. I don't mean a one-sided monologue; I mean real honest-to-God give-and-take conversation. Maybe I even mean arguments. I threw caution to the winds. "Really," I said. "I mean, does anybody *re-ally* understand relativity?"

"I do," said Maria.

I ignored her.

"Count me out," said Isabel, coming to my rescue.

"Understand what?" said Mrs. S.

"Relativity," I said. "They throw it at you over and over in school. I've seen countless PBS programs on Einstein. I've even tried to read a couple of books on the subject. But I still don't understand why the guy in the spaceship comes back younger than the guy who stays behind."

Mark grinned hugely.

"And your point is?" said Maria.

"That Daniel's right. If you're forced to accept a theory of the universe that you simply can't wrap your mind around, it gets easier to accept that toenail shakes or healing waves or whatever might actually work."

"Blame it on Einstein," said Lyman.

"Coq au vin?" asked the waiter.

WHILE THE ENTREE was being served, Mrs. Sefton laid a hand on my arm. "Dear, before I forget, I noticed you talking to Dottie Beekman when we came in. Are you a friend of hers?"

I explained that I knew her but hadn't seen her for several years.

"Well, since we were talking about alternative medicine, I wondered if you knew she'd been very, very ill?"

I said I was sorry to hear that. I was only half listening; I wondered why the waiter hadn't cleared the table settings from the unoccupied places.

"Yes, very ill. Which is quite, well, *ironic,* because the

place she went to was supposed to make her live longer, and that's not the way it turned out at all."

"I see," I said, although I didn't. I thought I'd seen a familiar face at the door. The speakers would be starting in a few moments. They always started the program before people could finish dinner and get up to leave.

"Although of course it might have been just a coincidence," Mrs. S. continued, intent on her story. "I mean, she might not have gotten sick from the treatments."

I nodded politely.

It *was* a familiar face. I smiled. It was Taylor Anderson. What could he be doing here?

"It might not have been Dr. Crystol's fault at all," she said.

I swung around to look at her full on. "Pardon me?"

She knew I hadn't really been listening, but she took it in good part. "I was telling you how Dottie Beekman got sick," she said helpfully.

Out of the corner of my eye, I could see Taylor crossing the room in our direction. The empty chairs beckoned. "She was being treated by Dr. Crystol? Dr. Bobbie Crystol?" I asked.

Mrs. S. nodded. "I believe that was the name. Do you know her? She's famous, isn't she? But as I said, I can't be sure—"

Involuntarily, I laid a hand on her arm. I gasped. Taylor was definitely heading for our table. And in his wake, tricked out to the nines, was my bête noire, odium made flesh, Carole Cushman Pratt.

Mrs. Sefton, her narrative momentarily stilled, took note. Her nose wrinkled. "That's Carole Pratt," she whispered. "She's such a climber. She was married to a surgeon at the hospital, and I understand he left her a very rich widow. She's a big donor, but frankly I can't stand the woman."

A *big donor*. With my children's tuition money. Well, maybe that wasn't fair, but I was so aghast at seeing her there with Taylor that fairness was the farthest thing from my mind. With *Taylor*. With Taylor, who had just advised me not to try to overturn the trust *or* the trustee. Who had to have known and chose not to say anything.

Maybe there was a perfectly innocent explanation—like they had just met at the bar and started talking and discovered a mutual passion for medical charities, and Carole had just happened to be on her way to this event, and . . .

And maybe Mike Tyson was a closet Quaker.

Taylor blanched when he saw me, but it was too late to sit somewhere else. Carole had an I'm-a-big-donor smile plastered on her face and ignored me, by which I knew she'd spotted me before Taylor had and had time to prepare.

Initially we were all quite civilized, at least about the introductions.

"Of course I know Becky," Taylor said jovially, not meeting my eye. "She's one of the top associates in my law firm. Has everyone met Carole Pratt?"

"Only by reputation," said Isabel serenely.

"Maria Oblomova," said Maria. "Pathology."

Carole was unfazed. "I'm so pleased to meet you, Dr. Oblomova," she said. "I've heard such wonderful things about your work."

I hoped she got to experience it firsthand. On the slab.

She gave Mark a long, assessing look that boded ill, and smiled. "And naturally I've heard of you too, Dr. Lawrence."

Had Richard told her *everything*? Or was I just imagining that she knew about our connection?

"Dr. Lawrence was particularly helpful to my late husband's family at a time of crisis in their lives," she said to the table generally. "But of course it wouldn't be appropriate to go into *that*."

She knew.

"No, it wouldn't," said Mark.

"You're too modest, Mark," said Maria. "I'm always saying so."

The chicken was being cleared from the table. The taste in my mouth was sour and acidic. I took a sip of ice water. The evening appeared to stretch on into eternity.

"I hope we didn't miss anything," said Carole, turning toward Lyman with unmistakable interest. "Taylor had to work late tonight, so we couldn't get away."

Taylor decided to stop being intimidated by the fact that he had sold me down the river, not to mention failed to note that he was dating my ex-husband's widow. He was, after all, my employer. He winked at me. "Our clients are very demanding, aren't they, Becky?"

I didn't wink back. "Yes," I said tonelessly. "Very demanding."

"With such busy schedules, how did you two find time to meet?" asked Isabel sweetly.

Carole waved a hand, which I noted was no longer possessed of the Pratt diamond. "On the tennis courts. At the Sport and Water Club."

"Of course," agreed Isabel.

"The program's starting," Daniel pointed out, to my relief. Whatever horrors might be revealed by the speaker—chunks of flesh inadvertently liposuctioned from strategic areas, amino acid injections Roto-Rootering the veins, duck liver overdoses giving new meaning to quack medicine—couldn't be any worse than sitting there wondering what potshots Carole was going to take at me next.

The waiter set down ambiguous dishes of something white and fluffy in front of us. "What is it?" whispered Lyman.

"Vanilla mousse," the waiter said.

I pushed it aside. I had no appetite.

"I'll just have a salad," said Carole.

"There aren't any more salads," said the waiter. "All finished."

Taylor whipped out his wallet and handed the waiter a rolled bill. "Please ask the chef to make us two salads," he said.

"Tell him it's for Mrs. Pratt," Carole added. "Mrs. *Richard* Pratt."

I was excessively sorry, at that moment, that the knives had already been cleared from the table.

Next to me, Mrs. Sefton heaved an audible sigh. I was beginning to find her take on life most appealing. Not only that, but she had information I wanted to pursue. I smiled at her. It was too late for conversation; the Welcome was already under way.

"Ladies and gentlemen, I am honored to be in the presence of so many distinguished professionals, generous donors, and . . ."

"Nuts!" Lyman cried suddenly, with a horrible strangling sound.

We all turned to him in inquiry. His hand was at his collar, pulling at his tie. He was glaring at his half-eaten mousse with what could only be called indignation.

"Nuts," he said again. He ripped open his shirt collar with both hands. The studs went flying.

"Oh, God!" Daniel said, jumping to his feet. "The dessert must have had nuts in it. He's deathly allergic. Where's your epinephrine syringe?"

Lyman waved his hand desperately and shook his head.

"Did anyone bring a bag?" Daniel asked.

All the doctors at the table looked at each other in despair.

Despite the commotion, the speaker was manfully launching into his pitch. "Before I introduce tonight's speaker, I would like to talk about some of the challenges Windansea Hospital faces in the new millennium. . . ."

Lyman was sweating and starting to shed his clothes, layer by layer. His coat lay on the floor in a heap. His shirt was opened halfway down his chest.

"Emergency room," said Mark briskly.

Daniel nodded. "Come on, old man; I'll take you."

"I'll come too," said Isabel.

"So will I," I said.

"No, don't," Daniel said. "It's not something you want company for."

"I'll take the two of you home," Mark offered.

I jumped up quickly. People were starting to turn around. "At least I can get your clothes," I said, leaning over the pile to pick up Lyman's coat and tie.

Behind me, I heard more than one startled gasp.

"Oh my God," cried Carole, in tones that were probably audible in Cleveland. "Look at what she's done to her dress."

CHAPTER EIGHTEEN

Dear Medallion Foundation:

Would you like to do someone else a good turn? I know a woman, the daughter of a gardener, who needs financial assistance to stay in school. She is thirty-two and worked in her mother's laundry to pay for her younger brothers' college educations before she went to law school. She's been attending Stanford, but she might have to drop out. Her parents are Vietnamese and are very supportive of her goals; at the same time, her sense of duty to them and to the family has made it difficult for her to get by on her own financially. If you would consider giving her the same sort of financial assistance you've given me, I know she would put it to good use. In case you'd like to contact her, I've enclosed some biographical information.

Please forgive the importuning, but sometimes it's hard to make it unless somebody helps you.

I should know.

* * *

On the Monday morning following the fund-raiser from hell, Taylor buzzed my office.

"I'm in Escondido at a board meeting," he said crisply. "I'd like to see you later today."

"I don't know if I can make it," I said. "My mother's being moved into her assisted living facility this afternoon. I have to be there."

"You're taking time off from work?"

"I cleared it with Jamison Roth," I said. Jamison Roth was like everybody's favorite grandfather—he never said no to anything.

"I need to talk to you," he said. "I'll come by your house."

"I don't think so," I told him. "It wouldn't be appropriate." Boy, did I enjoy saying that.

"You're angry, aren't you?"

No duh, as Allie used to say at a particularly inarticulate juncture of her life. "Look, Taylor," I said, with what I hoped was professional hauteur, "you are my employer. That places certain constraints on whatever emotions I might feel in my dealings with you."

It was a perfectly judicious reminder, and he knew it. "You are angry." He sighed. "You're overreacting."

I didn't say anything.

"You're not going to do anything stupid, are you?"

Like what? Jump off the Coronado Bridge? Run naked down Prospect?

"Becky?"

Bring him up before the bar ethics committee for failing to disclose a monumental conflict of interest? Ah, I had it. Like quit, and take Bobbie Crystol with me. As if. Still, it wouldn't hurt to let him think it possible.

"I'm sorry, Taylor," I said with exquisite politeness, "I really have to go. I have a client waiting."

"Eight o'clock tomorrow morning," he said. "My office. Be there."

DUNEWOOD, MY MOTHER'S new home, was used to dealing with the difficult transitions that lead to the end of life.

"We're so pleased to have you here, Mrs. Weston," said Mrs. Fay, the residence administrator. We were sitting in the reception area, a pleasant tiled room full of potted plants and mock-Impressionist paintings. I was pleased to see that the administrator did not use my mother's first name uninvited. "We all hope you'll be very happy here," she added.

My mother's expression said she found that an unlikely prospect, but Mrs. Fay was used to doubters. "Let me show you to your room. Your daughter has already approved it, and I think you'll find it very attractive."

My mother's arms folded over her chest. She set her face mulishly. She sat in her wheelchair, which the nursing home had provided for the trip between facilities, but in Dunewood she would have to make her own way around. "We provide a safety net," Mrs. Fay had explained to me when I interviewed her (or she interviewed me) regarding my mother's placement. "We try to give people the highest level of independence they can handle. But we aren't set up to provide more than a certain level of care. Your mother will have to meet certain standards of mobility and autonomy in order to stay."

"And when she can't?" I'd asked her.

"We keep an eye on them," she said, meeting my

gaze. "When they need more help than we can provide, the next step is a skilled nursing facility."

I suppressed a shudder. "Like the one my mother's in now."

"We can assist you in finding a facility your mother will like."

"I doubt that," I said.

She smiled. "You'd be surprised."

Although she herself had never been one for sentimental mementos, I had put framed family pictures around my mother's room, Still, it was far from homey. I was struck by how few things she had, other than her clothes, and by how bare her life had been, living with me. I felt guilty. Maybe I *had* been too wrapped up in my own problems to realize she'd never made a life of her own after she'd come to my house.

"Look, Mother, isn't this nice?" I asked, using the same tone I'd employed taking Alicia to her first day of school. My hearty cheer hadn't convinced my daughter either. She'd hung back and clung to my hand as if that tenacious grip would keep her from being swept away from me, into the future.

"Very lovely," said my mother without enthusiasm. She looked pointedly at a teddy bear that was sitting on the bed. "And where did that come from?"

Mrs. Fay beamed. "It's a gift from all of us here. We always like to welcome our new residents that way. I think you'll find us a very friendly community. We care about each other, and we try to show it."

"Sweet," said my mother.

"Now I'm going to leave you to get settled, and after your daughter has left, I'll come back to take you to the dining room and to introduce you to the activities director. Do you play cards?"

"No," Mother said.

"Garden? Golf? Quilt?"

"No."

"Well, never mind," Mrs. Fay said gamely. "I guarantee we'll find something you like to do."

When the door had closed behind her, my mother looked at me with bleak despair. Her misery was the worst kind of rebuke.

"I'm sorry," I told her.

"Take me home," she said.

"I can't, you know that."

She looked at me. "Take me home, and I promise I'll die within two weeks. Three weeks at the outside."

I didn't know whether to laugh or cry. "Oh, Mother," I said, despairing. I didn't have the strength to fight her; I was no match for all her needs.

"How can you just walk away from here and leave me like this?" she demanded.

I sat down on the bed and took her hand. "I'll do what I can to make things better for you, but this isn't something I can control. This situation can't be cured, it can only be managed." As I said that, I felt the kind of relief you feel when you realize that you have somehow stumbled onto the truth. I'd been trying too hard to control a lot of things that couldn't be controlled. Sometimes you just had to adapt.

"Don't you care if I'm happy or not? I won't be, I can tell."

"Of course I care. I love you. I want you to be happy and dignified and proud of the life you've made. But I can't make that happen for you. Only you can do that."

"That's easy for you to say," she said. "You don't have to stay here." She sighed. "Do you know that your father made coffee for me every single morning of our married life? He brought it to me in bed."

I smiled. "I remember that," I said.

"He always took good care of me," she said.

"I miss him too, Mom," I told her.

"Now I have to do this all alone." She looked sadly at the stuffed animal on her bed. "I hate being old."

"I know," I told her helplessly. "I understand."

"No, you don't," she said. "But you will."

MARK LAWRENCE CALLED me almost the instant I walked through the door of my house. "How did it go?" he asked.

"Okay," I said. "I feel like I just dropped someone off at camp. Everything's cheery and upbeat, and the adults keep talking about all the fun activities. But underneath, you know the campers are homesick." I stopped. "How did you know?"

"You told me, remember? After you finalized the arrangements."

"Oh. Yes. Of course." I'd almost forgotten that he was the one who'd recommended Dunewood in the first place. "I'm sorry. It's not that it isn't a very nice place. I'm sure it is. It's just hard to leave her there when she's so determined not to be happy."

"Ah," he said.

"You sound like a therapist," I told him.

"Why is that?" He didn't sound flattered.

"Because you listen and don't talk. Most people jump in with advice or anecdotes when you tell them something personal."

He laughed, but then I heard a change in his voice, a kind of withdrawal, a distancing. "Do you *want* me to sound like a therapist?"

I knew what he meant. He meant, did I want to start seeing him professionally again?

I considered. "No," I told him finally. "Definitely not."

"Good, because then I can tell you all about what happened when my great-aunt died in her own house in the small town where she'd grown up and lived all her life."

"Anecdotes," I said.

"Anecdotes," he agreed.

"Okay, I'm game. What happened?"

"The caregiver my family had hired forged a check for twenty-five thousand dollars on my aunt's account and ran off with a boyfriend. The townspeople came in after my aunt was dead and stripped the house of valuables, right down to the wedding ring off of her finger. Do you remember the scene like that in *Zorba the Greek*?"

"Jesus," I said.

"The point is, there are no perfect solutions. Your mother will be well cared for at Dunewood. That may be the best you can do."

I let out a relieved breath. "Actually, I'd sort of come to that conclusion myself. It's very frustrating that I can't make her happy. But I can't change the way things are. Even if I gave up everything—my whole life—to take care of her, to be with her every day, I still couldn't change the facts. Even that might not be enough." I was breathing harder, suddenly serious and urgent. "The truth is, I don't want to give up everything to take care of her, even if they'd let me. Do you think that's really, really selfish?"

"Becky—"

"No, don't answer that," I said. "It's not a fair question. You're not my therapist anymore." I laughed. "Not that you would have answered it anyway. I have to let go of this myself."

He said nothing.

"I want to age like Georgia O'Keeffe," I told him. "I don't want to end up frightened and unhappy."

"You want to end up with some handsome, much younger man who'll take care of all your needs?" he asked. I could hear his smile through the phone.

"It sounds heartless, doesn't it?" I asked.

"You're not heartless," he said kindly.

"There is one thing I wanted to ask," I said, after a moment. "Not about my mother."

"What's that?"

"You remember the other night?"

He laughed.

"Dumb question," I told him. "Of course you do. By the way, thank you again for taking me home. And for lending me your coat. I hope it didn't ruin your evening." It might not have ruined his, but it certainly didn't thrill Dr. Oblomova, who had obviously entertained more interesting hopes.

"No problem," he said. "I'm just sorry I didn't come equipped with safety pins. Did Lyman go back to Texas?"

"I guess so," I told him. "He sent me an E-mail this

morning. He's already heard from the hotel's attorney, the charity, and the waiter. Apparently the waiter didn't know the nuts were in the mousse either. Nobody told him. He felt terrible."

"I hope nobody's suing," Mark said. "Or is that a terrible thing to say to a lawyer?"

"Oh, Mark, not you too! Give me a break."

He laughed. "You wouldn't care to make any bets about it, would you?"

"Actually, no," I confessed. "Anyway, that's not what I wanted to ask you about."

"Chicken," he said. "What's up?"

"Do you know Dorothy Beekman?"

"Not very well," he said.

"Do you have any idea what's wrong with her?"

"Excuse me?"

I sighed. "Sorry. I put that badly." I explained what I'd heard about Dorothy Beekman and Bobbie Crystol from Mrs. Sefton.

"Why do you want to know?" Mark asked me.

I started to explain all over again, thinking I had not made myself clear.

"Yes, but *why*?" he said, interrupting. "What would you do with this information if you found out something to the detriment of Dr. Crystol?"

"I don't know," I told him. "I just want to know. It's been sort of nagging at me since Mrs. Sefton brought it up."

He was silent. I was beginning to appreciate the eloquence of his silences, which were neither critical nor demanding. *Patient* is probably the closest word to describe them.

"I'm not sure why," I added truthfully.

"And I'm not sure I can help you. You know that if I'd learned anything about her medical condition through the hospital, it wouldn't be ethical to tell you. But the truth is, I don't know anything. I thought she looked unwell and rather tired, but that's as much a social opinion as a medical one."

"Well, let me ask you this. Do you think it could be possible for someone to get sick from anti-aging treatments? Just generally, I mean?"

"Becky, it's *possible* to get sick from Tylenol or aspirin. Anything you put in your body can do you harm. Look at poor Lyman. One reason the medical establishment worries about alternative remedies is that these things haven't been through rigorous FDA testing because they aren't officially classified as drugs. People have no idea what the effects will be over the long term. There are all kinds of dangerous substances masquerading as cures. So sure, it's possible. It depends on what you mean by *treatments*."

"Maybe I should talk to her," I said.

"Excuse me for saying so, but I seem to remember that the last time we had this conversation you were a little defensive about criticism of Dr. Crystol."

"Yes, and you told me to watch myself," I replied. "Maybe that's why when Mrs. Sefton started her little story an alarm bell went off."

"That wasn't an alarm bell. Those were the sirens, coming for Lyman."

"I'm serious," I said.

"Hmm," he said noncommittally. "Just don't jump to conclusions. Even if Dorothy Beekman drank Crystol

Potion Number Nine and fell swooning to the floor, it doesn't necessarily mean anything. *After* doesn't equal *because of* in the scientific world. And anyway, patients are notoriously unreliable about cause and effect."

"Mark?"

"Yes?"

"If I do find out anything, could I run it by you?"

"Sure," he said. "Should I ask, why me?"

"Because you're a skeptic, but you're a fair skeptic."

"Thanks, I think."

Also because he had seen, and kept seeing, all the very worst things about me and hadn't blanched. But I wasn't about to mention that. "Mark?"

He laughed. "What?"

"Do you think I should just forget about it?"

"That depends," he said, after a moment.

"I hate that answer," I told him.

"Okay, try this one," he said. "Remember Pandora?"

CHAPTER NINETEEN

I SURPRISED TAYLOR IN HIS OFFICE AT A QUARTER TO eight, before he was ready for me. "I'm here," I said, standing at the door.

He'd been bending over one of his paper piles with his back turned. He jumped, although he tried to cover up the fact that he was startled by bustling around with some folders.

So far, so good.

He straightened a stack of papers on his desk deliberately. "Please sit down," he said formally.

"I think I'd rather stand if you don't mind," I told him.

"Whatever you like," he said, making me feel as if he was humoring some childish whim. Score one for Taylor.

I moved a book off the client chair and sat.

"I'm sorry you're upset," he said.

I waited. I had to be careful until I knew all the facts. Until I decided what to do.

"I probably should have told you as soon as I realized, but frankly, I didn't see the point," he said.

Take big slow breaths, I told myself. *Don't be rash.* "You didn't see the point of explaining, when I came to you for advice about my children's trust fund, that you were dating the trustee?"

His face hardened. "My personal life is my own business," he said.

"You didn't think there might be a conflict of interest in telling me to forget about trying to do anything about it?"

"I know it might seem that way to you," he said calmly, "but try to look at it from my point of view. You're a lawyer; try to separate yourself from the emotion and look at the facts."

"Which are what?" I said deliberately, lawyerlike.

"I have a duty to Carole, as well as to you." I bet he did. "Not to reveal what I know about her business affairs," he added. "Which, let me assure you, is not all that much."

"Fine, but couldn't you just have said, 'I'm not able to advise you' or something like that? Did you have to go out of your way to discourage me?"

"Are you suggesting that I told you what I did because of some loyalty to Carole?" He seemed shocked at the very idea.

"I'm suggesting that you had a legal and ethical duty to inform a client that you were not in a position to give an objective opinion," I told him. "The bar ethics courses are very clear about this kind of situation."

He stared at me, taking in the implied threat. "And I, if you will remember, made it equally clear that you were not a client when I gave you advice."

I flushed with anger, remembering what I should have

remembered already—his insistence that we were having an "informal chat" between colleagues. Finally I understood it. He'd been protecting himself even then.

"Very good advice, I might add," he continued. "Look, Becky. I did you a favor. I gave you my opinion about what you should do. Check with any trust and estates attorney; he'll tell you the same thing I did. I could have avoided saying anything, just as you suggested, but I felt I owed it to you to be honest. The fact that I've been seeing Carole socially doesn't—didn't—affect my opinion at all." He folded his hands on the desk in front of him. "I can imagine that you see this as some big conspiracy against you on the part of Carole and myself, but I promise you that's not the case. I didn't even make the connection between Carole and you until I looked at the trust documents. It's not as if you use your ex-husband's name, and I didn't realize . . ."

I stared at him. The man had no scruples at all.

"What about the investments?" I asked him.

"The investments?"

"The offshore investments. The ones that lost all that money for the trust."

"What about them?" Taylor had suddenly become uncharacteristically obtuse.

"Did you have anything to do with them?" I demanded.

He looked at me. "Of course not. I would have said something. Really, Becky, I'm scarcely involved in this at all. Also . . ."

"Also?"

He looked down at the desktop. "Naturally, I'm very reluctant to get involved in your business because I don't want to make you uncomfortable, but I want you to know I've tried to intercede with Carole on your behalf."

I'm sure. "And how would that be, exactly?"

He didn't meet my eyes. "Well, I asked her to reconsider about the tuition amounts."

I almost laughed. "And did you have any success?"

He hesitated. "I'm sure she'll consider it. I don't think I'm entirely without influence in this case." He smiled.

No success. "I see," I said. I didn't smile back. I felt dizzy with a mixture of emotions—all of them unpleasant.

"Look, Becky," he said again, as if the repetition of my name would set me at ease. Or make things all right. "We're colleagues. You have a great future here at RTA, I'm sure of it."

I heard the unspoken threat, this time his. *If you don't blow it.*

"You've brought in a major client, an excellent start." He cleared his throat. "Crystol Enterprises needs *both* of us to make it a success. We have to work together. Do you understand what I'm saying?"

I understood all right. Play ball, and the game can go on as before. What I was wondering was, *did* Crystol Enterprises really need us both? Was Taylor trying to make himself indispensable to the client so I couldn't take her to some other firm? What would happen if I tried? What . . .

"Becky?"

"I understand what you're saying," I told him.

"Good," he said, sounding relieved, as if I'd agreed to something I hadn't intended. "Think it over."

"I will," I told him. "You can bet on that."

* * *

"I DON'T KNOW if I can go on working there," I told Isabel when I called her to report on my meeting. We'd had a lot to discuss since the fund-raiser, which had revealed, in so many senses of the word, so many things.

"He threatened you?" she asked.

"It was more subtle than that," I told her. "He reminded me that my future at the firm depends on my cooperation."

"Could you sue him or tell the other partners or something?"

I sighed. "He was really careful to keep just within the boundaries, even if he violated the spirit of attorney-client ethics in spades. The other partners might just think I had hurt feelings or something like that. You know how these things can be slanted. As for suing, even if there were grounds, I couldn't do it without having another job. You watch *60 Minutes*. You know what happens to whistle-blowers."

"What will you do, then?" Isabel asked.

"I don't know. Unless Taylor leaves, I'll probably never make partner now anyway. He'll find some way to ding me. I've made him look bad, even if nobody else knows about it. I don't think he'll forget it."

"You don't think you're overreacting just a bit?" she asked. "He may not have that much power."

"Maybe not, but I wouldn't bet the farm," I told her.

"So what will you do?" she asked again.

"Well, I can't afford to quit now, whatever happens," I told her. "Particularly now that I have to find some way to get the money Carole's lost or is refusing to disburse from the trust. But I think I have to start exploring an exit strategy. Taylor's afraid I might take Bobbie Crystol away from the firm," I said. "I don't know if I could, but he thinks I might be able to."

"Now we're getting somewhere," she said.

"Not entirely. I'd have to have somewhere to take her, assuming she'd be willing to leave with me." I was suddenly so tired. It was all too much. "I'm not surprised at anything terrible Carole does to me," I told her, "but I can't get over Taylor. I mean, I had *feelings* for the guy, in a remote sort of way. I knew all he really cares about is the firm, but—"

"Then you shouldn't be surprised at his consistency," Isabel said with some asperity. "Or did you think you could change him?"

I laughed. "I don't think I'd gotten that far in the fantasy."

"Good. You'll live. You know what he is and how to deal with him now. End of story. Besides, you know—and he knows—that workplace romances are the worst."

"Boy, those grapes sure look sour," I remarked.

"Then don't take a bite," she said.

"I'm still mad as hell," I told her. "I'm positively *glowering*. This whole thing just isn't any fun anymore."

"Well, don't move too fast," Isabel said seriously. "Think how long it took you to get where you are."

I didn't need the reminder. "Weren't you the one urging me to open myself up to new experiences?" I chided her.

"I said, 'Be flexible,'" she told me. "As in *pliant* or *resilient*. I don't remember that *rash* was any part of the conversation." She paused. "Shit," she said, in a distant voice far from the receiver.

"What's up?"

"Nothing. My book fell off the desk and hit my toe."

"We lead such glamorous lives," I told her. "What are you reading?"

She mumbled something indistinct.

"What? I didn't hear you."

"A novel," she said, sounding a little strange.

"Why are you sounding all prissy? What is it? Danielle Steel? Jackie Collins? Confess."

"Michener," she said.

"You're reading Michener?" I asked, surprised. Usually she preferred books that were a little more piquant.

"I'm allowed," she said, sounding touchy.

"Don't bite my head off," I said. "What—" I suddenly realized the reason for her embarrassment. "*Texas!*" I said. "You're reading *Texas,* aren't you?"

"It's very interesting," she said formally.

"I'm sure it is," I agreed. And long. She must be more serious about Daniel than I realized.

"Want to borrow it when I'm finished?" she asked.

WHEN I HUNG up, I checked my voice mail. The results were not cheering.

"This is Carole," said the voice that was coming to haunt my darkest dreams. "I warned you." *Click*.

So much for Taylor's influence. What next? If Carole was progressing to telephone threats, she must have something really nasty in mind, a prospect I could not encounter with any degree of calm, much less levity. I was almost afraid to hear the second message.

"You haven't RSVPed to Opening Weekend," Bobbie Crystol said in an accusatory tone. "I really expect you to be there. Taylor is coming and some other people from your firm. Give me a call."

Christ, now I would have to go, whether I wanted to spend the weekend checking out the life-extension powers of hot-rock massage or not. I really needed to be exploring what to do about the trust money, but I didn't want Taylor moving in on Bobbie, my best hope of landing a halfway decent job at another firm. The only trouble was, I wasn't entirely happy with the role of Bobbie Crystol as lifeboat. Mrs. Sefton's little hints about her at the fund-raising dinner—dropped, admittedly, at a very distracting time—continued to nag at my conscience, demanding to be explored.

DOROTHY BEEKMAN WAS surprised to hear from me, as well she might have been, since we were never on chummy terms even in my more social days. Still, she was too much of a lady to act anything less than pleased, once I had made it clear who I was.

"I was hoping we might get together for a chat," I told her. I liked the word *chat*. It didn't sound threatening or particularly lengthy. Plus it was vaguely archaic, like Dorothy. I explained that seeing her had reminded me how out of touch I'd become socially, and that I hoped to remedy that gradually—perhaps by volunteering for a committee? I told her I was trying to interest my mother, just recuperating from a fall, in some appropriate charitable work as well. I hoped Dorothy had not heard about my escapade with the dress, as it might seriously undermine my credentials for social rehabilitation.

She said she would be happy to do lunch.

"Umm," I said, faced with the inescapable obstacle of no longer having lunchtime totally free, "that might be a problem."

"Are you on a diet?" she asked.

"Well, ah, I work," I told her.

"Oh, yes," she said, as if I had confessed to being an eccentric species of animal that needed humoring. "Of course. I remember. But my dear, just now I'm not getting out that much at night. I haven't been in the best of health."

I said I was very sorry to hear that, and what about afternoon tea?

"What a charming idea," she said.

"What about tomorrow?" I asked her. "The U.S. Grant? Three-thirty?" I would have to come back to the office afterward, but I thought it could be managed.

"Lovely," she said.

AFTERNOON TEA IS not an institution usually associated with Southern California, where the appropriate symbolic drink of choice might be tequila imbibed under a palm tree, preferably at sunset. Even Gatorade is more of a contender. Tea requires cups and saucers, not plastic glasses, and it doesn't go with chips, much less with guacamole. You can't drink it on the beach, and all those scones and little sandwiches are Bad for You. Still, there are several great tea places in metropolitan San Diego, with harpists and white tablecloths and silver tea services. The U.S. Grant, a downtown hotel, is one of them.

Dorothy was waiting for me in the lounge. She was wearing a close-fitting St. John knit dress that was attractive but accentuated her thinness. On me it would probably have looked like a sausage casing. She seemed relieved when she saw me.

"I hope you haven't been waiting long?" I asked her.

"I'm always early," she said graciously. "And this is such a lovely place to sit."

"Our table is right over there," I said. She wobbled a little when she stood up, and I took her arm and guided her.

"I feel so foolish," she said. "I've been a bit light-headed lately." She shook her head. "But let's not talk about that."

I decided to get right to the point, in retrospect a foolish decision. "Actually, would you mind if we did?" I asked her.

She looked alarmed. "I can't see why it would interest you," she said.

"Bear with me," I said.

She drew back in distaste. "You didn't ask me here to try to get me to bring some dreadful lawsuit, did you?"

I blushed for my profession. "No, no, it's not that. But I'm afraid I wasn't perfectly straightforward with you about why I did want to get together."

She relaxed a little. "I knew that already," she said with a tight smile. "No one *ever* volunteers to be on committees unless they want something. It's the biggest problem we have. All the younger women work or have other interests, and no one has time for charitable activities anymore. Plenty of people will give money, but no one will give time. It's very sad. I don't know what will happen when our generation is gone."

I felt vaguely ashamed of my subterfuge, and now I was going to have to volunteer for the cleanup committee or something equally undesirable to make amends. "I'm sorry," I said.

The waiter brought our pots of tea—Lapsang souchong for me, Earl Grey for her. The sandwiches were delicious.

"So what did you want to talk to me about?" she asked when he had gone. "Not really the state of my health, surely?"

"As a matter of fact, yes, if you don't mind. Mrs. Sefton"—what was that woman's first name?—"was the one who told me you'd been ill, and—"

She looked seriously displeased.

"Please don't be annoyed with her," I said, wondering what I'd started. In certain circles, if you cared to move in them, Dottie Beekman's disapproval was tantamount to dismissal. "We were talking about alternative medicine, and your name came up."

"In what context?" she asked carefully.

"In the context of Dr. Bobbie Crystol and her anti-aging treatments," I told her.

She held off a bite of scone with her fork as if it were a menacing object. "I don't want to talk about it," she said. "It was entirely my own fault."

"Please, I need to know if there's anything, um"—I struggled for the right word—"upsetting about her treatments."

She looked at me. "Why do you need to know?"

That was a complicated question, and I wasn't exactly in a position to tell her the complete truth. I had a duty to the client. But I felt horrid about lying to her. Again. Actually, I wasn't really sure of the answer myself. Did some part of me just want to prove that Bobbie Crystol was a dangerous egomaniac? Was I jealous? Was it Mark's warning? I couldn't really say. But somehow Mrs. Sefton's comments had struck a nerve. "I can't explain why, not entirely," I told Dorothy Beekman. "It's a lot to ask you to trust me, I know. I can tell you that one reason I want to know is that I'm thinking of going to her spa myself."

She patted my hand. "Aren't you a little young for that?"

I smiled. "Thank you for the compliment, but according to Dr. Crystol I've already missed my chance for a timely start. So tell me, *is* there anything I should be concerned about?"

"You mean did her treatments make me sick?" she asked directly.

"Well, in a word, yes."

"Nothing like that can be answered in a word," she responded. "I went to her clinic in Georgia when I visited my sister in Atlanta. Everyone was talking about it. Dr. Crystol gave me a diet and a great deal of pampering—herbal wraps, massages, facials. It was quite wonderful. Blissful, in fact."

I waited.

"I felt very good, full of energy. I even started getting up earlier. I decided to stay on for a month or two in Atlanta and continue with a more intensive program. The second part of the program deals with your attitudes, I suppose you'd say. Things like eliminating fears from your life and healing illnesses by harnessing your own consciousness. It was . . . interesting." She looked away.

"What happened?" I prompted her gently.

"My blood pressure went up," she said. "Rather seriously, in fact. I developed a heart arrhythmia."

"What did Dr. Crystol say?" I asked.

"She monitored me very carefully," she said. "She

said my pulse was trying to tell me that I was living too fast, that I should try to slow down. She said my health was in my own hands and that I should try to eliminate anger and hostility in my life. She said I was holding too much in and that I was in danger of developing heart disease." She sighed. "Unfortunately, she was right."

"You developed heart disease?"

She nodded. "I wasn't able to follow her advice. She told me what to do, and I couldn't do it." She shook her head. "I don't want to go into it, but there is someone in my life I can't forgive. I've hung on to that anger. I've made myself sick."

Her acceptance of the blame for this facile diagnosis made *me* angry, but not at her. "Did you see a doctor?" I asked her.

"Dr. Crystol is a doctor," she pointed out.

"A cardiologist, I mean."

"Oh, yes."

"And what did the doctor say?" I asked gently.

She smiled. "Oh, well, you know how doctors are. Pessimism is their defense against uncertainty." She lifted her cup to her lips. "This Earl Grey is delicious, isn't it?"

"Just one more question?" I asked her.

She sipped her tea, saying nothing.

"Did you take anything while you were being treated by Dr. Crystol?"

She blinked. "Take anything?"

"Drugs? Vitamins? Anything like that?"

"Oh, yes. Some people got injections and we all got drinks. Dr. Crystol called them Health Shakes or Life Shakes or something like that. I can't really recall."

"What was in them?"

She looked at me in surprise. "I don't know. Herbal supplements or vitamins, I assume." She raised her eyebrows. "I can see what you're thinking, Rebecca, but I'm sure there's no connection. None whatsoever. Now, shall we get down to business? Which is it going to be?"

"Going to be?"

She nodded. "Leukemia? Diabetes? What about the fashion show to benefit Family Recovery? I have vacancies on a lot of committees."

"Surprise me," I said.

CHAPTER TWENTY

MY MOTHER WAS NOT ENAMORED OF HER NEW LIFE.

"The food sucks," she said.

"Oh, Grandma," said Allie, laughing. I didn't blame her. I had never in my life expected to hear my mother, who had once actually washed my mouth out with soap when I'd said, "Shit," use that expression.

My mother looked rather pleased at Allie's reaction. "The boy that cleans my room told me that's what young people say now," she said proudly.

I hoped my mother had sense enough to be nice to the staff, but I doubted it. "Does it really?" I asked her. I had toured the dining area and the kitchens at mealtime, and the food had looked just fine.

"The vegetables are undercooked," she said.

I tried not to smile. My mother's generation regarded any vegetable that retained its shape after cooking with suspicion and disapproval.

"Eeuuw, gross," said Allie dutifully.

Lest I find myself in the unenviable position of urging two generations to eat their vegetables, I decided to let it drop. "How are you feeling?" I asked her.

My mother closed her eyes. “It hurts,” she said.

“What does, Mother?”

She sighed. “Everything. My leg. When I walk.”

“I’m sorry,” I said. “Maybe you haven’t quite healed after your fall. The doctors said you were cleared to walk, but if it keeps on hurting we’ll have them check you out again, okay?”

“I’m only entitled to an hour a day of assistance,” she said.

“What?”

“An hour a day. That’s what it works out to. What I’m paying for. After that I’m on my own. I have to do things for myself.”

“Don’t you want that, Grandma?” Allie asked her.

“I want to go home,” she said, looking at me.

“Have you met anyone here? Have you made any friends?” I asked desperately.

My mother looked away. “How could I? There’s no one here I want to know,” she said.

MRS. FAY, THE residence administrator, was more sanguine about my mother’s adjustment. “Some people just take more time to settle in,” she said as Allie and I sat in her office off the reception area. “Physically, she’s still very slow to make her way around, and she complains a good bit. I expect that will pick up soon, after she’s healed from her fall. I know we’re keeping an eye on her after her TIA, but otherwise she seems to be adapting reasonably well.” She sighed. “A lot of younger people come in here and say, ‘Oh, I’d love to live in a place like this, with everything taken care of,’ ” she said. “But look, it’s hard to give up your home and your independence. All your choices. A lot of people resist that, the way your mother has, and I really don't blame them."

I felt vaguely rebuked. "I'm just worried that she isn't meeting anyone. She doesn't go out, doesn't participate."

Mrs. Fay smiled. "Is that what she told you?"

"She certainly implied it."

"Did she tell you she's learning Spanish?"

"No, she didn't. In fact, I sort of had the impression she never left her room."

Her smile broadened. "I told you before, we have lots of activities. It's usually just a matter of finding the right one. Carlos is one of our best volunteer instructors, and his beginning Spanish class is very popular. It also doesn't hurt that Carlos is a dead ringer for Ricardo Montalban," she added.

"Who's that?" asked Allie.

Mrs. Fay and I exchanged sympathetic glances. "An actor, dear," she said. "A very handsome one."

"So are you saying that my mother is socializing some?" I asked her. "That I don't need to be worried?" I felt like the parent of an underachiever at Back-to-School Night.

She folded her hands together on her desk and looked at me kindly. "I'm saying that your mother may be misrepresenting things a bit because she still expects you to take her home. After all, if she's happy here, there's that much less incentive, isn't there?"

ALLIE WAS SILENT for much of the drive home. I knew most of her silences—there were leave-me-alone silences and please-ask-me-what's-wrong silences. I thought this was the latter.

"Anything wrong, honey?" I asked, turning down the volume on the radio.

She was quiet a few moments longer. At last she said, "Grandma doesn't like it there, does she?"

"Not much," I admitted. "But it's a nice place. She'll probably like it more in time."

"Does she have to stay there?"

I looked at her. "For the moment, yes."

"That sucks," she said, sounding like her grandmother. I had told her a zillion times that that was not my favorite expression, but I let it pass.

"Sometimes people have a hard time getting used to living with strangers, particularly when they get older," I told her. "And it's difficult for them to admit they need help. But you *know* Grandma needs help. You remember how she was at home."

She frowned and then turned to look out the window. "Mom?"

"Yes?"

Her voice was so low I could barely hear her. "You didn't put Grandma in that place because of me, did you? I mean, I know I said it was boring taking care of her and I wanted to have a *life,* but I didn't mean that you should send her away."

I pulled the car over to the curb and turned off the engine. "No, Allie, it wasn't because of you," I told her firmly. "The social worker at the hospital evaluated her and said she shouldn't be by herself or just with you anymore. I should have seen that myself."

"I still feel really, really terrible," she said.

"So do I," I told her.

"Really?" she asked.

"Sure," I said. "I feel sorry that she has to be someplace she doesn't want to be. I also feel guilty that I'm relieved that she's there so I don't have to worry about her all the time. I feel guilty that I put too big a burden on you long after I should have. All of that makes me feel terrible."

She nodded thoughtfully. "I guess I feel guilty for feeling relieved too. I mean, I miss Grandma, but . . ."

"I know," I told her. "It's complicated. Sometimes you have to do things for people you don't particularly feel like doing, no matter how much you love them. Usually it all balances out." I smiled. "I don't suppose Grandma was too thrilled with changing all my dirty diapers either. You have to look at the big picture."

"Is that like a 'Circle of Life' thing?" she asked.

Philosophy à la Disney. "Sort of," I told her. I turned the key in the ignition. "Okay now?" I asked her.

"I guess so," she said. "Mom?" she asked again.

"Yes?"

"Is it too late to get a dress for the prom?"

"You asked somebody?" I tried to keep my voice noncommittal and low-key.

She nodded. "A guy in my Advanced Algebra class. He's not one of the jocks or anything. He's just a nice person." She looked at me in wonder. "He said okay."

"Good," I told her carefully. "I'm glad."

She settled back comfortably against the seat, her happiness spilling over into a nonstop grin. "This is so awesome," she said.

I smiled too, relieved. And then I thought, I should remember this moment. The smallest minute of inattention and I might have missed it—it was so hard to keep everything in focus at once. But life has a way of slipping things under your guard, and here it was all of a sudden—the evidence that my baby girl had a life of her own and a heart to be touched or broken. I thought with a pang that loving your children is about having and losing them at the same time. *Circle of life,* I thought, and then I had to laugh at myself.

"So do you think we could still get a dress?" she asked me, confident of the answer.

"What do you think?" I said. The questions—*What's his name? Who will be driving? What time will you be home?*—and the worries—*Will there be drugs involved? Alcohol?*—could wait for later. I didn't want to spoil the magic.

"Let's call Grandma when we get home," I suggested. "She'll be very excited."

"Do you really think so?" she asked, wanting to believe.

"I know it," I said, and suddenly, I did.

"YOU DID *WHAT?*" Lauren asked me. We were having our lunches outside on the RTA patio. We both had salads encased in plastic containers—chicken for her, mixed greens for me. No dressing. Most of the men, both partners and associates, went out for sandwiches or took clients to lunch at upscale restaurants, but nobody ate big. It was bad for productivity, not to mention arterial plaque.

I had by now figured out that Lauren was my designated mentor, officially and unofficially, because of the number of times she dropped by to see how I was doing. I certainly appreciated it, but a part of me held back, wondering how much she reported to the upper ranks.

I could see at once that I should have held back now.

"I didn't tell her why I was asking," I said. I had just given Lauren a brief summary of my tea with Dorothy Beekman. I thought she'd be interested, since she harbored a certain skepticism about Bobbie Crystol herself.

She put down her fork. "Never, never, never divulge anything about a client to someone outside the firm," she said. "It isn't ethical, and it's very bad business practice."

"I didn't divulge anything except my interest in the subject," I protested. "She doesn't know Crystol Enterprises is a client. Besides, what she told me was inconclusive. Even I could see that."

"That's something, anyway," she muttered. "So tell me again why you did this."

"I heard something, and I wanted to check it out," I told her. "Wouldn't you want to know if Dr. Crystol had given people something that would make them sick?"

She looked at me with her clear, direct gaze. "No, I would not," she said firmly.

"Really?" I asked, surprised.

She looked resigned but disappointed, as if I were a tolerably nice pet who couldn't quite get the hang of obedience training.

"Really," she said. "Look, Becky, the essence of good lawyering is not asking a question unless you know what answer you're likely to get."

Then what's the point of asking? I wanted to say, but I didn't. I said, "I don't get it."

"Well, let me give you an example in the context of criminal law. If you are O.J.'s lawyer, do you ask him, 'Did you do it?' "

"I take it not," I said.

"Right. Because if he says yes, even though it's privileged, you can't put him on the stand and let him perjure himself. So you don't ask. It's better not to know."

I twirled greens on my plastic fork, thinking. "So you think it's just better not to know if your client might have done something wrong?"

She sighed. "I'm saying it makes it a lot easier to represent them. What could you do if you found out that your wildest suspicions were true? Knowing something damaging is not an advantage in this situation; you must see that. Just make sure nothing illegal is going on now. Period. Protect yourself, but be careful where you go poking sticks."

"I suppose," I said doubtfully.

"Trust me," she said.

"But—"

"No *buts,*" she said firmly.

Even I knew better than to argue with that. I said nothing. If she wanted to think that silence meant consent, then I wasn't going to stop her. Under the circumstances, I certainly wasn't going to tell her that I wasn't about to abandon my attempts to get around the trust somehow either, even if Taylor got dragged into the unpleasantness. I felt as if I were walking on eggshells with everyone.

"By the way," she said after a few moments during which we both got through the awkwardness by pretending enthusiasm for our salads, "there was something else I wanted to tell you. Remember my gardener's daughter? The one who's in law school?"

"Sure. The one who might have to drop out?"

"I *knew* you were the one I'd told about it," she said. "The most amazing thing happened."

"What?" I asked.

"She's been invited to apply for a fellowship. No, not invited, *encouraged*. Some foundation contacted her. If she gets it, she won't have to drop out."

"That's wonderful," I said. "What's the foundation?"

"I think it's called the Medallion Foundation or something like that. I don't think she'd ever heard of them before. It's something of a mystery how they even got her name."

I shrugged. "I say take the money and run. It sounds like she deserves it. Why look a gift horse in the mouth?"

She looked at me suspiciously. "You wouldn't happen to know anything about this, would you?"

I raised my eyebrows. "Me?" I shook my head. "I heard it here first," I told her.

CHAPTER TWENTY-ONE

DEAR MEMBERS OF THE BOARD . . . I SAT DOWN TO write to the Medallion Foundation. I got stuck after the salutation. I was gratified by the response to my request, but I was unnerved too.

Someone was listening.

I mean, originally I'd made up the character of Pendleton Silverbridge and endowed him with an imaginary interest in my little life so that I could indulge myself by sending, over the years, what amounted to one long journal about my career in law school. And a number of other things too, now that I came to think of it. I'd been embarrassingly confessional on occasion, I'd made bad jokes and snotty comments, mostly because I believed, deep down, that the letters were a pro forma exercise and were discarded unread.

Well, now I knew better. There was somebody out there. It was like the difference between a respectful belief in the Prime Mover and "Sinners in the Hands of an Angry God." One was impersonal; the other wasn't.

I wondered if I'd made them cringe all those years—

Pendleton or Helen or Jackie or Paul—and how I should address them now.

Nobody's listening till you make a mistake.

On the other hand, they *had* listened, maybe in spite of the mistakes. They had done something I'd asked them to. Maybe I shouldn't mess with success.

I tried again.

Dear Members of the Board:

I meant to write you a simple note thanking you for responding to the request I made when I last wrote. Thank you for your generous consideration of a very worthy young woman. I'm sure she'll requite your kindness with success.

Oh, hell. I might as well say what was really on my mind.

Thank you for listening. Not just this time, but all those years. I inflicted all my worries and regrets and observations on you like some juridical Samuel Pepys because, the truth is, I wasn't sure anyone was really reading them, and I have to admit, those letters did me an awful lot of good. I don't know who you are or where your sensibilities—collective or individual—lie, and for all I know I trampled on them right and left. If so, forgive me.

I wondered if I should, in fact, inflict my doubts on them one last time just for old time's sake. *L'affaire Taylor* had made me more than a little cynical about staying on in the life I had chosen, particularly since I was having a few doubts about Bobbie Crystol too. I had the impression from Lauren that not only was I supposed to dedicate myself to Work for the rest of my life, but I was also supposed to turn a blind eye to client foibles if I knew what was good for me. *Don't ask a question unless you know what answer you're likely to get.* I'd get little in the way of loyalty in return. And not a lot of laughs either.

I thought about all the lectures I'd given Allie and David over the years about making yourself do what you had to do, even if you didn't feel like it. It didn't seem like such a wonderful life plan now. So should I quit my job? After six years of struggle? When I could barely meet my financial obligations as it was? And—not to put too fine a point on it—to do what?

I studied the letter. Should I tell them? Nah, I thought. Time to grow up and handle things on my own.

> *Thank you again for your generosity. I wish you all the very best.*

I'd been putting off telling David about Carole's reduction in payments and, more to the point, my inability to date to do anything about it. I told myself I didn't want to upset his studies, but the reality was that I hadn't been in a rush to share the news. I knew he'd be angry and disappointed. Still, it was important that he know so he could make plans.

I drove up to L.A. on a Sunday so smoggy that my eyes felt scratchy as soon as I hit the Harbor Freeway. By the time I got to Pasadena the pollution had invaded my body, lounging in my lungs and irritating my stomach. I met David at his apartment; his roommates were away for the day. This wasn't the sort of news I wanted to impart over the phone. The sight of him—happy, relaxed, confident—twisted my heart. College had done that for him. It was just what Richard and I had hoped for when we made our plans.

"What's up?" he asked me after he had bent over and kissed me affectionately. He was a very big man; taller than his father had been by at least three or four inches. He didn't look like either one of us much, although he had Richard's curly hair. We sat down on an old brown couch that had clearly come out of someone's attic to furnish the apartment. I'd called before I came, so there were no unspeakable piles of laundry or discarded pizza boxes in evidence. David's sloppiness had driven me wild when he lived under my roof; now it seemed endearing and manly.

"Bad news, I'm afraid," I told him.

He touched my arm. "Is it Grandma?"

I shook my head.

His face changed. "Are you okay, Mom?" he asked, in a tight voice.

"No, no, it's nothing like that. I'm fine. It's the money." I explained about the payment reduction and showed him Carole's letter.

"Fuck her," he said finally, throwing it down on the coffee table. He looked at me. "Can't you do anything about it?"

I'd been prepared for the question, but it still came as a blow. "Some of the principal *has* been reduced—the accountants confirm that. I've looked into trying to break the trust or get her removed as trustee before she can lose any more. I'm a lawyer, Davey, but I'm not an expert in trusts and estates. I asked someone at the firm. I've been advised that trying to do either would be very difficult. Not only that, but it would cost a lot and eat into the capital in the fund."

"Fuck," he said again. "So that means you can't do anything, right?" He sounded angry and bitter.

"No," I told him. "It doesn't mean that. But it means that right now I don't have the answer. I promise you I'll do everything I possibly can to fix it, but I can't make a problem like this vanish this instant."

"Christ," he said. "Now what?"

I took a breath. "Well, you have some choices to make. You could try to get a loan. You could get a job during school as well as during vacations. Or you could . . ."

"Drop out," he said morosely.

"Transfer, not drop out," I said firmly. I paused. "I'm so sorry, David."

He shook his head vehemently. "No, I'm the one who's sorry, Mom. I'm acting like a baby. I'm taking this out on you, and it's not your fault. It's not your problem either." He straightened up on the couch. I never felt more proud of him than at that moment, because I knew he was signaling something more than taking responsibility for the tuition problem. My children were constantly surprising me. I felt a little misty-eyed.

"David—"

"I mean it, Mom. It's my education. I'll think of something. I mean, it's not like *you* didn't have to work to put yourself through law school. Try not to worry. You've been a good example." He smiled and patted my hand solicitously. "I just reacted badly because that witch always gets under my skin."

I decided to skip the treat-your-stepmother-with-respect lecture. "Mine too," I told him.

"Mom?" he asked, looking vulnerable again.

"Yes?"

"Dad wouldn't have wanted things to work out this way, would he?"

"Of course not," I told him, with a little more certainty than I felt. "I know your father wanted a good education for you, no matter what. Besides, one thing I am absolutely sure of is that your dad would have been really, really proud of you at this moment."

He blushed. "Oh, Mom," he said.

ON MONDAY, WHILE I was attempting to deal with megastacks of papers (mostly writing up corporate minutes, scripted in advance, the bane of every new associate in the corporate field), my direct line rang.

"Rebecca Weston," I said, although it was usually Allie.

"Ms. Weston, good afternoon," said the plummy voice at the other end of the line. "This is Scott Forsby at Ranier Associates." He paused. "We're an executive and legal search firm."

A headhunter? I was silent.

"Well, ahem, I've been asked to approach you to see if you might consider accepting what we consider a highly advantageous employment offer at a very prestigious firm."

I almost said, "Me?" but decided this was not the moment for excessive humility. Still, I felt there must be some mistake. First-year associates at third-tier law firms are not normally recruiting targets, even if you discount the hype about prestige and advantage.

"Are you there, Ms. Weston?" he said.

"I'm here," I said. "You've just caught me a bit off guard."

"I understand," said Plummy Voice. "Would you like to discuss this at another time?"

"What is it precisely that we're discussing?"

"For starters, an annual salary of two hundred thousand plus a substantial bonus."

I gasped. "Where is this firm, Saudi Arabia?"

He chuckled. "Newport Beach," he said.

"A firm in Newport Beach wants to pay a first-year associate more than two hundred thousand a year? That's a high starting salary even for New York. What's the catch?"

He coughed. "You're a first-year associate?"

Suddenly I knew what the catch was. But I would let him spell it out.

"I am," I told him.

"I just need to verify one or two things," he said.

I smiled into the phone. "Go ahead."

"We understand that you are currently the billing attorney for a substantial piece of business," he said.

"That's correct," I said.

"You haven't signed any agreement not to take clients with you in the event you leave your present position?"

"Correct again," I told him.

"Would you say that there is a high likelihood that your personal clients would want to follow you to another firm?" he asked.

"I don't know," I said truthfully.

"The offer would be contingent on that circumstance," he said carefully.

"I'm sure it would be," I said with a laugh. "I don't think anyone would be courting me otherwise."

He seemed relieved that I understood the realities of the situation. "And may I ask about your employment before your current position?" he said. "Summer internships, that sort of thing."

I said dryly, "I was the receptionist at my current firm for six years."

"I'm sorry? The what?"

I smiled. "The receptionist. You know, the one that picks up the phones and says, 'Roth, Tolbert and Anderson.' On a slow day I'd empty the wastebaskets too, but it wasn't part of the job description."

"Remarkable," he said.

"Not your usual client profile?"

He laughed, sounding human for the first time. "Not at all," he said. "More power to you."

"Thanks."

"Are there any questions you'd like to ask?"

"Sure. Tell me something about the firm."

He did. Looking to build a high-profile practice. Celebrity clients. Possible branch offices. Up-and-coming. Et cetera.

"What is the average number of billable hours per year for an associate?" I asked.

"Between twenty-five hundred and three thousand," he said proudly.

Twenty-five hundred to three thousand hours annually worked out to about ten billable hours every single day if you didn't work weekends (ha) and took a four-week vacation (standard). Ten billable hours a day is not how long your body is at the office; it's how much work you do for clients, in addition to lunch, bathroom breaks, walkabouts, personal phone calls, and shooting the shit with the other lawyers. If you're honest, that means at least twelve or thirteen hours every day at the firm. And that's just the average.

It was much worse than the time I was putting in now, and that was bad enough, which may be why, instead of shrieking "Salvation!" my first reaction was a kind of dread. Still, the money, the silver seat belt that kept you in place, was amazing. I could pay for my mother's care and make up some of David's tuition. I could take a vacation in lodgings that didn't require setup and assembly. I could buy Burdick Fancy Feast instead of the supermarket brand.

All I had to do was bring in Crystol Enterprises and stay best buddies with my old friend Bobbie.

"We'd appreciate it if you'd keep this confidential," he said. "But at least say you'll think about it."

"I don't imagine I'll be able to help it," I told him.

He laughed. "For the record, I'm very, very impressed that someone in your position could bring in such a substantial piece of business," he said. "I've checked, and I know you're not related to . . . the client."

"You know a lot," I told him. "How did you even hear about this? How did you get this number?"

"Trade secrets," he said calmly. "It's my job."

"ISABEL," I SAID. "How would you like a glorious spa weekend in sunny Mexico?"

"What's the catch?" she asked.

"You wound me," I told her.

"What's the catch?"

I sighed. "I have to go to Bobbie Crystol's Opening Weekend at Casa Alegría. She invited me to bring a guest."

"Why do you want me to go? It's a business event, isn't it?"

"There'll be lots of different people there," I said. "Anyway, I'd be interested in your opinion of the place."

"That bad? What's up?"

"Actually, I don't think it will be bad. I'm sort of looking forward to some aromatherapy and a good massage. Well, I'm not really up for Bobby's sick-minds-make-sick-molecules shtick. And I'm not terribly eager to massage her ego all weekend. But—"

"And I am?"

"You wouldn't have to do any of that. You could just sort of keep your ear to the ground while I'm sucking up to Bobbie."

"Why don't we just go somewhere else and forget it?"

"I can't afford to abandon her to Taylor." I told her about the headhunter's offer, swearing her to secrecy.

"Wow, Becky. Congratulations! Are you going to take it?" she asked.

"Do you think I should?" I asked, surprised.

"Get real," she told me. "Don't turn them down till you've thought about it. It's a lot of money."

"I know. Visions of sugarplums keep crowding out more urgent considerations, like getting my work done. I mean, if I took this job, I might not even have to worry about Carole or the trust. Maybe the devil really does reside in Newport Beach."

"He certainly has enough disciples there. It's the scam capital of California."

"Anyway, you see why I have to go on this weekend."

"I do," she agreed. "And you see why I can't. You have to stay totally focused on Bobbie Crystol if you want this new job. Besides, you don't need me to find out if Taylor Anderson is trying to take over your client. You know he is."

"I'm worried about more than that. What if she's doing harm to some of her patients? If I take this new job, I'll have to swallow whatever she's dishing out to the world, as long as it's legal. My entire livelihood will depend on keeping her happy. I have to be sure that's something I can live with."

"You're trying to dig up the dirt on your client? The one who's going to make you a partner?" She sounded amused.

"I wouldn't call it 'digging up the dirt,' " I protested. "It's more like wondering. Anyway, I'm really hoping there's nothing to worry about."

"The best way not to find something is not to look," she said.

I'd already heard that advice from Lauren. "You think I'm crazy, don't you?"

"It's too early to tell. Go to the spa and do what it takes to keep the client. Just keep your eyes open. You can always make a grand renunciation later if you have to, but it's better to start from a position of strength."

Good advice on the whole. I decided to switch gears. "So how's Daniel?" I asked casually.

"I don't know," she said. "He's home visiting."

"Home being . . ."

"Right. The *T* word."

"Maybe it's not so bad, Isabel. It's just a place. It doesn't mean Daniel bites the heads off of rattlesnakes or something like that."

"You know what Phil Sheridan said about Texas?" she asked gloomily.

"Who's he?" I asked.

"*Was*. Who *was* he. He was a general in the Civil War, but before that he served in Texas. He said, 'If I owned Texas and hell, I would rent out Texas and live in hell.' "

I laughed. "That's sort of what Satan said about heaven in *Paradise Lost*. That doesn't mean heaven's a bad place, does it?"

"Humph," she said.

WENDY RICHARDS BUZZED me as I was taking out my half sandwich (turkey, mustard, lettuce, and nonfat mayonnaise), preparing for what is euphemistically called a working lunch. In reality I had to clear the papers away momentarily lest I drop blobs of honey Dijon on my documents.

"There's a Mark Lawrence on the outside line," she said. "I didn't know if you'd want to be disturbed."

I licked my fingers to avoid getting the phone sticky. "Put him through, please," I said. I loved it that Mark didn't announce himself as Dr. Lawrence, the way every other person with an M.D. degree did, at least in my experience.

"Hi," he said when I came on the line. "I know it's very late notice, but if you haven't eaten yet, I'm only a couple of blocks away. I wondered if you'd like to have lunch."

I looked down at my sandwich, not too much the worse for wear. I pushed the ends of the wrapping back together. "I'd love to," I said. "I haven't done anything about lunch yet." I looked at my watch; it was one o'clock.

"Great," he said, and named the restaurant where we should meet.

After I hung up I wondered whether I should have accepted with such alacrity. Despite being out of what is politely known as "circulation" for a period too lengthy to dwell upon with any degree of comfort (if you don't count the fix-ups like Lyman, and look how *that* ended), even I knew that you weren't supposed to seem too available and eager. It was the old I-don't-want-to-join-any-club-that-would-let-me-in routine overlaid by the omnipresent admonitions of *The Rules*. It's not as if it were a date or anything, but I didn't want Mark to think I was interested in him, because it would just cause embarrassment later. Heaven knows he didn't need another woman chasing him, and I . . .

I was acting like a dork, or maybe a dorkette. It was just lunch.

CHAPTER TWENTY-TWO

MARK WAS SITTING IN A BOOTH NEXT TO THE WINDOW, SO I could see him from the sidewalk as I approached. Already I could see there were obvious advantages to lunching with him; by myself, I always got seated near the men's room or up against the cart where the busboys stacked the dirty dishes.

He saw me too and waved. He was wearing shorts and a light blue polo shirt. He had chest hair. I tried not to gape. I had never seen him dressed so casually.

"Hi," I said as I sat down across from him. "What are you doing downtown?" I almost said "like that," but I caught myself in time.

"I've got jury duty," he said. "I have a couple of hours till I have to go back. I'm so glad you could join me. Jury duty is so boring. All you do is sit and wait for hours."

"You mean you're just in that giant holding tank with everybody else?" I asked him. "You're not there to be an expert witness explaining why the accused was really in a fugue state or something when he shot up the postal clerk convention?"

He smiled. "Nope. Those people get *paid*. I'm just a draftee. I never get on a jury, because one side or the other is always afraid I'd have mystical powers of persuasion once we retired to the jury room. It never fails. People have the oddest views of psychiatrists. I always get excused, but once every few years I have to go through the motions anyway. The truth is, I wouldn't mind being on a jury. It might be interesting."

"I've been on one a couple of times, at least I was before law school. Criminal cases. It gave me a really jaundiced view of humanity. Nobody listens to the case or the judge's instructions. They just vote with their prejudices."

He raised an eyebrow. "Is that why you didn't go into criminal law?"

I shook my head. "I went with Roth, Tolbert and Anderson because I already worked there, and they offered me a job. Also because in law school you find out that most people who come to trial are guilty, and it seemed equally dispiriting either to prosecute them or to try to get them off."

"That sounds cynical," he said.

"Is that a professional opinion?" I asked him.

He put down his breadstick. "Relax, will you, Becky? I'm not sitting here judging you. And I'm certainly not here in some professional capacity." He looked a little sad and disappointed.

"I'm sorry," I said. "I'm not very good at this."

"It's just lunch," he said.

"I know, but I feel a little awkward around you," I blurted out.

"Then I'm sorry," he said. "Maybe this was a mistake. I thought it had been long enough since I saw you professionally that we could be friends."

I was horrified by the way things were going. I'd made a big uncomfortable scene out of nothing. "It's not that," I protested.

"Yes?" he asked kindly.

"Well, maybe it is that, in a way." I looked at him. He looked normal and friendly and smart but not intimidating. I felt encouraged. "It's just that the balance is off," I told him.

"The balance?"

I nodded and took a sip of my water. I brushed the menu away with an extravagant gesture. "I don't know anything about you, even though I've known you for years. How do you think that makes me feel in a situation like this? I mean, you know practically *everything* about me, most of it bad." There, I'd said it, what had been worrying me ever since we started exchanging more than perfunctory greetings at mass gatherings.

He sat back against the seat and opened his mouth. Just then the waitress came up, pad in hand, so we did a quick fumbling with the menu and ordered the daily special. When she had gone, I said, "I read in an article that seventy percent of diners will order the special, no matter what it is."

He ignored me. "First of all," he said, looking disconcerted, "how could I know everything about you? I haven't seen you professionally in more than five years, and even then . . . And besides, what do you mean by 'most of it bad'? That's absurd."

"I told you things I never told anyone else," I said, meeting his eyes.

"That's how it was supposed to work," he said, "but give yourself a break. You talk about a jaundiced view of humanity? I've seen it, baby. You can't imagine. And that's the point. You can't *imagine*. And that *is* a professional opinion."

"Thank you, I think," I said. "But still . . ."

He started to look amused. "You want me to tell you bad things about myself to even the score?"

I laughed. "Yes, I think I do. Good things too, but bad things first."

He looked at the ceiling. "I snore," he said.

I shook my head. "No good," I told him. "It has to be something you can help."

He paused. "When I was in med school, I stole something from the bookstore," he said.

"Better," I said. "What was it?"

"A really, really expensive textbook."

"Don't make excuses," I said. "Did you ever pay it back?"

He looked embarrassed "Yes, as a matter of fact."

"Keep going," I said.

"You want more?" he asked incredulously.

"Does that exhaust your repertoire? Your soft palate vibrates and you once had a momentary flirtation with shoplifting? Which you rectified, I might add."

"Okay," he said soberly. "Last one: I haven't been honest with someone I care about a great deal."

"A big lie or a little lie?"

"A pretty big one."

"That's enough," I told him lightly. "You're off the hook." I was ashamed to press him further. If the "someone" was the Mystery Lady from Jonathan's or, worse,

Dr. Oblomova, I didn't want to know about it. "Unless you want to confess to a passion for beets or Brussels sprouts, in which case, I'm out of here," I added.

"Loathsome and revolting, both of them," he said gravely. "You'd have to be *seriously* demented."

"My sentiments exactly," I told him. The waitress brought the specials, which turned out to be swordfish brochettes. We both looked at our plates with approval.

"Just one thing," he said, when she had gone.

"Broccoli?" I asked.

"I'm serious."

"So am I," I said, but then I gestured, *go ahead.*

"You were right about balance. I should have thought of it myself. If people tell you secrets about themselves and you don't reciprocate, if they need you in ways you don't need them, it makes them vulnerable. That's okay for therapist-patient, though it gives you a responsibility not to abuse it. But it's not okay for friends. I should have made it easier for you."

"Well now you have," I told him. I didn't tell him that he had put his finger on precisely what had been wrong about my marriage too. Counseling was over. He still looked worried, so I added, "I'm sorry if I made a big deal about it."

"No, you were right. I was insensitive."

"You can stop now," I told him. "I don't want to know any more bad things."

"Not even about the time I talked my sister into going to a Halloween party as a black widow spider, and then I tied her extra legs together under the table so tightly she couldn't lift her arms to eat?"

"What a brat," I said.

"That's what my mother said. She made me stand next to my sister for the whole party and feed her with a fork whenever she wanted anything."

I laughed, remembering how many times David had set Allie up for embarrassment when they were little, only to have it backfire. "Where's your sister now?"

"Costa Rica, off and on. She's a biologist doing entomology research for the University of Pennsylvania."

"So maybe you inspired her," I offered.

"I like to think so," he said, taking a bite of his brochette.

We chewed companionably for a while, confessions for the moment being at an end.

"I have a revealing activity in mind, if you're interested," he said after a while. "My favorite weekend outing. Care to come along some Saturday?"

"Do I get to know what it is first?" I asked him.

He grinned. "Do you want to? I thought you might like to be surprised."

"It's nothing to do with snakes, right?"

"I promise. I can also assure you I've outgrown my interest in arachnids."

"In that case, I'll trust you. You can surprise me." He'd surprised me already. I hoped it wasn't obvious how much.

"Next Saturday?" he inquired.

I shook my head. "I can't next Saturday. It's Casa Alegría's Opening Weekend."

"Casa Alegría? The House of Joy? That sounds like a whorehouse."

"Does it?" I laughed. "It's Bobbie Crystol's new longevity spa. I think it sounds better in Spanish."

"You're going for the opening reception?" he asked.

"For the three-day weekend. It's a miniversion of her total program," I told him. "It's pretty much a command performance."

He looked serious, as he invariably did whenever Bobbie's name came up. "Why is that?" he asked.

"Because my glorious future in the law is probably tied to keeping Bobbie Crystol happy," I said. I was tempted to tell him about the job offer, but I'd promised not to. (Telling Isabel didn't count. Any woman would understand that.)

He smiled. "The prospect doesn't appear to excite you."

I sighed. "It would have doubtful appeal in any case, but I'd feel better about it if I were one hundred percent sure she was harmless."

He looked serious again. "And you're not?"

"Well, no, not after talking to Dorothy Beekman. And frankly, I'm still suspicious about her reasons for picking me to do her legal work." I saw his expression. "I'm not being overly modest or anything like that. It's like having Arnold Schwarzenegger ask you to do his heart bypass operation when you're a first-year resident in cardiology. It doesn't compute."

"I take your point," he said.

"Believe me, it would be a lot better for me to ignore any doubts I might have on this subject," I told him. "I can't even tell you how much better. The law firm's policy is not to ask a question if you don't already know what answer you'll get."

"And does that work for you?" he asked gently.

"You sound like a shrink," I said.

He smiled. "I am a shrink."

"And I'm a lawyer, but I don't think I want to be that kind," I told him. "Not if I can help it."

"Good," he said.

Something about his expression tipped me off. "You *do* know something," I told him. "I knew you had something against her. You've been trying to warn me off her since her name first came up."

"I don't know anything for certain," he said scrupulously.

I waited. I was not letting him off the hook now.

"It's a long story," he said. "I have to get back soon."

"Summarize," I told him.

He took a big swallow of water. "These are only things I've heard—okay?—but I've heard them from several sources I usually find reliable."

He looked at me to see if I'd absorbed the disclaimer. I nodded.

"It all goes back to drugs," he said.

I sat up straight, startled. "Bobbie takes drugs?" I wouldn't have believed it. She looked too healthy.

He shook his head vehemently. "No, no. *Legal* drugs. Pharmaceuticals." He sighed. "Before managed care, if you were a pharmaceutical company, you could raise your prices almost at will for your drugs, so you didn't have a lot of incentive to develop new products. Now, with the squeeze on drug prices, there's a big push to increase the number of drugs you sell. And that means a lot of new drugs in development. Are you with me so far?"

"Yes, but I don't see—"

He raised his hand. "You will. Drug development is

big business. Very big business. It costs more than half a billion dollars to bring a product to market. After the research and development phase—the discovery and the preclinical testing on animals—you have to have clinical trials on human test subjects."

"Human guinea pigs," I suggested.

He made a face. "It's necessary," he said, "and it's voluntary on the part of the subjects. At least it's supposed to be."

"Aha!" I said.

"Don't jump to conclusions," he said, but he smiled. "Anyway, there's enormous pressure to come up with new blockbuster drugs—like Viagra, for example—and to be first into the market. To do that, the companies have to speed up the process as much as possible. One way to speed things up is to bypass the traditional way of finding test subjects, which used to be to go to the medical schools and ask them to design the protocols and carry out the tests. Now drug companies are approaching private doctors directly, asking them to sign up their patients for the clinical trials. For which the doctors are handsomely compensated, of course."

"Of course. Define *handsomely*," I said.

"You can get anywhere from hundreds to thousands for every patient. You get bonuses for enrolling them fast. If you hustle, you can bring in an extra half million to a million a year."

"Nice," I said. "Let me guess: the handsome sums involved may tempt doctors to be less than scrupulous about who gets enrolled in these studies."

"Well, it sets up a certain conflict of interest, to say the least. Medical professionals are enticing patients to enter these studies at a point when they're exceptionally vulnerable and probably have no idea their physician has anything other than their best medical interests at heart."

"It's the balance thing again," I told him.

He smiled. "It is?"

"Sure. The doctor has all the power in the relationship. He has knowledge and you don't. You don't want to hurt his feelings or make him mad at you, plus you think he must know best. So of course you say yes."

"You've thought about this a lot, haven't you?" he asked me.

"Am I right?"

"Probably," he conceded.

"Well, I was married to a doctor. That's undoubtedly what started me off."

"That's right. I forgot," he said tactfully.

Liar, I thought, but I didn't hold it against him. "So the only thing standing between the poor, trusting patient and some risky study that might actually harm him or be bad for him in some way is the doctor who's getting paid to sign him up. Is that what you're saying?"

"I might not put it that way, but that's what it can boil down to. There's a lot of potential for abuse," he said. "There are testing companies that contract with doctors as clinical investigators, regardless of their specialty, so you can have people conducting trials in areas they know nothing about. There are lots of issues about the quality of the data, and the monitoring systems are patchy, to put it kindly. There is also," he said slowly, "a real possibility of faking the data, because it stands to reason that if the trials work out, um, *felicitously* for the new product, you're a lot more likely to be invited back as a researcher."

"My God, you've made me scared to take cold medicine," I told him.

"People have always been too cavalier about drugs," he said seriously. "And that includes over-the-counter stuff."

"So where does Bobbie Crystol fit into all of this?" I asked him.

He consulted his watch surreptitiously. "Well, these are private contracts, not public documents, so it's very difficult to know for sure. But one of the benefits to doctors of conducting the research is that you get your name on academic papers describing drug studies, even though the companies really write the papers. Dr. Crystol's name is on an awful lot of papers."

"Meaning she's conducted a number of these studies?"

"A very large number. Many of them in areas outside her specialty. It's probably how she financed her original clinic." He shrugged. "The rest is really just rumor. But the scuttlebutt is that there were a lot of problems."

"Such as?" I pressed him.

"Adverse patient reactions, enrolling people medically inappropriate for the studies, that sort of thing."

"Which she could cover up by convincing the poor patients that it was their attitude that caused them to be ill or have the adverse reaction or whatever." I told him about my interview with Dorothy Beekman, although I had been planning to save it until I had more information. I thought it was fair to divulge what I knew, despite Lauren's admonitions, since I hadn't learned it through legal work I'd done for Crystol Enterprises.

Mark shook his head. "You can't draw any useful conclusions. At this point, there's no way to tell what she took, and it might very well be just a coincidence that she got sick after something Dr. Crystol gave her. I warned you about that before."

"Well, *something* had you worried enough to be dropping hints all over the place. Why didn't you tell me when I asked you earlier?"

"I knew what this client means to you, Becky," he said quietly. "If I'd known anything . . . concrete, I would have told you. I told you I had concerns about the psychological manipulation of patients that goes on with some of these anti-aging, mind-body-spirit gurus. There's a little too much charisma and not enough science for my taste. And throw Mexico into the mix . . ." He raised his hands. "They don't exactly regulate the legal drug industry, and just about anything goes." He grinned suddenly. "Which you would have found out for yourself if we had stayed for the speaker at the fund-raiser."

"I was busy trying not to fall out of my dress," I reminded him.

"I noticed," he said in a voice that sounded surprisingly, gratifyingly unprofessional.

"I DON'T KNOW," I told Isabel later. "I don't think so, but I could have just imagined it."

Isabel made a sound precariously close to a snort. "He asked you to lunch, he asked you on some mystery date, and he's falling all over himself scoping out your little trip to Crystolandia, and you're worried you're just imagining that he's interested in you?"

"Well, he kept emphasizing the part about being friends," I told her.

"That's a really good sign," she said.

" 'I like you as a friend' is what I told Russell Garon in sixth grade when he kept wanting to carry my books home from the bus stop. Ever since then I've always thought of it as a surefire turnoff."

"Why didn't you let him carry your books?" she asked me.

"It wouldn't have been fair," I told her.

"Jesus, Becky," she breathed. "Sometimes I can't believe you." She sighed audibly into the phone. "Look, didn't you give him a pretty hard time about being your shrink?"

"Former shrink," I corrected her. "Yes, I did."

"Well, you probably scared the poor guy to death. Made him feel like he violated the canon of ethics or something like that."

"Isabel, it was years ago," I protested.

"You don't have to convince *me,*" she said. "Anyway, the *f* word is a good sign. Men who just want to manipulate you into bed don't talk about being friends."

"What do they talk about?" I asked, feeling as if I were in high school again.

"They tell you how hot you are and lick your earlobes," she said.

I burst out laughing. "Be serious," I said.

"You think I'm not? Do you want me to name names?"

"Yes," I said.

She did.

"I'm convinced," I told her, a little embarrassed. "Maybe he is interested in me, I admit it. What scares me is how perfect he is. I mean, I don't want to blow this. I'm afraid if I actually put it into words I'll jinx it."

"Aha."

"Don't 'aha' me. I've just spilled my guts."

"Well, you *know* he isn't perfect," she said.

"I do?"

"Of course. Doesn't the part about lying bother you a little?"

"Oh, right. Sure," I said. "It bothers me a lot. He made it sound as if he hasn't told his mother he's gay." I tried to make it sound like a joke, unsuccessfully.

"You seriously think that's a possibility?"

"Do you? You've met him."

"No," she said.

"Neither do I. He would have told me," I said, certain this was true. "But there's something."

"Want me to check him out? It is my business, after all."

"No," I said emphatically.

"Are you sure? People have been surprised before this. I can do it very discreetly, and he'd never know."

"I'd know," I told her. "The man is as honest as they come. I want to trust that. About everything else I'm willing to be surprised. Besides, I really like the way I feel when I'm with him. I don't want to do anything to jeopardize that."

"Uh-oh."

"What's 'uh-oh'?" I asked her, torn between amusement and annoyance.

"You've got it worse than I thought," she said.

"I haven't the vaguest idea what you're talking about," I told her.

CHAPTER TWENTY-THREE

THE DOORBELL WAS RINGING WITH MADDENING PERsistence. I was late getting started departing for Opening Weekend (despite years of being almost late for innumerable events, I always cut things too close), and now I would get stuck in traffic. I hadn't used my suitcase in so long I'd forgotten the combination of the lock, and I'd wasted twenty minutes hunting it down. My hair was a mess. I couldn't find Burdick, and I couldn't leave until he was safely enclosed in the house.

Ding-dong.

I yanked open the door.

Ron the postman (or postal carrier, if you want to be precise)—computer genius, polymath, and all-round decent guy—took one look at my face and stepped back a little.

"Sorry," I muttered. "I'm just late for something."

"I'll hurry," he said, meaning he wouldn't tell me any jokes today or inquire why I was home early on a Friday afternoon. "I've got a Return Receipt Requested for you to sign." He looked at me. "It's from *her*."

People obsessed with what's happening to personal privacy on the Internet should realize that their suburban postman might have been keeping tabs on them for years. I mean, talk about personal profile. How can you have secrets from someone who knows what magazines you read and what packages you get, whether or not you get collection notices, and how messy your garage is—not to mention someone who is, through unavoidable proximity, privy to the odd argument with your neighbors, your family, or your ex-husband's new wife?

I knew exactly who he meant by *her*. I made a face. "Thanks," I said, signing for the envelope.

"Good luck," he told me.

When I had closed the door, I held the envelope by the corner, wondering if I should open it then or just stick it in my suitcase and deal with it later. Like Carole's earlier letter, I knew it boded ill, particularly after that "I warned you" phone call.

Under the circumstances, I was afraid to put it off. I slit open the envelope, getting a paper cut on my finger.

I skimmed the contents of the letter. *Advised to inform you*, blah blah. *Addition of beneficiaries to the trust,* et cetera. I put the paper back in the envelope, marring it with a smear of blood as I did. I could deal with it later. At least she wasn't closing the checkbook altogether or suing me for defamation of character. I stuck it in the side pocket of my purse. I would figure it out when I got to the spa.

CASA ALEGRÍA SAT in the dry brown hills east of San Diego and south of the border, far enough away from the coast to escape the less upscale elements of Tijuana—

the desperate hordes of sick, impoverished native women selling yarn bracelets and Chiclets for pennies, the feral children swarming over your car when you stopped for gas, the determined packs of American college students hell-bent on getting drunk, not to mention the political assassinations and narco-murders. (I haven't even started on the poor donkey spray-painted to look like a zebra, so tourists could get their pictures taken with something wild.) Perfectly nice people lived in Tijuana, went to church, and raised their children, but you wouldn't meet them driving through. It was not the sort of place to site a well-heeled life-extension clinic.

Alegre, the town closest to Casa Alegría, had been spared both the blights and the pleasures of urban life. There was little more to it than a plaza with a fountain, a band shell, the requisite pigeons, and one or two scruffy dogs.

The clinic lay at the end of a long road out of town, its Coyote Colonial splendor visible behind wrought iron gates. There were pots and pots of exuberant hot weather flowers—petunias, geraniums, bougainvillea—without a single dead bloom in sight. Maybe the plants had gotten the message too.

I approached my destination with a mixture of curiosity and dread. Maybe I was a little—okay, a lot—excited too. Spa weekends had been pretty thin on the ground the last few years, but that wasn't it. The entire weekend had the air of some kind of adventure, and adventures had been hard to come by lately. Despite the fact that I was there to make my stand as Bobbie's attorney of record, her legal right-hand woman, I was still arriving with an envelope full of Carole's latest venom, not to mention a domestic house of cards that could tumble at any second. I could use a break. If only there didn't turn out to be something *not right* about Bobbie Crystol, something more to the spa than aromatherapy and lectures on senile fruit flies.

If only Bobbie's cure for aging didn't turn out to be some kind of ghastly cosmic joke.

And if there was something, what would I do then? *Don't ask a question if you don't know what answer you're likely to get,* Lauren had said. If I asked and I didn't like the answers, I'd probably find myself out of a client, not to mention a job.

Mark said . . .

I stopped, realizing how often he had found his way into my thoughts lately.

You've got it worse than I thought. When Isabel had said that, I felt as if I'd been caught penning love notes to the most popular boy in the class. I hadn't felt that way in so long I didn't recognize the feeling until it had sneaked up on me. One minute the pilot light was barely lit, and the next minute, *whoosh*, a full-fledged flame.

The second you have something to lose emotionally, all the worst-case possibilities leap vividly into your mind. Mark was seriously interested in Maria (*call me Pathology*) Oblomova or the woman (*Marky!*) from Jonathan's. He was still grieving for his dead wife and had vowed never to marry again. He—and this was the worst of all—felt sorry for me because he knew, well, everything, and he thought I needed a friend.

These unsatisfying scenarios came as naturally to me as breathing, but I decided it was time to let go of bad habits. I hadn't done so well playing shrinking violet on the one hand and trying to keep everything under control on the other. I might as well try something else. I remembered one of the mantras of self-help I'd read in a magazine article: *There is no room I fear to enter.*

I might as well start with that.

I DROVE THROUGH the gates and onto the circular drive that led to the front door of the reception area (marked by a tasteful sign bordered in talavera tile). A Jimmy Smits look-alike—a hard body in a guayabera, the dress shirt of the tropics—leaped for my car door. I handed him the keys while a bellman removed my suitcase. He smiled with just the right degree of familiarity when I tipped him. His youth was the real thing, and his manner managed to convey that it was the merest accident that he was parking the cars instead of arriving in one. So far, Casa Alegría was more luxury hotel than clinic.

My room was very beautiful, with Mexican paver tile floors and a decorated tile bathroom with twin hand-painted sinks. There was a sitting area with two over-stuffed chairs, and a mini dining area with a huge bowl of fruit. The refrigerator was stocked with bottled water. Just in case, I took out two bottles and put them in the bathroom, for brushing my teeth. In Mexico, even in up-scale surroundings, what comes out of the tap is iffy, to say the least.

The afternoon sun came through the window, giving a soft glow to the room. I took off my shoes and walked around barefoot; the tile floor felt incredibly soothing to my feet. It was so perfectly restful and lovely that I considered stretching out on one of the beds for just a moment and . . .

"Hi," Melissa Peters said, dragging her suitcase across the threshold—*my* threshold. "Hope you don't mind. They didn't have enough rooms for everyone. I said we'd double up."

Missy was clearly outfitted for getting the drop on longevity. She had on skintight pants, an abbreviated T-shirt in a leopard print, and strappy sandals that showed off gold-painted toenails. She looked fully capable of biting the heads off of small animals.

"No, no, of course I don't mind," I told her insincerely. Her manner to me had been much less condescending since I'd snared Crystol Enterprises, but she was far from my ideal roommate.

She smiled with equal duplicity. "Don't worry, I don't plan to be around much," she said. "After all, this is a *working* weekend." She picked up the schedule and menu of offerings from the table. "Opening reception, five o'clock," she read. "And look at all the different kinds of massages they have, and two pools, and yoga classes, and that doesn't even count the medical treatments and the mind-body lectures." She looked around. "Bobbie's done an excellent job here," she said. "You'd never believe this place used to be a shark cartilage clinic."

"This was the house of the guy who ran the clinic," I reminded her. "The clinic itself was just part of the entire complex. It shows you what kind of money you can make on bogus cures," I added.

"True." She bent over her suitcase and removed one . . . two . . . *three* pairs of running shoes, which she set side by side in the closet.

"Why so many?" I couldn't help asking.

She looked at me. "I take my running very seriously. It's important to me."

I vowed right then and there to get undressed in the bathroom. With the door closed. "I guess so," I said.

"Weren't you ever athletic?" she asked me.

I noticed that past tense, but the answer was still the same in any case. "No," I told her.

"Pity," she said. "You might like running. It keeps you younger than any of Bobbie Crystol's wacko theories."

I resolved to be nice. "But you don't even have to worry about aging yet," I said. "You still *are* young."

She looked at me with a kind of pity. "It gives you an edge," she said, as if speaking to a slow-witted five-year-old. "Your thirties is when you start to lose it." She consulted her watch. "I wonder if I have time for a run before the reception. . . ."

THE CENTRAL RECEPTION area of the spa/clinic opened into two wings, one for men and one for women. Each wing had lockers and treatment areas and its own indoor pool and hot tub, where—the ubiquitous staff members told us—it was equally appropriate to appear with or without "swimming attire."

In your dreams, I thought. Still, the idea seemed to appeal to Melissa. The relaxed attitude toward clothing apparently extended to the grounds as well, where we were encouraged to wander around in the thick white cotton robes and slippers with the Crystol emblem (the infinity sign enclosed in a crystal) embroidered on the pockets and toes.

For the opening night reception, however, dress was definitely casual chic. Bobbie herself was wearing a shimmering Grecian shift that bared one shoulder and strongly suggested she might be auditioning for the part of Aphrodite. She made her way toward us, rustling softly, arms extended. "Ah, my *lawyers* are here," she said dramatically, swooping in to kiss my cheek and bestow a slightly less exuberant peck on Melissa. I spotted Taylor across the room balancing a tray. "Circulate, try the food," she said. "I want to know what you think of all this."

All this was pretty impressive, I had to hand her that. The tables were piled high with foodstuffs stamped with the Crystol seal of approval: lobster salad with daikon sprouts and fruit salsa, asparagus spears with morels and currant tomatoes, wild raspberries in balsamic vinegar. One table, about which a number of people seemed to be clustered, appeared to offer nothing more than various kinds of salad greens.

I wandered closer to see if it was true, while Melissa went off in search of . . . whatever it was Melissa was looking for. Four middle-aged women, possibly the product of a multiple birth, turned around to greet me. They all had almond-shaped eyes, aquiline noses, and lips so full they seemed to be inflated. I asked if they were sisters.

"Oh, no," one of them said to me in tones of displeasure. "Of course not." They all turned back to the produce, leaving me to wonder what I had said wrong.

Someone tapped my sleeve. "They were all 'touched up' by Dr. Greene," my informant whispered. "He has a signature line. You can always tell."

"Remarkable," I gasped, wondering how many other Greene clones were walking the earth at this moment. Did he have some Platonic ideal of beauty in mind that he tried to create over and over? It boggled the mind. "Thank you for telling me."

My informant extended her hand. "Clarissa Harlowe," she said. She herself was rather unusual looking. She was quite beautiful, but her mouth and eyes stayed almost motionless as she spoke. It made her seem grave and impassive, like a buddha.

"You're probably wondering about my face," she said.

I made a noncommittal noise and hoped I hadn't been staring.

"Botox," she said.

"Pardon me?"

"Botox injections," she said, barely moving her lips. "The botulism toxin. It smoothes out wrinkles." She made a broad, resigned gesture with her hands. "They screwed it up. Put the needle in too close to the mouth. Now the muscles are paralyzed."

"My God," I said. "Is it permanent?"

She laughed, or I thought she did. "Nah. It wears off in a couple of months. But I can't work till it does."

"What do you do?" I asked politely.

"I'm an actress."

I told her I could see how facial immobility might have its disadvantages, unless you were Gary Cooper. She didn't get it, naturally.

"Anyway," she said, "I'm really excited about the Crystol program. I tried sheep parts, and I liked them, but this is better. It's *spiritual*, you know?"

"Sheep parts?" was all I could think of to say.

"Sure, you know, adrenal glands, veins . . . I felt really invigorated. I can't wait to try Dr. Crystol's supplements."

"What kind of supplements does she have?"

She leaned forward conspiratorially. "I don't know, but I've heard they're great. Like speed or something. Unbelievable bursts of energy. You feel years younger, that's what I've heard."

"Are you going to take them without knowing what's in them?" I asked.

She shrugged.

"What if they made you sick?"

She slid her eyes back and forth in their motionless sockets. "They couldn't. I think Dr. Crystol would say that it's your mind that's sick, not your body. It's ayurvedic. You harness your consciousness as a healing force, and then you're not sick anymore. Or old either."

"What if you took poison? Could you heal yourself then?" I asked her.

She gave me an assessing look. "You don't take any anti-aging treatments, do you?"

I summoned the quelling demeanor I had often seen my mother use in response to questions she felt were impudent. "What do you mean?" I asked her, drawing myself up. "I'm seventy-five years old."

Her jaw dropped, or it would have if the muscles had been working. "Really?" she asked me. "You're kidding, right? What do you take? What?"

AFTER A COUPLE of hours of this it became apparent that most of the invitees were wrestling with aging *mano a mano* and weren't about to give in without one hell of a fight. There were a handful of celebrities and one famous romance author whose picture I had seen on book jackets. It was a photographic triumph; in person she looked something like a mummy, with shiny skin stretched over her cheeks and forehead like very expensive leather.

Clearly, there weren't too many skeptics in attendance.

Most of the conversation was shoptalk—head transplants (if only someone would volunteer), healing waves, valerian root, DHEA—in which I had little part. I wondered how Taylor was taking all this. I caught sight of him once or twice engaged in apparent backslapping male bonding rituals with some of the older executive-looking types.

"Having fun?" asked Bobbie, appearing like a magnificent moth at my side.

"Sure," I said. "I've been circulating. It's very interesting."

"'Interesting,'" she mimicked. "Can't you just let yourself go a little? *Try to believe.*"

"Believe what?" I asked her. It was decades too late to save Tinkerbell. But I knew what she really meant. *Believe in me.*

She swept her arm dramatically. Her crystal earrings clinked. "In possibility," she said. "In transcending the known limitations of the body. In the future." The speech had a rehearsed quality. I didn't say anything.

"Look at you," she said finally, "standing here like a wallflower at the party. Don't you want to change your life?" She said it with such satisfaction that I knew that lonely, unhappy Barbara Collins was enjoying a bit of revenge.

I smiled. "This is your show, Bobbie. I'm your lawyer, not your client. The clinic is beautiful and your guests are happy. What more do you want from me?"

She studied me. "Enthusiasm," she said.

She meant she wanted another longevity groupie, but I couldn't oblige her. I spread my hands placatingly. "I am extremely enthusiastic about your potential. We all think you've done a wonderful job with this place."

She made a face. "That's lawyer talk. I meant enthusiasm over my program."

"Your supplements, you mean? I've been hearing about them."

"That's part of it. I think my longevity supplement therapy could do a lot for you. In addition to giving you more energy and sex drive, it reverses the outward signs of aging. You should notice it in your skin." She smiled. "And your butt won't droop so much."

Not in this lifetime, although the butt thing was the first thing I'd heard that made me consider it even momentarily. This crowd might jump at ingesting mole testicles, or whatever, but Clarissa's masked features were only one example of the downside of incaution. I figured I was doomed to failure as an anti-aging groupie anyway. Bobbie had my number; I didn't believe. I'm not saying that if someone invented a magic pill that took away gray hairs, a drooping ass (Bobbie was right about that), arthritis, osteoporosis, presbyopia, et cetera, *and* guaranteed a hundred and fifty years of healthy, pain-free life, I wouldn't be first in line to take it. I'm no fonder of age spots than the next person. But it seemed to me that the frantic pursuit of longevity was occurring at the expense of living. I mean, look how much time all these people had spent in the cultivation of the perfect body. The catch was, some Instrument of Fate—a truck, say, or a meteorite, or a misdirected golf ball—could come hurling out of nowhere while you were concentrating on how to keep from getting any older and—*kapow*—wish granted. And look what you would have missed while you were focused on preserving the unpreservable. What would your tombstone say? *I thought I would live forever, but I was wrong. . . .*

"I still have to pass. But I would like to know what's in them," I told her. Or not. The death knell could be tolling for my professional career at that very moment.

She gave me a toothy grin. "Later," she said. "I have to get back to my guests." She floated a few feet away and turned back. "By the way, Taylor has been extremely helpful to me. I just thought you should know."

"That's great," I said, through gritted teeth.

SOMETIME IN THE middle of the night I awoke from a troubled sleep. It might have been Bobbie's comment about Taylor that had disturbed my subconscious, but when I opened my eyes, I saw Melissa standing by the window, facing out. I hadn't seen her since we'd entered the reception together. When I'd gone to sleep she still hadn't come in. "What time is it?" I asked in a befuddled voice.

"Sorry," she said softly. "I didn't mean to wake you."

"That's okay," I told her. "Are you just now coming to bed?" I sounded exactly like my mother.

"No. I couldn't sleep."

Something in her tone made me sit up in the bed. "Are you all right?" I asked. I couldn't see her face. It was too dark.

"No," she said.

"Want to talk about it?" I asked, as lightly as if she'd been Allie.

"I'm an idiot," she said.

This was promising. I got up and put on the Crystol robe, tying the sash tightly around my waist.

"It's got to be a man, then," I said. "Would you like something to drink? Hot chocolate? Coffee?"

"I brought some scotch," she said.

"Perfect," I agreed.

We sat at the table on our enclosed patio in surprisingly companionable silence, sipping scotch. It was warm, and the air was very dry. A nice night for looking at the stars, which was only possible when you left the city.

When I was very young, my parents and I would lie out on blankets on the lawn while my father pointed out the constellations and made up silly stories about each one. Suddenly I had an image of my mother on her blanket, in her dress and high heels, arms spread out at her sides, laughing at his jokes. Why did I always picture their relationship as one-sided? You could never tell about anyone else's life.

"I'm sorry," Melissa said at last. "I shouldn't bother you with this. I hardly even know you."

"You don't have to say anything," I assured her.

"I just can't believe I let him treat me this way. I can't believe I fell for it!"

Whatever the circumstances were, I couldn't believe it either. Melissa didn't seem like the type to be manipulated easily. I made a noncommittal noise of encouragement.

"It's not as if I didn't have other offers. Plenty of other firms—top-ranked firms, not third-rate ones—tried to recruit me."

She'd lost me. "I don't . . ."

She shrugged. "He's the reason I picked RTA. Well, most of the reason anyway."

Oh, dear. "You mean . . ."

"Taylor Anderson. I came here to be with him this weekend, and now he tells me that after all the time we've been together since he left his wife, he's not ready for a commitment. He denies it, but I think he must be seeing somebody else."

"I think we'd better go inside," I told her.

CHAPTER TWENTY-FOUR

"YOU'RE SHITTING ME," MELISSA SAID.

"I'm afraid not," I told her.

"He really told you to forget about trying to remove the trustee and didn't happen to mention that he was sleeping with her?"

I nodded. "I'm really sorry, Melissa. This isn't a nice way to find out about Carole. Not that there is a nice way." I *was* sorry too. Despite her know-it-all demeanor, it was clear that she had a lot more invested in her relationship with Taylor than dreams and fantasies.

"Don't be. I might have been an idiot, but I'm not such an idiot that I'd rather not know. I asked him, and he flatly denied that he was seeing anybody. I didn't believe him, but *still*. And now this. In a way it makes me feel better, since he dumped me, to know that he doesn't have any character. You know?"

I knew.

"Not that he actually *dumped* me," she said. "What he said was, I'd misunderstood. He wasn't ready for an exclusive commitment. We should both see other people and test our feelings for each other." She took a sip from her glass and looked at me. "That's dumping, isn't it?"

I sighed. "I think so. It's been a long time since I've navigated these waters, and Taylor and Carole both look like sharks to me. But the truth is, I can't be objective about it. I'm sorry." This was one of the weirdest conversations of my entire life. I mean, here I was swapping confidences with Missy Perfect Peters—the last person in the world I'd ever expected to lose her head over a man—over a bottle of scotch in the middle of the night. We could have been a couple of sorority sisters. Or mother and daughter. Or even colleagues.

We were silent a few moments.

"If it's any consolation," I offered after a while, "the worst punishment Taylor could possibly receive is to end up with Carole. They deserve each other." I filled her in with a few of my best bits of Prattiana.

She smiled grimly. "You're a real dark horse, Becky. I had no idea any of this was going on. So what did you do about the trust?"

I told her about the accounting statement and Carole's letter. "I've been sort of mulling over what to do," I told her. "I don't exactly have a lot of resources to put into fighting her, so I have to be careful. And now I have to figure out what she's up to with this latest move."

"Want me to have a look?" she asked.

I wondered if it was the whisky talking. On the other hand, she did have a first-class legal mind, even if her judgment in men was even worse than mine. And in her place, I'd be trying to thrust a spoke into Carole's wheel too. I could certainly use an ally in spoke thrusting. "I'd appreciate it," I said. "It didn't come till this morning, so I haven't done more than glance at it myself. Now?" I asked.

She nodded. "Why not?"

I took the letter from its envelope and spread it on the table under the light. I held it by the edges, in case something noxious rubbed off on my fingers.

We both read it through.

We looked at each other.

"Christ," I said. "I should have read it more carefully. Is this as bad as I think it is?"

She rubbed her eyes with the heels of her hands. "Don't panic," she said. "You're sure she does have the power under the trust to add beneficiaries?"

I nodded.

"I'll have to think," she said.

MELISSA WAS UP at the crack of dawn, propping her foot up on the back of the chair and bending forward over her leg to stretch out her hamstrings and calf muscles. Her spandex shorts left little to the imagination, so I could see, through eyes half open, that everything appeared to be working satisfactorily. I couldn't believe, after the events of the night before, that she was vertical, much less active. Morning people always manage to rebuke you with their virtuous energy. My own horizontal posture suddenly seemed infinitely comfortable and desirable. I turned over and closed my eyes.

"I'm going for a run," she called from the door.

"You were up half the night," I protested.

"I told you, it gives you an edge."

"Bye," I murmured into the pillow.

"Don't get too comfortable," she said. "We've got work to do."

* * *

THE FIRST ORDER of the day (after breakfast—papaya, toast, and herbal tea) was a session in the Bodygraph, a sort of benchmark Barcalounger that purported to measure your brain waves and muscle strength to determine where you belonged on the Crystol Aging Scale. A white-coated attendant read the results from the computer printout with professional cheerfulness. If my "biological age" made me a fit mate for Methuselah, she didn't let on. "If you were a regular client, this would help us design the program perfect just for you," she said. She carried each printout into the next office.

"Ms. Weston," the attendant called, beckoning me through the door.

I followed her into another tiled sanctuary. A fountain outside the window made soothing water noises. "Come in," Bobbie said.

"This is beautiful," I told her. "I was expecting something more clinical."

She smiled. "Surprise is part of the therapy," she said. "I'm glad you like it." She turned around and picked up a sheaf of papers. She set it down next to me. "Do you remember Barry Norton? From school?"

I was relieved to see that her accusing tone from the night before had evaporated. "Not really," I told her. "Why?"

"You used to go out with him," she said.

"Did I? Oh, maybe so. But only once or twice."

She sighed. "You don't even remember. Amazing. I had the most incredible crush on him."

"Did you?" I asked. "I didn't know."

"No," she said. "How could you?"

She gestured toward the mound of papers.

"What's that?" I asked.

"Your schedule for this weekend, plus options," she said. "I know you're here in your professional capacity, but you might as well get something out of it too."

"Options?" I inquired.

She smiled. "Some people take HGH—human growth hormone. I'm sure you know what that is."

I knew. I wondered if that was what was inspiring such enthusiasm among Bobbie's followers, but I doubted it. "Is it safe?" I asked.

"It's FDA approved, though not for this application. I think it's far more dangerous not to take it, frankly."

"Is it expensive?" I asked.

"Not this weekend. It's part of the program. If people want to continue, and almost everyone does, it costs about seven hundred dollars a month if you do the injections yourself."

"Wow."

"It's far cheaper than a long-term illness," she said.

"Is this what you meant by your supplement therapy?" I asked.

"That's part of it. The rest is vitamins and some other supplements," she said.

"One of the guests was talking about a big 'energy boost' last night."

She smiled. "We have all kinds of things to 'youthen' your metabolism. We like to start from the inside out. Want to change your mind and try some?"

I shook my head. "No, thanks. But what's—"

"I didn't think so," she said. She consulted my printout and made some notes. "We can chat later, but I do want you to try the hydrotherapy tub to detoxify your body and improve your circulation. After that, lunch, and then I've scheduled you for a seaweed wrap. Following that is my class for everyone on using your mind to heal your body. Any objections to any of that?"

I shook my head. "It's a very full schedule, isn't it?"

"You've got a lot of catching up to do," she said seriously.

MELISSA CAUGHT UP with me in hydrotherapy.

"I didn't want to miss this," she said, climbing into the tub. "I do my best thinking in a hot tub. And this feels really *great,* don't you think?"

"I'm not sure," I told her. Actually, I had a lot of trouble hearing her over the sound of fifty-four jets of water hitting my body simultaneously. I was afraid to ask, "Why fifty-four?" so I took it on faith. "It's a little hot, isn't it?"

"That helps you sweat out the poisons in your body," she said, intent on adjusting herself so that the spray hit her from all angles. "All the preservatives and fat and chemicals." She was obviously a veteran. "Just relax and go with it. You'll feel really good."

I had a little trouble relaxing against the spurts of water poking into all parts of my anatomy, but I had to admit that by the end of the session my skin was tingling and I did feel very loose of limb. In fact, it was an effort to stand up. My heart pounded a little with the exertion.

"All right?" asked the attendant.

I nodded. Melissa practically leaped out of the tub in a single bound.

"Move slowly," cautioned the attendant.

"Time for lunch," I said.

"I'm not really hungry," Melissa said. "I'm too nervous to eat. But if you want something, I'll go with you.

Then we could sit on the grass and talk. I've been thinking about your trust."

"You should eat something," I told her, my maternal instincts coming to the fore unexpectedly. I remembered not being able to eat when Richard and I split up. I'd been making up for it ever since. Besides, I was actually touched that she was still interested in helping me, even after the whisky bonhomie had worn off.

"I'll be okay," she said.

With so many poisons exiting my body all at once, there seemed to be a lot more space opening up in my stomach. I did my best to fill it at lunch, and then Melissa and I took our fruit juice out on the lawn.

"Well, back to business," she said. "Can you get a copy of the original trust amendment adding the beneficiaries?"

"Probably," I said. "We must be entitled to it."

"I think you should." She looked grim. "I'm sure you realized last night that Carole's really screwed your children, right?"

I nodded. "By amending the trust to say that the assets go to her grandchildren as additional beneficiaries, my children won't see any of the principal till they're in nursing homes, if then. The trust doesn't terminate until the death of the last to die of Carole's grandchildren. I probably won't even be alive by that time. But look," I told her, "the principal doesn't concern me as much as the income. Now is when they need the money. They were always going to have to wait for Andrew—Carole's son—to grow up before the assets were disbursed."

"That's true," she agreed. "But what you want is a lever to remove her, right?"

"Right."

"Well, this might give you one," she said.

"How?"

"There's an argument that she's just using her power to add beneficiaries to keep your children from ever effectively benefiting from the trust. That would violate your ex-husband's intention in setting it up. The courts don't like that sort of thing. They might be willing to reform it, and they'd probably remove her as trustee."

"Would that really work?" I asked, excited.

She shrugged. "You'd most likely end up in court spending a lot of time arguing over what 'equity' should require and what the drafter's intent was. It would take some time, and it would cost. But it might be worth a shot."

"Definitely worth a shot," I told her.

"Don't get too excited. I'm not an expert in this area. But I do know someone who is. We could run it by him."

"Not someone in the firm," I insisted. I wasn't going down that road again.

"Oh, no. This guy is brilliant, really. He knows tax law inside out, and he used to be a really big name in trusts and estates."

"Do I know him? Where does he practice?"

She shook her head. "You don't know him. Nobody knows him now. He got in a little hot water with the IRS and decided to take 'early retirement.' He keeps a lower profile these days."

"Oh," I said, unsure if this was the sort of person I wanted to advise me. "Would he even want to talk to me, then?"

She looked away. "He will if I ask him to. He's my father."

* * *

AFTER LUNCH, I reported for my seaweed wrap. I started the treatment stretched out on a table behind drawn curtains. The technician, a slender, attractive young woman with the intensity of a zealot, had told me that the seaweed and oils would probably ruin my underwear, but I could leave it on anyway if I preferred.

I said I would live dangerously and take it off. Since it was physiologically impossible to hold in my stomach, thighs, and rear all at the same time, I didn't make the effort for more than a minute and a half, and abandoned myself to her ministrations.

Rosa, the technician, applied large blobs of cold seaweed from a bucket, slathering it on my body with gusto. In addition to the chill, which was considerable, and the color and texture, which were reminiscent of salad greens left far too long in the refrigerator, there was the smell, which might have been extremely alluring to sea otters and barnacles but did absolutely nothing felicitous for me.

"Yuck," I said. "*Eau de kelp.*"

"It is very beneficial." Her tone was disapproving. She slapped on another big glob with her gloved hand.

I hoped so, because an entire forest of the stuff must have been sacrificed for the cause. There was even seaweed between my toes.

"Now turn over," she said, and started wrapping me in—I swear—Handiwrap. She twirled it round and round me until my briny body was totally encased in plastic. Then she put a large heated blanket over me. I felt like someone's bagged lunch, or maybe a seaweed enchilada. The only nonvegetable-covered part, my face, extended out from the top of the blanket. She patted some "extract" on that too, for good measure.

She set the timer and put it down on the table. "Forty

minutes," she said. "I'll be back to help you into the shower and give you a rubdown with oils." She looked at me. "It's strange at first, but try to relax. All the impurities are being drawn out of your body. Think of something beautiful and perfect."

At first all I could think of was what if there was a fire while I was lying there doing my Mirabel Morgan Meets the Little Mermaid routine. I was practically paralyzed by the plastic wrap, but I rationalized that at least it would melt off as I was hopping away from the flames. After a while the forced immobility quieted my mind. Then thoughts of Carole and her plans to keep the trust money away from my children till I was moldering in my grave began to seep in unbidden. I tried to shake them off. I wondered what beautiful and perfect things I should think of instead. My daughter's face on her first day of school. Hanalei Bay on Kauai. Franz Biebl's "Ave Maria." A perfectly ripe piece of Camembert on a water cracker. Chocolate eclairs . . .

My stomach rumbled and I opened my eyes. I closed them quickly and opened them again.

Taylor Anderson was still there, looking down at me. "Sorry," he said. "I wasn't sure it was you."

"What are you doing here?" I asked. The extract had hardened on my face like a mask and made my skin taut. The mask cracked when I moved my mouth. "This is the women's side."

"Sorry," he mumbled, looking away. "Have you seen Melissa?"

"Not recently," I told him.

"What? I can't understand you."

"Not since lunch," I enunciated. The mask broke up into shards. "Shit."

He scuttled backward. "Sorry, sorry. I'll keep looking."

"Fine," I said, pulling a small dagger of hardened extract off my lower lip. It was a measure of how far I had come that I didn't even care that Taylor had seen me green and slimy and smelling like an overripe fish tank.

When he had gone, I tried to recover the chocolate éclair mood, but for some reason my mind kept drifting back to law school and—worse—the bar exam. A dreadful ordeal by anyone's standards, an odd thing to think of from the forced idleness of a Handiwrap straitjacket. So much of all that elaborate preparation—the notes, the briefs, the classes, the bull sessions—was overkill. It was hard not to become a victim of your own excesses. I've heard lawyers twenty years out of school say their stomachs still turn over whenever they catch sight of one of those oversized bar review outlines.

The ownership of Property is the first principle of Western societies. . . .

And for the last week before the exam, no untroubled sleep, no properly digested food, no time, no confidence.

Rules regulating the ownership of Property are not easily altered without upsetting the entire social system.

And on the big day, sitting down with a room full of bright young things, feeling absolutely sure you are somewhat less intelligent than everybody around you.

And afterward, comparing notes with the other exam takers, finding out that you answered three questions with a discussion of the Rule Against Perpetuities, and nobody else thought it even applied to one.

And then . . .

Oh, yes! Thank you, Subconscious! The Rule Against Perpetuities! Maybe all that preparation wasn't wasted after all. The meander down memory lane had triggered a real "aha" moment. Now I just had to find Melissa and check it out for sure. I pulled myself up to a sitting position like some mummy in a horror movie. "Hello?" I called. "I need to get out of this plastic wrap. I can't move."

Rosa came in tsk-tsking. "It's not time yet," she said.

I felt too squirrelly to wait. "If I lie here much longer, my seaweed coating's going to harden into concrete," I pointed out. "Besides, there's something I need to do."

"You might ruin the entire detoxification process," she insisted.

"I'll take my chances."

She cut the wrapping down the back with scissors, gave me a stiff brush, and pointed me toward the shower. She said she would rub in the oils afterward, so my skin wouldn't be damaged by prolonged exposure in its chrysalis state.

An eternity later, my skin looked as if I'd spent an unprotected hour in the desert at high noon, but at least the briny smell was gone. In its place was something vaguely herbal and not at all unpleasant. It was time for Bobbie's mind-over-body lecture, but I decided to skip it in favor of a powwow with Melissa, if I could find her.

Things were definitely looking up.

CHAPTER TWENTY-FIVE

NONE OF THE DOORS HAD LOCKS AT CASA ALEGRÍA, SO I rapped on the door to our room before I entered—slowly. If Taylor and Melissa were by any chance reconciling under the covers, I wanted to give everybody plenty of notice.

Melissa was lying on her bed with a bag of ice on her head. She looked at me and swung her feet over the edge, sitting up.

"Oh, sorry," I said softly. "Do you have a headache?"

She put the bag of ice down on the table with a gesture of disgust. "I thought you were Taylor," she said. "He's been chasing me all over the place, wanting to 'talk.' It was the only way I could think of to avoid him."

This was not the Melissa Peters I knew. "I know," I told her. "He even broke in on my seaweed wrap to ask where you were." I laughed. "He won't do *that* again. But seriously, couldn't you just ask him to leave you alone?" I asked.

"Sure, but it's dangerous to piss him off." She sighed. "This is why you should never get involved with somebody you work with. I'm going to have to look for another job, and I can't afford to have him annoyed at me till I've landed the next one. He has to think he's still in charge. Taylor can be a bad enemy," she said.

Oh, great.

She smiled suddenly. "On the other hand, Taylor has to keep me reasonably happy too, at least until I move on, because if he doesn't I might slap him with a sexual harassment suit. It gets pretty complicated."

"Um, do you think it will be hard to find another job?" It was not a disinterested question.

"Of course not," she said, in a tone brimming with her old confidence. "There are legal jobs going begging. So many lawyers want to be dot-com tycoons—or at least they did—that big-time law firms are having to pay first-year associates a hundred sixty K just to show up. Somebody like me won't have any trouble." She gave me a shrewd look. "Even you could probably find something without too much difficulty. I could help you."

This was vintage Melissa, putting me down and offering me help in the same sentence. It was a relief in a way. "Thanks," I said, with a small smile. "I wanted—"

"Actually," she interrupted, looking serious, "there's something I wanted to talk to you about."

"I want to talk to you too. But you go first." She would anyway.

She sat cross-legged on the bed. "While I was playing hide-and-seek with Taylor this afternoon, I went for another run," she said.

"Christ, why were you jogging again?" I asked her. "You've already run once today."

She shrugged. "I didn't feel like sitting. I had all this energy. I just wanted to run. The problem is, there isn't really anyplace to go—I wasn't exactly thrilled with the idea of running off into the Mexican desert by myself—so I just ran around and around this place. Guess what I saw?"

Someone with a better pair of jogging shoes. "What?" I asked her.

"Did you meet that woman with the frozen face last night?" She pulled her features into a likeness of glacial immobility.

I laughed. "Clarissa Harlowe. The one whose Botox treatment went bad."

"Well, something worse than that has gone bad today. I saw them taking her away in an ambulance."

"Really? Something serious? I wonder what happened."

"I don't know. The attendants were all jabbering away at her in Spanish. When she saw me, she called me over and grabbed on to me like a barnacle. They kept trying to shoo me away, but she wouldn't let them."

"What did she say?" I asked.

"She just wanted reassurance, mainly. She kept putting her hand on her heart and saying, 'Something's not right.' She said she could tell there was some arrhythmia." Melissa looked at me. "She said she thought she might have taken too many of Dr. Crystol's supplements."

"Uh-oh."

She raised her eyebrows. "I didn't get any more than that, because just then Bobbie came out and started her try-to-relax, let-your-mind-participate-in-the-healing routine. Bobbie told me, politely of course, to mind my own business and move away. She said she—Clarissa Whosit—needed quiet so she could focus her mind and spirit on healing. Then they drove off in the van, which, I might add, had the Crystol logo on the side. It was all a bit slick, if you know what I mean."

"You mean you think they're a bit too prepared for this eventuality," I suggested.

She shrugged. "It's a thought. It's probably not a huge deal, but I thought you should know if there's going to be a lawsuit or something like that. This is your client, after all."

"Not for long, if Taylor has anything to say about it."

She smiled, not even bothering to deny it. "Well, it's possible it could turn into a be-careful-what-you-wish-for kind of thing."

I didn't want to go into all the doubts I'd already been harboring about Crystol Enterprises just yet. "Thanks for telling me. I'll see what Bobbie has to say about it." I hesitated. "If you're up for it, I did have another idea about the trust," I said.

"Sure," she said. "What is it?"

"The Rule Against Perpetuities," I told her.

She stared at me, as well she might. The Rule Against Perpetuities is the elusive White Buffalo of estate planning, a legal prohibition against tying up property in trust forever (or for an excessive period of time) whose meaning is so complicated the lucky can glimpse it only occasionally. It is so difficult to explain that the California Supreme Court once ruled that writing a will that violated it did not constitute attorney malpractice. In California, the rule essentially requires that a trust terminate and have its assets distributed within twenty-one years after the death of everyone who's living at the time the trust was created. Or at least that's what I thought it required.

I could see Melissa's mind working. "So how old is Carole's child?" she asked me.

"Preschool," I told her.

"Jesus, Becky, that really could work. If she's added this kid's children as beneficiaries to the trust, by the time it terminates it could violate the rule. Maybe. I can't be sure," she said. "We'll have to check with my father." She gave an annoyed little cluck. "How come you thought of that and I didn't?"

I raised my hands placatingly. "I'm closer to law school than you are. It was on the bar exam. I think."

"Well, good for you," she said grudgingly.

"Yes, but if Carole *has* amended the trust so it violates the rule, then what?"

"I think the bottom line is that California's version is biased toward allowing the courts to reform trust documents that violate the rule," she said. "So she may have handed you the key to unlocking the trust and getting the court to appoint someone as trustee who will do a better job of looking out for your kids."

"What should I do?" I asked her.

"Let's get the document first. Then we'll run it past my father and see what he thinks. Don't say anything to anybody about it—you don't want her trying to change it back. Let her think she's getting her way for the time being."

Boy, did I like this scenario. Carole might be undone by her own greed, and the longer she thought she'd triumphed, the worse it would be for her in the end. But then I thought, *She must have had an attorney draft the amendment, right? So why didn't he or she catch the violation?*

Melissa shrugged when I put the question to her. "So we don't get our hopes up too far. Let's see what happens. In the meantime," she smiled, "in the meantime, this could actually be fun."

* * *

I DECIDED TO waylay Bobbie at dinner, the last scheduled activity of the day, to find out what had gone on with Clarissa Harlowe. The shrimp in citrus sauce with pomegranate seeds was delicious, but Bobbie was nowhere in sight. Maybe she'd transcended the need to eat. I went to her office, but no luck there either. The person on duty at the reception area told me that Dr. Crystol was meditating in her room and could not be disturbed, period.

I asked if I could leave a note. She looked dubious, as if it were a major infraction.

I said it was important.

She gave me a pen and paper with the Crystol crest. I wrote, *I need to talk to you*, and handed the paper back to her.

Bliss weekend was coming to a close, and I wanted to get to Bobbie before she flew off to her next appearance in Sedona. Most of all, I wanted a direct answer regarding what was in those supplements and whether they had any connection to what had made Clarissa ill.

When I awoke Sunday morning, my note had been pushed underneath my door. At the bottom, Bobbie had written, *Later*. She'd also added, *P.S. I know why you want to talk to me. There's nothing to worry about.*

"Make her level with you," Melissa told me. "You can't let the client get the upper hand. You have to maintain control."

I went for a swim after breakfast and sat out on the lawn reading while I dried. I passed up the morning class, Biofeedback for Beginners, in favor of the latest Elinor Lipman novel. Checkout time was noon, so I went back to reception and asked to see Dr. Crystol before I left.

She'd left very early in the morning, the man told me. Would I like to leave a message?

No, I would not.

Would I like to make a contribution, then?

Contribution to what? I asked him.

He smiled broadly. Many guests liked to leave contributions to Dr. Crystol's ongoing work when they checked out, but of course it was purely voluntary. "Or," he added, "you might like to sign up for one of her long-term programs."

I smiled with equal ferocity and told him I was Dr. Crystol's lawyer, not her patient.

"In that case," he said, showing teeth like bullets on a cartridge belt, "we must thank you for helping to make possible Dr. Crystol's work." He said it reverently, in the tone all of Bobbie's employees seemed to have mastered.

"You sound very proud of her," I suggested.

"She is the Joan of Arc of anti-aging medicine," he said seriously. "All the doctors are against her, but she is willing to sacrifice herself to save others. She works so hard," he said, clearly impressed by this anomalous behavior. "She is very noble."

I had to suppress a smile at the thought of Bobbie's auto-da-fé and told him I was sure Dr. Crystol appreciated his admiration.

He beamed. "I almost forgot," he said, extracting a thick manila envelope from beneath the counter and extending it in my direction. "Dr. Crystol instructed me to give this to her lawyer. That is you, yes?"

"Yes," I said, reaching for it.

For the time being, anyway.

CHAPTER TWENTY-SIX

I DROVE STRAIGHT BACK TO LA JOLLA, PICKED ALLIE UP at Isabel's, stopped in to thank my neighbor for feeding Burdick, and called for pizza delivery. It was still early evening, so I telephoned Dunewood to find out how my mother had fared over the weekend.

"Finally," she said, when she picked up the phone. "I thought you'd never call."

"I was in Mexico for a couple of days, remember? I just got home."

"They don't have phones in Mexico?" Her voice had an edge that sounded like something more than irritation.

"Is something wrong, Mother? Are you all right?"

"Of course I'm all right," she said. "Under the circumstances."

"What circumstances?" I asked her.

"I told you," she said. "I hurt." She paused. "They don't like me here. I can't do what I'm supposed to do."

"What do you mean?" I asked her. "I don't understand. What are you supposed to do?"

She was silent on the other end of the phone.

"Mother?"

"I don't want to talk about it," she said.

"Would you mind if I came over on my way to work tomorrow?"

"Why would you want to do that?" she asked.

"Because I love you, and I want to make sure you're all right."

She sighed. "You can come," she said.

MRS. FAY, THE Dunewood administrator, was gracious about seeing me without an appointment at seven-thirty in the morning.

"Come right in," she said. "Most of our residents get up early, so I'm usually here by seven. Besides, my office is always open to members of our extended family."

I took a seat opposite a gigantic jar of candy and an oversized chartreuse stuffed animal of indeterminate species. Mrs. Fay didn't remark on either, so neither did I.

"What can I do for you?" she asked.

"I'm just wondering how my mother is getting along," I told her. "Now that she's had some time to settle in."

Mrs. Fay was no dummy, despite her taste in office decor. "Is there any particular reason you're asking now?" she said.

I folded my hands to keep them from gesturing maniacally, a habit I had when I was nervous. "I know my mother can be difficult to please," I began.

Mrs. Fay smiled and said nothing. She waved her hand, *go on.*

"She says she can't do what she's supposed to do," I said apologetically. "I'm not exactly sure what that means. But she thinks people don't like her here."

Mrs. Fay stopped smiling. "I think she's overstating the problem," she said.

One hand escaped from my lap and made its way through the air, taking my arm with it. "The problem?" My voice came out all squeaky. "Oh dear, she *is* being difficult, isn't she?"

Mrs. Fay shook her head slowly. "I wouldn't say that. As I told you before, I think she likes it here more than she'll admit to you, at any rate. It isn't that."

"What, then?"

She sighed. "I believe I told you when your mother was admitted that we require certain levels of performance in order to qualify for both admission and continued residence. I wasn't going to bring this up so soon, but it appears that your mother doesn't meet all the required tests."

I closed my eyes. "Which tests, specifically?"

"Well, for one thing, she takes far too long to get from her room to the dining area. We've timed the walk at a sedate pace and added a generous amount of time to that number. But I'm afraid your mother doesn't even come close to meeting the standard."

"Maybe she just stops and talks to her friends?" I asked, without much hope that this was true.

"Sometimes, perhaps, but certainly not for every meal."

"Have you talked to her about it?" I asked.

"Of course. She says her leg hurts and she can't go any faster." She looked down at her hands, then back up at me. "That may very well be true. But you must understand that we don't have the staff to assist our residents every time they leave their rooms. That seems to be what your mother requires, or at least that seems to be what she wants."

"I'm afraid to ask what happens now," I told her.

"Well, it's a bit premature to take any action. I think we should adopt a wait-and-see attitude for now. But I'm afraid that if things don't improve . . ."

She didn't have to spell it out for me.

I WASN'T CERTAIN what mood I'd find my mother in, so I tapped on the door very gently. She was sitting in her chair, reading a copy of *You Don't Have to Die*.

She looked up. "You're late," she said.

"I was talking to someone," I told her, torn between amusement and annoyance. "Where did you get that?"

She put down the book. "From the prison library, where else? The woman's short a sheet," she said. "You can't imagine the things she suggests in here."

Yes, I could. "Then why are you reading it?"

She looked at me shrewdly. "Did you talk to Mrs. Fay?" she asked.

I nodded.

"Then you know why I'm reading it. This Crystol woman is famous. She's your client. She sent me that 'I care' card." She sighed. "I thought this book might have something to make me feel better. Younger. How did I know it would be a bunch of mumbo jumbo? She was on the *Today* show."

"Oh, Mother," I said helplessly.

"Your friend Bobbie says that negative emotions like anger can make you sick." She looked at me. "That must be the reason I can't make it to the dining room fast enough. I'm mad at you for putting me in this place," she said.

"I'm sorry," I told her. "I know you don't want to be here. I'm just trying to do what's best."

"You're always trying to do what's best," she said.

"Maybe you should just relax a little. Maybe Dr. Crystol's book is right. I've spent a lot of time being mad about things I can't change." She shrugged. "Maybe it's all in my head, but my leg still hurts," she said. "I mean that, Becky. And if I can't cut the mustard here, they'll put me in a nursing home, right?"

"Probably," I said.

"Do we have the money for that?" she asked.

"I don't want you to worry about that," I told her, trying to keep the panic out of my voice. "We'll do what we have to do."

"That means no, we don't have the money," she said. "I didn't think so." She sighed again. "Maybe I should give Dr. Crystol's ideas a whirl," she said. "What have I got to lose?"

"Do you honestly believe anger is at the root of your problem here?"

She shook her head.

"Don't worry," I told her. "I'll think of something."

MARK'S PHONE CALL caught me just as I arrived at the office. I was late after my visit to Dunewood—not the best image for an associate on the make—but I was too tired and worried to care. Mark's voice acted on me like a tonic.

"Hi," I said. "I'm glad you caught me. I just got in."

"Why didn't you call me?" he asked. "I've been a little concerned. How did the weekend go?"

I gave him a capsule summary, skipping some of the more colorful details, such as my rapprochement with Melissa and the whole trust issue. I ended up with Clarissa Harlowe's untimely departure.

"Clarissa Harlowe?" he asked with a laugh. "Isn't that a character in the most boring novel ever written?"

"Bingo," I told him, impressed. "Although I think *Finnegans Wake* gives it a run for the money."

"Philistine," he said.

"So what do you think it could have been?" I asked him.

"Sorry?"

"That made her sick? I mean, if anything Bobbie gave her was responsible."

"*I* don't know. What was Bobbie handing out?"

"People were getting shots of human growth hormone. Everyone there seemed really into them."

"That wouldn't cause arrhythmia," he said.

"There were pills too," I said.

"What did she say was in them?"

"She didn't. And after I heard about the incident, I couldn't find her to pin her down. I'm really worried about this, Mark. I didn't feel comfortable with what I saw down there."

"What will it take for you to get comfortable?" he asked softly.

"The truth," I told him.

"Whatever it costs?"

"Yes."

"Then put it to her," he said. "Tell her you have to know. Did anybody else show any unusual reactions?"

"I don't think so. There was a whole group of people there—some of them people you'd recognize—clamoring for treatments." I described the opening night reception, exaggerating a bit, but only a little.

"It sounds like the bar scene in *Star Wars,*" he said. "All kinds of aliens under one roof."

"True," I said. "But I don't think any of them woke up twenty again, whatever they might have taken."

"God forbid," he said.

"I liked being twenty," I told him. "It was what came later that wasn't as much fun."

"I was a geeky premed," he said. "All I knew how to do was study."

"I don't believe you," I told him. I didn't. He had always seemed so balanced, so fully developed, even when I knew next to nothing about him.

"I assure you," he said. "My parents didn't want me to be a doctor, and I was determined to prove them wrong."

I laughed. "You must have had the only parents in America who didn't want their son to be a doctor," I told him. "Did they object for religious reasons or something like that?"

"No, they wanted me to go into the family business instead."

"Wow. What was it?"

He sounded uncomfortable. "Oh, just business," he said. The way he said it, I wondered if it had been cement. He clearly didn't want to discuss it further. "And speaking of family, how is your mother doing?"

I explained—with some reluctance, since he'd been the one to suggest Dunewood—about my mother's problem, which naturally led to my concern about what was I going to do if she couldn't stay there when they wouldn't let her live with me and I couldn't afford nursing-home care. By the end, my eyes were watering slightly. I was glad he couldn't see me.

"Sorry," I said ruefully when I had finished my tale of woe. "I guess there's something about talking to you that brings out the confessions." Another minute and I would have divulged the entire sordid trust story too, and the probability that I would be jobless before long. I thought our fledgling personal relationship was still a bit too tender for that. Besides, there were some things I needed to take care of by myself.

"It's the couch," he said. "It's too comfortable. Everybody says so."

"I'm not on your couch," I pointed out. "I'm at my desk, in my office."

"The *figurative* couch," he said. He paused. "Could you bring your mother into the hospital day after tomorrow?"

"I guess so. Sure."

He gave me a name. "I'll get you an appointment with this woman. She's the tops in orthopedics. I'll call you back with the time as soon as I talk to her."

"Thank you," I said. "What are we looking for? She was checked out pretty thoroughly after her fall, and they said there was nothing physical other than the TIA."

"Anything. Who knows? You can't be too careful. Something might have been overlooked. If we can't find anything, we can get a psychological evaluation."

I was grateful, and I was impressed at his confidence about getting an appointment, but I wanted to ask him if the insurance would cover it. It seemed crass, so I let it go.

"Don't worry. I'm sure it's covered," he said.

A mind reader, in addition to his other attributes. "Thanks," I said again. I looked at my watch. "I should be going," I told him. "I have a lot of work to do. I can't begin to tell you how grateful I am, Mark. You've done so much for me. I really appreciate it. I mean it."

"Please, don't, Becky."

"But—"

"Please."

"Okay," I said.

"So, are we on for this weekend? Saturday?" he asked lightly.

"Sure," I said. After my longevity weekend, I'd almost forgotten. I was glad he hadn't. "When?"

"Saturday? About four-thirty?"

"Great," I said. "That will give me time to check in on my mother beforehand."

I could hear the smile in his voice. "Four-thirty A.M., Becky."

My jaw might not have dropped, but it loosened a little. Dawn was a time to be spent in bed, with REM up and eyelids down. "Your favorite activity takes place at four-thirty in the *morning*?"

He laughed. "Trust me," he said. "You wanted to be surprised, remember?"

I did and I had, but still. "What should I wear?" I bleated.

"Layers," he said firmly. "And sensible shoes."

CHAPTER TWENTY-SEVEN

IT WAS ONLY TEN O'CLOCK, BUT I ALREADY FELT AS IF I'D been in the office half a lifetime, and I hadn't even started any work. There were so many other things going on in my life—the trust, my mother's health problems, my future at RTA—that it was hard to focus on actual legal work. I looked at the pile on my desk with dismay. If I was going to be looking for another job, it wouldn't help matters to look as if I was slacking off in the one I already had.

I took the top envelope off the pile, the envelope handed to me by Bobbie's minion at Casa Alegría. I'd assumed it contained copies of some lease agreements she'd wanted me to look at—a pro forma exercise, since Jamison Roth, the real estate expert, had already signed off on them. All I needed to do was check them over to make sure they conformed to the agreed-upon terms.

I slit the envelope with my letter opener without any sense of premonition.

So much for ESP.

The documents in the envelope were not lease agreements. They were bank statements, confirming two accounts in the Cayman Islands. One, a new account, was in the name of Bobbie Crystol, with an initial deposit of $1,624,987. The other showed the transfer of $50,000 from the Crystol account to another Cayman Island account.

The name of the second account holder was Taylor Anderson.

I sat back in my chair (a cheap one, which creaked) to consider the implications. The documents were pretty clearly meant for Taylor. "Dr. Crystol instructed me to give this to her lawyer," the man had said.

Not me, obviously.

I wondered what to do next. I couldn't just give Taylor the documents and leave it at that. I mean, there might not be anything illegal per se about Cayman Island accounts, but the transfer of money to Taylor—which looked an awful lot like an off-the-books payment of some sort—smelled to high heaven, to say the least.

Res ipsa loquitur. The rat in the soft drink bottle. The thing speaks for itself.

Not only that, but Taylor had told me to my face he'd had nothing to do with *Carole's* Cayman Island investments. The coincidence was too great to ignore.

The question was, what to do about it? I had to have help—I needed to know more than I knew before I could proceed. But whom to ask? Lauren? Melissa? Whom could I trust to help me uncover the dirt on Taylor? Somebody who loved the law firm, or somebody who loved Taylor?

Or had, anyway.

I dialed the extension number. "Are you alone?" I asked.

"Of course not," Melissa snapped. "I'm here with Ryan. We're going over some things. Why do you ask?"

I took a breath. "I'm sorry to bother you, but I think I may have screwed something up on Jason Krill's financing."

"*What?*"

"I was wondering if you could help me with it when you get some time," I said.

"Christ!" She mumbled something—presumably to Ryan—that I couldn't hear. "I'll be right there," she said.

"Jesus, Becky, I was just talking to Jason," she said, blowing into my office like a dust devil. "What's the problem here?"

I knew I could count on her. "Would you mind closing the door?" I asked mildly.

She looked momentarily taken aback. "Yes, sure," she said, closing it behind her. "I didn't mean to yell at you. I know we all make mistakes, but—"

I raised my hand to stop her. "Relax," I said. "I haven't screwed anything up, at least not that I know of."

"That's good," she said, "because Jason is very interested in hiring one or both of us." She looked at me. "So why did you tell me that?"

"Because I needed to get you in here with the door closed without arousing anyone's suspicions," I said.

Her eyes narrowed. "And you could predict my reaction?"

I didn't say anything.

"Well, never mind. What's up?"

"Does anyone at the firm set up offshore accounts?" I asked her. "Is that part of our practice?"

"Not that I know of," she said. "Why do you ask?"

I handed her the documents.

She looked at them and raised her eyebrows. "Where did you get these?"

I explained about the mix-up.

She frowned. "This doesn't look right. Why should Taylor be getting a fifty thousand dollar fee transferred into some private offshore account? That's not how our legal fees are collected." She handed the papers back to me with a shrewd look. "So what do you want from me?" she asked. "I'm out of here just as soon as I get another job."

"Advice," I said.

"Okay. Before you say another word, here it is: Let it go. Let me help *you* find another job. Let Taylor twist in the wind, and if he's up to anything he shouldn't be, let it come out in the course of time. The world does not reward a whistle-blower, and there isn't enough here to blow the whistle on anyway."

"Bobbie Crystol's my client, or at least she was," I reminded her. "If she's up to something illegal, people might think I'm in on it."

She shook her head. "Not likely. You're too low-level." She looked at me. "Sorry. I didn't mean it quite that way. But it's true."

By now I was getting used to Melissa's habit of speaking her mind. "I'm not offended," I told her. "You're right. But I am the attorney of record. Besides . . ."

"Besides?"

I explained to her about the offshore investments that had drained the Pratt trust of a good chunk of its principal. "It's a recent thing," I said, "and I can't help wondering if there isn't some connection. What if Taylor is helping Carole *and* Bobbie hide some assets in Cayman Island accounts? The accountant told me it's virtually impossible to penetrate the accounts because of the islands' privacy laws. I'm not some vigilante Clytemnestra, but if there's something like that going on with the trust, I want to know about it."

She looked at me and sighed. I could tell that the specter of Carole had kindled her enthusiasm for helping me. "I've got to meet this woman," she said.

"I'm sure it can be arranged," I told her.

"Okay, Plan B, then." She picked up the documents again. "First, we make copies of these bank statements." She tapped the envelope with a perfectly manicured nail. "Then we get a new envelope, seal it up, address it to Taylor, and sneak it into his in box. If he asks about it, I'll tell him Bobbie gave it to me to give to him. Under the circumstances, you don't want him to know you know anything about it."

"Definitely not," I agreed.

"I'm sure it goes without saying that it would be highly unethical, not to mention unwise, to say anything about this to anyone," she cautioned.

"I agree. What next?"

"Next we go looking through the chron files," she said. "Just to see what turns up."

The chron files were the firm's daily files of all the work done by its lawyers, filed by date. "You mean, to see if there are any offshore account billings or anything like that? Do you think there will be anything there?"

"That depends on whether it's legitimate work undertaken by the firm," she said. "We'll see." She smiled. "And after that . . ."

"After that?"

"We'll see what Daddy has to say about it."

* * *

THE CHRON FILES were essentially a backup to the firm's files for each client. Their advantage for sleuthing was that the secretaries usually did the filing, while the lawyers sometimes kept their own client files. Secretaries, for obvious reasons, made much better filers than lawyers.

Melissa and I took alternating days from the past week. There was a surprising amount of paper to look through—the firm's partners and associates accounted for a lot of work every day.

Melissa proceeded more slowly than I did, pursing her lips and shaking her head over some of the documents she found. It was obviously tough to be smarter than so many of your peers, because your sensibilities were always being outraged. My focus was somewhat different, so I made more progress.

After about half an hour, Melissa glanced at the clock. "I'm sorry, but I'm going to have to quit after this bunch and finish later. I left Ryan working on something important, and I don't want to leave him unsupervised very long. I'll try to get back to it later this afternoon. I only have one more day to check."

"That's okay," I told her. "I really appreciate whatever help you can give me. I—"

"What are you two up to?" inquired Wendy, stepping into the room. She looked taken aback to find us together, as if Sonny and Cher had somehow reunited. "Can I help you find anything?"

"No, thanks," Melissa said, returning her glance to the papers she was holding. I remembered why she was not popular with the staff.

I smiled at Wendy. "We needed some backup on some work Taylor did for Crystol Enterprises," I said. I prayed that Taylor was not in his office, raising the awkward question of why I didn't just check with *him*. At least Bobbie was nominally my client, and anyway, I was pretty sure I could trust Wendy not to get me in trouble.

Wendy looked surprised. "Well, you won't find it in there, or at least you shouldn't."

Melissa's gaze appeared to be riveted on the papers in her hand. She didn't look up. "Really?" I asked Wendy. "Why not?"

Wendy gave Melissa a sidelong glance, then looked at me. I nodded. "All the secretaries know. Taylor's stuff only goes into his personal files. Without exception." She lowered her voice. "A few weeks ago one of the temps filed some trust documents in the regular files. He made a *huge* fuss about it."

Melissa did look up at that. "Really? What kind of trust documents?"

Wendy shrugged. "I don't know that, Melissa. I didn't see them. The temp was so embarrassed she refuses to work here anymore. That's all I do know."

I of all people should have remembered the first rule of law firm society—if you want to know anything, talk to the secretaries. They know everything and they're not unwilling to spill it.

"Thanks," I told Wendy. "You've saved us a lot of time. If we decide we really need this document, we'll check with Taylor about getting it. I don't think we'll bother him right now."

Wendy smiled. "Whatever you say, Becky."

"Now, that was interesting," I said to Melissa when Wendy had gone. "I imagine it means we won't find anything here."

Melissa was still looking at some papers she was holding. She laid a hand on my arm.

"What is it? Did you find something?"

She looked at me and raised her eyebrows. "Yes and no. Not what we're looking for, but something interesting nonetheless. You told me your ex-husband's name was Richard Pratt, right?"

I nodded, with a sense of foreboding.

"Well, guess what eminent San Diego law firm amended the Pratt trust last week to add beneficiaries?"

"What?"

She handed me the papers. "There it is in black and white. The attorney was Ryan, and the amendment was made 'as per client instructions.' "

My mouth hung open. I'd never suspected that Carole had used RTA. "Are you sure it wasn't Taylor?" I asked her. "Using Ryan doesn't make any sense."

She pointed out the name of the billing attorney. "Using *RTA* doesn't make any sense," she said.

"Well, it does, in a way, if you're Carole," I said grimly. "She probably wanted to stick it to me with my own firm. I would have found out anyway as soon as I got the official documentation. It's just an extra thrust of the knife."

"I'm sure Ryan didn't know it was your family trust," Melissa said. "He's a twit, but he's not that cruel. In fact, the way I'm envisioning this is that she didn't ask Taylor because he would have refused. So she called and asked for a tax or T and E associate. After all, it's supposed to be something simple. Ryan saw his big chance for independence." She laughed suddenly. "Of course, you were incredibly lucky that it *was* Ryan and not Taylor."

"I am?"

"Sure. If Taylor had done it, he wouldn't have screwed it up. Ryan might have handed you the way to get the entire trust reviewed. You should get down on your knees and thank him for his incompetence."

I felt more like socking him in the nose, but I didn't say anything.

"Of course, it does present us with something of a dilemma," she said.

My life was so full of dilemmas lately I didn't know which one to focus on. "What?" I asked.

She looked amused. "Well, ethically speaking, I'm sure you can see that if we've identified a potential problem in some other RTA associate's work, we might be obliged to divulge it. On the other hand, if we do, our friend Carole might try to scramble around and alter the trust in such a way that it doesn't violate the Rule Against Perpetuities, and then you'll have a harder time getting a court to review it. So what do you think we should do, Becky?"

Let's see, my loyalty to the firm versus my loyalty to my kids. "Technically speaking, we don't *know* there's any problem, right?" I said. "Not till we get someone expert to confirm it." I looked at her. "I think we should hurry up and talk to your father," I said.

She smiled. "You're thinking like a lawyer, Becky. I hope that pleases you."

"I'm sure that will be very useful in my next job," I told her.

"I'M A GENIUS," Isabel proclaimed when I picked up the phone late that afternoon.

"Undoubtedly," I told her, "but it's customary to let other people point it out first."

"I don't have time for that sort of phony modesty," she said. "Wait till you hear what I've done."

"I'm all ears."

"While you were gone, I posted a note on HumbugWatch inviting people to share problems they've had with Dr. Crystol's program," she said. I'd called her when I got home the night before, so she knew about the incident at the spa.

"What's HumbugWatch?" I asked her.

"It's a website devoted to alleged medical quackery. There's quite a bit about anti-aging on it. People can post their comments on the site. So now you might find out more about people's experiences with Dr. Crystol."

She sounded so excited I didn't want to tell her that whatever Bobbie did or didn't do was now largely irrelevant to my future. Besides, I did have an obligation—one that I would honor—not to say anything about my suspicions concerning Bobbie's offshore accounts.

"That *is* brilliant," I said admiringly. "Do you think anyone will respond?"

She laughed. "Check your E-mail," she said.

I gasped. "You didn't post my address?"

"I told you I was a genius. Of course not. I just forwarded the first of the comments to you. I threw out the obscene suggestions and the obvious cranks, but I included the who-do-you-think-you-are-to-invite-criticism-of-such-a-fine-humanitarian messages. There are a lot of those. In the future you can check them yourself."

"So most of the response was positive?" I asked.

"I wouldn't say that. There are a number of people who think they got sick from the therapies." She paused. "There is also one from someone who claims she used to work next door to Bobbie's office and heard a lot of things from her employees."

"Don't torture me, Isabel. What kinds of things?"

"That she cut corners and invented data while running drug tests for pharmaceutical companies. Kept blood and urine samples in the office fridge so she could fake the results if necessary and give the companies the answers they wanted."

"That's possible. Mark said he heard rumors about her clinical trials. I'm afraid Bobbie's scruples are suspect, to say the least."

"You sound down," she said. "Is there something else?"

"It's just been a bad day." I told her about my mother. "And just when I'm going to need the money, I have to face the fact that realistically I'll be out of a job soon. Very soon, probably. And I absolutely won't be taking Bobbie with me, for reasons I can't explain right now, so I'm going to have to do it on my own. The only bright spot is this thing with the trust. It might work out. But there are consequences you don't know about."

"Don't borrow trouble," she said. "One thing at a time. It's a great job market—if you get fired or have to quit, you'll find something else."

"I know. I might even have a lead on a job in a high-tech company. But you know what those guys are like, Isabel. They regard sleep deprivation as a stimulus to creativity, and they've all got this singular and ruthless devotion to work, uncluttered by inconvenient attachments. That's okay for Melissa Peters—she'd probably thrive on it—but I don't think it's really me."

"I don't think it's really you either. What does Mark say?"

"I haven't discussed it with him."

"Why not?"

"I don't want to sound needy and dependent. He's already helping with my mother. I have to take care of this one myself."

"I think you're too hung up on the fact that he used to be your therapist. You don't have to keep proving to him that you're tough. He knows you."

"Thanks, I think. Want to get together this week over a bottle of wine?"

"Okay," she said. "But I can't do it until after I correct a hundred and fifty-two math tests and check out the bona fides of some guy claiming to own a sixty-thousand-acre spread in Montana." She sighed. "So what's he doing selling cars in National City? I mean, some people will believe *anything*."

"Love may be blind, but at least she's checking him out. Does that count as one eye open?"

"Just a squint, I'd say." She hesitated. "Do you want to hear my latest Texas quote?"

"Isabel, where are you getting these things?"

"You type in *Texas*, and up they come," she said. "Do you want to hear it or not?"

"Shoot."

"That's not funny, Becky. Do you know what J.B. Priestly said? He said that Texas was a world so contemptuous and destructive of feminine values that women had to be heavily bribed to stay there."

"Bribed with what? Spareribs?"

"Shops. Like Neiman Marcus."

"That's totally ridiculous. You can find Neiman Marcus lots of places, including here. Why are you tormenting yourself trying to find bad things about Texas?"

"You know why," she said.

"But Daniel doesn't even live there," I pointed out. "He lives here."

"He might want to go back. It's where his roots are."

"Isabel, will you listen to yourself? You can't get an impression of someplace by amassing a collection of quotes from a bunch of dead guys. If you want to know what it's like, you should go there and see for yourself. And besides, aren't you just looking for reasons not to get involved with Daniel?"

She laughed. "Becky, it is so tacky to throw my own advice back in my face. What is this, the zeal of the convert?"

"I guess so," I mumbled.

"What did you say? I didn't hear you."

"I guess so," I told her.

CHAPTER TWENTY-EIGHT

I saw your invitation on HumbugWatch. You're just like all the rest of the bureaucratic, so-called medical profession, trying to keep genuine revolutionaries like Dr. Crystol out of the limelight because you're afraid of being shown up as narrow-minded hacks. You should be ashamed of soliciting negative information about Dr. Crystol, whose research will liberate us from the limitations of our aging bodies. She is the true humanitarian, misunderstood in her own time, like Freud and Elvis. I hope you get chin hairs the size of toothpicks and have to get up fifteen times a night to pee. Then we'll see who has the last laugh. . . .

Dr. Jackson, Mark's orthopedic whiz, was elated. She waved the X rays in front of my nose as triumphantly as if they were da Vinci drawings authenticated on *Antiques Roadshow.*

"I knew it," she said happily. "I knew as soon as I examined you, Mrs. Weston, there had to be a break there somewhere."

"My leg is broken?" asked my mother from her wheelchair.

"Not your leg," said Dr. Jackson, sobering up. "Your hip. I'm sure you fractured it when you fell. It's been getting worse all this time. No wonder you've been feeling pain."

I thought my mother herself would feel a temptation to gloat at having been proved right after all, but she looked worried.

"This is good news, right?" I said encouragingly. "If something is broken, you can fix it. Isn't that right?"

"Well, yes," said the doctor. "I'd recommend hip replacement surgery. And if you're not on something for your osteoporosis, I'd recommend that you start."

"Hip replacement," said my mother in a leaden tone.

"It's not so bad," said the doctor brightly. "After some rehabilitation, you'll be back to walking just about normally again, with much less pain. Won't that be an improvement?"

"I have to go into the hospital," said my mother. "And a nursing home."

"Well, yes, Mrs. Weston. It's not the sort of surgery you can do on an outpatient basis."

I knelt beside her chair. "It'll be okay, Mother. You'll see. It's only temporary."

She looked at me skeptically and then turned her face away. "I don't have any choice, do I?" she said to the wall.

"Of course you do," said Dr. Jackson. "But if you don't have the surgery, the pain will get worse and you'll end up unable to walk at all. In fact, I'm surprised you've been able to get around as well as you have been. It must have taken a lot of willpower."

"They said I had to," said my mother.

I put an arm around her shoulders. The thought of my mother bravely making her way down the corridors on a broken hip in order to meet some arbitrary fitness standard just about unhinged me. "I am so sorry," I said. "I should have listened to you sooner. You told me you were in pain, and I thought because the tests hadn't shown anything, there was nothing physically wrong." I looked at Dr. Jackson. "Why *didn't* the earlier tests show anything?" I asked.

She shrugged. "It was probably a hairline fracture, and now it's been made worse by your mother's efforts at getting herself around. We try, but we don't always catch everything."

"How soon would you want to operate?" I asked.

She did some mental calculations. "Hmm. Today's Thursday. I'll have to check my schedule, but I would imagine we could do it on Monday or Tuesday." She turned to my mother. "You'll need a special hip prosthesis, Mrs. Weston, because of the break. It will take a day or two to get here. I'd like to get you admitted today, however, so we can get the hip immobilized and run some tests," she said. "Because of your history, we want to be extra careful." She bent over my mother. "Is early next week all right with you, Mrs. Weston?"

My mother clutched at my hand.

"Don't be scared, Mom," I whispered, though I was scared too.

"I just want to say . . ." my mother began.

"Yes?"

"I told you so," she said.

* * *

MARK CAUGHT UP with us in the hospital lobby. "Sorry," he said. "I couldn't get away. How are you doing, Mrs. Weston?"

"I have a broken hip," my mother said proudly.

"Ah, they found something," Mark said. "Dr. Jackson's the best." He looked at me. "Surgery?"

I nodded.

"Feeling scared?" he asked my mother.

"What are you, a shrink?" she asked.

"This is Dr. Lawrence, mother. He came to visit you after you fell, remember?"

"No, I don't. Did you bring flowers?" she asked.

"I'm afraid not," Mark said.

"Candy? Balloons? A card?"

"Mother—" I said.

"Cheapskate," she muttered.

Mark laughed.

"Mother," I said, horrified. "Mark got you this appointment."

My mother shrugged.

"I'll bring flowers and a card next time, Mrs. Weston. I promise," Mark said. He consulted his watch. "You need to go get her checked in," he said. "Can I meet you in my office or somewhere afterward? We need to talk."

"I could stop by your office in an hour," I said.

"Nobody has the decency even to wait till I'm gone," said my mother.

"I DON'T KNOW what's the matter with her," I said to him when we met an hour later. "One minute she has me feeling horribly contrite because she's been bravely soldiering on with a broken hip, and the next minute she's acting like a cranky two-year-old. I don't know how to treat her. I'm sorry she was so rude to you."

He laughed. "I'd say she was pretty smart. You can bet I'll show up with an armload of goodies next time. Anyway, don't worry about it. She's scared, and she's lost control of her life. That can make anybody cranky."

"Don't I know it," I said.

He smiled.

It was strange being in Mark's office after such a long time, especially as a visitor and not a patient. The furniture was all a newer version of what had been there before—generic, comfortable, tasteful but not extraordinary. In fact, it conveyed absolutely nothing about its owner—a blank slate each patient could fill in for himself. It had to be intentional.

"I never noticed before," I told him.

"Noticed what?"

"That there's nothing personal here in your office. It's very nice, but nobody could ever guess anything about you from seeing this."

He looked embarrassed. "I try to keep my personal life at home, at my house. Especially since . . . Well, it helps you keep your professional life separate. You need to, in this business."

I thought he'd been going to say "since my wife died." I said, "Like Dorian Gray, in reverse," striving for a lighter tone. "This place gets the bland exterior and your house gets all the telling knickknacks."

He laughed. "My house is *not* full of knickknacks," he said, "telling or otherwise."

There was an awkward pause, during which I wondered if he thought I'd been hinting to see his house. To cover it, I said quickly, "What did you want to talk to me about?"

He stopped smiling. "I have a friend who's a top consultant in the biomedical industry. I asked him to do some checking into drug companies that might be running clinical trials on something that fit your description of Bobbie's supplements."

"That's great. Did he find out anything?"

"He says a company called SINALMA Pharmaceuticals is testing an anti-aging product with a formulation that doesn't exist in any product currently on the market, possibly just for distribution outside the United States. He doesn't know who's doing the clinical trial—SINALMA's not his client."

"What's in it?"

"The exact ingredients are secret, naturally, but the scuttlebutt is that it's an ephedrine-related alkaloid and caffeine," he said. "Along with some less significant things."

"Explain," I told him.

"Ephedrine and related alkaloids are structurally similar to amphetamines," he said. "They rev up the metabolism—the blood pressure and the heart. They're usually found in weight loss products and 'energy boosters.' If you've got cardiac arrhythmia or high blood pressure or diabetes, they can be very dangerous."

"Is it illegal?"

"Not really. A version of an alkaloid, pseudoephedrine, is found in just about every cold product on the market. This could be a more dangerous cousin, but ephedrine is still approved as a bronchodilator for people with asthma. The FDA is trying to remove oral ephedrine drug products from the OTC market, but you can find these products on the Internet right now."

"So if that was what was in the pill, do you think it might have caused that woman's problems?"

"It certainly could have. Particularly if she exercised excessively and she didn't eat. Did you ever drink way too many cups of coffee and make your heart pound?"

"That much coffee doesn't exist," I told him.

He smiled.

"So what's the point?" I asked him. "Of the pill, I mean."

"Oh, well, if you don't get hypertension, coronary spasm, respiratory depression, or convulsions, you feel incredibly energetic."

"What do you think Bobbie's up to?" I asked.

He sighed. "What she says, I imagine. It's not a magic pill, but you could argue that it does make people feel younger, at least temporarily."

"If they survive it."

"The only sure way to avoid growing old is to die young," he said. He touched my arm. "You saw how people were clamoring for these treatments, Becky. They don't care if they're dangerous or not."

I remembered the group at Opening Weekend and knew he was right. Still, I hated to leave it like that. "My leverage with Bobbie Crystol has gone from low to nonexistent," I told him. "I don't think there's much I can do if she is the one doing the clinical trials, particularly if she confines her treatments to Mexico."

"I know that," he said. "I didn't tell you because of that. I told you for you."

"Because I said I wanted to know no matter what." I

smiled. “I wonder how many people regret it after they say something like that.”

“Lots of them,” he said. “I’m sorry.”

“Don’t be. I’m on my way out with Bobbie anyway. I’ve been supplanted in her legal affections.”

“How does that make you feel?” he asked, in his therapist’s voice.

I looked at him, but the professional mask was gone. He just looked concerned.

“Relieved,” I said. It was the truth.

“Really?”

“Really.” I didn’t say any more. I could save my job worries for another day.

“So what now?” he asked.

“I have to decide what I want,” I told him. “But first I have to go shopping for some sensible shoes.”

CHAPTER TWENTY-NINE

MELISSA'S FATHER, ERIC PETERS, CHUCKLED WITH GLEE at the documents we brought him. "I haven't thought about this stuff in ages," he said.

"You're not practicing, then?" I asked, ignoring Melissa's warning look.

He waved his hand. "Oh, no, darling, I'm in real estate now. My lawyering days are over for good."

We were sitting in the living room of his trailer in Happy Village Trailer Park in Santee, a suburb of San Diego many miles inland and as far from La Jolla in every respect as it was possible to get. It wasn't what I'd been expecting, to say the least.

Mr. Peters seemed to read my mind. He smiled. "I'm in my minimalist period now," he said, looking around the room. "Everything is secondhand. It's unbelievably refreshing."

Melissa closed her eyes.

"All right, my dears, we have *lots* to talk about." He practically rubbed his hands together, making his stomach jiggle beneath his shirt. Wherever Melissa had gotten her stunning good looks and commitment to fitness, it wasn't from Daddy. It made me wonder if she'd been adopted. He put the trust amendment drafted by Ryan down on the battered coffee table. "Now let's look at this first. Becky"—he raised his eyes and looked at me—"Missy tells me you figured out that this might violate the Rule Against Perpetuities. Is that right?"

"Well, I wondered," I said.

"A first-year associate, imagine that! It didn't occur to Missy to wonder, did it, darling?"

"No, it didn't," Melissa said tonelessly.

Uh-oh.

His voice took on a sharper tone. "Well, what *you* saw, Becky, and others didn't was that even if it doesn't *sound* outrageous to amend the trust to add the trustee's grandchildren and terminate it at the death of the last to die of the grandchildren, it violates the rule because any grandchildren (bless their little hearts) could very *easily* die more than twenty-one years after the death of whoever is the last to die, the trustee or her four-year-old son. In other words, the trust has to be distributed prior to twenty-one years after the death of everyone living at the time your friend Carole made these changes or it violates the rule."

I was very happy to be right, but I didn't like being used as a weapon in some war between father and daughter. "It was a lucky guess," I told him. "But thank you for clearing it up."

"Nonsense," he said.

Melissa shot me a look I couldn't interpret.

"So what should I do now?" I asked him.

"We'll get to that. First we get to the really interesting stuff." He waved the copies of the bank statements under our noses, like something we should smell. "Now, I want you to understand that here we're entering the realm of speculation. There is nothing concrete to go on but two bank statements for offshore accounts. Nevertheless, we can entertain some very delicious suspicions, based on our experience and the unlikely coincidence of Mr. Anderson's . . . um . . . involvement with two unscrupulous women with accounts in the Cayman Islands." He looked at me. "Melissa will have told you, I assume, that I am not totally lacking in experience in this somewhat dubious practice myself."

"I didn't provide any details," Melissa said.

"Nor do you know any, my child. And we're going to keep it that way. It's enough to mention that I know, shall we say, what I'm talking about."

I nodded. It seemed the most appropriate response.

"All right, then. Let me say at the outset that there are lots of legitimate reasons to have offshore accounts, the primary one being to diversify investments. You're probably aware that most hedge funds are formed offshore, even by the most reputable investment advisers, as a way to avoid—legally—onerous U.S. securities laws."

I wasn't, as a matter of fact. My finances didn't exactly put me in the hedge fund category, and my knowledge was limited to the ones that periodically made headlines for nefarious reasons. Still, I nodded again to prove I was listening.

"Nevertheless, the biggest advantage of these accounts if you're up to something you shouldn't be is the secrecy laws of the offshore country. You can knock on the door, but nobody's going to tell you anything." He looked at me. "Now, suppose you're the trustee for a fairly substantial amount of money, but your trustee days are numbered because, say, you're planning to marry again, and under the provisions of the trust your position will terminate upon your marriage. Or maybe you just hate the other beneficiaries so much you don't want them to get their hands on any of the principal. Ever. Anyway, with the help of an adviser of questionable virtue, you decide to salt away some of that money for yourself, thereby accomplishing two goals—feathering your own nest, and denying the other beneficiaries their rightful due. So how would you go about doing that?"

I didn't know the answer, but I could see how smart he was. He'd already pulled all the significant facts out of what I'd told him about Carole and the trust, and he'd constructed a believable hypothesis.

"I'm sure you're going to tell us," said Melissa.

"Yes, darling, but bear in mind what I said about speculation, won't you? It's only a theory." He smiled. "Inference. An educated guess. What have you. Anyway, here's what you might do. You take a substantial portion of the trust assets and buy some investment—stocks, annuities, mutual funds, something—outside the United States. Then you claim that the investment has gone bad, thereby reducing the principal considerably. With the aid of your adviser, you bogus up some documents—stock certificates, investment advices, insurance policies, annuity contracts, whatever—that look just like the real thing but are really fronts behind which the money is hiding. You provide your legitimate accountant with the name and contact of the agent in the Caymans who sold you the investment, but when that person is contacted he is prevented from giving information because of the secrecy laws of the islands. Meanwhile, you shuffle off a nice payment into another overseas account for your adviser, who doesn't declare it on his income tax. The beneficiaries get an accounting statement showing a loss for the accounting period with a corresponding reduction of principal. They are very sad, they may even be suspicious, but what can they do? If no one talks, it's not that hard to get away with it."

I sat back in my chair. "Oh, wow." I was absolutely, completely, entirely certain he was right. I could feel it in my bones. My anger took my breath away.

"What strongly suggests the possibility, of course, is the presence of these two accounts for Crystol Enterprises. Mr. Anderson appears to have been disbursing his favors rather freely. Careless of him. Now, in this case, Dr. Crystol may be thinking of running the same scam, or she might just be hiding some of her payoffs from the pharmaceutical companies to avoid paying tax, or she may be setting up a legitimate offshore investment. The size and nature of Mr. Anderson's off-the-books payment throws a little shadow over her legitimacy, but it's not conclusive." He turned to Melissa. "You're not by chance still enamored of this rogue, are you?"

She flushed. "I hate his guts," she said.

Mr. Peters raised his eyebrows. "That's perhaps fortunate, because if our suspicions are correct, I fear the Internal Revenue Service will have more than a passing interest in his activities."

"Well, what can I do?" I asked. "I can't let them get away with it! If no one will talk, how can we prove anything?"

"If there's anything to prove," he reminded me. "You know, the wonderful thing is, people do talk. They tell other people in their families about these accounts, or they brag about what they're getting away with. They leave inconvenient records of their transactions. If there isn't supposed to be any money in the trust, finding an account that isn't supposed to exist is extremely helpful. There are all kinds of ways. The IRS"—he gave a little shudder that appeared to be genuine—"has its methods, I promise you." He smiled. "But you, Becky, are fortunate."

"I am?"

"Yes indeed." He folded his hands across his stomach. "Would either of you like a soft drink? I think there's some grape soda in the refrigerator."

It was my turn to shudder. I tried to suppress it. "No, thanks," I told him.

Melissa made a face and said nothing.

"Well, then," he continued, "let's assume for a moment that my little story is true. The evil trustee has stashed away a portion of the trust that rightfully belongs to the beneficiaries, depriving them of—well, whatever it's depriving them of."

"A private school education, for example," I suggested.

He spread his hands. "What have you. Now we come to the lucky part. Not content with stealing some of the principal for herself—and of course she can't steal it *all*, because that would look very suspicious—the trustee devises a plan whereby the hated beneficiaries will never be able to get their hands on any of the principal, at least till they're too old to need it for anything but orthopedic shoes. Her adviser has probably told her to lie low for a while to avoid emphasizing the connection between them, and he certainly wouldn't be involved in anything so blatantly self-destructive as changing the terms of the trust. But she can't help herself. Her loathing for the first wife and her stepchildren festers in her till she has to do *something*, so she asks an associate in the firm—an ignoramus, but an innocent ignoramus—to amend the trust at her direction. The fact that it is the firm where her rival also works adds immeasurably to her satisfaction." He looked at me. "Liking this story so far?"

"*Liking*'s probably not the right word," I told him. "I'm waiting for the denouement."

He laughed. "Are you seeing anybody?"

"Yes," I said, probably too quickly.

"Pity. I like smart women."

"Get on with it, Dad," Melissa prompted him.

He sighed. "All right. The great thing about this story is that the trustee's greed will be her ultimate undoing. Because now she's gone too far, and her attempts at selfishly tying up her late husband's assets in perpetuity come up against the laws designed to keep people from doing just that. People really do want to control others from the grave, you know. It's quite remarkable. You can't believe some of the conditions I've seen people impose on beneficiaries and trustees. The restrictions are limited only by the trustor's imagination—or paranoia. I—"

"Dad," Melissa said again.

"Oh, Missy, you're always spoiling my fun. As I was saying, thanks to some very sharp lawyering on the part of the trustee's rival, the violation of the Rule Against Perpetuities has been uncovered. Now the trust gets into court, and a complete accounting, probably including an auditlike review by a Special Master, will undoubtedly uncover the sort of shenanigans we've been postulating here. If they've been up to something they shouldn't, it's unlikely to escape the auditor's notice, especially with a little prompting from interested parties. If the investment losses *were* on the level, at the very least you'd get the court to review the trust and, undoubtedly, remove Carole as trustee."

"That sounds like a no-lose situation," I said excitedly. "How do I get the court to review the trust?"

"You go to this person whose name I will give you and get him to file a motion for accounting. Then you wait to see how the chips fall." He put the tips of his fingers together and lifted his eyes to mine. "I wouldn't be too sure about the no-lose situation, though. In my experience there's no such thing. Either way, I doubt RTA will be very happy with you. And—"

"I'm helping her find another job," Melissa interjected.

"And you may get your client Dr. Crystol into a lot of trouble. Of course, you may feel she deserves it since she's clearly setting you up."

"Setting me up?" I asked, with a sinking feeling in my stomach.

"Well, it certainly looks that way. I take it you know why she wanted you to represent her?"

"I assume the answer is not because we were old school friends?"

"*Were* you old school friends?"

I laughed. "No, not really."

"Well, forgive me for being blunt, but why pick an inexperienced lawyer in an unlikely firm to hand your business to? Does the term *scapegoat* mean anything to you?"

"Dad—"

"No, it's okay," I said. "He's right. I've always suspected there was something fishy about it."

"Attagirl," Mr. Peters said. "So go get 'em. This is

one of those 'biter bit' stories. Don't let 'em get away with it."

"I won't," I told him.

"SO WHAT DID you think?" Melissa asked me as we left the trailer park in her BMW M-5. She seemed hell-bent on proving the manufacturer's claim of zero to sixty in under five seconds. The g forces were pinning me to my seat.

A loaded question if I'd ever heard one. "He's very smart," I said cautiously.

"He is, isn't he?" she said. She looked over at me. "He was impressed with you," she said.

I had to bite my tongue to keep from screeching at her to keep her eyes on the road. "I'm sure he was just being nice," I muttered.

"Actually," Melissa said, "he isn't a particularly nice person. And he has very exacting standards."

Everybody's relationship with their parents is so complicated. I couldn't think what to say. "It must be hard for him, losing so much," I said.

She smiled grimly. "Don't fall for it," she said.

"Excuse me?"

"That minimalist crap. The trailer park. Grape soda." She snorted. "The whole bit. He's a fake and a fraud."

"I don't . . ."

"It's an act. A pose."

"For whose benefit?" If it was an act, it was a good one. That living room was pretty shabby. I doubted that the bedroom was secretly done up in Louis Quinze.

"For the benefit of people who might be interested if they thought he had money stashed away in accounts somewhere." She shrugged. "He wouldn't tell me, of course, but I don't believe for one second that he doesn't have the kinds of offshore accounts we were talking about today. He's far too clever."

"Oh." I longed to ask Melissa what her mother was like, but I didn't dare. Since there was no sign of her at Happy Village, I assumed she was no longer in the picture. It was interesting how transparent other people's hang-ups were, as opposed to your own. Melissa had clearly rejected a lot of what her father represented (like junk food and big hips), while at the same time she tried to gain his approval for her mind and legal skills. I had a swift, painful vision of Allie and David, far in the future, sitting around some kitchen table dissecting their relationship with *me*.

"Changing the subject," Melissa said, taking her right hand off the wheel and resting it on the gearshift, ready to zap the competition at a moment's notice, "I've followed up with Jason Krill. He really is interested in employing both of us. It could be very exciting, Becky. His company could be the next global IT powerhouse. You'd be in on the ground floor getting your get-rich-quick credentials in order." She pushed her hair back from her forehead. "Of course, you'd have to pay your dues for a while. You have to work really hard to get started and then to keep from getting obsolete. You have to stretch yourself pretty thin. But the payoff is worth it."

I looked out the window, watching the world go by at eighty-two miles per hour. You couldn't see much. I had to do something—my future at RTA was written in sand—and I could certainly use the money, but I was already giving up so much to work. When would I have time for my children? Allie still had at least two more years at home. My mother? I hadn't talked to her about anything meaningful in at least fifteen years. I thought maybe I should try before it was too late. Myself? I only had half a life now, or maybe only a third of one.

"I'll think about it," I told her. "But thanks—I really appreciate your help."

"What's to think about?" she asked.

"You'd be surprised," I told her.

CHAPTER THIRTY

EARLY MORNING ALWAYS MADE LITTLE POUCHY THINGS under my eyes that would not be smoothed away by any level of diligent application in the makeup department. I considered answering the door in sunglasses, but at 4:22 A.M. this would very likely be seen as an affectation. I put the sunglasses in the pocket of my windbreaker for later. I turned off the porch light so I wouldn't stand there blinking like a mole.

"Hi," I said cheerily, opening the front door. I'd already warmed the croak out of my voice with coffee, but my brain was still barely plugged in.

"Hi," Mark said. I was happy to note that he had on a jacket nearly identical to mine, so I must be dressed properly. He eyed me. "What do you have on under your windbreaker?" he asked.

I laughed. "Isn't it a little early for that?"

He laughed too, but he squeezed my arm, exploring the fabric.

"Layers," I told him. "A T-shirt, a sweater, and this. It's waterproof," I added. I felt as if I were auditioning for an Eddie Bauer ad.

"Good," he said. He looked at my feet.

I stuck out one running shoe–clad foot for his approval.

"Perfect," he added.

He was starting to make me nervous. All this emphasis on outdoor attire pointed to some exceptionally athletic activity, a sphere in which I did not shine.

Burdick, scenting opportunity, leaped out of his basket in the kitchen and made a beeline for the front door. I reached around Mark and pushed it shut, stumbling a little as I tried not to step on the cat. Mark caught me before I tripped. "Sorry," I said. "He's an opportunist."

"You don't let him out?"

"Only in the daytime," I said. "At night he mixes it up with the skunks and possums, so he's confined to quarters."

Mark bent over and picked him up, supporting his tail and hind legs with his arm like an expert. "Hey, big guy," he said. He looked at me. "What do you feed him, Mighty Cat? He's gigantic."

"The vet says he's just muscular," I insisted.

He smiled and put the cat down. He looked at his watch. "Ready to go?" he asked.

"Do you want some coffee to take with us?" I asked.

He looked alarmed. "I should have told you," he said. "You don't want to have a lot to drink."

IT WAS STILL dark when we exited the freeway. When the car slowed for the off-ramp, my palms started sweating.

I knew where we were going and why we had to get up at the crack of dawn.

"This is where we're going," Mark said. "Can you

guess now?" I could hear the delight in his voice, although it was too dark to see his expression clearly.

I hoped the dim light hid my sudden pallor as well. "Ballooning," I whispered. About the only neurosis I'd never gotten around to confessing to Mark was that I was terrified of heights, unless there was a wall and a window between me and the possibility of falling. The sensation was both physical and mental—a weird, unpleasant tingling in the stomach and groin, a feeling that the ground was drawing me down to meet it and that I was powerless to resist. It came randomly—not in every circumstance—but often enough to make me wary of bridges and cliffs. A balloon—with nothing between me and mortality but a bag and a basket—was so far beyond the pale that I'd never even considered trying it.

"Have you ever been before?" Mark asked me.

I told him no.

"You'll love it," he said confidently.

I considered backing out of the excursion. I could picture how it would go. He would be kind and understanding. He might gently try to talk me into going anyway, to work through the fear. I would refuse, and he would be nice about it. A good friend. A good psychiatrist even. But he would be disappointed.

And so, I realized suddenly, would I.

"I'm a pilot," he said happily, unaware of my inner struggle. "I've been in several cross-country races."

I thought, *If I keep seeing him socially, I'll have to do this more than once.*

"But today is just for fun," he said. "Someone else will be in charge." He turned to look at me as we pulled into the parking lot. "You're awfully quiet," he said. "Are you all right?"

"Fine," I said, forcing the incipient panic out of my voice. "I'm naturally reticent before sunrise," I told him in a more normal tone. "Is there someplace I could go to the bathroom?"

He pointed to a chemical toilet on the edge of a large field. He bent over and handed me something from the glove compartment. "Here," he said. "Take a flashlight."

WHEN I CATAPULTED out onto the field (never take a flashlight into a chemical toilet; ignorance is preferable), there were miniature balloons bobbing around the launch site like eager guests at a birthday party. It was starting to get light. Several men were stretching a garishly colored balloon out on a tarp next to what looked like a burner and an oversized wicker basket. A huge fan that appeared to be an errant part of a jet engine stood nearby. I thought that if I focused intensely on the mechanics of the process, I might be able to ward off imagining the ascent.

"What is all this stuff?" I asked Mark, who was helping the others.

He straightened and smiled. "Those are 'pibals,' or pilot balloons," he said, gesturing at the party guests, now departing the scene. "They show you the wind direction and velocities. This is the burner. It's attached to the gondola—"

"The gondola?" What I wouldn't have given for a nice safe ride across some sewage-infested Venetian canal.

"The basket," he said. "And then the basket is attached to the balloon."

"How does the bag fill up?" I asked him.

"The bag is called an envelope," he said. He pointed to the jet plane detritus. "That's a big fan. We crank it up, inflate the envelope with cold air, and then light the burner to heat the air. As the air heats, the balloon starts to rise until it pulls the basket upright."

I could guess what happened after that. "How do you steer it? I don't see any steering wheel or a rudder or anything like that."

"Well, um, you don't actually steer it," he said. "There isn't any way to control lateral movement in a balloon. They go wherever the wind takes them. All you can do is heat or cool the air in the envelope to enter a different layer of air and move in whatever direction the current is going."

"You mean it just *drifts*? How do you get back to the starting point?" I tried not to sound as alarmed as I felt.

He grinned. "In the chase vehicle, usually. Part of the adventure is not knowing exactly where you'll end up before you go."

"So it's an envelope with no return address," I joked feebly.

"That's the spirit," he said.

"It must take a long time to get all this set up," I said hopefully.

He pointed eastward, where the light was starting to illuminate the tops of the hills. "We'll be up right after the sun," he said.

THE FAN MADE a terrible noise, clattering and roaring in the morning's gray stillness. Mark and the rest of the crew held the balloon open with gloved hands as it filled with cold air. When it was partially full, they ignited the burner, which shot a long narrow flame into the envelope.

"What's the envelope made out of?" I shouted to Mark

over the din. I hoped it was something nonflammable.

"Ripstop nylon," he shouted back. The balloon started to stand up.

I liked the sound of *ripstop,* except that it necessarily implied the possibility of rips. I didn't want any holes in something that was going to be holding me aloft.

One of the crew grabbed the attached rope as the balloon was standing up. It dragged him sliding over the ground. Visions of Passepartout dangling from Phileas Fogg's balloon as it sailed away made me cry, "Look out!"

"It's okay," Mark said. "He's just providing weight resistance, so the balloon doesn't pop up too quickly." He took my hand. "Ready?"

I nodded, not trusting myself to speak.

He introduced me to a guy in dark pants and a black T-shirt and jacket who looked scarcely old enough to have a driver's license. "This is Perry," he said. "He's our pilot today."

"Hi," Perry said. He was chewing gum.

"How do you get to be a balloon pilot?" I asked him, trying to sound casual. I hoped it wasn't something you could learn in summer school.

They both laughed. "A balloon is an aircraft regulated under the same FAA regulations as all the other categories," Mark said. "Pilots have to get a commercial license."

"With a minimum of seven hundred hours of flight operations," Perry added.

I thought he looked as if seven hundred hours would have put him back on the Little League field, but I didn't say anything more.

* * *

PERRY HAD HIS own section of the cabin, right under the burner, and separate from the passenger portion of the basket, so I didn't get to see exactly what he did to make the balloon go up. I anticipated a sensation like riding the elevators in New York's World Trade Center or the throttle-to-the-firewall thrust of an airplane takeoff. I closed my eyes, expecting to see the world from ten thousand feet up when I opened them. Instead we were only about thirty feet off the ground, and Mark was shouting something at the ground crew, who were shouting back.

Sort of an anticlimax, after all that anxiety.

The fear subsided to a kind of fizziness in my stomach, like champagne.

"How fast does it go?" I asked Mark.

He turned to me and smiled. "As fast as the breeze," he said. "Maybe about twice as fast as a walking speed on the ground."

"This is the perfect antidote for control freaks," I told him. "You can't direct where you're going, where you're going to end up, or how fast you'll get there."

He laughed. "You're cured or you're driven nuts," he said.

"Do you think this is a metaphor for something?" I asked.

"Probably," he said.

"It's so quiet."

It was. There was a lot of frenetic activity on the ground—the distant freeway, crows flying beneath and around us, a few people moving on the hillsides and beaches. But the balloon hung motionless in its air mass, and there was no sound other than the occasional *whoosh* of the burner as we rose in gentle stages, like climbing stairs. There was absolutely no sense of motion or sway as we drifted. It was as if we were part of a celestial Christmas ornament pinned to the sky, while the earth moved on beneath us.

The sun rose high enough to light the ocean, turning it a light turquoise.

My heart swelled, like the balloon, with a sense of peace and happiness I hadn't felt in a long time, filling up empty spaces I hadn't even known were there. My eyes blurred with tears.

"I can't believe this," I told Mark. "I've never felt anything like it."

He took my hand. "I'm glad you like it," he said. "Most of my colleagues think I've taken leave of my senses."

I took a deep breath and smiled. "If this is taking leave of your senses, I'll be the first one at the railing waving good-bye." I looked out at the horizon, giddy with the twin sensations of unexpected pleasure and fear overcome. "It's so beautiful," I said. "I'm trying to put a name to this feeling. Everything is so . . . harmonious. What do you think it is?"

"Perspective," he said seriously, watching the world spin past.

The words popped out of my mouth before I knew I was going to utter them. "I'm quitting my job," I told him. "I'll probably get let go anyway, but I'm quitting first. As soon as possible."

He turned to me and smiled. "Why?" he asked.

I spread my hands. "Because it's no way to live," I said. "At least not for me." It was true. I just skipped the part about being made a possible scapegoat if I chose to stick around.

He didn't say anything. The balloon went lower, drifting westward.

"You're not surprised, are you?" I asked, watching him.

He looked at me. "No," he said. "Should I be?"

I shook my head. "I've been sidling up to this for quite a while. I just didn't know I was ready to announce it till today."

"What will you do?"

"I don't know," I said, gripping the sides of the basket. "I'll think of something. I've got a sort of an offer from an Internet start-up, but I'm not sure that's what I want." I looked out at the distant ocean. There were a few early surfers bobbing on the waves. "I've spent too much time being scared about things at RTA. Scared I'll mess up, scared I won't have enough money, scared I'm not doing enough for the firm, scared I'm not doing enough for my family. Bobbie even has me scared of getting old. The list goes on, but I just don't want to be scared anymore." I raised an imaginary carrot into the sky. "As God is my witness . . ."

He laughed. "You've got a bad case of ascension euphoria, Scarlett."

"Is that a real psych term?" I asked him.

"Sure. It's the geographical opposite of rapture of the deep."

I couldn't tell if he was serious or not.

I looked him squarely in the eye. "I am feeling sort of . . . rapturous," I said.

He smiled and kissed me, the way he was supposed to do.

"I might be taking advantage," he said, pulling back a little.

"Good," I told him.

"TELL ME ABOUT your job offer," he said a few minutes later.

Despite the fact that I had just announced my intention to shuck my legal career, I was less interested in talking job prospects at that moment than I otherwise might have been. I had to force myself to concentrate. "What?" I asked dreamily.

"From the Internet start-up."

"Oh." I told him about Jason Krill and Melissa. "But that kind of job might be better for somebody in a different period in life. I'm not sure it's for me." As a matter of fact, I was pretty sure it wasn't. I thought of Melissa and her father and how her whole life in some way was trying to measure up to the impossible standard she thought he held for her. I realized that my entire legal career had been a kind of ongoing dialogue with my ex-husband. A dead man. I'd needed to prove I was a professional—with a capital *P*—the way he'd been. Well, I'd proved it, at least to my own satisfaction, and I didn't need to make partner or a zillion dollars at the expense of everything else in my life just to keep the conversation going.

"Why do you ask?" I asked him.

"I was wondering if you could use some help finding something else."

I shook my head vehemently. "No, thanks. This is something I have to do by myself." My career choices were complicated by my involvement with Bobbie Crystol and Taylor and whatever happened down the line. It didn't seem fair to entangle anyone else in that, at least not yet.

He looked away with a pained expression.

"I'm sorry," I said, touching his sleeve. "I didn't mean to be so abrupt. It's complicated. Right now I just feel . . . overwhelmed by all this." I gestured vaguely, encompassing the sky, the view, the balloon, life in general, and him in particular. "And besides, you've done so much for me already."

"Don't make me out to be some kind of noble philanthropist, Becky," he said. "I don't want your gratitude. If I've helped you, I did it for my own sake as much as yours."

Whatever he might say, I thought of the difference that kind of generosity had made in my life at a time when I had nowhere else to turn.

And suddenly, just like that, I knew what I wanted to do.

"I have an idea," I said. I was having lots of them, spilling all over themselves demanding attention. "I think I know what kind of a job I'd like."

He smiled. "Balloon pilot?"

I laughed. "Not in this lifetime." I looked at him. "I have a long-standing relationship with a charitable foundation. They helped me pay my way through law school, and I know they've helped others too. I was thinking of approaching them to see if they need someone to do their legal work or raise money or something. If they don't have anything, they might recommend me to some other foundation."

He didn't say anything.

"What's wrong? Don't you think it's a good idea?"

"Sure," he said. "It's great."

"Then why aren't you more enthusiastic?" I asked, trying to hide my disappointment.

"It's not that. You don't understand," he said.

"I guess not," I told him.

He took my hand and held it against his chest. I thought it was the most romantic gesture I had seen in years, but I was hardly objective. "I'm not saying this right," he said.

"You're doing fine," I said encouragingly.

"I haven't been honest with you," he said.

"You don't have to tell me," I said. "I know what you're going to say."

His eyebrows went up. "You do?"

"Sure. There's something you don't want to come out."

He looked almost amused. "What led you to that conclusion?"

"You told me, remember? You said you'd lied to someone you cared about." I looked at him. "You don't have to tell me what it is if you don't want to. I said I didn't know anything about you, but that's really not true. I know all the important things." I told him with my eyes how I felt. Even someone far less clued in than a psychiatrist couldn't have missed the message.

He got a wild look on his face, as if he might burst into hysterical laughter or tear his hair. I wondered if his big secret might be worse than I thought. "Becky, I—" He stopped and looked down at the ground, or at where the ground should have been. "Christ," he said, looking around. "We're heading toward the ocean."

"We're not supposed to be?" I asked.

Just then Perry came out of his compartment of the gondola, holding three life jackets.

I guess not.

"What happened?" Mark asked him.

Perry looked at him. "It's just a precaution. I can't find a current that's blowing any direction but out to sea."

Now that there might be something to worry about, I felt a strange kind of exhilaration but not the apprehension that would have been a sensible reaction under the circumstances. I was also discovering that Eros and Thanatos can coexist quite comfortably in the same experience. I would have to get Mark to explain it to me. "I take it we can't just turn around," I said. I laughed. "Oh, right. No return address. I remember."

Mark and Perry looked at me oddly.

"I'm okay," I said.

Perry turned to Mark. "What do you think?" he asked.

"Try going up," Mark said.

Perry shrugged and opened the burner. The balloon rose gently. Very slowly, after an eternity, it started to turn east.

I was almost disappointed.

Mark put his arm around me. I couldn't feel it because of the life jacket, but I moved close to him anyway.

"You were saying?" I said to him, when it was clear we wouldn't end up heading for China in a bag of hot air after all.

He tightened his arm around my shoulders. "It can wait. I think we've had enough excitement for one day."

"Chicken," I said.

He didn't laugh. "Are you ready to descend?" he asked.

"Let her rip," I told him.

CHAPTER THIRTY-ONE

MY MOTHER HAD A VISITOR.

Lauren was sitting next to the bed in her wheelchair, resting her head on her hand. My mother was telling her in some detail about her triumph over the forces of evil at Dunewood. "And they made me walk," she said, "when I had this fracture. Can you imagine?"

Lauren was gazing at her with an expression of apparent interest. I recognized the look from RTA—it meant her mind was elsewhere. She made a small noncommittal sound. "But you'll have this operation, and then you'll be able to walk very well, won't you?" she said to my mother encouragingly.

My mother sighed. "I don't want to have it, but the doctor says if I don't I'll end up in a wheelchair. I wouldn't want that," she added vehemently, oblivious.

"No, you wouldn't," Lauren agreed.

"Sorry," I told Lauren when we'd excused ourselves and gone into the lounge to get some coffee. "I keep making all these resolutions about what I'm not going to be like at eighty. Think it will do any good?"

"Of course not," she said. "Ten to one your mother made resolutions too."

"My mother's never been big on introspection," I said. "It was nice of you to come and see her. What are you doing down here?"

"Tom's aunt had emergency gallbladder surgery. He's with her now." She smiled. "If you think it's hard to listen to hip stories, you should try gallstones."

I laughed. "You're a good sport, Lauren."

"I try."

"I'll miss you," I said.

She turned her head and looked at me. "That sounds valedictory."

"I'm going to leave RTA," I said.

She didn't scream or faint with surprise. "And do what?" she asked calmly.

"I'm not sure yet. I just know I'm not cut out for this. I'm not the type to sharp-elbow my way to the table and perform heroic metabolic feats in order to put in enough billable hours to someday, maybe, make partner."

"Have you told anyone yet?" she asked.

"No, just you."

"I'm flattered," she said. "But why don't you wait a bit and see if you change your mind? It's a big step."

"I won't," I told her. I couldn't tell her that waiting around to see if Bobbie and Taylor tried to make me a fall guy was not an option.

"I see," she said. She paused. "Will you be taking Crystol Enterprises with you?"

I laughed. "Not a chance. Bobbie's part of the reason I'm leaving. Not that she'll want me to represent her anymore anyway. Taylor has more or less assumed responsibility for her legal affairs."

"I'm sorry, Becky. I know she was your client. This doesn't have to mean that you're cut out entirely."

"It does in this case. I'm not sure she ever *was* my client, really. Look, Lauren, you've been good to me. I want to level with you. I think there's going to be trouble," I said. "Not now maybe, but sooner or later." I tried to give her a capsule summary of my misgivings and concerns, as well as my feeling that some embarrassing discovery about Bobbie's methods, some juicy lawsuit-in-waiting, was practically inevitable. "She's been careless," I said. "People are talking. Some witness will turn up, or some child whose mother has died, and the public will turn against her. Not only that, but she's callous as well. She's not terribly worried about who gets hurt." I didn't tell her about Bobbie's offshore accounts, but I thought this was enough to put her on her guard. "Protect yourself if you need to," I added.

She put her head in her hands. "Oh, God, Becky. I warned you not to go poking around in this mess."

"I know you did," I told her. "I wish I could follow your advice, but I can't. Melissa told me recently that I'd started thinking like a lawyer. I didn't understand what that meant initially, but I think I do now. I can make arguments. I can find a reporting position, a way to stay within the law. What I can't do if I stay in this job is decide who to make the arguments for. And I want to be able to do that."

She sighed. "Well, at least you know what you want."

I nodded. "I want some joy in what I do. I hope that's not too much to ask."

She smiled. "The best of luck to you. I'll watch my back. There is one thing, though."

"What's that?"

"Before you go, you have to get Bobbie's affairs in some kind of order, even if you think Taylor is handling her now. You have to square things with her. It's your obligation. Not only that, it protects you for the future."

"She's in Sedona conducting a workshop, as far as I know."

"As soon as she gets back, then, assuming you're really planning to leave sometime soon. Okay?"

"Okay," I said.

"Will you need some help finding another job?"

"Probably," I said. "I have some ideas, but I'm not so well fixed that I can just leap off the deep end without any definite prospects at all."

"I'll put out some feelers," she said.

"That's really nice of you," I told her. "You're the second person who's offered today."

"And?"

"I turned the other guy down."

"Ah. Why?"

"Well, he's a friend, but . . ."

"You're hesitant?"

"This probably sounds silly, but . . . it's just that he's already done so much for me. I'm not sure it would be a good idea to keep on accepting his help."

She waited.

I studied my coffee cup. "I think I might be in love with him," I said glumly.

She smiled. "I'm afraid I don't see the problem."

I tried to explain. "Years ago, when I was getting divorced, he was my therapist. He helped me through that. He helped me get my life back on track. Now he's reappeared and helped me find a place for my mother. He helped me with these issues with Bobbie. How can I let him get involved with my job too?"

"I'm still not getting it," she said. "It sounds as if he might be in love with you too. What's troubling you?"

"The equation is off," I said. "I mean, what is there left to do for *him*? Besides, if it works out, how will either of us ever know how much of what I feel is love and how much is gratitude?"

She was silent a moment. "You've been tactful enough not to ask me how I got in this chair," she said. "When I was twenty-one years old and Tom and I had been married six months, we were taking a walk around our neighborhood. It was a very nice neighborhood—quiet, full of trees, lots of children. One of our neighbors set up a target in his garage and decided to try out his new rifle, just at the very instant we were walking by." She gestured at the lower half of her body. "That's how I ended up this way," she said, as dispassionately as if it were a story about someone else. "He missed the target. The bullet went through the garage door and lodged in my spine. Part of it is still there."

She looked out the window. "I had three operations that summer. Between them, I lay in our bed listening to this neighbor—the one who'd shot me—batting tennis balls against his fence, riding a bicycle, doing all the things I'd never do again. He got probation and community service, and he got to go on with his life." She took a breath. "I got . . . a life sentence. I don't think I could have made it through any of it, except for Tom. He stayed with me, he told me that I was beautiful and he would never leave me, he bathed and changed me before I learned to do it for myself. He wouldn't let me despair." She turned to me. "So how about *that* for an unequal equation?"

"Christ," I said.

"You can't repay people for loving you, Becky," she said. "It's not as simple as two plus two equals four. The only way to balance the inequity is by loving the person back."

"What did you do then?" I asked her. "How did you get over it?"

She smiled. "Well, I didn't exactly get over it, did I? I just went on with my life. With the settlement money from the insurance company, I went to law school. Not because I had visions of avenging myself by prosecuting criminals or anything like that, but because a life of the mind seemed like the best way out of my . . . dilemma. Tom supported me in that too." She looked at me. "As it happened, I loved law school. I love being a lawyer. I love what I do now. So we've just made the best of everything else. My point is, I don't think there's any love that isn't at bottom a grateful one. And besides . . ."

"Besides?"

She looked at me. "If you want to sleep with him, there's probably *something* more than gratitude involved, isn't there?"

ISABEL CALLED ME before I had even brushed my teeth the next morning. "I left three messages," she said indignantly. "Allie told me your mother was in the hospital again."

"She's okay," I said. I told her the circumstances. "The operation's scheduled for tomorrow afternoon."

"So where were you yesterday morning? I called you again at six and I woke Allie up. I didn't have the heart to grill her, poor child."

"Ballooning," I said.

"Ballooning? I thought you were afraid of heights."

"It was special," I told her. "And anyway, why were you calling at six A.M.?"

She said something I couldn't hear to someone else in the room. She sounded distracted. "I forgot," she told me. "It was eight A.M. here."

"Are you okay? Where are you calling from?"

There was a pause. "San Antonio."

"San Antonio? As in Texas?"

"Yes," she said.

"Gathering quotes?"

"Very funny. This was your idea, remember?"

"So how is it?" I asked her.

"It's awesome," she said, sounding almost giddy. "Oh, Becky, I've been such an idiot."

"Are you alone?" I asked.

"No."

"Good," I said. "Say hi to Daniel, have fun, and call me when you get back."

"Give your mother my best wishes," she said.

"I will," I told her.

ON SUNDAY NIGHT I wrote my letter of application to the Medallion Foundation and dropped it into the box. First thing Monday morning I went to see the attorney Melissa's father had referred me to.

"Thank you for seeing me so early," I told him. "My mother is having hip replacement surgery this afternoon, and I have to get to the hospital as soon as possible. But I don't want to delay getting started with this."

He looked at the trust documents in his hands. "I can understand that," he said. "Eric has briefed me on the circumstances." He folded his hands on the desk. "If you're prepared, I'll file the motion for accounting as soon as possible."

"I'm prepared," I said.

"The retainer will be five thousand dollars, payable today," he said.

In appearance and style he was in every way the opposite of Melissa's father. He was thin and pale, and he sucked in his cheeks while he looked over the documents, making him look even more cadaverous. As far as I could see, he was totally without humor, although perhaps it was too early to tell. In a way his desiccation was almost reassuring. I wanted someone as far from flamboyant as possible, someone who regarded the Rule Against Perpetuities as appropriate nightstand reading material.

I wrote out the check and handed it to him. I tried not to wince.

Unsuccessfully, apparently. He managed a dry little smile. "From what I've heard, I believe it will be worth it to you," he said.

"I hope so," I told him. "And after you've filed the motion, what happens then?"

He looked at me solemnly. "We wait for events to unfold."

"And will they . . . um . . . unfold, do you think?"

"Oh, yes," he said, showing a glint of zealotry for the

first time in the conversation. "I can practically guarantee that the court will review this case. They take a very dim view of this sort of thing."

"And if there is anything untoward about the offshore investments, will that come out too?"

"I believe so. And if not . . ." He put a finger up and touched his bow tie. "Well, let me put it this way. The IRS can always audit someone for whatever reason they want. In this case they would probably get a very reliable tip, one I have every reason to believe would be acted upon quite promptly." He looked at me. "Will that be satisfactory?"

"Perfectly," I told him.

"Ahem, Miss Weston," he said as I was leaving.

"Yes?"

"I have quite a bit of work now, really far more than I can handle myself." He tidied the papers on his desk, squaring the corners of the pile. I bet he ironed his underwear.

"That's wonderful," I told him.

"Yes, yes, but what I meant to say was, I might be interested in taking on a senior associate. Eric Peters speaks very highly of you, and while Eric is admittedly a bit . . . unconventional . . . I've always found him an excellent judge of ability. What do you say?"

"What do I say?" I asked, temporizing.

He nodded. "Do you think you'd be interested in the job?"

What I thought was that Melissa's father had just thrown me a safety net. I hoped I didn't have to fall into it, but I was still grateful.

"Thank you," I told him. "Could I think about it?"

"Of course," he said, fussing with the papers again. "You'll want to see how your case progresses. Most understandable. We can discuss it further when you're ready."

"WE HAVE TO talk," I said to Bobbie in dangerously untoadying tones when I reached her by phone in her new office. It took some doing; the more money you have, the more people you can employ to shield you from unpleasantness. "Tell her it's her *attorney*," I'd insisted as I was passed up the line. "Tell her I need an appointment right away."

"What are you talking about?" she asked coldly when she came on the phone. "What's so urgent it couldn't wait? Taylor didn't say anything."

"This isn't about Taylor," I told her. "At least not directly."

"Then forgive me, but I may not need to hear it," she said.

"You need to hear it," I told her.

I could hear an exhalation of breath, as though she were smoking. "What is it you're trying to say, Becky? Just because we're old friends—"

"Cut the crap, Bobbie," I told her. "We're not old friends."

She laughed suddenly. "Well, well. I wondered how long it would take you to get around to this." Another puff.

She *was* smoking. "Are you *smoking*?" I asked her.

"I do now and then, under stress." She sounded amused at my reaction. "Is that what you wanted to ask me about?"

"No," I said. "But I can't talk now. I wanted to schedule an appointment. I'm at the hospital. My mother's having surgery this afternoon. Are you free later this week?"

"I suppose I could be. How about Friday at ten?" She paused. "Do you want me to come visit your mother in the hospital?"

I was speechless.

She laughed again. "I'm well aware of what you think of me, Becky. But you can credit me with a decent impulse. I promise you it's genuine."

"Well, thank you," I mumbled. "But she's already sedated."

Puff puff. "Until Friday, then," she said.

CHAPTER THIRTY-TWO

MY MOTHER'S HIP REPLACEMENT OPERATION WAS A SUCcess, if that's the right word for it. She emerged groggy but unbowed, dissatisfied with the nursing care and the food but inordinately pleased at once more being the center of so much attention. The orthopedic surgeons had made her a video of the entire operation, which she played more than once on the VCR in her hospital room. It rivaled the gore content of *The Texas Chainsaw Massacre,* but as far as she was concerned, it might have been *The Sound of Music.*

"And right there is where they ream out the socket," she said with relish, like someone pointing out the good parts in a summer rerun. "And then they put in the cement."

Allie and I had brought Allie's just-purchased prom dress to show to my mother, since she was going to have to miss the event itself. We hadn't taken it out of the box.

"That's great, Grandma," Allie said gamely.

I went over to the window and opened it a crack.

"Look at all the cards I've gotten," my mother said

when the tape was over. "And I've had lots of visitors." She looked at me with a hint of accusation. "Except for that psychiatrist you introduced me to."

"He sent flowers, Mother." He had. The biggest, gaudiest bouquet in the room, just what he knew she would love. "But I told you, remember? He left a message for me saying he had to go out of town. Some family emergency. He'll be back in a few days." I tried not to let on that I was as disappointed at not seeing him as she was. After our balloon ride, I'd only seen him briefly for a few minutes at the hospital.

"Does she know about him?" Allie whispered.

"I told her," I whispered back, "but she's probably forgotten."

"There's no need to whisper about me," said my mother. "It's rude to talk about people behind their backs. Where's David?" she demanded.

"He had to go back to school," I said. I'd already told her that too. "He was here on the day of your operation. He stayed as long as he could."

"Look at my dress, Grandma," Allie said, coming to the rescue. She took it out of the box and shook it out. The blue satin spilled to the ground like a waterfall. "Isn't it beautiful?" she asked.

It was, and so was my daughter's face as she held it. "Yes, it is," said my mother, her eyes misting. "I'm so sorry to miss your dance, Alicia. By then I'll be in rehab." She sighed. "It sounds like someplace you go when you have a drinking problem or take pills. But after that the doctor says I can go home."

I reached for my mother's hand. "I'll move heaven and earth to make sure you're with us, Mother. There's a chance we'll be selling the house, but it won't be till the school year is over and you've recuperated enough to be comfortable with the move."

My mother patted my hand between hers gently. "I don't want to hurt your feelings, Becky, but what I meant by 'going home' was going back to Dunewood."

"Dunewood?" I asked blankly, as if I'd never heard of it.

"That's where I live now," she said patiently, as if explaining to a child. "Look at the cards and the flowers. Mrs. Fay came to visit me yesterday. They want me back. They're keeping my room for me."

"Is that what you want?" I asked her.

"Want?" She made a small derisive noise, as if I'd brought up something vulgar. "I think it's best. I hope you're not too upset." She smiled almost coyly. "Besides, I haven't learned the past tense yet."

"The past tense?" I asked. "I don't understand."

"In Spanish," my mother explained. "Carlos was about to get to it when I left Dunewood. I just couldn't bear to disappoint him after he's gone to so much trouble preparing the lessons." She frowned. "Also, some woman sent me a note before I got in here. Dorothy somebody. She wants me to be on a committee to raise money for some charity. A bunch of us at Dunewood are going to call people. So you see, I couldn't think of leaving now." She looked at me. "I hope you understand."

"THAT WAS WEIRD," Allie said to me when we left the hospital.

"What was?" I asked, although I could guess what she was going to say.

"That Grandma wants to go back to that place. I thought she hated it."

"I think," I said carefully, "that what she hated most was the idea of it. It's a big transition, and it's leading somewhere no one likes to think about."

"Death, you mean," she said solemnly.

I nodded.

"That's sad," she said.

"That's life," I told her.

"What do you think made her change her mind?"

"I'm not sure," I said. "It sounds trite, kiddo, but maybe she decided that it's what you do on the road that counts, not the destination." Also, I realized that intentionally or not, my mother was letting me off the hook. I could stop feeling guilty. Or at least I could try.

"Cool," Allie said. She was silent a moment. "So what are we going to do after we sell the house?"

"I'm not sure," I said. "I'm looking for another job. We'll probably invest the money we get from the sale and rent an apartment or a condo until you get out of school. If necessary we can live with Isabel—we'll just have to see."

"Mom?"

"Yes?"

"Are you going to be seeing that balloon guy?" she asked.

"I certainly hope so," I told her.

"Then don't you think I should get to know him? I mean, shouldn't you invite him over or something?"

"I might be able to arrange that," I said.

To: MedallionFoundation@jps.net
From: RebeccaWeston@RTA.com

SUBJECT: YOUR INVITATION

DEAR MEMBERS OF THE BOARD:
OF COURSE I WILL BE HAPPY TO COME! I AM PLEASED TO HEAR FROM YOU SO SOON. AFTER SO MANY YEARS, IT WILL BE SUCH A PLEASURE TO MEET—AND THANK—YOU FACE-TO-FACE.

I WILL BE AT 741 WILLOWSAND ROAD NEXT WEDNESDAY AT FIVE O'CLOCK. I KNOW THAT'S IN A GATED RESIDENTIAL AREA—SHOULD I JUST ASK FOR MEDALLION? IF NOT, PLEASE LET ME KNOW.

P.S. HAVE YOU ALWAYS HAD MY E-MAIL ADDRESS? THERE IS SO MUCH I DON'T KNOW ABOUT YOU!

It was ten A.M. on a Friday morning, but Bobbie was loaded for bear. She was wearing a white silk pantsuit with a lemon-colored tunic top and enormous sun disk earrings that managed to flash even under the fluorescent lighting. An ankh symbol in what appeared to be platinum and gold was suspended from a heavy chain around her neck. If she'd been struck down by a car on the way to the office, she could have gone straight into the pyramid without further ado.

"I hope you don't mind the cameraman," she said when we walked into her conference room. "We're filming a documentary—remember, I told you I was busy." She looked at me. "Do you think this might be a good thing to include?"

I smiled. "No."

"I'll tell him to come back later," she said.

She sat back in the leather conference chair that had probably cost more than my entire suite of living room furniture. "So what is this about, Becky?"

"I'm getting to that," I said. "Other than Taylor, do you have any other legal representation?"

"Are you still my lawyer?" she asked.

"Until close of business today, yes, I am," I told her.

"Ah." She clasped her palms together and touched the tips of her fingers to her chin, providing me with an exceptional view of a whopping chunk of yellow topaz set into a ring. "No," she said.

"What about Largo and Longueur?" I asked. "Weren't they representing you when you came to RTA?"

"We had a small difference of opinion over legal strategies," she said calmly.

I bet. "I'm going to go over some things with you," I told her, speaking carefully. "I'm going to put them in writing. You might want to review them with another attorney."

"Other than Taylor?"

"Yes," I said. "I'd recommend Lauren Gould if you want to use someone at the firm, but outside representation might be best."

"Why are you being so serious about all this?" she asked.

"I'm trying to scare you," I said. "I'm not kidding."

She folded her hands and looked at me. "I'm listening."

I handed her a piece of paper from a manila file in my briefcase. "This is a model release form. I want you to have each one of your patients sign something like this before you give them any experimental medications.

You'll have to specify the ingredients and the possible side effects."

She glanced at it. "The contents of the drug are perfectly natural," she said. "It's an herbal base in combination with naturally occurring caffeine and some other beneficial components. There have been some problems with pure ephedrine, so the company is experimenting with another alkaloid form."

"Nevertheless, you have to let people know what they're taking."

"I think you'll find," she said, "that people sign a brief consent form when they check into the clinic."

I remembered the stack of papers that were part of the check-in procedure. I myself had only given them a cursory glance. "No one reads those things," I told her.

She laughed. "That's a hell of a thing for a lawyer to admit."

I drew in a breath. "The thing is, I don't think that would meet the test of informed consent."

"It would, and it has, in Mexico," she said confidently. "Look, Becky, you're worrying about this too much. Clinical drug trials have used unproved remedies with unknown effects on human subjects for years. And lots of conventional treatments were used for decades without anyone knowing exactly why they work. Look at aspirin."

"Aspirin doesn't cause heart attacks."

"Aspirin can cause all manner of bad things, and people gobble them up anyway whenever they have a pain. You had a chance to meet some of the clients. Do you think they give a flying fuck what some statistically improbable side effects might be when you're giving them back their youth? Stand there with your doomsday message and watch them trample right over you to get to the pills. What I do is far too important not to run a few risks. I'm sure you can see that."

"Then the laws are there to protect people from themselves," I told her. "As your attorney, I'm advising you to do this. I can't be any clearer than that. Besides, you must know there are rumors that something has been wrong with your clinical tests for drugs."

"Absurd," she scoffed. "I have everything documented." She paused. "I'm completely covered, do you understand me?"

I did. She meant no one could prove anything.

"You're probably right," I told her. "But sooner or later, if there's something to find, someone will find it. Then you could have a mammoth lawsuit on your hands, or worse. You're the only one who knows what there is to find, Barbara. You have to consider whether you want whatever it is out there in public." I hoped she would notice my use of her college name, a reminder of where she had come from and what I knew about her. I bet that of all the things in her past, what rankled her most was sad, unpopular Barbara Collins.

"Look," she said again. "I had to do the drug trials to finance my clinic. There's nothing amiss, I assure you, but the way things are going now, I could stop anyway after this one. Frankly, my patients like the way they feel on Evergreen—that's what it's called, by the way—and I'm inclined to go on offering it as part of the program. But that's not the entire basis for the life-extension program, by any means."

"Then give your patients the basis for an informed

consent. It's the legal, moral, and just thing to do." I looked at her. "You might even come out ahead for doing it," I told her. "Do you really want a lot of people having heart problems after they've been to your clinic?"

She studied her hands for a moment and then picked up the consent form again. "You can't possibly understand, Becky. This won't make one iota of difference. People want their youth back. They come to me because I can help them. Nothing else really matters."

"Then they can charge ahead like lemmings," I said. "All I'm asking is that they get a chance to see the Dangerous Cliff sign first."

"I suppose I can do that," she said after a while.

"There's one other thing," I told her.

She looked at me with something like amusement. "Just one?"

"It's a big one," I said.

She smiled sourly. "What is it?"

"Make sure your accounts are on the up-and-up," I told her.

Her hands stilled on the tabletop. "Why are you telling me that?"

"Because it's my duty as your attorney to make sure you understand the consequences of any irregularities."

"As my attorney? Until close of business today, you mean."

"Exactly. I'm going to leave RTA in the next week or two, but you and I are finished as of now. This is our last meeting, Bobbie. I don't want you to misunderstand anything I'm saying."

"You've found another job?" she asked.

"Not yet," I told her.

"You're going to leave even before you have another job lined up?"

"I'll find one," I said. I had to smile. I sounded just like Melissa.

"What kinds of consequences were you talking about just now?" she asked, studying her nails.

"Serious IRS-type consequences. The ones people go to jail for."

"I see," she said. She met my eyes. "I underestimated you."

"I know."

"Can I ask you a question?"

"I guess so."

"Did you really not remember Barry Norton?"

I almost laughed. I wasn't expecting the sudden switch. "I remember him. He was a creep."

"I know," she said. "I ran into him at a medical convention three years ago. He had no idea who I'd been. He's a podiatrist, for God's sake. He talked about *corns*." She looked at me. "I had the impression that you might have been interested in Taylor once."

"Once upon a time, it might have seemed like a good idea," I told her. "Not anymore."

She looked annoyed. "You're so straight-arrow, Becky," she said. "If you had let me, I could have changed your whole life."

I looked at her and smiled. Should I give her the satisfaction or not? *Why not?* I thought.

"As a matter of fact, Bobbie, you already have."

CHAPTER THIRTY-THREE

THE MEDALLION FOUNDATION, LIKE SOME MODERN-DAY Manderley, was not visible from the gates. They slid aside, inch by sublime inch, operated by an unseen hand. As I proceeded down the drive I entertained myself with my last imaginings of benevolent, pink-faced Pendleton Silverbridge. In a few moments I would have a real face, or faces, to put with the foundation name.

Behind a wall of cypresses the house rose like a glass tower next to the sea. I could see right through it to the horizon. I caught my breath. No kindly old gentleman in a sweater lived in a building like that. I parked the car on the circle drive and walked across the limestone pavers, my steps sounding loud in my ears.

The door (massive and framed in some expensive-looking dark wood) was answered by a pleasant-looking woman in a T-shirt, cotton pants, and running shoes. "I'm Becky Weston," I told her.

She looked blank, although not unfriendly.

"The Medallion Foundation?" I inquired. I hoped I had the right address.

She laughed. "Oh, sorry," she said. "Of course. The offices are upstairs. I'll show you."

She led me into an atrium with a ceiling a good twenty feet high. On one side was the Pacific, on the other was a long pool lined with deep blue tile. In the middle of the room was a large etched-glass sculpture like a cross-section of the ocean, complete with tropical fish and coral. It was one of the most beautiful things I'd ever seen. "That's stunning," I told my guide.

"It's by a local artist," she said.

"The setting is perfect," I said sincerely. In an ordinary house it would have been overwhelming, but here it was dramatic and appropriate.

She took me up the stairs, passing all manner of doors I was dying to open. She stopped at last in front of one of them. She tapped on the door. "Mr. Henry Sutton's away just now," she said to me.

Sutton? As in "the family owns half the real estate in Southern California"?

I didn't have time for further speculation. She opened the door. "Ms. Weston to see you," she said, stepping out of the way. . . .

"COME IN," MARK said, rising from behind his desk.

I stared at him uncomprehending. I thought that somehow the foundation had arranged for him to be there to . . . To what?

"I don't understand," I told him.

"I'm sorry," he said, "I know it must be a shock. I feel terrible about this. I tried to tell you the other day, but . . . I couldn't."

In an instant it flashed over me. About six years late. "It was you?" I gasped.

"Sort of," he said apologetically.

"I have to sit down," I said. "You . . . you were the foundation? You did all that for me?"

"I hope it's not *that* hard to believe," he said. "Anyway, it wasn't really me. I only set things in motion."

"It's like finding out your parents are Santa Claus after believing in some magical elf," I said. "I'm in shock." I shook my head, thinking of a thousand things that might have clued me in. "I don't know what to say." I looked at him. "Why didn't you tell me? It was unfair not to."

"I know," he said seriously.

"And you even let me go on and on about the foundation the other day and never said a word," I pointed out.

"I know," he said again. He spread his hands in a helpless gesture. "I should have said something, I know it. But you'd just refused my help, and you made a big point of wanting to take care of things yourself. And I remembered what you said about the balance of power being all on one side because I used to be your therapist." He hesitated. "I thought . . . I was afraid that if I told you the truth . . ."

"What? What were you afraid of?"

"I was afraid I'd lose you before we even got started," he said.

Okay, so he wasn't perfect after all. He'd lied to me and by omission had misrepresented himself. On the other hand, he'd helped me in every possible way you could help someone, and he'd just confessed he had feelings for me. Maybe it balanced out the equation a little that he had a few faults.

"Why did you do it?" I asked him.

"Because you deserved a chance, Becky." He leaned forward across the desk, but he didn't touch me. "I want to make that clear. At the beginning that's all it was. The . . . rest came afterward."

"The rest," I said. I was having trouble taking it all in. "So the foundation is just a made-up thing?" I asked after a moment.

"Oh, no," he said, sounding surprised. "There's a foundation. My uncle's the head of it. Uncle Harry makes all the final decisions, including about you. I just make recommendations. My sister and I are members of the board. I fill in for him when he's not here, but that's the extent of my involvement. We've been anonymous till now, but now he'd like to move into the public realm. That's why we need to enlarge the directorial staff."

"You and your sister? The black-widow spider?"

He laughed. "That's the one. I want you to meet her today, because she's back from Costa Rica. Our grandmother died in Florida last week. That's where I've been since I last saw you."

"I'm sorry," I told him.

"Don't be," he said. "She was ninety-seven and very ill. It was past time."

I had a thought. "Did you read my letters too?" I asked. I blushed, remembering all the things I'd put into them.

"What letters?" he asked.

I looked at him. His expression said, "Not guilty."

I decided to believe him. "Never mind," I told him. "I don't get it. Where does the money come from for this foundation? Why haven't I heard of it?"

He looked embarrassed. "It's family money," he said.

"The Lawrence family?"

"Um, actually, Lawrence is just my middle name," he said.

"Your last name's Sutton," I ventured.

He nodded. "We're just a lesser branch," he said. "But there's enough."

I looked around at the house. "I guess," I said. "Why the subterfuge?" I asked him, although I could imagine.

He shrugged. "I think I told you, the family wasn't too keen on my going to med school. And after I chose psychiatry, I knew a background like that would create a lot of issues for my patients. So I decided to use Mark Lawrence professionally instead of my full name. I'm sure I remember telling you that I like to keep my private and professional lives separate." He looked at me. "Besides, sometimes a lot of money just gets in the way."

I knew what he was saying. He meant that he wanted to be liked for himself. Since he apparently liked *me* in spite of all the things he knew about me, that put us on an equal footing. Sort of. "Who lives here?" I asked him. I almost hoped he didn't. All the opulence was a bit much.

He read my mind. "Not me," he said, laughing. "The house is available to anybody in the family who wants to use it. There's a year-round staff. Uncle Harry has a place in New York; he's not here all the time. As I said, that's why he needs someone to help direct the operations, particularly now that we'll be adding Granny's money too. The primary foundation offices are here, so this is where you'd be working. That is, if . . . Well, anyway, the house is Uncle Harry's *hommage* to the sea, or something like that. You get used to it."

"I'll take your word for it," I told him.

"Can you forgive me for lying to you?" he asked after a moment.

"Yes," I said seriously.

He reached out and touched my cheek with his finger. "Thank you," he said.

"This isn't exactly what I thought you were lying about," I said when I'd recovered my equilibrium. "I thought you might be hiding a polygamous history or a secret passion for Wayne Newton," I said. "I was all ready to be extremely compassionate and understanding."

"About Wayne Newton? That is broad-minded."

"Luckily we won't have to put it to the test," I told him. "I—"

A very attractive dark-haired woman about my age stuck her head around the door. I recognized her at once as the woman from the grocery store.

Mark beamed. "Here's my sister," he said. "Mary, come in and meet Becky."

My cup overflowed. "Hi," I said, extending my hand.

She clasped it warmly and flashed me a grin. "Mark"—she said it so carefully I knew she usually called him Marky—"has told me a lot about you. Are you going to work for Uncle Harry? You'll adore him, I promise you."

"We were just discussing it," I told her. "I'm still sort of stunned."

"If you hang out with Mark, you'll get over that fast," she said with a sisterly lack of reverence. We were both busy looking each other over while pretending to talk about other things. I liked what I saw.

"There is one thing," I said.

"What?" they both asked at once.

"Your uncle. Mr. Sutton. If he's interested in hiring me, doesn't he want to meet me first?"

"Oh, he had you checked out already," Mary said.

"Mary!" Mark exclaimed.

"Well, it's true," she said.

"He had me checked out?" I inquired.

"On the Internet," she said.

Mark winked at me.

"Ah, well," I said, hiding a smile. This was not the moment to confess my misgivings about the accuracy of an Internet search.

"And anyway," she said, "he said he already knew enough about you to be sure you were right for the job. Something about a mouse in a bottle or something like that? Does that make any sense?"

They both looked at me. "It's a legal term," I said, trying to look serious.

Mary looked at her brother. "I know you two have things to talk about. It was great meeting you, Becky, but if you'll excuse me, I have a rhinoceros beetle to dissect."

"What an exit line," I said to Mark when she had gone.

He looked into my eyes. "I hope you'll be very good friends," he said.

"So do I," I told him.

He put his hands down on the desk with his fingertips resting about one inch from mine, but he didn't touch me. Still, I could almost feel the electric current flowing between us. "So you'll really consider taking the job?" he asked softly.

"The job?" All this honesty in the atmosphere was like too much oxygen. I was finding it hard to think.

"You'd work for the foundation? Help expand the giving, set up new programs, that sort of thing?"

"Will I have a contract?"

"Of course. I think you'll find the salary and benefits are generous. Uncle Harry insists on treating his employees well."

"Then sure, I'll consider it." I said.

"You will?" He seemed surprised.

I grinned at him. "Are you having second thoughts already?"

His hands closed over mine. "There are no strings attached, of course, but I think I should warn you there's every possibility it could turn out to be a package deal."

"I'll take my chances," I told him.

TAYLOR MARCHED INTO my office and scooted a client chair up to my desk. "I'd like to talk to you," he said.

The temperature around the office had turned frosty after I told Jamison Roth I would be leaving the firm at the end of the week. Even nice old Jamison was distinctly cool. "Whatever happened to firm loyalty?" he muttered. I might have asked the same thing about Taylor's hanging me out to dry with Carole and Bobbie, but bitterness was the last impression I wanted to leave. I told him how grateful I'd been for the chance they'd given me, and I meant it.

"Fine," I said to Taylor. In fact, I'd been avoiding him

since I made my announcement to the partners. If the ax (in the form of the auditors) was about to fall on him, I didn't want to tip him off by anything I might say.

"Seriously."

"Okay."

He looked at me. "I know you've been exceptionally close-mouthed about where you're going when you leave here, but—"

"That's because I didn't know for sure myself until a couple of days ago," I said, interrupting him.

"But the word is out," he insisted. He named the Newport Beach firm that had solicited me through the headhunter.

I waited to see what he would say next.

He rested his elbows on the armrests and studied me from under his perfect eyelashes. "Before you embarrass yourself, there's something you should know," he said.

"What's that?" I asked in an interested tone, letting out the rope a little.

"You won't be taking Crystol Enterprises with you," he said.

I told him that was scarcely news to me, but he clearly didn't believe me.

"Bobbie asked me to handle her legal affairs some time ago," he said. "We had a long talk about it, and everything was finalized." He could scarcely suppress a smirk. "So you see, you won't have much to sell to your new firm. It's tough luck, Becky, but that's what happens when you try to play in the big leagues."

I looked at him. "Have you discussed this with her recently?" I asked.

He looked startled. "There's been no need."

"I think you may find otherwise," I said.

He reddened. "You mean you've been trying to undermine me with Bobbie the way you did with Melissa," he said. "Well, I promise you, you won't succeed."

"Then you have nothing to worry about, do you?" I asked reasonably.

He glared at me. "Don't think I can't do your career a lot of damage, even at this point," he said.

I ignored the threat. "Look, Taylor, no one *needs* to undermine you with anyone else. You do that all on your own. And your boring personal life is of no interest to me whatsoever." I spread my hands. "As for Bobbie, she no longer interests me either. I've fired her as a client."

"That's absurd," he said coldly. "They won't take you without Crystol Enterprises. And neither will anyone else."

"As a matter of fact, I'm not taking *them*. And you're wrong about everybody else. It's a whole new world out there, Taylor. I've already had three other offers."

"Then what firm are you going to?" he asked, in a tone that suggested *Prove it*.

"I'm not planning to go to another firm," I said.

"You're not?" he asked, surprised.

"That's what I'm trying to tell you. I'm not even in the sandlot. I'm not going to practice corporate law."

"You won't be practicing corporate law?" he repeated, as if I'd announced an intention to spend eternity in an iron lung.

"No," I said.

Taylor frowned. "I had you figured all wrong," he said.

"Good," I told him. "Want to hear my parting wisdom?"

"Not particularly."

"Here it is anyway: What goes around, comes around. Remember that." I hoped he would when the time came.

He made a face. "What is it you said you were going to do after you leave here?"

"Have fun, I hope," I said.

He looked uncertain, as if he couldn't tell whether I was joking or not.

WENDY GRABBED ME on my way to the ladies' room. "Did you get canned?" she said. The staff, in theory at least, was not yet privy to my departure plans.

"No way," I told her. "I quit."

She let out her breath. "Good for you," she said firmly.

"How did you know I was leaving?" I asked.

"Ryan told me."

I smiled. "Of course."

"He says Melissa's leaving too."

I didn't say anything.

"You're not going off together?"

"No," I said, still smiling.

"Becky?"

"Yes?"

"Take me with you?"

I remembered how she had tried to warn me about Taylor. "Anywhere?" I asked.

"Anywhere."

"Deal," I told her.

CHAPTER THIRTY-FOUR

I WAS STRADDLING THE FLOWER BED CLUTCHING A FIST-ful of spurge when I heard the car pull into the driveway. Burdick, whose assistance in the garden usually took the form of rolling on his back in the dirt, straightened up and bolted for the side of the house.

I turned. Carole emerged from the Lexus and went around to the backseat, where she opened the door and unfastened Andrew's seat belt. Then she grabbed him firmly by the hand and headed for my front door.

Oh, shit.

"Hi," I said, coming out from behind the junipers, where, if I could have managed it, I would have remained in cowardly seclusion. I knew what was coming. Carole had never, in all the years I had known her, come to my house, though I wouldn't have put it past her to drive by and crow a little. Andrew's presence was as clear an admission of guilt as I could wish for. She never would have risked the contamination otherwise. Maybe I should have relished the encounter, but even the Count of Monte Cristo had his limits.

Carole regarded my muddy hands with distaste, so I didn't extend one. "I've been weeding," I said unnecessarily. "Won't you come in?"

I opened the front door and they trailed in after me, careful not to touch the handle where I had opened it. "Allie," I called. "Are you here?"

My daughter came into the living room and stopped dead. "Hello," she said in a wooden voice. I knew what the effort at civility cost her. I was making it myself.

"Andrew," I said to the child. "You remember your sister, Alicia, don't you?" He saw her so seldom I couldn't be sure.

He nodded solemnly.

"She's going to take you across the street to the park and show you where the squirrels live," I said. "Okay?" I said to Carole.

"I would prefer he not leave the house," she said sourly.

"And I would prefer not to have this discussion in front of him," I told her. "It's just across the street. It's tiny. You can see him out the window."

"All right," she said. "Thank you, Alicia," she added, barely moving her lips.

"You can trust her. She's a good kid," I said when they had gone. I hoped it made her feel guilty. "Would you like to sit down?"

"I'd rather stand," she said. She folded her arms and looked at me. "What have you done to us?"

"That isn't the appropriate way to frame the question," I told her. "You're not some victim here. I've asked for a court-supervised accounting of the trust."

"I've been suspended as trustee," she said.

"That's normal," I told her. "It's part of the review. Do you have a lawyer?"

"Taylor—"

"*Not* Taylor," I told her. "You should get one."

She lowered her eyes. "Look," she said, "I know it must be costing you a lot of money to bring this kind of motion. . . ."

"It is," I told her. "I might be selling the house."

Her eyes flicked around the room. "I thought you were worried about money for your kids," she said.

"I am," I told her. "That's why I'd sell it. To make sure the money is there for their educations."

She balled her hands into little fists. "Maybe we could come to some kind of arrangement," she said.

"I doubt it," I told her.

"I know I wasn't always fair about the payments. I could make up for it now. We . . . I . . . could even settle some money on Alicia and David. Right now, so there would be no question of an inheritance or money for school."

If I'd had any doubts that she'd been fiddling with the trust funds, they vanished with her offer. "Don't go on with this," I said. "It's demeaning."

"You could withdraw the motion," she said. "Before things go any further."

"I couldn't stop it now even if I wanted to. David and Allie are the beneficiaries. The motion is on their behalf. If . . . if there is something to come out, it will come out. It's too late for anything else."

She looked desperate. In spite of everything she'd done to us, I managed to feel a little sorry for her. "People could get hurt. Andrew. Your children even," she said.

"I'm sorry, Carole. What did you expect? You have only yourself to blame. You can't buy me off, not with threats, not with guilt, and certainly not with money. And anyway, I don't want to go back to worrying about getting the money we need from somebody else. I didn't like it with Richard, and needless to say I haven't liked it with you. I won't live like that again."

She leaned against the back of an armchair, her diamond tennis bracelet cutting into the edge of the fabric. "I could lose everything," she said in a hoarse voice.

I was starting to lose patience. "Know what? I've been there. Sometimes everything isn't everything after all. So here's my advice, and then I'd like you to go. Get a lawyer, the best one you can afford with Richard's money. Then do what you have to do to make things right. For your own sake, not just for ours. After that, get a job."

"That's easy for you to say," she said petulantly. "You're a professional. What am I going to do?"

The words *Frankly, my dear, I don't give a damn* came to mind, but they'd already been used. I thought of something else.

"Start over," I told her. "It worked for me."

CHAPTER THIRTY-FIVE

IT'S MAY, AND THE BREEZE IS BLOWING OFF THE OCEAN, stirring things up. It's a little chilly, but Allie is taking no chances on wrecking the line of her dress with some superfluous wrap. She drapes a stole over her arm for later, after she's been seen. She holds it away from her wrist corsage, as if she's been managing formal wear all her life. She is fifteen going on twenty-five.

The limo has pulled up in front of the house and her date emerges. She turns nervously to the mirror and then to me. *Okay?* her eyes ask.

"You look incredible," I tell her. She does.

She smiles.

Mark comes out of the kitchen with the camera.

The doorbell rings. The curtain rises.

I open the door, and her date is standing there wondering what to say. He is not Leo DiCaprio; he's just a boy with longish hair and a face I like. I start to relax. "Hi," I say encouragingly. "I'm Alicia's mother, Becky Weston."

He steps into the house, smiling awkwardly.

Allie sweeps forward to rescue him. "Mom, Mark, this is Jeff," she says.

"I'm Jeff Jennings," he says, extending his hand to Mark. "It's nice to meet you, Mr. Weston, Mrs. Weston."

My heart stops for a minute, but Allie giggles. "No, Jeff, I *told* you, remember? This is Dr. Lawrence. He's a friend of my mom's."

"Sorry," Jeff mutters.

"No problem," Mark and I say together.

Jeff is staring at my daughter with something akin to awe. "You look great," he says softly.

She blushes. "Thanks. So do you." Her voice is scarcely more than a whisper, but I hear the emotion in it. I can hardly bear it, but the pain is sweet.

"Picture?" Mark inquires gently.

Jeff and Allie look at each other in resignation. *Parents,* the look says. *What can you expect?*

"Sure," Jeff says, touching her arm. She moves next to him, floating.

They pose obligingly—three or four shots—but their thoughts are out the door already. Soon enough they are moving down the path toward the waiting car.

I look at Mark as the door closes behind them.

There is so much to say and never enough time, but I want to tell him what I've learned:

That sometimes having it all doesn't mean what you think it does.

That pibals are useless. All the planning in the world won't keep your balloon aloft if the thermals aren't going your way.

That love means having to accept the necessity of putting your heart into the care of somebody ultimately unknowable, not just once, but over and over again.

That that's the fun of it.

EVERMORE: THE VOICE OF THE LONGEVITY MOVEMENT
"People in the News," February 16, 2—

Longevity superstar Bobbie Crystol announced yesterday that she is temporarily moving the base of her operations to Moscow, with the intention of establishing a chain of life-extension clinics throughout the former Soviet Union. Crystol, the author of *You Don't Have to Die,* is closing her clinics in the United States. "I have to concentrate my energies on this important new project," she stated. "Russia needs me." Crystol says she has no plans to return to the United States for at least two years.

KRILLINFO HOLDINGS INC. ANNOUNCES GIFT TO MEDALLION FOUNDATION
Commerce Wire Copyright © 2002

SAN DIEGO—COMMERCE WIRE—March 3, 2—. KrillInfo Holdings, Inc.(NASDAQ: KRIL), a Delaware corporation, today announced a gift of two hundred thousand shares of its common stock to the La Jolla–based Medallion Foundation.

Since its initial public offering early last year, the company's stock price has increased steadily, currently trading at $24 per share. Melissa Peters, former general counsel and current COO of KrillInfo, as well as wife of the company's founder, Jason Krill, said the gift is in fulfillment of a longtime pledge to use the fruits of the company's success for benevolent social purposes. "We would like to see the money go to extend technology into America's classrooms," Peters said, "but there are no strings attached. We trust the foundation to use the gift as they see fit."

Rebecca Weston, codirector of the Medallion Foundation, says she sees no problem using the gift as Krill and Peters suggest. "We at Medallion are very excited—and very grateful—to have the chance to bring the entrepreneurial spirit of the Internet into the schools," she said. "We hope more children will want to become a part of the high-technology industry."

Neither Peters nor Weston provided a reason for the selection of the Medallion Foundation as the recipient of the gift, but the two were formerly legal associates together at the San Diego law firm of Roth, Tolbert & Anderson (now Roth, Tolbert & Gould), which recently reorganized following a tax fraud scandal involving one of the firm's partners. Both declined to comment.

More Irresistible California Dreaming with the Sensational Catherine Todd

"[She] illustrates the humor, irony, disasters and unexpected joys life can throw at women."

Romantic Times

MAKING WAVES

"A can't-put-it-down novel with a sense of humor (and reality—this woman is busy!). MAKING WAVES is for every woman who's had to mend a broken heart and *get even."*
Redbook

What's a loyal, 40-year-old California housewife to do when her shark lawyer hubby tells her he wants out? If she's Caroline James, she holds her panic at bay with a makeover and a massage. Until a dire warning from the unpleasant ex-wife of her spouse's law partner has Caroline nervously preparing to fend off a slew of unscrupulous settlement tactics. And when the whistle-blowing divorcé turns up suspiciously dead, Caroline suddenly has a lot more than a custody battle to worry about.

I WAS A BLANK SLATE. MY NAME TAG, WHICH HAD "CAROline" printed over a background of muted peach and salmon, had no other information, certainly not my history or my taste in books (Jane Austen and Barbara

Kingsolver) or whether I had always dreamed of being a blonde (I hadn't).

Inside the Treatment Room, I scrutinized my face under the fluorescent light. What would Signor Eduardo whom I was trusting to unearth the new me find there? Despite years of scarcely disinterested inspection, I hadn't a clue.

Well, that's not quite true. There were hints enough—the little runways of gray at each temple, the blotch of brown pigment on my forehead, the lipstick oozing into the tiny crevices the years had formed around my lips. Still, I didn't really know what I looked like. Pictures usually startled me. My nose was bigger and my hair shorter than I remembered, though the general effect was not displeasing. But whether or not he could find any characteristics on my face that I had failed to observe on my own, I couldn't say.

I didn't really care so long as my face wasn't a signboard for the real truth: Middle-aged. Separated. Abandoned. Scared.

You might think "sex-starved" or some other cliché for the newly partnerless would not be inapt, but the fact is that ever since my marriage had succumbed to domestic attrition or whatever it was, the south end of my body had pretty well closed up shop. Fear and humiliation were scarcely the most potent aphrodisiacs, despite the unsuitable opportunities that almost immediately presented themselves, just the way all the books said they would. The prospect of a quickie with the mailman was scarcely the appropriate tonic to my battered pride. No wonder I needed a makeover.

Still, I was more than a little embarrassed to be handing over the task of renovation to an image consultant. I had always distrusted interior decorators, despite the hulking black leather couch that took up too much space in my family room and other mistakes that, presumably, expert advice would have saved me from. Look at all those pictures in *Architectural Digest*; not a single perfect room ever contains more than three books or a few discreetly arranged magazines, even if the owner is Susan Sontag. Besides, decorators always want to put sago palms or pampas grass or some such thing in the living room, and I am really bad with plants. So how could I trust a total stranger—albeit a highly paid and, as I was shortly to discover, extremely confident one—to turn me into something I liked better than what I was?

Because I was desperate.

Not only that, but my mother-in-law had bought me the session about a year before our separation three months before, and ever since then she had not failed to ask me about it every time I saw her. The message was scarcely subtle, and she had gotten a deal on the makeover because the cosmetic company that employs the image consultants is one of the law firm's biggest clients, but nevertheless she managed to make me feel guilty. The unspoken rebuke was that if I had acted more quickly, my perilous grip on a shaky marriage might never have faltered, and her son might not be spending his weekends squiring flight attendants round the breakwater on the firm's yacht, leaving his children to run wild in the streets of La Jolla.

She might even have been right. So add "guilty" to middle-aged, desperate, etc, etc.

Signor Eduardo's origins were probably a lot closer to Guadalajara than Fiesole, but his mauve silk shirt and slim-cut Italian pants exuded an enviable air of fashionable certainty. His hair was pulled back in a ponytail. He raised one slender wrist and frowned at his watch in disbelief. "My clients are never late. Never!" His accent, like his style, hovered somewhere between two continents. He was a half hour late himself.

I smiled apologetically, although it was not my fault.

He did not appear to be mollified. "We must begin," he announced, with the air of a symphony conductor raising his baton. My renovation could not wait a moment longer, apparently. "Clarice," he said, reopening the door of what I had come to think of as the Examining Room, "when Signora Hampton arrives, if she arrives, please show her into Giorgio's room. She must begin with him."

I started. "Signora—Mrs. Hampton? Is that Eleanor Hampton?"

He consulted a typed card surreptitiously. "Signora Eleanor Hampton, *sí*. She is a friend, perhaps? If so, I may make an exception and allow her to come into my session late. I have found that my ladies are more confident in the company of friends."

I shook my head, more to clear it than in denial. I was trying to find a way to explain Eleanor Hampton. "Her ex-husband and my . . . husband are partners in Eastman, Bartels, and Steed."

He looked politely blank.

"It's a law firm," I told him. "They do the legal work for this company."

His nostrils quivered a little, as if I had presented him with a piece of moldy cheese. "I do not concern myself with such things," he said with finality. "I live only for beauty and loveliness. I find beauty in every woman," he added firmly, though I was not inclined to dispute it. I did wonder, though, what he would find in Eleanor Hampton.

Eleanor Hampton was the divorced woman's Dorian Gray. The portrait, not the character. Every wounded feeling, every urge to hurl the *spaghetti al vongole* in the bastard's face, every outraged rebellion against being quietly replaced with some pliant bimbette, was magnified and given (ample) flesh in Eleanor Hampton. Ever since Barclay had left her for his legal assistant, she had made Medea look like Anne of Green Gables. Her obsession with her ex-husband, his new wife, and the life they had stolen from her was her only topic of conversation, and the lengths to which she would go to harass and pursue them (sample: She had hired herself out as an assistant to the florist who furnished her husband's wedding, and then she sneaked ragweed into the bridal bouquet.) made her a social pariah. I don't suppose too many people sat down to dinner with the Furies, either. Still, she served as a kind of a safety valve for the rest of us. She did what we could only imagine doing, and her excess reassured us that no matter how neurotic we felt, we still had not "gone too far," like Eleanor.

STAYING COOL

"Cross private eye Kinsey Milhone with Scarlett O'Hara."
Detroit Free Press

When the guilty verdict came in, forty-something juror Ellen Santiago Laws was relieved. After all, she helped convict the murderer of Natasha Ivanova, a flashy matchmaker who brought love to Southern Californian movers-and-shakers. But afterwards, Ellen learns that Natasha may not have been the virtuous businesswoman the prosecution made her out to be. So the usually reserved Ellen decides to dig up the dirt on the deceased, and for the real low-down, she must penetrate the chic matchmaking service by enrolling as a love-starved client. Ellen soon finds that at her age dating is like Russian roulette—with each new tryst being a miss rather than a hit. When Ellen realizes that the real killer is on to her, she must stay cool—to stay alive.

AMBIGUITY GOT NO RESPECT IN THE JURY ROOM.

There were no shades of gray, no "maybe it happened, maybe it didn't."

"It's cut and dried," said Leo, the foreman.

I was leaning forward attentively, more out of politeness than necessity. I hadn't been cooped up with him for days for nothing; I had already guessed how he was going to vote.

The fluorescent light cruelly illuminated the knobby ridge of his pate, despite what had obviously been painstaking efforts to conceal it with hair combed over from one side of his head. His face shone with sweat and a measured enthusiasm. He sold insurance.

Under the circumstances, "cut and dried" was probably not the most tasteful expression to have used, but he did have a point. The state had put on a convincing case against the defendant—Jesus Ramon Garcia—and the Jury Room held an air of conviction.

Leo let his words hang in the air a minute and then turned to the rest of us for confirmation. That had been his pattern throughout the period of our unnatural intimacy: first bluster, then a pause for approval.

Next to him, Hazel, an elderly housewife, nodded agreement slowly. She was very sincere, the sort of retired person who likes to serve on juries because it is "interesting." She had confided to me at the beginning of our service that she owned a very valuable thimble collection. She'd invited me to come and see it when "this was over." I'd said I would.

"If you mean," she said precisely, "that Mr. Garcia appears to be guilty, I'd have to agree. But—"

"What do you think, Alvino?" Leo interrupted. Every man on the jury interrupted every woman on the jury whenever he felt like it. Maybe it was a Deborah Tannen thing, because the men never seemed to notice they were doing it, and, of course, the women were too chicken to bring it up. It was bad enough to be confined with a group of strangers day after day without picking fights over nonessentials.

Alvino Louis owned a very successful exotic car agency in San Pedro. He was black and lived in Palos Verdes, haven of the affluent and gentrified. He had more than once expressed his determination to "get this over with" as soon as possible, although he had promised to give his fellow jurors a "good deal" on a car if we stopped by afterward. He usually exhibited a salesman's buoyancy, but today he looked grim. I suppose we all did.

He glanced at his watch, then back at Leo. "Guilty." He rolled his eyes. "The dumb bastard."

"Marta?" Leo asked.

We all looked at her. Marta was the only one who came close to fulfilling the "jury of his peers" requirement in that she was a pleasant, grandmotherly Latina from a part of town not generally distinguished by its prosperity. That hardly made her the peer of an eighteen-year-old punk with a juvenile record as long as the phone book, but the counsel for the defense had fought to keep her on the panel, as much as he had fought for anything. A court-appointed attorney for an indigent defendant could hardly be expected to muster the enthusiasm or the resources to mount an all-out attack on the prosecution's case, especially given the weight of the evidence and the unfortunate air of undesirability that hung about his client. He did his best, but he had the hangdog aura of a predetermined loser.

Marta appeared uncomfortable under the scrutiny. She ran her hands over the edge of the Formica table. It was dark brown, like the paneled walls. It was not a room for levity. "I don't know," she said heavily. "I think . . . I think he is not so bad a boy as he wants everyone to believe." She shook her head. "But there is so much evidence. The police . . . the weapon, everything." She sighed.

"Does that mean you think he did it?" Alvino asked impatiently. Leo glared at him.

Marta nodded. "I guess so."

"It" was bashing in the head of a prominent Westside businesswoman when she (presumably) discovered the defendant burglarizing her office. The weapon was an Erté statue—a female figure with elongated, outstretched arms and dressed in a romanticized twentieth-century version of Egyptian costume.

In most of the crime novels I'd read, the lawyers seemed to spend a lot of time on the victim's life. The prosecution wants to do it so the jury has some emotional involvement with the dead person; the defense is looking for something that lets their guy off the hook. One of the troubles with having read a lot of Patterson or Turow or Grisham is that, when you end up on a jury, you see how you're being manipulated, or at least you think you do. No one asks you about your taste in fiction when they're doing voir dire (except perhaps in the OJ case, where they asked *everything*), but maybe they should.

Leo drew himself up. "Hazel?" he asked.

She looked away. "I'm not . . . I need . . . I'm not quite ready," she pleaded.

"A woman is dead," Leo said sternly. "Do you want her murderer to get away with it?"

Hazel gripped the table in panic.

"Come back to her," said Alvino. "I'll start, okay? I vote guilty."

Leo turned his head ostentatiously away. "Eric?"

"Guilty."

"Marta?"

I could almost hear her swallow. "I agree. Guilty."

"Ellen?"

This is what I remember: The fluorescent fixture hummed. The tabletop had lines of fake wood grain stretching unbroken the entire length. A chair scraped against the leg. The air-conditioning blew down my collar from the vent above. Everybody was looking at me expectantly. My mouth was very dry.

But that's it. No crisis of conscience, no inner voices not even an accelerated heartbeat. Not a single clichéd emotion. No hesitation, or not much. No doubts, reasonable or otherwise.

"Guilty," I said.

No excuses.

EXIT STRATEGIES

"A slick, sassy book . . . Todd's characters are dead on."
Sunday Oklahoman

How can one woman be mother, daughter, breadwinner, ex-wife, widow, attorney-at-law, single, and dating in the course of an average day? Becky Weston Pratt's not even sure who she is any more! And to top it all off, her sole new client, a new-age spa impresario, seems to be involved in some dirty dealings. Becky's beginning to wonder what she's gotten herself into, and more importantly, how she's going to get out!

THE MEETING HAD STARTED WITHOUT ME. I SNEAKED A peek at my watch—I was still one minute early. I flashed Taylor Anderson—partner in charge, Armani Adonis, and the object of countless fantasies, including mine—a rueful smile, which he appeared not to notice. I took a seat. The client, Jason Krill, head of a tiny Internet start-up company, looked at me expectantly. Members of the legal team, no matter how junior, are usually introduced.

Taylor went right on talking. Krill's company was trying to raise venture capital, the kind of shoestring deal that could explode profitably overnight given the right combination of luck and more luck. The venture capitalists wanted seats on the board of directors and a reasonable amount of stock. The CEO wanted to give up as little as possible. Taylor was explaining the Facts of Life.

"This isn't Silicon Valley," he said apologetically. "I'm afraid you have to give something to get something back."

The client had the geeky look of someone who had spent a lot of time in front of his terminal and not much outdoors. He probably wasn't a day older than twenty-five, with a hint of stubble on his chin that spoke of neglect rather than style, but in a year he might be driving a new Bentley Continental SC and squandering vast sums on a vintage pinball machine collection. Or not. That was the fun of start-up companies.

Melissa Peters, my senior in experience but not in years, crossed her admittedly awesome legs beneath a skirt that was definitely born the runt of the litter. "You might want to rework your business plan," she suggested.

The leg-crossing appeared to have short-circuited the client's brain. He stared at her, his mouth opened slightly. She obviously did something for his hard drive.

Melissa (called "Missy" by her friends, but not by me) and her ilk are the reason a lot of men in positions of authority treat their female colleagues with a wary formality inspired by fear of lawsuits. She gave off so many conflicting signals you were derailed before you knew what hit you. Her awesome self-confidence in her own ability was no less irritating for being justified, at least most of the time. On the other hand, instead of the you-touch-me-you'll-be-sorry professional demeanor of a female associate on the make, she had a kind of postfeminist exhibitionism about her body. She could stop a firm meeting dead (and had) by hitching up her skirt and massaging her calves. She was also taking classes in Tae Kwan Do and early Norse literature. For fun.

Taylor frowned momentarily. I knew what was the matter—the rule for associates at Roth, Tolbert & Anderson was that in meetings with a client, silence was not only golden but mandatory. Only one person at a time speaks for the firm, and it better not be you. My job, as the lowest in seniority, was to sit in the corner like Jane Eyre and take notes. Melissa's was to nod sagely at everything Taylor said. She wasn't supposed to make suggestions on her own.

"The firm feels that a review of your plan might be helpful," Taylor said, resuming command. He glanced in my direction. "Becky, could you get Mr. Krill's business plan for us?" He turned to the client. "Jason, can we get you anything? Coffee? Tea? Soda? Wine?"

Jason closed his mouth and swallowed. "Do you have Sprite?" he asked hopefully.

I stood up. Taylor caught my eye and then he stiffened. I knew, and he knew I knew, that he'd forgotten I was the lawyer and not the gofer.

Again.

If I'd come into the firm in the normal way, fresh out of law school at twenty-four and incandescent with ambition, I wouldn't have had these problems. Instead I'd spent the last six years becoming the oldest new associate in the law firm where I had, not incidentally, spent the same six years working as a receptionist while putting myself through law school at night. If I hadn't received a foundation grant for older graduate students returning to the workforce, it would have been more like eight and a half, or never. Not such a lofty pinnacle, I admit. But if this wasn't success, I didn't have a clue which way to turn.

The trouble was, for all those years I'd been a fixture at the front desk—a pleasant fixture, probably, but only slightly above the Italian-style furniture in rank. Receptionists come in two categories—twenty-year-olds who didn't go to college and can't get another job and forty-something divorcées who went to college years ago and can't get another job. Moreover, firms like the forty-somethings better because they don't chew gum into the phone, don't come to work wearing halter tops, and don't (usually) throw themselves at the partners. Anyway, when you're used to seeing—or, more accurately, not seeing—someone in a certain way, it's difficult to alter your perception.

It was bad enough that the attorneys sometimes forgot to take me seriously, but worse by far was the attitude of most of the staff. Putting yourself through law school at night—however grueling, grinding, or boring the process—is seen as a kind of rebuke, a suggestion that being a secretary or a receptionist isn't Enough. It isn't, financially, but that's beside the point. I mean, how much did the stepsisters like taking orders from Cinderella after the ball? I hadn't married the prince, but it was like pulling teeth to get anybody to do my work.

Not that I wasn't grateful. The firm paid for me to take the bar exam and gave me time off to study. I didn't have to uproot my children from their schools or my mother from her security. I could stay in La Jolla, home of the improbably fortunate, even if only on a shoestring. Jamison Roth, the only partner over sixty, took me to lunch. In a burst of optimism, I even allowed my college roommate, the alumni class secretary, to publish news of my promotion in the Class Notes. So what if all the other first-year associates called me "ma'am"?